The Dog won't fish anymore.

After five years of self-imposed exile on the rivers of America, trout bum Ned "Dog" Oglivie has burned his waders and hat, given away his rod, and turned his lumbering Cruise Master RV toward home. The waters Hemingway made famous in Michigan's Upper Peninsula didn't receive the Dog the way he expected—his Nick Adams baptism failed to wash away his guilt.

Bound for reconciliation with his past, the last thing Dog expects to find in his bunk is a dead man. But there lies Heimo Kock, the big-shot guide who locals called "The Governor of the U.P." With a vodka-Tang fire in his belly and an admittedly skewed view of justice, Dog dumps the body where he figures it'll be found.

He didn't figure on the local sheriff, a varmint-faced water thief, and the sheer "doggedness" of the local librarian ...

Also by John Galligan
Red Sky, Red Dragonfly
The Nail Knot
The Blood Knot
The Clinch Knot

THE WIND KNOT

The Wind Knot

John Galligan

For Fung —
Hope you're enjoying "the Dog."
another outing with "the Dog."

TYRUS
BOOKS

Published by
TYRUS BOOKS
1213 N. Sherman Ave. #306
Madison, WI 53704
www.tyrusbooks.com

Library of Congress Cataloging-In-Publication Data has been applied for.

15 12 13 12 11 1 2 3 4 5 6 7 8 9 10

978-1935562306 (hardcover)
978-1935562290 (paperback)

In memory of Tom Helgeson, a difference-maker in the causes of good fishing, good writing, and the good life where the two flow together.

1

Dog quit fishing that night.

Dolf Cook came by in a bathrobe and slippers, toe-stubbing drunk through the campground from his summer cottage on the other side. He said, "Here's your money."

Dog counted it. The bills added up to a thousand dollars. Dog put the cash in the glove box of his Cruise Master RV.

"Stop over before you go," Cook told him. "I want to give you something. When you leaving?"

Dog arranged pine twigs in a teepee around a crumpled map of the Upper Peninsula. He was done with the place. He stuck his lighter in there and got a flame going. "About an hour."

"Where in New York is that again? I used to fish the Finger Lakes when I had a hit restaurant up in Rochester. Christ, I used to top-line stickbaits for Atlantic salmon in there, catch fish my brother never even dreamed of. He never landed the Prince of Salmon. Sure, he's a big-name guide around here, but there's a lot of fish he never caught that I did, and you know, my good friend, if you coulda seen my dumb brother ..."

On went Cook into his nightly logorrheic coma. All topics led to the man's famous brother and festered there. This was the sixth night running.

Hungry flames licked up through the pine twigs as Dog laid in kindling the thickness of his thumb. This was going to be a fast, hot fire—just what he needed. "Not New York. Massachusetts," he interrupted Cook. "I'm going back home. Take care of some personal business." Dog paused. He was still finishing the idea. "For a long time I've been trying an approach that doesn't work. Now I'm going to do the right thing."

"Atta boy," Cook slurred.

Dog looked at him across the leaping flames. Cook swayed. His fire-shadow thrashed against the pine trunks behind him. Now and then he raised his flask and the shadow of his left arm slashed across the outhouse and darkened the bear box that held the trash cans.

"I met your brother," Dog said. "This morning at the Rainbow Lodge. I asked him about the West Fork of the Two Hearted."

"What'd that peacock sonofabitch say?"

"He said it was barren. No trout in it."

"Shit, everybody knows that. Not a goddamn trout in the whole river. Hell, I'm not a famous guide, but I coulda told you—"

"So I went up there. Caught about a dozen brookies over twelve inches. Best fishing I've had on the peninsula."

"Hell," Cook said. He lurched toward the fire. "I coulda told you that." Dog watched the sloppy mental flip-flop. "Like I told you, my brother lies. It's all about him and his celebrity clients. He doesn't have time for me. I only own restaurants in fifteen states. I never fished with Coach Bob Knight or did it in the woods with Miss Michigan. Sonofabitch hasn't fished with me since Billy Sims ran for the Lions."

That morning Dog had recognized Cook's brother, Heimo Kock. The living legend who locals referred to as "The Governor of the U.P." had nearly knocked Dog over as he barreled out of the Rainbow Lodge with a half pint of Bailey's Irish Crème in one fist and several spools of Berkeley Tri-Line in the other. The brothers looked alike, but Heimo Kock was handsomer and more robust, richly silver-haired and dressed like a sales rep for outboard motors. What Dog had wondered about was the wee bottle of girly liqueur. But he didn't want to start Dolf Cook on that topic.

Instead he asked, "I'm curious. Who changed the family name, you or your brother?"

"I was born Adolf Kock. You want a name like a goddamn Nazi porn star?"

"But—Heimo Kock?—your brother doesn't mind his name?"

Cook leveled a soused glare across the fire. "Perfect fit," he said.

Dog turned to his woodpile. Earlier he had dragged big, awkward branches out of the forest. With a saw and an axe, he had made a decent stack. "Maybe what you want to give me, you could bring over here."

"Aw, come on."

"I'm not drinking tonight."

"You've been drinking my liquor all week." Cook shook the flask. "Where's your cup?"

This fire was moving. Dog had to stay with it. "I packed it," he said, circling, laying on arm-thick branches.

"First day of the rest of your life and all that crap." Cook let go a presumptuous chuckle. He was one of those lonely guys Dog met on the road who tried to take shortcuts to fellowship. He had appeared across Dog's fire the first night in a fishing hat and pinstriped pajamas, bearing two Cohibas and a flask full of Glenlivet. To a complete stranger he had brayed: "How'd we do today, partner? We knock 'em dead, did we?"

"Two days from tomorrow morning," Dog told him now, "my son would be ten years old. These last six years I tried to heal the pain of losing him in a way that hasn't worked." He was composing this explanation for himself, knowing Cook didn't care. "Fishing seems to do the job, but then this time of year comes around again, and I realize a helluva a lot of trout have suffered for nothing. I've decided to try something different."

Cook chuckled again, shaking his jowly head as if there were great ironies in the air. "Rewrite history and yada-yada, yakity-yak. Been there, done that. Christ, back in '81 I brought this nice lady and her sixteen-year-old daughter here up to the cottage for the summer—and goddamn if my brother didn't somehow get his gaff into the daughter behind my back. I thought that lady was going to be Missus Cook number three, but she dumped me because of it. I never forgave my sneaky, horn-dog sonofa—"

Dog threw on a big log that splashed sparks up into Dolf Cook's face.

"I'll come over and get whatever it is," he said. "You go back and wait."

A few hours earlier, Dog had navigated upstream five miles along the sand road beside the West Branch of the Two Hearted River. He had been a fool to drive in that deep. He was always a fool, this time of year. The road became a soft-bottomed roller coaster, interrupted by hard patches where heavy tree roots humped across the narrowing track. Dog turned the engine off at the base of a sand hill that his eight-ton RV could not climb. The road there sloughed into bog on either side. The river was a nasty bushwhack to the southeast. Dog left the vehicle like a cork in the road. He was unsure how a person would turn around. But he didn't worry about it. It didn't matter.

He geared up and fished, productively and in total isolation. He smoked Swishers to fuddle the mosquitoes. He saw two eagles, a kingfisher, a porcupine up in a tree, and a Detroit-to-Shanghai jet in the high blue sky. This time of year he became aware of exactly where he was on the calendar. Eamon's birthday was three days away.

He fished streamers down to where a shelf of the Canadian Shield planed the river into a sheet of root beer candy. That smooth brown water wanted to buckle his knees from the back. As the current shoved him along, Dog found himself recontemplating the Hemingway story that had sent him on this six-year fishing trip in the first place. "Big Two-Hearted River" had stoked in him a hope that was just intense enough to keep him looking ahead. At last he had come to the story's sacred source—only to discover that there was no Big Two Hearted River.

There was a North Branch of the Two Hearted, a West Branch of the Two Hearted, a South Branch of the Two Hearted, and a Little Two Hearted—all of them willow-clogged, sand-bottomed, peat-stained affairs, with low densities of small trout—but no majesty, no gravity, no *Big* Two Hearted River, the place where Hemingway's Nick Adams figured things out and got better.

Nothing on Dog's horizon anymore, in other words.

And here came Eamon's birthday around the calendar again, asking its annual question.

Dog had overshot his streamer into hostile brush and snapped it off. He had waded on with his line trailing. Eventually the shelf narrowed, clogged with snags, and dropped off, pouring the West Branch into a deep, chaotic froth.

Dog had stared at the swirling turmoil. His sadness would not leave him, he decided. It never would.

He laid aside his rod and hat. He unbuckled his wader belt and stepped in.

When Cook had gone, Dog built up a waist-high bonfire and first burned his waders. The campsite now stank of inhuman pro-ceedings. He drizzled a hundred trout flies over tall orange flames, watched the flies sizzle and vanish, then dropped in his battered plas-tic boxes and stepped back from more foul smoke.

He forged on. He emptied vest pockets one by one: strike putty, leader wallet, tippet spools, each creating its own quality of flame. Most spectacular was the squeeze bottle of Uncle Z's Tropical Bug Dope, which caved in and then erupted like a tiny bottle rocket.

That junk didn't work on U.P. mosquitoes anyway. Nothing did but Swishers.

The vest was too soggy to burn, but Dog was patient. He hung that tattered sack of pockets over his lawn chair. He paced around the campground's dark little circle, smoking and thinking while the vest dried out.

He couldn't go through Canada. You needed a passport these days. And word was out that the Mackinac Toll Bridge to lower

Michigan was closing at night for repairs. So Chicago, via Wisconsin.

He tossed his fishing hat into the fire. It crackled like bacon. Red sparks jumped through the flaming hoop of his landing net. Eventually the vest was dry enough. In no time it was white ash and orange buttons. Dog stripped the line off his reel. That line had held about ten thousand trout: browns, rainbows, brookies, cutthroat, bull, golden, dolly varden, apache, grayling, greenback, steelhead, coasters. A good number of chubs and whitefish too. Plus one large snapping turtle, several bats, a swallow, and a six-foot water snake. He balled the line into a handful and lobbed it into the fire. It melted fast, squealing like a live thing. Dog's heart hurt. But if he fished again, nothing would be the same. He would start over: gear, purpose, and all.

Now that was it. His rod was graphite, wouldn't burn. He snapped it into a handful, like fat black spaghetti, and dropped the pieces into the campground trash can. He let the lid on the box slam down.

That left just him and his pistol. He retrieved that from the Cruise Master's glove box and stood in the chill beneath the stars. Last chance for a bear attack. Going once. Going twice. He kicked his lawn chair into the fire. He fit the pistol into a jacket pocket. He turned his back and walked over to Dolf Cook's place.

The frothing plunge pool on the West Branch of the Two Hearted River had twisted Dog around and pulled him upstream before it submerged him. He had a view of tannin-stained river pouring over bedrock—smooth as dark beer from a bottle. Then it punched him under.

Dog went limp and spun like a coin flip. His waders sucked against him. Something rough along the bottom nearly took his head off. Then he felt water rush down his left leg. In a few seconds that foot became heavy as a stone. Anchored and twisting, Dog felt his knee wrench. His eyes bugged open. Centered in the fastest current, he was trapped flotsam. Anything in his vest not pinned or zipped—floatant, indicators, cigar butts—streamed around him. His torso whiplashed frenetically, at the mercy of the river.

Then he came loose.

No explanation for it. He was tumbling, knocking his skull along the bottom in an arc from the center of the pool. In the next moment he was sitting in the shallows, a minor riffle plowing up his nose. He corkscrewed out of the current and staggered to his feet. His rod and hat and wader belt sat tidily upon a boulder not twenty feet away. His knee was tweaked but stable. He was hardly out of breath.

And there Dog had decided. He would go home and see Mary Jane, and he would stand with her at Eamon's grave on his birthday. Maybe he had to go into the agony, not away from it.

Dog called the man's name and waited. Cook wasn't in his summer cottage. A satellite television showed news of a drought in the southwest. The worst dry spell on record. Crops and animals dying of thirst. A Phoenix man had stabbed a neighbor for stealing from his hose.

Dog looked around Cook's place. Phony crap crowded the shelves and walls. An antique deer rifle, circa 1850. A Mauser machine gun from the Great War. A shadow box full of historical salmon flies. The dusty severed head of a musk ox. It was real stuff, but God only knew where it came from. Cook was a drunk and a cheat.

Dog snooped around for the photograph. The day before, Cook had hired Dog as a fishing guide. The man had obsolete gear and no skills. He could hardly draw water with a cast. Steady nips on the flask had nursed out his purpose: "A thousand bucks, partner, you catch a nice one for me."

They were on the Sucker River, at an upstream sweet spot Dog had discovered. For about three times a normal guiding fee he would catch a nice one with his bare hands if need be. He had ordered his "client" bank-side. There, finishing his flask, Dolf Cook had yammered about his brother non-stop while Dog teased a brush heap with a Mickey Finn and hooked a monster brook trout. It was better than a "nice one." It was the kind of fish that fed by moonlight, eating mice and baby wood ducks. It was the kind of fish you saw in photos laid out on a car hood, in Hemingway's time. Cook might have peed his waders. At least Dog could smell something.

He had landed the trout without serious difficulty. The old man held it. Dog took a picture with Cook's camera. Cook swore Dog to silence and then reached for his wallet. Oops. No cash. But he was good for it, the old man said. This had turned out to be true.

Now, here on Cook's dining table lay the fish porn. Cook had printed the photograph at eight-by-eleven: in his rabbit felt fedora with the gamecock feather, sunglasses on a lanyard around his neck, his sleeves rolled up, his sloppy mustache and his drunken blue eyes, his soft little hands where Dog had positioned them because the man had never held a fish that large. It was a fine fish and a fine photo. The trout, an instant later, had tail-whipped Cook in the face and escaped beneath a reef of submerged alder. Dog had caught up with Cook's soggy hat about thirty yards downstream.

Cook startled him. "Even the great Heimo Kock never caught a fish like that!"

Dog turned from the cluttered table, thinking *neither did you*. Tottering in the same doorway that Dog had come through, Cook was a sight. His robe was twisted, and he looked wet. Mosquitoes clung to his face. He was out of breath. He held out his old push-button Pflueger fly reel.

"I must have dropped the darn thing outside," he panted. "Hell to find it in the dark." He extended the reel to Dog. "You admired this. I want you to have it."

"No thanks. I'm divesting."

"Take it. I insist." Cook lurched forward and caught Dog by the shoulder. "C'mon. You're my friend."

Dog took the damn thing.

"Thanks."

"Hang on to that, it'll be worth a fortune."

Cook tottered downhill to his liquor cabinet. He splattered more Glenlivet across the tops of two Detroit Red Wings shot glasses. Dog took the drink to keep it off his shirt.

"You're really leaving, right, partner? Now that you got all that money? Driving out to New York?"

Cook slung a soggy arm around Dog's shoulders. Dog peeled it off. "Massachusetts." He produced the pistol from his back pocket. It was a modest thing, a short-barreled Colt automatic, easy to carry but probably not enough hammer to stop the black bears that sometimes marauded through Cook's cottage. Shoot to scare, Dog was about to explain. But Cook had shrunk away against his booze supply. He aimed a trembling finger at Dog

"I ... you ... I won't be blackmailed."

Dog downed the Glenlivet. What the hell. He removed the pistol's magazine and placed it with the pistol on the table.

"Well, good for you," he said. "But here's a little something to wave around if someone tries."

He walked out. He tossed the Pflueger into a kindling box inside the front door, thinking: *blackmail?*

Back at his own site, Dog knifed open an ancient package of Krazy Glue. The glue was still good. He squeezed the entire contents of the tube onto the flat nose of the Cruise Master. He gobbed that glue on right between the wipers. He attached his beloved fly reel, the only thing he was keeping, in the hope that it would spin and click in the wind when he got up to speed.

It did. It spun and clicked all the way down through Seney, Manistique, Rapid River, Gladstone, Menomonie, and Marinette.

Later, as the Cruise Master leaned through a cloverleaf in Fond du Lac, Dog had the idea that he was spiraling inward and backward toward some essential center, some fiery forge where, hand-in-hand with Mary Jane, everything would be destroyed and remade.

He would phone her in the East Coast morning. Let her know he was coming.

There was no place on earth less like a trout stream than ex-urban Chicago, Dog observed at sunup. He entered a bland, nesting-doll landscape as he curled off the interstate, one no-place inside another no-place, inside another no-place, until he parked the Cruise Master in the outer lot of a Road Ranger truck stop. There he faced a fence that faced another fence that faced another fence. The fences seemed to keep patches of dead grass and concrete from trespassing against each other. This was the outer ring of agony, Dog thought.

The reel stopped spinning and he got out. He rattled a fistful of quarters, yawning and snapping his knee joints. Out of the Cruise Master behind him wobbled the last few U.P. mosquitoes, drunk on Dog blood. They were in trouble now, he thought. This was different. This air would kill them.

He stood for a minute. He watched people traverse asphalt. The surface appeared smooth. Yet these people appeared to struggle, like into current. Dog shook himself. When he stepped toward the red-glowing Road Ranger mini-mart, he felt like a man on the moon, bounding through zero gravity, moving almost too easily.

"Excuse me, ma'am." He got the attention of the young woman clerk inside. "I can't seem to locate your pay phone."

"My what?"

"Your public phone."

"My what phone?"

Dog rattled his quarters and smiled. She called security.

"Oh, they took them things out years ago," the old Per-Mar gentleman said. "Them're long gone."

"Depends where you are," Dog said.

The old gentleman put a shaky hand on Dog's elbow. He made a gesture toward the great outdoors. Dog caught his own reflection in the glass. The image startled him. "So let's just move along," the gentleman said. "Heckuva day outside here. There we go."

This was Schaumburg, Illinois. At that one moment, six airplanes plied the sky. A thousand cars and trucks streamed and swirled, pursued by the next thousand. The headlines in the newspaper boxes were all about the drought in the southwest. Golf courses were dying, and apparently this was a national concern.

Dog took a walk around the chain-link perimeter. The truck stop featured a play area with a weedy sandbox and swings, a rusty slide caked with road smut. One bloated kid about ten slumped on a landscape timber, thumbing a device.

Dog made an offer. "All these quarters if I can make a phone call with that thing."

The boy squinted up. Dog went to a squat and stacked out four dollars and seventy-five cents on the tarry timber.

"Are your hands clean?" the kid asked him.

"I'll go wash them."

In the Road Ranger men's room, Dog washed his face too. He strained a few bits of cobweb from his patchy beard. He rinsed a smashed and bloody mosquito from his temple and tried to put a little fluff into his hat-bent hair. There was another dead mosquito on his neck. His skin had gone to dark jerky everywhere except where his sunglasses had preserved a goggle-shape of nude flesh. He had fished himself into quite the handsome specimen.

The kid had to dial for him. At Mary Jane's number, a man answered and went to fetch her. Dog could hear him calling out "sweetheart" and "baby" and "Hey, what the hell? You gonna answer me?" but getting no response.

"She must be in the can," he told Dog. His voice was all Boston. "I take a message?"

Dog swallowed. "Yeah," he said. "Yeah. Tell her I'm going to be there at the cemetery this time so we can do it together. Tell her I'm on my way."

M.J.'s man was silent. Dog too. Both of them reflecting.

Then from Boston: "This who I think it is?"

"More or less."

"Your ex don't want to see you, pal. Get it? Your *ex*."

It was true. He and M.J. were official. Harvey Digman had sent him the final papers last winter in New Mexico.

"It's not about what she wants," Dog said.

"She don't need it neither."

"I called a year ago," Dog informed this one. "It wasn't you that answered. It was a guy with a British accent. Believe he said his name was Colin. The time before that, middle of the night, it was my old friend Patrick. I guess you've been around M.J. what, a couple months?"

"Five."

"So you've got no idea what she needs," Dog said. "But a few weeks from now when the locks change, you'll get a better idea of what she doesn't."

"How about you eat me, jerk?"

The phone changed hands. Mary Jane was there, sounding hoarse and exhausted.

"You're on the way home, to stand with me at the grave? That old story again?"

"I'm really coming this time."

"Ned," she said, "you are such a—"

"Just hang up," said M.J.'s man in the background.

"Hands off, Ray." She continued to Dog: "Seriously, you are such a ..."

"Gimme the phone. I'll tell him what he is."

"Get away!"

"I said hang up!"

Was that a slap?

Dog said, "I'm on my way, M.J."

"You are not."

"I am," he said, but she was gone.

Such a dog, he finished for her. I know. Bad. Lost. Feral. Runaway. But now I'm homeward bound.

He was nearly at the Cruise Master when the kid yelled, "Hey, mister! Some guy called you back!"

Dog put the device to his ear. A frail and grizzled voice said, "So you've finally fished your mind away?"

"Harvey?"

"M.J. just called me. You're coming back, fine, but coming back to *see her*?"

It was good to hear Harvey Digman's voice, his Boston accent getting sharper, like cheese. The old man was Dog's tax accountant, counselor, sole believer, and overall spiritual irritant. He was nearing ninety.

"And this is how I find out? From the beast herself?"

Dog glanced down. This fat kid had his hand out. Dog shrugged: no more coins.

"I was going to call."

"You were going to call. And I was going to grow my teeth back."

Dog heard muffled voices away from the phone. Harvey had cut out of the conversation to tell some young lady—an elbow therapist, a macrobiotic bowel coach, a private hula teacher—where the no-fat yogurts were in the refrigerator.

He returned now. "M.J.'s a mess, Dog. She's toxic. Christ, I talked to her six months ago—she wants alimony that you don't have—and afterward I had to get my liver flushed. Burdock and dandelion root. You ever try that?"

The fat kid had begun to circle, whining for his device back. Dog turned away.

"Harv, listen. Did you read that Hemingway story I told you about? The two-part one, where fishing heals the guy?"

Dog endured a silence. Vaguely, he tracked the kid's urgent waddle toward the Road Ranger.

"You didn't read it. Well, anyway, I don't feel better. It's not happening."

"Oof," Harvey said. "Thank you, dear. That was lovely. No, I did read the story." He said *starry.* "I read it a couple times. Here's my analysis. It's a starry."

"Of course it's a story. But come on, Harvey. Don't you see how fishing makes the guy better? I tried that. Now I have to try something else."

"I see. Like extreme—oof!—and pointless suffering."

"Come on, Harvey …"

Dog heard a shriek from outside the Road Ranger. A large woman in Illini sweat clothes plodded toward him, her lump of a son wrenched along by his arm. Her other arm ended in an index finger that jabbed across the blacktop at Dog.

"I figured out that I need M.J. to get over Eamon's death," he said. "That's what I'm saying. And she needs me."

"Oh … my … Lord," Harvey Digman grunted out. "And what starry is *that* from?"

Dog surrendered the device and his entire collection of toll booth change, leaving just his ten hundreds from Cook. He needed to rest now. He emptied his bladder inside the mini-mart, earning a third and clearly less cordial defenestration from the Per-Mar gentleman.

Inside the Cruise Master's galley kitchen, Dog fixed himself a vodka-Tang and smoked a nap-time Swisher. He walked a tired circle, pulling shut his curtains. He took his socks off, wrinkled his nose at the reek. He had to go outside and pin the socks beneath his wipers in the sun.

When he came back inside the Cruise Master, the bad smell was still there. It puzzled him. Five years of road was its own sour and musty thing. This smelled like river mud and body odor.

Dog thought about it. Maybe it was the mosquito protection he had hung across his bunk area. The netting was salvaged from a wind-wrecked screen tent, dredged from a swampy corner of the Two Hearted downstream of the campground. He had cut out a wide piece of mesh, rinsed it and dried it. Duct taped around his bunk, the tent-shred had become the perfect sleep shield. It was bug-proof and opaque, but it breathed. Now it stunk too, apparently. He had to get rid of it.

Dog finished his vodka-Tang in one gulp. He pinched back a curtain, checked the lay of the land. About a hundred yards away against the back of the mini-mart was a dumpster. But the gentleman from Per-Mar Security seemed to be pointing from the gas pumps straight toward the Cruise Master. Beside him was a police officer.

Dog yawned. Hell. Just stuff the mosquito net in a trash sack for the time being, set it outside the door. He didn't need trouble. He needed rest.

He peeled up a corner of duct tape, ripped it sideways, and down came the net.

In his bunk lay a man.

Dog froze, his mind stunned and blank except for one thought:

no pistol.

The man was big-shouldered. He lay on his side facing away, half covered with Dog's sleeping bag.

"Hey ..."

No movement. He made himself jostle the man.

"Hey ... pal ... come on."

Dog clenched a fist and held it like a club. He rolled the man. The sleeping bag came around too, stuck to skin and clothing. The fetid body odors billowed out. The man's face was bruise black. His neck was encircled with fly line wrapped about a dozen times, cutting into skin. He was way dead.

Dog's mind slung itself backward. How had he missed this?

His fingers moved on their own. The fly line that killed the man was an ancient one, pale orange and cracked. From its end trailed a damaged leader, bumpy with wind knots created by the gruesome casting of an unskilled fisherman.

He rolled the body over and—it was Dolf Cook.

How?

The blocky silver-haired head. The blue eyes. The jug-handle ears and stiff gray moustache. The drunk's nose.

But no.

It was not Dolf Cook.

This man was bigger. Firmer. This man wore an Evinrude jacket and a Skoal belt buckle and had presence, even dead. This was the "Governor of the U.P.," the big-shot guide, the one who kept his Finnish name and stayed home to nail Miss Michigan and fish with Bobby Knight.

This dead man in Dog's bunk was Cook's brother, Heimo Kock.

2

Outside Sheboygan, at a beach on Lake Michigan two hours north of Chicago, Dog pulled over and threw up.

He dragged out his sleeping bag, his fouled foam mat and its stained plywood support sections. He lit all this afire in the sand and drove on. He had other plans for the body. In the scrambled civics of the moment, Dog clung to this: he had paid too much for death already. This one was on Dolf Cook.

With every backward mile, Dog became more enmeshed in his course of reaction—and more uncertain of it. But what else could he do? His deadline was fixed in his mind. His primordial re-beginning wouldn't wait. He pictured Eamon's headstone, the timeless engraving, the horrible date. And he pictured M.J. sprawled on a floor, her face swelling. Never mind Harvey Digman. It wouldn't work unless she stood with him.

The corpse of Heimo Kock, swaddled in a plastic tarp, slid on the corners. Miles trickled through Dog's odometer. His gut seared. He could not stop the chatter.

Do what instead? Call over that City of Schaumburg policeman? Tell him what? "Hey, I brought this stiff down from the U.P.

Didn't know I had him, honest. You guys can take it from here. I gotta go. I'm innocent. Promise."

He would be tied up in no-man's land for days. Maybe even weeks.

If Dolf Cook had done a half decent job of framing him, he could be tied up for a lifetime.

The Cruise Master broke the tape into Upper Peninsula Michigan at mid-afternoon. Desolation followed. Dog chewed a Swisher stump, trying to stay awake another fifty miles.

By the Seney Swamp, he was certain he could dump the body anywhere. Bears and coyotes would take the flesh. Flies would oviposit. Maggots would scour the bones. Porcupines would gnaw for salts.

Dog could visualize the entire procedure, right down to Heimo Kock's massive set of photogenic teeth, perched for eternity atop a hummock of bog sedge, preserving the fishing guide's wide and boastful grin.

He pushed on. He had to play it as straight as he could. At least he had to leave the body where it could be found. His plan was to unload Kock upstream from Dolf Cook's cottage, give justice and closure a floating chance. Wasn't that half right anyway? Inside his plastic cocoon, Heimo Kock was silent, shifting ever-so-faintly on the corners.

Luce County occurred, to the indifference of the landscape. It began to rain. Fat drops steamed on asphalt. Then the road was awash, Dog's wipers unable to cope. Then it stopped.

Runty pines blurred the roadside. Dog needed nourishment and relief. He dropped rocks of Tang straight into Smirnoff's. He nursed on the jug, moonshine-style, getting good and logical. Keep moving. Here was the upper North Fork of the Two Hearted. Getting close.

At about Mile 37 on State 410, Dog picked out a logging road that looked wider and less sandy than average. He eased in, knowing this was his biggest gamble, an eight-ton RV on a sand road with no turnaround. But he had managed it before. He had to do it again.

Getting in was not bad. The road hit the river at a high bank about a quarter mile upstream of the Reed and Green Bridge Campground, where he had spent the last week. This was the same distance, approximately, from Dolf Cook's cottage. River depth and current were decent. The rain had helped, putting more push in the river. The Two Hearted was swollen, almost red.

Heimo Kock made egress from the Cruise Master with his head banging down the steps like a rock. Dog grabbed the tarp, dragged the body. With his boot prints straddling, the course to the high sand bank left a track like a colossal turtle. He would have to wipe that out.

At the edge of the bank, Dog maneuvered Heimo Kock sideways. He held onto the tarp's open end and let it unroll, launching the body into a thirty-foot tumble and then a splash. The river did its work. Heimo Kock floated out and away.

Dog shook the tarp. He cut out the grommets with his Leatherman and threw them in the river. He marinated the remaining tarp in diesel and lit it afire. It burned well, but with copious black smoke. Dog looked up. Visible for miles no doubt. *Go, Dog, go.*

He scouted the area for an exit plan. He backed the Cruise Master onto a crackling scrum of deadfall branches that gave good traction. He pulled forward onto a rocky knoll just wide enough to support his front wheels. He eased back into the deadfall once more. He pulled forward, now turning, one wheel up on the rocky knoll and the other sinking into sand. He goosed it. His rear tires spun. A dead branch shot back, shattered against a tree trunk. The Cruise Master tilted, engine racing and tires spitting sand. Then the old RV jerked forward, punched its nose into a tangle of sumac. Dog's windshield was shrouded with serrated red leaves. *Calm down. Calm down or else.*

His rear wheels—where were they? He got out. His rear wheels had emerged solidly into the narrow roadway. They should be ok. But the burning tarp would get involved if he backed his gas tank into it.

Dog worked two rocks loose from the sand. He measured, positioned, then backed up the Cruise Master until the rocks stopped his tires.

He got out again. His front end had ripped out a mustache of sumac leaves. He cleared these, feeling the ground ahead with his boots. Very soft. He wished he had waited to burn his plywood bunk supports.

He used his galley table and bench top instead. He tore them out and shoved them under the front tires. He heard them crack and splinter as he pulled forward. He tried to stop just before he came over the front end. He got out to look.

He needed to do the same thing again. He tore off his cupboard doors, discovering he had forgotten, last night, to immolate his collection of roadkill fly-tying materials and his leader-building kit. Later. Backing, he eased onto the doors, listening carefully to their slow ruination. He stopped just right. He forwarded the busted galley table and bench. Then the cupboard doors once more. Then with a risky spurt of gas he was out, facing home.

But there were all those tire tracks and footprints behind him. He parked the Cruise Master a short distance up the road, walked back and found a bristly deadfall that worked like a giant broom. He swept in circles around the fire to the high bank. He looked over at the river. The body had hung up on a sand spit about fifty yards downstream.

Dog slid down the bank. He waded out but quickly bogged down in muck. He crawled to the bank and worked his way downriver through dense brush to the sand spit. The mosquitoes were trying to make a goddamned citizen's arrest. He took Heimo Kock by the shoulders and pulled him into deep water, let him go again. That was all he could do. He fled the river bank.

Dog recovered his deadfall broom, walked backwards to his driver's door, dragging the broom behind him. Now it looked like a UFO had landed and tried to take off again—close to how Dog felt about his whole U.P. experience.

Yet he was going to make it. He visualized: out the sand logging road, down the dirt highway to the gravel highway, down the gravel highway to the pavement, down the pavement through Newberry, Engadine, and Manistique, through Escanaba, Marinette and Green Bay, back through lovely Schaumburg around midnight, around the Horn of Gary, east into a turnpike sunrise—

But an old green bus barricaded his path to the dirt highway.

Not an old green bus. Different. Modified. Doors fore and aft on the side facing him. Solid body in between. Windshield in two angled pieces, wipers at the top. Antique, wallowing, misplaced thing. Dog slowed, squinting. Lettering on the side of it.

Unbelievable words.

Really? On this occasion? Here?

The Luce County Bookmobile?

Dog blew his horn.

Into the window of the front flap door, a young woman's face popped into view, then out, then in again—a pigtailed redhead—then out again to stay.

Dog horned hard. She did not reappear. The driver's seat remained unoccupied. He considered ramming the thing. But old attachments paused him in neutral: all that Dr. Seuss in there, all that Curious George. The sacred texts, *The Wind in the Willows*, *Goodnight Moon*—he took his foot off the gas.

The bookmobile door was locked. Dog pounded. A shrill voice inside told him, "You're under arrest, buddy!"

"The hell I am. Move this thing."

"I'm calling the sheriff right now!"

"Move it."

"I saw what you did!"

Dog circled, cussing in large, hair-curling terms. He stood on the front bumper and cupped his hands to the glass. Keys hung from the ignition. In the rear of the bus, a wiry young woman flattened her body against a loaded bookshelf, a cell phone open against her cheek. She met Dog's eyes with a hot glare. Dog lingered inside his hand-tunnel, eyes adjusting. Her frightened face was spotted with huge freckles, framed in coppery hair shaped in square bangs and weird, horizontal pigtails. She wore a patchwork shift, mismatched knee socks and clod-hopping boots.

All this looked vaguely familiar. But he couldn't place it. He jumped off the bumper. He tried to take the Cruise Master around, through the brush-clogged ditch. He went at speed, embedding the front end in a tangle of small-bore limbs and stumps until his wheels spun. Backing out, he sheared off his far-side mirror. His keepsake fly reel snapped off between the wipers. Something popped between his ears. His brain went fizz.

When he emerged from the Cruise Master this time, he carried his camp axe. He hopped the bumper. He inserted the camp axe through the bookmobile's divided windshield with one crisp chop.

She shrieked. "Fucker!"

Dog shoved his head through broken glass. "Never heard that word in a library."

She shrieked again. "Get away you fucker!"

"You parked me in." Dog elbowed safety glass to the side. "That's not nice."

"You are under citizen's arrest!"

"The hell I am. I'm moving this bus."

"Stay—fucker!—stay where you are!"

Dog kicked in head first over the window seal. He hung upside down, reaching for the keys. Her big clodhoppers clunked. She was coming. He grabbed the steering column to stop himself from somersaulting. He strained for an extra inch. She snatched the keys from his grasp.

Boot-clunks scampered back. "Now he's got an axe," she informed someone through her phone. "He's coming in."

Dog let go into the somersault. He hooked glass, tore his pants from crotch to cuff. He came up lunatic with pain and desperation. Yes, he did have an axe. He raised it for emphasis.

"Give me those keys."

"No! Yes! State 410, a little west of Reed and Green! I've got him blocked in. Tell Margarite. She's where? Oh, shit."

Dog inched toward her. "I didn't kill that guy."

"I saw you."

"I had nothing to do with it."

"I saw the smoke. I walked in there and I saw you dump him in the river." To the phone she said, "I know you have to tell the sheriff. Just tell Margarite too."

"Give me the keys."

"You were burning evidence."

"You read too many books," Dog said. "Why don't you give me the keys, and mind your own business."

She clipped the keys to a lanyard around her neck, where they hung with an ID card. She reached behind her. She hurled a heavy book past his head.

"Ok," she said into the phone. "Put her on."

She hurled another book. Very accurate. Dog felt the spine graze his shoulder.

"Stay where you are, fucker. Stay back. Margarite? Jesus, Margarite—you're all the way in Brimley? With Julia? Not with Julia. Fishing? Not fishing. Ok. Ok. Yes, I have the pager. I didn't think of it. Ok. But wait—it's behind him."

Breathing fast, she eyed Dog up and down. "Yes, an axe. About six feet and thin, sunburned, green eyes maybe, shaggy brown hair, and a dirtball beard. Forty or so. What? Yes. But he's right there in front of that, too. Ok—ok, I'll try."

She folded the phone with a pop that charged the air between them.

Dog said, "I don't want to hurt you."

"Sure." Those weird pigtails emphasized the incredulous tilt of her head. "I'll bet you've said that before. Right before you started chopping limbs off."

Dog leaned the axe against Local History. He tried to settle himself. "I'm not dangerous. Please. You're a librarian. Is that right?"

"I do have a degree in Information Sciences, so that's right, fucker."

"I've heard it's bad luck to hurt a librarian."

"Oh, it is," she said. "The worst. Don't mess with us. Or me, in this case. I'm the only one in Luce County, and they've cut me back to part time. How about that?"

"Keys," Dog said, holding out his hand. "You won't be letting loose a criminal. I promise. I'm a good guy. It will all work out."

"You've got all the lines, axe man."

She began to creep those clod-hopping boots toward a little checkout station at the rear door of the van. Meanwhile she was changing tones, keeping Dog off balance.

"I'll bet you just need a chance."

"You're right. I do."

"You just need a break. Just this once."

"That's it."

"Someone to believe in you."

"Right."

"You haven't done anything all *that* wrong. Anyway, you didn't *mean* to."

"Not really, no."

She was near the desk, near the door. "Lately, I'll bet, you've done a lot of soul searching."

"More than you can imagine. And stop fucking with me. Give me those keys."

"And ... you've changed," she said. "You really have ... honest."

"Look ... why don't we just move this bus and let the cops worry about me."

Dog had followed her in little dry-fly stalk-steps. Again he reached his hand out.

"Just give me the keys. Please?"

"Ok." Suddenly teeth and dimples. "You convinced me."

She raised the keys, jingled them, and threw them over his head. No, she didn't. She faked him. They never left the lanyard. When Dog turned back, she had punched the rear door and jumped.

Dog followed. When he got out, she was heading back into the bookmobile by the front door. Dog arrived just as that door locked.

"Fucker!" he heard shrieked from down by the rear door, which was now locked too.

Dog howled his own terrible words into the cool purple of a U.P. dusk. Mosquitoes descended.

He went back to the Cruise Master and looked at his map. He considered hoofing it, running from here to Dolf Cook's, grabbing the picture of Cook and the brookie, digging in the wood box for the old Pflueger reel, the one Cook had tried to plant on him, with its cracked pale-orange line to match the one around his brother's neck. But Brimley—where this "Margarite" was—Dog guessed was forty minutes away. There was time to work this out. This was a damn bookmobile, after all. This was a librarian, in pigtails and magic marker freckles, terrified, with her knee socks falling down. How hard could it be?

But when Dog dropped once more through the broken wind-shield, she shoved a vintage shotgun in his face. She had his axe too, filed behind her in Psychology. She showed him a small, black pager.

"Hey, fucker. Welcome back." The pager buzzed. "There we go. The sheriff's department now has your exact GPS coordinates."

She pulled up a little stool from the kiddie section and got comfortable. Her legs folded smoothly beneath those baggy knee socks, one black, one brown.

"You too. Sit down."

She adjusted her aim until with one squeeze she could shelve Dog's head in Self Help. Then she gave him the perfect, perky, story-time smile.

"So ... let me guess, Mister ..."

"My name is Ned Oglivie. I've been calling myself Dog."

"Oh, how sad," she said. "Because deep down you're just a lost puppy who's in a lot of pain. Right? Fucker?"

3

Esofea Maria Smithback watched him check her up and down, boots to pigtails, with bloodshot eyes surrounded by sunburn and rimmed in a mask of pale, dirty skin the shape of his sunglasses.

This she called "varmint face."

She had seen it a thousand times.

This was the taxonomic mug shot of the Yooper hose monkey as he woke up in middle age on the verge of renal failure and a permanent vehemence against all things that frustrated him, primarily women. It was a fact that her boyfriend, the hose-monkey varmint-face fucker Danny Tervo, was currently diagramming his big passage into man-hell, and he was planning to take her with him.

She was calming down, her brain beginning to work again. She had seen this "Dog," this canine member of the Tervo brotherhood, drag a large man's body off a little hump of sand and let it go into the river current. She had felt frightened, then she had felt filled with civic outrage, then frightened again—but now she felt mostly sick with exasperation. She had so been here before.

He ran a dirty hand through his dirty hair and looked around the Luce County Bookmobile. She had reorganized the old bus that morning, while it was parked outside the county office. She had put all books with *Edmund Fitzgerald* shipwreck references together on the Focus Shelf. These had been for the Crisp Point Light Historical Society luncheon. She had snuck in books on U.P. Indian massacres and the epic deforestation of the white pine, making a backdoor point about *real* tragedies, the kind that kept on happening. After the luncheon, she had dressed up and done a "Hop on Pop" at a birthday party in Deer Park—slipping a little Pippi Longstocking into that one.

This varmint was exactly what Danny Tervo was planning to be in another few years—wasted, stupidly criminal, but still thinking he was smooth. He said, "Let's calm down. So, you fish?"

"What makes you say that?"

"*Salvelinus fontinalis* on your ears." He nodded. "Your earrings."

"Is that what they are?"

"Brook trout."

Esofea didn't know brook trout from Brooke Shields. Her new girlfriend in the Sheriff's Department, Deputy Margarite DuCharme, a lesbian, had given the earrings to her. Platonically, it was understood.

"So you think you can flirt your way out of this? Is that it? Fucker?"

"I thought we could get to know each other a little. See if that helped any."

He glanced at the shotgun, probably wondering if she knew how to use it. She released the cross-bolt safety at the rear of the trigger guard, to convey the fact that as a Smithback woman, she did know, and she had, and she would. He tried to act unimpressed. Old ground.

"Brimley is a long way off," he said. "What else are we going to do?"

"Maybe you could beg for your life."

"You're some kind of librarian."

"Yeah?" Esofea said. "Which kind?"

"In my experience, yours are a peace-loving people."

She studied him a while. Dirty, dangerous, lippy, and clever—yes, she did have a weakness. She and Deputy DuCharme had discussed these things—tendencies and patterns—over instant coffee in the break room of the Luce County office.

"So who did you kill?"

"Nobody. But that was Heimo Kock."

"Bullshit."

"I've seen Heimo Kock. Looks just like his brother Dolf Cook but in better shape. Silver hair and red face. Dressed in boat-rep swag."

She was truly astonished. If this were true, it was perfect. If Heimo Kock was dead, no doubt Danny Tervo was involved. With this "Dog." Amazing how these fuckers found each other.

"You offed Heimo Kock …"

"I didn't off him."

"Unbelievable. Somebody finally offed Heimo Kock."

"I didn't touch him until he showed up dead in my vehicle."

"You're a hero. And a dead man." These elemental Yooper truths just came to her. "Assassin to the 'Governor of the U.P.' What a feeling, huh?"

He just shook his head, no.

Esofea sat back on the kiddie stool to give the shotgun a little more room. Remarkable how these fuckers could claim they had not done what they had obviously just done. Their trick was they believed their own bullshit. She tried to recall if Pippi, including the movies and all the Swedish TV episodes, had ever held a psychopathic criminal at gunpoint. Times like this, Esofea had a mantra for herself. What Would Pippi Do? WWPD, for short.

"Can I have a lollipop?" the fucker asked her.

They were in a basket behind her. "Those are Jolly Pops," she told him, "and there are no Jolly Pops for bad boys."

"Come on. Toss one over here. Purple."

"Purple, huh? Your favorite?"

"No."

"Then why purple?"

He waited to respond, building drama. "Well," he said at last. "Well," he repeated, "shit." His shoulders slumped. "Ok, I'm going to tell you." And here came the classic hose-monkey-varmint-face shift to the quivering voice and the teary eyes. To the tender man grief. "You know where I was headed before you parked me in?"

"Hmm ... Mexico?"

"Walnut Hills Cemetery, Boston, Mass."

"Oh, good boy. You visit your victims."

She tossed him a green Jolly Pop. He gave her this deflated look, as if to say: *Green? How could you?* Danny Tervo made that same face when she nailed him, like it just *wasn't fair* to turn over the rotten log of his soul and watch the bugs squirm. And half the time the fucker would get an apology out of her, complete with her special acrobatic make-up sex. That was the sickest part, really. Her gullibility. Her guilt and loneliness. Her inability to take the risk and cut him off forever. And this all went way back.

Discussion points, all of these, with Deputy Margarite, who was now on the cell phone, updating. Just out of Brimley, coming up on Raco. Thirty minutes. Was she ok? Did she have her varmint gun on the suspect?

"He whacked Heimo Kock," she interrupted the deputy. "Can you believe it?"

Margarite was silent a moment. "Well, hang on to him," she said finally. "For the sheriff's department, obviously, but for his own good, too. Know what I mean?"

"No shit," Esofea said.

Varmint Face, watching her for a weakness, repeated, "I didn't kill him. I haven't done anything wrong. I made a bad decision, but I didn't kill anyone."

Funny: even green eyes like Danny. "A sheriff's deputy will be here in three minutes," she lied, dividing the situation by ten.

"Can you listen to me? Can I tell you what happened?"

"Sure. We can make it story time. Go ahead."

"I was at the campground. I was the only one there except for Dolf Cook. I left about midnight. I drove down to Chicago and that's where—"

"Don't give me the 'I-didn't-do-it' story," Esofea interrupted. "You can try that one on my friend the deputy. She's a lesbian. Not having had the pleasure, she might be more sympathetic. As for me, the story I'm game for is the 'I-couldn't-help-it' story. It's my favorite. I hear it all the time."

He swallowed. Looked hurt still. "You," he said, "ought to be driving something like a parking enforcement vehicle, not a bookmobile."

"I love kids," she said. "They really are innocent."

"They haven't double parked yet."

"Right."

"They're not so injured. Like me and you."

That slowed her down a beat. Like her? Injured? He could see that? Were the freckles too thin? Danny never saw it.

"After a certain point we're all in pain," he went on. "Some more than others." He narrowed his eyes at her. "My little boy drowned in the bathtub six years ago, while my wife and I argued about tulips."

Esofea squinted at the varmint. "Wow. Swinging for the fences right away. You don't even need to warm up?"

"He would have turned ten in two days."

"Oh, sure, and—"

"And I've been away," he talked over her, "more than five of those years. This Saturday his mother is going to drive through the gates of the cemetery, like she has every year, with flowers and balloons and toys, and she's going to wonder where the hell I am. This time I was planning to be there. But someone dumped a body on me—and here I am, trying to dump it back ... and be on my way."

Esofea scooted her kiddie stool a bit to the left. "Good story," she said. Funny how the fucker was so anatomically correct, with the tight brown forearms, the long-fingered hands, the slightly feral slouch. "Hemingway-caliber bullshit. My boyfriend Danny Tervo loves that macho pain junk. But I've built up my immunity."

She kept the shotgun pressed into her shoulder as she reached back, feeling along the Health and Wellness bookshelf with her left hand. The book she wanted was a heavy one, with a brittle dust jacket. She tossed *The Family Guide to Abnormal Psychology* across the floor. "Look on page eighty-six. And read," she said.

She re-established the shotgun. "Read. It's good for you."

Varmint Face read, "'A USC study has found the first proof of structural brain abnormalities in people who habitually lie, cheat, and manipulate others ... significant association with criminality and other antisocial pathologies ...'"

He looked at her without blinking. His kind could do that. "You think I'm lying? Right behind you. *Green Eggs and Ham*. Open it. I'll prove I was a father."

Esofea snorted and broke out laughing. She had heard all kinds of Yooper hose-monkey-varmint-face malarkey in her twenty-nine years but never had she heard of Tervo et. al. begging for a chance to prove paternity. *I didn't do it.* That was their motto. Suddenly here was someone different, refreshing actually, axing his way into her life.

She balanced the shotgun in one hand. She opened the Seuss book. "That's quite an offer, Dad. But it's gotta be perfect."

Dog had played a game with Eamon. For a while his little boy was obsessed with x-ray vision. So Dog had learned to close a book and pretend to read it through the cover. He would grunt and struggle, grit his teeth, shake the book. He would ask Eamon to massage his temples. He would spew nonsense. "I am a donkey." He would tilt the book to a new angle and improve to half-nonsense. "I am Rick." At last he would ask Eamon for a stiff slap to the back of the head—whap!—and finally Dog would get it right.

"I am Sam," he said now. "Sam I am."

The librarian was instantly unimpressed. "Never mind," she said, twisting abruptly to re-shelve the book. The shotgun never lost its vector at his head. "Everybody knows that. It's the only book most people can remember. Now where did you say you were from?"

"Boston."

"A father in Boston in would know Sterling Carpenter."

"I do."

She brayed an awkward laugh that seemed to hurt somewhere in her chest. For a moment she stared blankly at Dog. At last she said, "Of course you do. God, you are so much like Danny Tervo, knowing every goddamn thing a person can think of, or claiming to. Go on. Prove it."

Dog fumbled in his memory for a title, a topic, any purchase on the work of Sterling Carpenter, who was right up there with the *Make Way for Ducklings* guy—was it Robert McCloskey?—yes, right up there with McCloskey in the pantheon of local writers erected by the Boston Chamber of Commerce. Christ, there was a bronze statue of Mrs. Mallard in Boston Commons. Then he had it: the lobster. A plaque on the Boston Harbor Walk. *Ludwig the Lobster*, by Sterling Carpenter. About a silly lobster in the live tank at a grocery store, anxious to be selected.

Dog began, "'Pick me!' cried Ludwig the Lobster ..."

The librarian seemed startled.

"... as he tip-toed in the tank. 'I'm the nicest! I'm the brightest! I'm so much handsomer than Hank!'"

He looked at her. "More?"

"Of course more," she said, "fucker."

Dog ground his teeth. He wondered if the shotgun was loaded, if there had been time in the frantic moments before he had plunged back through the windshield.

He went on. "'Over here!' waved Ludwig Lobster, as he wiggled in the tank. 'I'm a singer! I'm a dancer! I'm so much fancier than Frank!'"

Now Dog summoned up in wrenching detail the wideness of Eamon's eyes as they had frozen on the picture of crackpot Ludwig, begging to be chosen for someone's kettle of boiling water. Eamon's alarmed expression, Dog recalled, had showed a nervous father just how vast was the innocence he was charged with defending, and maybe that explained why the words of Sterling Carpenter had never left his mind. Here came more.

"'I'm the one!' proud Ludwig signaled, as he swam around the brim. 'I'm oh so stronger! Oh so longer! Oh so healthier than Slim!'"

The librarian had him fixed in a grim squint. He noticed the whiteness of her knuckles on the stock of the shotgun. "And?" she said. "Next?"

"We closed the book then. We put it back."

"Why? Liar. It's hilarious. Sterling Carpenter is goddamn hoot."

Dog stared down the shotgun barrel into those pinched green eyes. "Yeah, well ... fatal ignorance, self-inflicted doom ... those concepts are hell on four-year-olds, I guess. My little boy was horrified."

She lowered the barrel a little. She shook her strangely pigtailed head side to side in mock admiration. "Wow. You're good. *Ludwig the Lobster*, not age-appropriate. That is developmentally correct, as a matter of fact. But probably this is just an aspect of your psychopathy, knowing just how children get messed up."

"Oh, I messed him up, all right."

Dog's voice trembled on the confession. But with a silent effort he bit off his grief. He could hurl the heavy reference book at her, he thought, then roll and dive for the shotgun. But not yet—now that she was sort of smiling at him, her elbows looking loose.

"Ludwig the Lobster escapes," she said. "Did you know that?"

He didn't know that. He drifted a hand beneath the book. "Yeah? How?"

"Someone falls in love with him. You know, with his self-delusion, his damaged behavior, his complete lack of a realistic worldview."

"Lucky Ludwig."

"You want to put the psych book down? Slide it across the floor? Put your hands behind your head? Fucker? Thanks."

With the effort of raising his arms, Dog realized he was weak on adrenaline, not much juice left in the gland. Still, he summoned an idea.

"You still think I'm lying?"

"Brilliantly."

"Then how about this. My boy's favorite book. Mine too. Right behind you again. *McElligot's Pool*." She re-tightened her grip on the shotgun. Dog clasped his hands exactly on top of his head. "Go on. Open it. You might have forgotten. It's about hope, and enthusiasm, about never giving up, and trusting what you believe."

"It's about fishing."

"Like I said."

She found the book by feel, right over her shoulder, its cellophane jacket cloudy and cracked.

Dog said, "Go to the page second from the end, the one with

all the fish in the sea." She paged. He waited. "With curly noses and feather tails and buck teeth. One with frog feet. One with a kung-fu moustache. How many fish are there in the sea?"

"How many fish in the sea? Just one." She gave him a cheesy smile—bitter cheese. "Just my man."

"On the page."

"'A number' it says."

Dog said, "My son counted sixty-eight. Is he right?"

The librarian looked down, her eyes roving over the Seussian throng of goofball swimmers.

"Go on," Dog urged. "Sixty-eight. Check him."

She sighed, "Ok, stop," and closed the book.

"Fucker," she muttered, glaring at him.

Dog let a breath out. "Is there a society of professional librarians?" he asked, "where I can report you?"

"If I let you go," she answered, "will you kill someone for me, too?"

"Sure."

"Liar."

"This boyfriend of yours must be a real asshole. What's his name again?"

He watched her eyes press shut. Quickly, silently, he un-knit his hands and sprang to one knee. But she caught it. She aimed the shotgun at his groin. "I believe you know him. Danny Tervo. And what was your son's name?"

"Ea—"

The word, the name, the first sound of it, made Dog's heart ache and his throat close. "Eam—" His airway stuck. His heart had ballooned up and choked him.

"The lollipop would be cute right now," she said, "while your eyes tear up."

Dog squeezed a breath in and out. A strange thought entered his mind: if he were ever free of this, he could ask this woman on a date—and strangle her.

"Eamon Theodore Oglivie."

This made two tears spill out and wander into his beard. Then a third.

"Fucker," she murmured. "You're a pro. You oughta teach the class. He was how old?"

"Four. Four-and-a-half."

"And he drowned in the tub? And you didn't kill yourself? See, I know something about the pain of that, and that's how I know you're lying."

Dog jaw fell slack. "What kind of person would lie about something like—"

"Danny Tervo."

Dog could not respond. The librarian seemed spent as well. They stared at each other. A chipmunk chattered outside. Then a dove began to keen. Dog wiped a sleeve across his face.

"Let me go," he said at last. "It will turn out ok."

"You're lying."

"Let me go."

"I wish I could help you."

"You can. You can trust me."

"What did you say?"

"You can trust me."

"*What?*"

"Trust me."

"Fucker. I hate those words. *Fucker.*"

She blinked rapidly. Breathed rapidly too. One of her legs, the one in the black stocking, jittered up and down at the knee, and her head began to shake along the horizontal plane of her pigtails. This went on while Dog weighed his options. Then her eyes fell shut. She seemed in some sort of trance.

Dog stood with extreme care. He waited for his balance. The gritty floor of the bookmobile made faint crunches as he moved in reverse. One step, two steps, three …

Then he spun. He hit the door. He sprang onto the deserted dirt highway.

He made three strides to the opposite shoulder, hearing a siren in the near distance. He was in mid-air, hurdling the ditch in a cloud of mosquitoes, when she shot him in the back.

4

When Danny Tervo heard about the corpse of Heimo Kock dumped in the Two Hearted River, he was just outside of Tucson, Arizona, six AM, heading north on Interstate 10 with an empty tanker, and he celebrated. He blew his horn and waggled the tanker's ass-end in the face of an airport mini-van behind him. He lit up an American Spirit—the organic one—and blasted his dusty wind-shield with a big, smoky "Ahhh!"

Sweetness. Heimo Kock was dead.

God Grand Coulee Damn. How lucky could he get?

His bud Conrad Belcher waited, mouth-breathing out of Tervo's prepaid phone.

"Belch, come on. You're not just shitting me?"

"I shit you not." Belcher was Tervo's man on the ground, so to speak, though the dude spent half his life in tree stands. Tervo pictured Belch in the U.P. dawn, cross-legged on a platform in the Seney swamp, a camo-skin cell phone to his ear.

"Shot?"

"Strangled."

"Perfectly righteous. They know who?"

Tervo heard a meaty slap. "Damn skeeters coulda done it." So maybe Belch wasn't in a tree stand. Maybe he was walking over a mud bog in his snowshoes with a bucket of bear bait. "But I heard they got some fly fisher dude from back east."

Tervo changed lanes to the right. He wanted to slow down and savor this. Some fly fisher dude from back east. How about that? All those U.P. tourism dollars finally paying off, everybody free to do business from here on without the hassle of Heimo Kock—everybody meaning especially him, Tervo, who had been in need of a Kock solution of his own. As a matter of fact, he had been planning to coffee-up and hatch something on the drive home.

But strangled by a tourist? And a fly fisherman? Belcher could have told him the Blind Sucker River had filled up with Oktoberfest beer and Danny Tervo could not have been more spliffed—or more eager to get back home.

"But, Danny, here's the thing."

Tervo wasn't totally listening. The problem with chilling in the right lane was the sleep-addled clowns who approached merging onto a highway like they were half-inch-to-ball-sac on Lake Superior and couldn't take the plunge. Tervo blew his horn for real, a long foghorn blast at some Outbacker who couldn't find his gas pedal.

"Yeah? What, Belch? The thing?"

"Well ... you and Esofea, where's that at these days?"

"Huh?" Tervo had to rattle his brain a little. "Uh, yeah, Esofea, lemme see."

His run to Tucson had been a big event. He had made his inaugural product dump at his ideal price point, and then he had met some people. These people had been holding some stuff. There had been a pool party, brown women, multi-lingual karaoke. Right now the U.P. seemed ten thousand miles away.

"The usual, I guess. I had the snip and she was pissed. I know I said some shit to her. Probably there was also some shit I didn't say. I just can't remember if we got back together or not."

"She might be mad at you, then?"

"Dunno."

"You gonna reverse the surgery?"

"Belch—what the hell? Whose side you on, brother?"

Anticipating the rush of early commuters at the North Tucson on-ramp, Tervo forced the truck back into the center lane. Belcher said, "I'm trying to help you here."

"Ok, Belch. Help me. What's the deal?"

"You check your regular cell?"

"Didn't bring it. Only the prepaid on business trips, Belch."

Belcher's voice was faint suddenly: "You want I give Esofea this number?"

"Hell, no. What? Belch—"

"—I heard she told one of the EMTs—"

Tervo shook the phone. Too far from a tower.

"Belch?"

One of the Upper Peninsula's national forests had swallowed the signal. Now down a curl of concrete onto Interstate 10 bumpered a new flight of Arizonans, swarming out of their drought-stricken suburbs, heading out to eat and drink and buy and sell as usual in this worst-ever, total water catastrophe.

The deepest drought in a hundred years, and nobody down here wanted to give up anything. There was big money in inertia, Tervo was sure. Big.

So Esofea told who what?

Danny Tervo drove a retired Golden Guernsey milk tanker, five thousand gallons, rebuilt Volvo engine under the hood, four hundred horses, chemically etched clean on the inside and repainted outside to say *The Essence of Soy*, except it wasn't paint actually, it was stickers, like the wraps they put on buses and trains these days, so Tervo could change stories as needed. He was *DSY Environmental* during a dry run of the pumping and dumping aspect. Early summer for an exploration of weigh station evasion techniques he got honks with *Moose Creek Maple Syrup*—having a little too much fun with it. Five thousand gallons of maple syrup? What the hell was he thinking? The idea was to *avoid* attention.

All the way up through Marana and Eloy, Tervo just spaced around in the afterglow of Heimo Kock's death. Talk about a perfect drought, however. It was dry everywhere southwest of Denver. And it was spreading. Some places had water under the ground, aquifers, but even the aquifers were in trouble. A few hundred miles north, beneath all that Kansas corn and wheat, the Oglala was the biggest underground water resource in North America. Five hundred feet below his truck sometime later in the wee hours would be an estimated twenty-three trillion gallons. But Tervo's research had told him even the Oglala aquifer was shrinking by about five percent a year. Amazing. Scary. Whereas Lake Superior was at three quintillion gallons and holding. So … money in the bank, right?

Off and on through recent history, according to Tervo's studies, some Arizona or New Mexico politician had suggested tapping the Oglala, floating the argument that the water resource belonged to everyone and had to be shared equitably, or at least traded on the free market. After all, didn't Arizona send microchips to Kansans who did not make their own? Didn't Florida share its citrus with Nebraska? But this bullshit was shot down by spectacular opposition. Now and then some idiot cowboy congressman mentioned diverting water from the Great Lakes Basin and thereby committed political seppuku, laid his bowels out on the desk of some CNN talk show. You didn't touch the Great Lakes. Not out in the open. Tervo had done the research. The Great Lakes were a *Swiss* bank.

At a co-op in Casa Grande, he had vegan eggs Benedict and a bottle of kombucha. He wired up on Korean ginseng and aimed for Phoenix. Lovely.

She didn't cross his mind, Esofea.

But Danny crossed and double-crossed her mind a dozen times until at dawn Esofea pulled the plug on a nightlong Xanax-vs.-nicotine throwdown in a ring of sweaty sheets and admitted she had shot someone who was possibly *not* Danny Tervo in absentia. Who was possibly innocent. Possibly.

To a girl with a pestilence—this was her problem—every man looked like a varmint.

Esofea Maria Smithback confessed this to herself, and got up, and looked at the Newberry Motors calendar that hung above the wood box in the kitchen of the old Frens mansion. She thought of this Dog and his trip to the cemetery in Boston. So his idea was to formalize his grief? To give it a place and a time and an action, so that it wasn't everywhere, all the time, in everything he did? It couldn't hurt her to try. She picked an anniversary date. Today. She knew the place, too.

She made coffee and fit the travel mug between the seat and the emergency brake in her rickety red VW Beetle—Danny Tervo sold it to her—and drove against the morning stream of empty pulp-wood trucks all the way to where the Two Hearted River joined Lake Superior. Her cell phone buzzed twice atop the passenger seat: Danny's pal Belcher. She loved Belcher. But she ignored it. She had the date and place. What would be her action, she mused, for grief?

After the turn east on 410, the roads became "Yooper freeway." That meant free of rules, free of signs, free of taxes, free of pavement. Esofea bent over the Beetle's ivory steering wheel and checked the sky. What she didn't need when driving the Beetle was the road soup that came with rain, also free of charge. But the clouds were high puffs, still pink on their eastern cheeks. She was ok.

She parked in the Mouth of the Two Hearted Campground. She walked over the river on the little suspension bridge. She crunched her way across the thickness of beach agates to the wave line where walking was easier. She took her shoes and socks off. Cold.

Cold, cold, cold, cold, cold, cold—until she reached the reunion of waters, where pale brown river swirled into pale green lake. There she stepped from the stinging surf and back onto beach rocks, which felt warm.

Here was her problem: there was no exact site of burial, not when living tissue simply left your body and entered the flow of shit and piss and eggshells through the sewer pipes. Esofea felt sick for a while, all over again. But this place seemed ok. For one thing—to be positive again—she had heard Sheriff Bruce Lodge report to Deputy Margarite DuCharme that the Coho were out there, schooling in the lake, getting ready to spawn. She thought of a million salmon, massing, building pressure, ready to squirt and race and struggle upstream to implant new life in the river bottom. This, the blunt ubiquity of sex, of drive, made her feel very small, but in a good way, as in not alone. Then there was the opposite motion, river flowing into lake, pretty clouds rising into limitless sky, an endless water cycle where the infinitesimal mingled into the vast and became new shapes and new directions. So the burial site for *her* baby was here then. The agates made a thousand-million lovely headstones. Only thing missing was the fucker, Danny.

Action? She should weep. Esofea knew that. She thought about it. Did he weep, her new friend Dog? She stretched her toes, lit a cigarette. She was afraid to weep. The ride was too wild.

Perched among the agates, her little red cell phone began to buzz, its window saying *Sheriff Dept … Sheriff Dept … Sheriff Dept …*

She expected Deputy Margarite, calling to arrange a follow-up regarding yesterday's events. Instead, Sheriff "Bruce the Moose" Lodge said, "Young lady, where you at right this minute?"

"The lake."

"Doin' what?"

She tossed an agate as high as she could. It peaked and fell, entered the lake with a short hard *tump!*—like all that heavy water had inhaled it.

"Nothing, I guess."

"Good. We're all tied up today. Do me a favor? I got a call from some folks at the Blind Sucker Campground about somebody shooting off a cannon from the other side of the flooding. You figure that's your Grandma Tiina with her punt gun again?"

See? She told herself she should buck up.

It wasn't like she totally lacked a family.

Esofea could confirm the noise complaint from the turn-in to the Blind Sucker Resort. Up on the deck of the main lodge, Mummo Tiina had Great-Grandpa Smithback's historical punt gun—a shotgun, ten feet long—propped on the rail while she loaded in a shell. The remainder of the Smithback clan—Uncle Rush, Aunt Daryline,

Cousin Caroline—milled around, ineffectually and with substances, as they did best.

Esofea pounded the wimpy Beetle horn as she cornered the Blind Sucker flooding, not wanting to get hit. That gun could shred an entire flock of geese with one pull. She gave the horn all she had. But of course Mummo Tiina pulled the trigger.

Esofea hit the brakes and ducked.

Waited.

Clear, she thought.

Continued.

But no—the shot had been aimed skyward. A sheet of raining lead clipped the tail of the Beetle as she made the turn by the boat-house, heading up the hill to the dilapidated family resort. *Blind Sucker Resort, Cabins, Boats, Trips, Est. 1937.* The sign was barely readable anymore. The resort made a fortune in its day, but lately most tourists turned around right here, at *Blind ucker ort,* while they still could.

Big old Mummo Tiina was swabbing out the punt gun's barrel with a mitten duct-taped to a musky rod as Esofea came through the great room of the lodge onto the deck. Uncle Rush rose from a peeling Adirondack lounger and claimed, "I told her to stop it."

"Hmm," said Esofea, moving around him, "but she just wouldn't listen to an unemployed man in his pajamas drinking beer at nine in the morning."

"You just come right in talking like that," Aunt Daryline observed from her own lounger. "Like you own the place."

"You're lucky I don't."

Esofea's grandmother, who did own the place, was preparing another blast. From a crate between her black ankle boots she produced a shotgun shell the size of Uncle Rush's sixteen-ounce beer can. She loaded the shell and sat back in a wheeled chair from the lodge office. She folded a pillow between the gun stock and her shoulder. Behind her, twelve-year-old Caroline performed a dramatic huff.

Esofea said, "Mummo, no. The sheriff called me. You're scaring people all the way across the flooding at the campground."

"These ain't pajamas," Uncle Rush argued.

Aunt Daryline backed him up. "Them are his hospital scrubs." She tipped a coffee cup and took a hit to the face from sliding ice.

"So Doctor Rush is doing surgery this morning?"

Caroline muttered, "Oh, my god." She was having a red Mountain Dew, quart-size, mostly gone. Esofea took it away, poured the rest off the deck.

"Hey!"

"How come you're not in school?"

"I missed the bus and nobody could drive me."

"Which nobody?"

Esofea turned to glare at Rush and Daryline.

"Get ready," she told the girl. "We're leaving in five minutes. Mummo Tiina, what are you shooting at?"

"Him."

"Him who?"

Daryline said, "Them are Rush's scrubs he got legally the time they sewed his tongue back together."

"Today we got bad backs," Rush clarified. "Me and Daryline both. Doctor's orders. That's why we ain't drove her."

"Caroline, go. Get ready. Mummo Tiina, which him are you—"

When the punt gun went off, Esofea lost all sensation. She reeled away into a brainscape of red-and-black zigzags, reminiscent of places Danny had taken her more often than she cared to remember. The fucker was always holding. Always.

When she had faculties again, Esofea discovered Mummo Tiina had been driven across the deck by the recoil—thus the wheeled chair, which was blocked from hitting the lodge windows by sullen Caroline. Having done her duty for Mummo Tiina, the girl turned to prepare for school.

"That'll fix you," Mummo Tiina said.

"Fix who?"

She pointed a gnarled finger toward those pink-cheeked clouds, beyond the flooding and over the big lake.

"Go to hell where you belong," the old woman scolded the shreds of some ghost she saw floating in the sky. "You old Heimo Kock."

5

Theodore (Ned) Oglivie, before he went feral, had been fired upon three times, and each time his life had changed.

The first two of these events took place during his previous life as CEO and sole employee of Oglivie Secure, his start-up corporate security firm in suburban Boston. Those bullets came his way at a time in company history when "corporate client" meant a Citgo station in a rough part of town, or a Lotto outlet that was too close to a liquor store, and before Dog was able to employ targets on his behalf.

The bullet at the Mopar Auto Parts warehouse in Roxbury was wide right by about twenty feet. The thief had been in flight with so much chrome that his aim was distorted. Still, the percussion, the out-of-the blue shock, had knocked Dog to the glass-speckled asphalt behind the warehouse, where he had lain among cigarette butts and flattened PET bottles while the Mopar manager ran around screaming Ukrainian blood oaths and waving a wicked shank of muffler pipe.

It was during these few moments that as a tenured boyfriend Dog had decided, hell, why not just propose to Mary Jane? It was clear he couldn't jump the fence and run, didn't want it quite badly enough. So what was he waiting for?

The second occasion was freakish luck. Dog and M.J. were still newlyweds. They were party people, spending the money they imagined they would accumulate later, no problem. Mary Jane discovered recreational drug use and began to make up for having been a clueless Catholic pretty girl at Mount Holyoke. Dog stuck to booze and felt righteous about it. The stock market was booming—actually metastasizing, as it turned out. But Oglivie Secure was gaining ground. Dog had nibbled off a little corner of the Raytheon market. He was guarding the parking lot at the Waltham facility. He worked sixteen-hour days. On weekends he interviewed for help.

Quality guards were tough to come by, though. The good ones were real cops. The bad ones Dog wouldn't trust to guard a turd in the toilet of the men's room during a Pats game at Foxborough. In the middle ground were ex-military, and those guys were a tough read. All yessir and nossir, fully capable, sir—with very little, often, to back it up.

There was one intense young man whose discharge papers "got screwed up in the system and hadn't arrived yet." Dog turned him down.

That Friday afternoon, when a bullet slammed through the window of the parking lot guard booth, Dog knew exactly who it was. The cops picked up Derek Stark, dishonorable discharge for extreme battery, within the hour. Raytheon was impressed. The firm lent him a couple of bonded older guys who quickly retired and went to work for Dog. And bingo. Gunplay the second, and Oglivie Secure was off the ground.

Those were the days of the contraceptive sponge. Dog's long fingers snagged one out of M.J. on a winter night, banked it into the wastebasket across the room. "You're right. Let's get on with our lives," he whispered into the cold cream fog around her ear. He might as well have followed his tail around in a circle before he lay down beside her.

The third time Dog was shot at he was deep in the hardwood forests of upstate New York, on a deer hunting trip with Mary Jane's father and two of her brothers. This was a few months after the loss.

Once again it was time to "get on with our lives." Angry, sad, and helplessly isolated in his grief, Dog was not following the script. He was not "supporting" M.J., who was using pills, snarling at him, and seeing a dangerously inane therapist who was telling her to live out, have fun, consider this a new beginning. Dog was drinking and reading Hemingway for the rugged self-pity, coming back again and again to "Big Two-Hearted River," parts one and two. He was dismayed with M.J. He was losing her. By that morning in the New York forest he was losing the business too. He had been sitting on a stump taking a nip of Wild Turkey when a rifle cracked across the foggy clearing from the direction of his in-laws.

Dog felt a crease in the air at his shoulder. Leave or die, he decided. Go fishing alone, like the kid in "Big Two-Hearted River." Or the other kid, in *McElligot's Pool*. Either one. Or both. He had bought the Cruise Master and was gone inside a week, leaving a long and tortured note that, he was sure, neither explained nor excused a damn thing.

And now a librarian had shot him. And Dolf Cook had tried to plant that Pflueger on him, frame him for the murder of the brother he couldn't live up to. And Mary Jane was expecting him. Expecting him to fail. And somehow his little boy Eamon stood observing, holding up a scorecard like a gymnastics judge: zero. This was not to be understood as a score, however, but a direction. *I'm heading up to the river*, someone said. *Right*, Dog replied. The words scrolled out perfectly: *Up the track and out of sight ... beyond the burnt hills of timber ... where it stretched away, pebbly-bottomed with shallows and big boulders and a deep pool as it curved away around the foot of a bluff.*

And then his brain, having assembled this nightmarish collage, went black.

After Sheriff Bruce Lodge allowed Fritz Shunk, Luce County Attorney and owner of the Log Jam tavern, to have a peek at Ogilvie—passed out on a special kind of bed, twitching and murmuring through the hole that cradled his face—the sheriff told Shunk, "I'm heading up to the river, give You-Know-Who a break."

"She still has a name, Sheriff. A nice one. It's Margarite DuCharme."

"Who's to say it's real, though?"

Shunk put up both hands like he didn't want to hear any more. He looked back through the hospital doors as they exited. Shunk was always worried about a lawsuit. He said, "Mind if I go up to the river too, have a look?"

They did not ride together. Sheriff Lodge stopped at Pickleman's. He was buying a red-and-white Daredevil spoon for spin fishing and a sack of teriyaki beef jerky when Shunk came in. It was awkward. Wonder what he was there for, Lodge mused, back on the road. Shunk had moved up from a suburb of Detroit three years ago and opened a tavern. Later he ran for County Attorney. A pretty nice fellah, but the sheriff had yet to figure out what he found so complicated about life. Maybe he was paying money for water, in a special bottle, with ions.

Sheriff Lodge did a loop through Oswald's Bear Ranch to get behind Shunk on the highway. Twenty miles later, he turned into the High Bridge state campground on the West Fork of the Two Hearted. It was after Labor Day. The campground was deserted. The sheriff's cruiser sank a bit and rode silently in the soft soil of the loop. The plastic bubble of the Daredevil package hit the bottom of the trash barrel. The trunk of Lodge's cruiser contained emergency flares, a cardboard box of D.A.R.E. pamphlets, a snow shovel, a shotgun, and an Eagle Claw rod and reel.

Large and gentle, seventy-two years old and not too agile, Sheriff Lodge sidestepped down the steep sand bank, avoiding ant hills, and ended up on a pitched slab of concrete from the old bridge that used to wash out about once a generation. Lodge had seen it swept away four times. Above him, sixty feet up, the new bridge, High Bridge, rumbled as a pulp truck rolled across it.

Lodge knocked the bail on his reel and flipped that big spoon upstream into the dark water swirling against the abutment of the new bridge. He counted three Eisenhowers and began his retrieve.

Nothing.

Second cast.

Nothing.

Three casts were all Lodge allowed himself. He was the sheriff, always on his way someplace. He flipped the spoon as far as he could, gave it an extra Eisenhower to sink.

"Come on, baby. Talk to me."

Something struck and Lodge struck back. The spoon launched out of the water with a brook trout about the same size attached. All this business flew toward the basswood behind the sheriff. Spoon-with-trout caught an outlying branch and hung up.

"Well, suck a duck."

Lodge tugged with the rod. The branch bounced. The little brookie wiggled with all its might. The sheriff tugged harder. No deal. Stuck up there. Not a keeper. He had to move fast. They said a trout could live about as long breathing air as a man could live breathing water.

Sheriff Lodge pulled his service revolver and shot the branch off, first try—reeled it in, freed the trout—wished it was like before, only a week ago, when he could make it a funny story to tell You-Know-Who.

He parked nose-to-tail with Shunk's Subaru wagon on the sand highway. The Luce County Bookmobile still blocked the logging road to the river, crime scene tape around it. T-boned behind the bookmobile was a recreational vehicle out of the early '80s, when Lodge was a middle-aged sheriff and gas was cheap. The Marquette County crime scene van was parked up the road.

Sheriff Lodge popped his glove box and stepped out of his cruiser with the package of teriyaki beef jerky. He and You-Know-Who had been having fun with this whole teriyaki thing. The whole world, Lodge complained, was going teriyaki. Shunk's car was teriyaki. Kids walked around with teriyaki haircuts. Coming next was teriyaki beer. But the joke seemed stale anymore. Lodge rattled the package at Shunk. Shunk said no thanks. More like no way. Lodge didn't want any either.

You-Know-Who's cruiser had been there all night on the opposite shoulder. A rind of frost went along the ditch and up and over the cruiser and back down into the ditch again, as far as Lodge could see along the flat, pine-flanked stretch of State 410.

He approached the cruiser's passenger window and scratched a hole in the frost. At least she wasn't in there making out with You-Know-Who-Else. That was good.

Shunk had an injury out of Viet Nam but he was a rapid little shitbird anyway. He speed-limped to the spot where the frost was rust-colored, formed over the suspect's blood. Sure enough sipping ions from shapely plastic bottle, the county attorney said, "Let me make sure I understand. He's bleeding, crawling along this ditch here, two hundred pellets of industrial grade Ice Melt in his back, and he's asking you to do him a favor?"

This was correct. "He was giving me a phone number," Sheriff Lodge said.

"Did you get it?"

"I called it this morning. Somewhere near Boston. Fellah asks me what I want."

"And?"

"Heck if I know. This fellah here with the salt in his back passed out after he gave me the number. I was telling him no, not here, trying to get him to crawl out before he put his face down in this nasty stuff."

Shunk looked down blankly. Teriyaki or no, some things never changed. Ions wouldn't help either. Downstaters still stepped in every kind of trouble they could find.

"It's poison ivy."

"Oh."

Shunk stepped back.

"He made it past the stuff," Lodge said. "I told the Boston fellah that I got the number from Theodore Oglivie and a woman starts screaming in the background. Fellah says he's going report me to the cops."

"Always fun."

"Yup. I got to say I *was* the cops. Fellah hung up."

Lodge realized he had put a shred of beef jerky into his mouth. He chewed it down to a paste and swallowed. "About ten minutes later, I'm running a CrimeNet check on the phone number—You-Know-Who's been teaching me computers—and the woman called me back. She's his ex-wife. And you know what our boy is?"

The sheriff looked at Fritz Shunk. Shunk was looking at his shoes, his pant cuffs, like he would be able to see poison ivy on them.

"He's a trout bum. Nothing but fishing for five years. Driving that thing around. Montana. Colorado. Wisconsin. Pennsylvania. Nothing but fly fishing. You know what fly fishing is? Fly fishing is what You-Know-Who does. Can you believe it?"

"Sheriff," Shunk said, "if You-Know-Who made whoopee with left-handed donkeys, she'd still have a name. Give it a break."

One of the evidence techs had emerged from the RV: a black woman, short and plump and scowling, her clothing way too tight. She stretched, raising blue latex hands into the foggy morning air. Lodge tipped his head her way.

"So is that gal one? I can't tell."

"You gotta stop this, Bruce. Seriously. I don't want to be defending the county against a lawsuit. We hardly have the money to plow snow."

"Did you know Julia Inkster was one?"

"Julia Inkster is something different. It's called bi."

Lodge shook his head. Old guy, sue him for being confused. That's what they'd do. Teriyaki up a lawsuit. Make him the one with the problem.

Shunk changed the subject. "Oglivie's ex-wife tell you anything else?"

"She had a message for him."

"Yeah? What?"

Lodge tried to remember exactly how the woman said it. But his mind took the long way, a frequent pattern of late. He had gone through Oglivie's vehicle last evening. He had found just under a thousand dollars cash. He had found vodka, Tang, instant coffee, bread, and peanut butter. He had smelled mud and sweat and tobacco. The vehicle had nearly three hundred thousand miles on it. Lodge had sat down in the driver's seat for a few moments, a little dazed, wondering what such a life was about. Now he had it: the exact opposite of his stay-put bridge fishing.

"She said, 'Tell him to go to hell.' I told her, 'Actually he's in custody at the moment for suspicion of murder.' She said, 'Then I guess he already made it there.'"

Shunk said, "Whoa. Was she high?"

"She said, 'So I'll see him soon.'"

"Seriously, was she effed up?"

Lodge looked at his county attorney. Here was a gray-haired man, semi-retired, who was still twenty years younger than the sheriff. Young enough to be a boy of his, living in another world. "Now, I wouldn't really know a thing like that, Fritz, would I?"

Shunk put a hand on his shoulder. "Let's go down to the river."

"Gotta call a wrecker for the bookmobile," Lodge said. "Then I think I'll rig up. Tell You-Know-Who I'll be there in a minute."

Deputy Margarite DuCharme had been inside the bookmobile most of the night, bundled in her duty jacket and her emergency blanket, reading. That was lucky, having something to do. She wasn't much of a reader, but hey. When the Marquette County evidence techs showed up around eight, she had put a paperback in her pocket and walked on numb feet down to the river, swinging her arms and clapping her hands.

She went along the high bank to a spot in the sun and positioned her back against the warming sand. Her chordite bulletproof vest worked perfectly for this. In the back it hunched up and supported her neck. In front, squared up to the sun, it acted as a heat sink. Plus, always thinking safety, if some Milwaukee gang banger erupted from the thick brush across the river and shot her in the chest …

Deputy DuCharme laughed at herself. She was out of Milwaukee now. Way out of Milwaukee. Still, she would never go on duty without the vest—never, ever, anywhere, any time, not even before breakfast in the middle of nowhere.

After about fifteen minutes in the sun, she was decently comfortable, except for her toes. She was yawning, finishing *Pippi in the South Seas*—finally getting her chance to follow up on one of Esofea's many recommendations. It was exhausting, making friends with a librarian.

"Hey, young lady."

It was Fritz Shunk on the bank above, a Pickleman's sack in his hand.

"You look comfortable."

"I'm getting there."

"Divers not here yet, eh?"

Margarite stood up and brushed herself off. "Nope." She squinted at the river. "There's a deep hole around that corner there. I'm thinking he went at least that far."

"Current really took him for a ride."

"I guess so."

"So full of hot air he must have floated like a cork."

Margarite climbed up the bank. From some long-ago injury, the county attorney moved like he was two different people, one trying to run and the other trying to sit down. He was hard to keep up with anyway. Margarite trailed him downstream to the wide patch of scorched earth that framed a partially burned blue tarp.

"What's with the fire?"

"I think he moved the body with this tarp. He tried to burn it."

Shunk hitched over to the spot where the high bank slumped into itself and formed almost a funnel. "I get it. He rolled the body down right here. Pretty slick. And what's all that?"

Margarite told him her theory. The splintered wood was pieces from inside the RV. He put it under his tires so he could turn that thing around. He was coming back out when Esofea blocked him.

"Anyway, here," Shunk said. He handed her the sack. Inside was an egg sandwich and a Coke from Shunk's tavern in Newberry, The Log Jam, plus a bottle of SmartWater, some gum, and a Pickleman's chocolate doughnut with multi-colored sprinkles.

"Thanks."

"Oh, you betcha."

"Perfect," Margarite said. "You're way ahead of me. I'll never get the lingo."

"I've been in that tavern almost three years, eh?"

Margarite snapped the Coke. It didn't feel right on her stomach, but it was something. It opened her eyes. Started a new view of things. The Two Hearted River, infused with sunshine, flowed blissfully inside its corridor of trees and brush in fall color, wet with melting frost. Pretty and sedate, like nothing ever happened.

"So where's the big guy?"

"He's coming. You freeze your ass off last night?"

"I was about ready to burn some books."

"The old boy's having trouble with the new status of things."

"I gathered that."

"He's calling you You-Know-Who."

"Great."

"He thinks you should have told him."

"I was taking it slow."

"He thought you and he were friends."

"Me too."

"Here he comes," Shunk said.

Bruce the Moose crested a bump in the sand road and eased down the near side with a spinning rod bouncing in his hand. He was a sweet old bear of a man who before last week tended to come at Margarite like she had jam on her face. She loved it. It broke her heart, what was happening. Made her furious, too.

"Morning, Sheriff."

Lodge squinted into the sun toward the Two Hearted. "Morning."

"No news on my end," Margarite offered. "Quiet night."

His eyes on the river, Lodge said, "Good deal. Figured while I wait for the divers to get here, I'm going to toss a few."

"There's a nice fish feeding out there," Margarite said.

"Where at?"

"It's feeding on insects though," she said. "Not on soup spoons painted red-and-white."

"We'll see about that." The sheriff shaded his eyes. "Where's it at?"

Margarite had seen the trout earlier, looking up from *Pippi in the South Seas* at a spot where a riffle piled up against the far bank. From there an eddy nosed its way counter-current until it rejoined the sand shoal that formed the riffle. She pointed toward that topmost pocket of sheltered water, where a good-sized brown fed on emerging insects, bulging the surface with its kiped snout.

"Uh-huh. That's a nice one. You see that, Fritz?"

Shunk sniffed and peered myopically at the river. The county attorney was a short and stocky man, bristly gray all over, making Margarite think of a badger. "Only fish I ever caught was in a fry basket," he said.

Margarite set her Coke down in the sand. She took a bite of cold egg sandwich. It stung her esophagus all the way down. Not fault of the sandwich, though. These last few days, acid roared on and off like a gas burner in her chest. She was livid with Julia. She was baffled with herself. And Sheriff Lodge hadn't looked her in the eye or said her name in the ten days since the Newberry Labor Day Brat Fest.

"Have her teach you that fancy fly fishing," Lodge told Shunk.

There it was. *Her.* Shit. When she was standing right here. When she had stayed here all night, doing her job above-and-beyond so the old man could go home, feed his kitty, have a beer, talk out loud to his dead wife and go to sleep.

"Her is too busy," she said. "Her is too busy sinning. It's all her does."

Lodge grunted. He had that big red-and-white Daredevil spoon speared into the cork of his rod. His massive pink hand went to it. Unsteadily, he freed the treble hook. He began to say something about a little brook trout but stopped. Everything had changed in the moment at the picnic when Julia, ripped on keg beer, had crawled onto Margarite's lap, straddled her tightly, leg-locked their groins together, and started eating off the opposite side of her sweet corn.

Margarite had spent the next few days in shock. After six months of trust-building, she had gone in six seconds from Deputy DuCharme to Deputy Dyke, doing it with a local chick who, as it turned out, nobody knew was gay—and who commenced to defending herself in bars afterward, telling people that Margarite had approached her, that Margarite was four-and-a-half years older than she was, that Margarite had taken this job to be with her, and that she was Margarite's third live-in girlfriend in the last five years, all of which was true. Coincidentally—sure—Lodge had swapped Deputy DuCharme off to Schoolcraft County for five straight shifts of high-way duty on the Seney stretch.

Margarite dropped the egg sandwich back in the bag. Screw it. Get to work. He kept it up, she would sue him. Period. "Let's go ahead and have a meeting since we're all here," she said. "The question is do we charge Oglivie."

"No." Shunk jumped at the point. "We don't even have a body yet," he said. "And Esofea could be wrong. Our 'victim' could be shacked up with a nineteen-year-old in L'Anse for all we know. Though from what I hear, nineteen is a little over-the-hill for Heimo Kock."

Margarite glanced at Lodge. He had been looking at her. Now he unhooked the Daredevil and it swung out, his big paw chasing. "I agree with wait," she said. "We have twenty-four hours to charge him and we've got a lot of questions. I think the cash in his glove box makes it possible he did this for someone. Every third car down the highway carries an enemy of Heimo Kock. Could be a lot going on here."

They both watched Lodge chase the swinging Daredevil with his hand. Margarite glanced at the river. The trout still fed, unaware of the impending air raid.

"Shit," Shunk said finally. "My dream case? That cretin Donuts Rudvig did this so Kock wouldn't sacrifice him for setting the Pine Stump fire. Rudvig killed his boss, paid a drifter to dump the body … No, wait. I have a better idea. How about this?"

Shunk adjusted his body angle and lowered his voice, cropping Lodge out of the discussion. Margarite felt the usual bolt of guilt, but the sheriff didn't seem to notice. Or maybe Bruce the Moose had just accepted the way things had become.

"We're dealing with a coup," Shunk hypothesized quietly, next to her ear. "Rudvig and the rest of Kock's swamp rats teamed up to kill the asshole and take over his business. Rudvig gets murder one. We nail the rest of the pack on conspiracy and it's game over, the end of an era. Then I re-retire."

Margarite couldn't flow with the fantasy, but she gave Shunk a stiff smile for trying. "That might be what happened. But the simplest answer is highway robbery."

Margarite remembered the Coke she had set down in the sand. She tried it again. Like pouring gas on a fire.

She raised her voice to bring the sheriff back in, if he cared to be. "I've got an interview with Esofea in an hour. She calms down, she'll start to make more sense. When I talked to her last evening she couldn't seem to make up her mind about what she saw, or why she shot the suspect."

Margarite paused. One hot summer night she had tasered a burglary suspect in Milwaukee. The guy fell, hit his head on the pavement, went into a grand mal seizure. He did live, sure. But the deputy easily recalled how when you hurt another person you were plunged into an altered state for a while, your head full of replays and what-ifs, logic clashing with remorse wrestling with denial angling for forgiveness. Esofea's mental state had to be a mess.

"Dolf Cook needs a visit too," she continued. "He may have seen his brother recently, or seen Oglivie in the campground, or both. Kock's wife will have some answers about what he's been up to, with whom, where he's supposed to be. I'm sure like everyone else she's been hearing all kinds of rumors since last night. Then I'll have to speak with whoever's in charge at the outfitter. That's Donuts Rudvig probably, so I'll go have a shit sandwich with him. Meantime, we need a vehicle. We need basic crime scene results. But most of all we need a body …"

Suddenly Margarite felt she might throw up. She closed her eyes and swallowed, feeling a chill on the back of her neck. First she didn't eat, then she couldn't eat. Since Labor Day, this is how it was.

She heard Shunk's voice. "What do you think, Sheriff? Wait until tonight to talk about charges?"

"Sounds like you two got it all figured out."

"You ok with that, then?"

"As to what I'm ok with," Lodge said, "that would be another conversation."

Zinnng! went the sheriff's spinning reel, and Margarite opened her eyes.

That fat red-and-white spoon soared over the Two Hearted on a shining filament of line. For an instant it was a graceful thing to see. For an instant, as the reel buzzed and the cast peaked, the Daredevil paused like a hummingbird, exactly over the trout.

Then it crashed down in a belly flop, tore the water and left it swirling. The trout was long gone before the sheriff said, "Ok, Fritz. Watch this."

Back in Newberry, Margarite parked at the north end of Main Street by Shunk's Log Jam tavern. She walked for the exercise under a huge pale sky to the Holiday station, where she bought a nine-ounce bottle of Pepto-Bismol.

That same number, nine voice mails, all from Julia, uploaded onto her cell when she turned it on. But Margarite put the phone back in her pocket. She was too tired to wrangle with Julia.

She peeled the plastic safety wrapper off the Pepto bottle. She threw that and the little plastic measuring cup into the public trash can outside the high school. She measured her pink stuff in glugs. One glug. Two glugs.

Maybe she could stop at two glugs, she thought, now that Heimo Kock was dead. Presumed dead. Maybe she should try.

She reached her cruiser. The day was warming up. She took her jacket off and put it in the trunk. She waved at Shunk's wife, Louise, who was back from a supply run to Manistique, lugging groceries through the back door of The Log Jam. Louise Shunk balanced a sack on her knee, freeing a hand for a thumb's up. This is a good day, she was saying. No more Heimo Kock. No more threats. No more fires in the Log Jam's pamphlet rack, where they displayed brochures for alternative U.P outfitters.

Margarite knew Louise Shunk was anticipating the best for her husband, for herself, for the restaurant, for Luce County. And maybe Louise was right. But the brilliant blue sky made Margarite's head hurt. Now, assuming Heimo Kock was dead, should she and Shunk pull out the stops, involve the sheriff, go after Kock's lieutenants and cronies and flunkies—mainly Rudvig—through a Pine Stump arson and homicide charge? If it went well, they could pull up Superior Outfitters by the root. Or should they drop Pine Stump, return the case to Lodge's conclusion of "accidental death," and hope that trouble in Luce County died with Heimo Kock?

If he was dead.

He was dead.

She hoped he was dead, Margarite confessed to herself. She had never before wished for a thing like that.

The next steps would depend on Shunk, whether the county attorney's approach to justice would turn out to be absolute or concessionary. The latter would make peace with the sheriff's style, for sure. Margarite had thought a lot about that style, trying to find words for it. From the start she had felt wrong about working with Shunk behind the sheriff's back, on an investigation the sheriff had closed. Then she learned about his fishing. Bruce the Moose fished trout from bridges, with spinners. He took a three-cast howdy-do and moved on, never caring if he caught a fish or not. To Margarite's mind, that said everything you needed to know about how Lodge had run the Luce County Sheriff's Department for the last thirty-some years. Get along, move along, and arrive home by supper.

Not a system equipped to deal with the fatal fire at Pine Stump junction. Lodge's conclusion of "accidental," supported by longtime county attorney Lars Peterson, Lodge's old friend, had ignored serious questions about Heimo Kock's involvement. Downstater Fritz Shunk, a retired civil rights attorney, having purchased the Log Jam for something to do, spent the better part of a year listening to nasty rumors from behind his new bar, and when Lars Peterson lost his faculties to a stroke, Shunk had decided to un-retire and run for the vacant county attorney seat on a "Clean U.P." slogan.

Shunk had received no help from Sheriff Lodge, and Paul "Donuts" Rudvig had quickly assembled the signatures and filed an affidavit of candidacy to run against him. This was a fact that Margarite was still trying to wrap her head around. To run for Luce County Attorney you had to be eighteen and a resident. That was it. Felonies—Rudvig had two: one drugs, one firearms—were not a problem. Body odor, bad habits, and general hatefulness were fine too, apparently. Legal experience not required. No doubt Luce County voters, knowing the great and mighty Heimo Kock was behind Rudvig, had found themselves in a fear-hope conflict. But in the privacy of the voting booth, exactly fifty-one percent had gambled that Fritz Shunk could take out "the Governor of the U.P."

Well, someone had.

Margarite sat down in her cruiser and dialed her cell phone. "I'm back," she told her new friend, Esofea Smithback, who had approached Margarite in the Luce County building after Margarite's outing at the brat fest. She had given the deputy some kind of spirit-healing geode and a hug. Next day Margarite had reciprocated with a pair of earrings she had decided not to give Julia.

"Meet you at the office?" Margarite asked her now.

Esofea's reply was small and sniffly: "Ok."

"Just like you told me the other day," Margarite said. "You are so much bigger than this. You'll survive."

"Ok."

Margarite started the cruiser and pulled onto Main Street. What developed next in the Kock saga was that Shunk had found himself unable to get any traction on the Pine Stump case as long he was working with Sheriff Lodge and the county's assorted part-time deputies. They were all too habituated to avoiding the wrath of Kock. So the new county attorney convinced the board to put a line in the budget for a full-time deputy. Enter applicant Margarite DuCharme, who, given her looks, and however she played them—up, down, or sideways—had gotten every job she had ever tried for, from sixth-grade president to sheriff's deputy. So there she was suddenly in the Upper Peninsula, living very privately with her new love Julia and investigating a 2006 fire that killed Farooq Kalim, the former dry-waller from Pontiac who had been burned beyond recognition trying to save his investment in the Pine Stump Motel.

Margarite worked for Shunk discretely over the next several months. She had felt insubordinate and guilty leaving her boss, sweet old Bruce the Moose, out of the loop. But Shunk seemed right in claiming that the sheriff didn't much want to know. Quite easily, she had turned up stuff the sheriff should have documented four years ago. She had given Shunk two "meetings" between Farooq Kalim and Heimo Kock. She had given Shunk affidavits from six others in the U.P. recreation business, establishing a long history of intimidation by Kock. As for Paul "Donuts" Rudvig (nearly the county attorney, Margarite had to remind her unwilling brain): she had placed Kock's right-hand-man near the scene one hour before the fire. Shunk had been just one link away from filing charges against the "governor."

Now what?

Margarite drove up Main and turned right onto West Harrie just as the high school let out for lunch. The kids used to wave. They would again. Eventually. Maybe. But today they nudged each other, whispered and smirked. There goes Deputy Dyke.

Margarite sighed heavily. New frictions chafed everywhere in the last few days, in formerly simple moments, expanding and bearing down. Goddamned Julia. How was this fair? Margarite had been taking care of her, protecting her. As Julia's partner, and payer of the rent, didn't Margarite deserve more than a sudden, vulgar exposure? Lately Kock, or someone on Kock's behalf, had tried hard to intimidate Margarite: a broken window, dead fish on the lawn, menacing phone calls. She had hidden these threats from Julia, knowing she would respond badly, get herself into trouble. But ... that whole dynamic ... secrets, assumptions, silent sacrifices, taking care of someone who did not reciprocate ... God, it felt familiar. Margarite's gut burned. What was wrong with her?

She stopped waving to the high school kids. She had other things to think about. Events could break quickly from this point. How it worked was the "Governor of the U.P." was a racketeer and an extortionist. He had established a world where all Upper Peninsula guiding and tripping, everything from fly fishing to sea kayaking to snowmobile tours, had to go through his company, Superior Outfitters. If not—as in the case of Farooq Kalim—then "meetings" took place to discuss the unwritten laws of the land.

It was such a shame. Margarite had learned that Farooq Kalim had been a natural for the U.P. Before leaving Pakistan in the '80s, he had hunted ibex, wild boar, deer, and ducks, and he had also done some fishing. He loved snowmobiles and hated government. He saved his money, bought and upgraded the failed motel at Pine Stump Junction, and immediately refused to pay his taxes, like a good Yooper patriot. But then Kalim's American dream went too far. He got an outfitter's license and offered bargains, packages, free trail maps, got his business written up in the *Daily Miner* and the *Detroit Free Press*. In the first off-season, deep February, after his apparently unsuccessful meetings with Heimo Kock, his motel caught fire. According to the fire inspector's report, Kalim's body was so charred, and the motel so totally devastated, that it was impossible to say what had prevented him from getting out. The case photos haunted Margarite.

She took a third slug of Pepto just on the memory. Still distracted as she rolled past Saint Gregory's Catholic Church, Margarite answered a live call from Julia, and Julia said, accusation in her voice, "Where are you?"

Margarite told her precisely. She was heading west of Main on Harrie, passing the church.

"Well, you don't have to be that way about it," Julia responded. "You just never tell me anything."

"Now I'm turning left into the county lot."

After a few seconds, the pissed-off silence on the other end was disrupted by the sounds of Julia twisting the cap off a beer bottle, the cap bouncing off the counter and rolling on the kitchen floor. Margarite couldn't help herself.

"How many is that?"

"You don't come home, you don't call—" Julia was going for the train wreck right off the bat "—what am I supposed to do?"

So many angry answers to that one. Clean the house. Cook something. Get a job. Get treatment. You have all these options, and yet you—

But anger chews holes in a person's stomach, Margarite reminded herself. So she took a deep breath and said, "I'm sorry," and then she broke it all down for Julia: Sheriff Lodge getting to the scene first, Margarite having to bust hump all the way from Brimley because she was over there taking complaints about extortion by Kock from a guy at the marina—meanwhile their bloody suspect crawling off into the bush, a pile of evidence on fire down that sand road, and what might be Kock's body rolling away along the bottom of the Two Hearted River.

Deep breath.

Honestly, she was too busy to even think of calling—though somewhere on Highway 28, yes, a whole half hour in the cruiser, it might have crossed her mind. But then the logistics got hairy. The sheriff went with the ambulance back to Newberry, gone before Margarite even arrived. That left her with Esofea Smithback to manage—

"Oh, your little librarian quote-unquote friend. I see."

—to try to get some straight answers out of a girl who had popped a couple of Vicodin or something, who Margarite had found sitting against the wheel of the bookmobile reading Dr. Seuss books and giggling through a stream of tears. So she called Tim Shrigley, who worked as a part-time deputy for special events, and had Tim come drive Esofea home.

"So nice, the way you think of her."

Then these borrowed crime scene people arrived from Munising and muddled around until dark. Bruce the Moose asked her would she mind to spend the night there, make sure no one messed around—which she had already decided was necessary. So she spent the night reading in the bookmobile, or walking up and down the road trying to keep warm, and by morning they had borrowed divers coming to look for the body in the river. So once Bruce the Moose got there to supervise that, she had to drive back down to Newberry to get on her computer, put the suspect into the system, let it work.

Then there was all this evidence to log. But for the moment she had to go interview Esofea—

"Oh, of course. Have fun."

Here came the lid off the Pepto bottle. Glug four. The pink stuff slid down.

"Sweetheart," Margarite said, "I love you."

Another bottle cap spun on the kitchen counter. "No, you don't. You hate me. You're mad at me."

"We'll talk tonight."

Esofea Smithback, heavy into a Xanax-and-Five-Hour-Energy mixer, replayed those twenty minutes inside the bookmobile over and over in her mind. She had the varmint, then she lost him, then somehow *he* had *her*, which got him shot.

But she found, under review—her loopy, anxious mind double-tasking while she reread Astrid Lindgren's lovely chapter called "Pippi Plays Tag with Some Policemen"—that she had not pulled the trigger in the midst of complete emotional anarchy, as she had first assumed. Shooting the man the news websites were calling "trout bum Theodore 'Ned' Oglivie, 42, of West Newton, Massachusetts," was actually not the single most confused and awful thing she had ever done. At least it was not only that. She had apprehended either the killer or an accomplice in the murder of Heimo Kock. She had dropped him with rock salt before he escaped into the bush—and therefore she had also saved his life. And that life, again upon review, seemed quite possibly worth saving.

No doubt she had saved him. The validation for that still made her pulse race uncomfortably. Only last summer an inmate had defeated security during a transfer at Newberry Correctional and made a dash into the vastness of the Lake Superior State Forest. The runner was an anonymous white man from Indiana, in prison for routine offenses involving drug dealing. But from the way the local asshats mustered their civilian militia, you would have thought a Black Panther had shot a Republican president during a Super Bowl game. Well ahead of the prison search unit and the state police, vigilante dog teams had combed the swamps around the upper Tahquamenon River for no more than a hour or two before a premium varmint named Donuts, Kock's bear hunting coordinator, had "regrettably" shot the unarmed convict five times "in self-defense" in a bog on Syphon Creek. Esofea's trigger squeeze had stopped a repeat of that scenario, no doubt.

And also, thinking in layers, she was at the same time saying to herself, Right here, this moment, is a good place to stop all this shittiness in my life, to find out why I am the way I am, face facts, and do something about it—and meanwhile her eyes were taking in the words that made Pippi dance away along the ridgepole of Villa Villekulla while two policemen dimly pursued. She was laughing out loud about this or perhaps about something else she hadn't thought of yet when Deputy Margarite DuCharme touched her shoulder and she jumped. It was kind of a blur, this state she was in, the aftershock of shooting someone.

"Thanks for coming in," the deputy said. "How about we sit outside?"

"Sure"

"You a sun or a shade person?"

"Shade."

"I'm sun," Margarite said. "Gotta have it. Hmmm, what shall we do?"

The deputy led Esofea by the arm out the front and around to the west side of the Luce County building. There a red pine cast its mid-morning shadow across the dry and bumpy lawn. The ground sloped awkwardly down into the asphalt lot where the bookmobile, with its shattered window, had been returned to its place beside the cruisers and the snow plows. That was no good, Margarite said.

Esofea dropped spacily behind and followed the deputy to the south side of the building, where they found only a few little streaks of shade behind saplings that needed water. Watering was custodian Derek Tapp's job to remember, Margarite commented, but at the current time Derek was having trouble remembering not to drink Jägermeister during work hours.

The west side was all sun, bees buzzing up from the grass in the early autumn heat. Margarite sighed, "Ahhh," but kept walking. Esofea liked the way she walked. It was perfect. Margarite DuCharme could pass, if she wanted to, for Cindy Crawford, 2002, People magazine, one of the 50 Most Beautiful—which made it just so cool, so in your face, that the deputy loved girls.

"I've got an idea," Margarite said, and waited for her. "Let's go across the street."

"Any place is fine."

"Not true," Margarite said, smiling at her. "A 'whatever' statement like that is never for real. I'm going to have to watch out for you today, I can tell."

A few seconds later, leading Esofea across West Harrie Street to the lawn of the Helen Joy Newberry Hospital, where the grass was green and shaded, the deputy fought a yawn and lost. Esofea yawned too. Margarite said, "Well, you probably did save his life."

"I know."

"I know you know. But I know that anyway you feel terrible and confused and not sure if you're in trouble."

"Am I?"

"Some."

"What kind?"

"Well, you shot him in the back. And he was unarmed."

Esofea was silent. She couldn't think of what to say.

Margarite, teasing her, said, "I know, I know. He's a good-looking guy under there. You didn't want to mess up the front," and Esofea felt herself smiling too as they sat down. But the ground seemed a long way off—and then it was right there, jarring her spine and shaking *Pippi* from her grip.

"You ok?"

"Yup."

The deputy smelled like overtime and Lady Speed Stick as she helped Esofea brush off. She leaned forward to pick up the book.

"This the good one?"

"It's the original. It's translated into over seventy languages. There are film versions of it in Sweden, the Soviet Union. It's in

Japanese computer games. It comes up in *Seinfeld*, *Austin Powers*, *The Simpsons*—"

Here she was chattering suddenly, in anxious librarian mode, trying to sell her girl Pippi. At Northern Michigan University, she had written her thesis on the original *Pippi Longstocking* versus *Goes on Board* and *In the South Seas*, two sequels that were sellouts by comparison, picaresque and shallow, caving to societal fears of authentic female independence. She could go on about this and had done so many times with her finger in the face of Danny Tervo, whose Mr. Hemingway never wrote a female character with one-tenth of Pippi's courage and spunk and who, truth to tell, in Esofea's opinion, was a rather shitty handler of female ... but Margarite's yawning silence finally registered and Esofea stopped talking.

The deputy's eyes were puffy and dark underneath. "I read all the Pippi last night," she told Esofea. "*South Seas* was my favorite. It probably shouldn't be."

Esofea's jaw felt stiff. Suddenly she had to hew words out of the resistant air in front of her. "That's ok. Everybody's different. Nobody's better."

"You are just all full of whatever today, aren't you?" Margarite said. "I'm not much of a reader. I already confessed that."

"I should go jogging or something," Esofea countered. "Be in shape like you." In her careening mind at this moment, it was exactly eighty-seven days ago and Danny was speaking, telling her why they weren't ready for their accidental pregnancy—that she needed about six months of detox and aerobics—that he needed to shore up his boundaries before she got too needy—that their relationship required time to reveal its true purpose. And then the fucker, without discussion, while Esofea was walking around in a diaper because the aspiration procedure made her bleed like a stuck pig, went and got his tubes snipped—and this is why he had to suffer.

"I should do Pilates," she blurted and started laughing. It came to her abruptly. God, she could take Danny by his empty balls now, couldn't she?

"You ok?"

"Yeah."

"That was a trick question. You shot someone," Margarite said. "You are not ok."

This was confirmed by a long silence between them while the Saint Gregory's bell rang eleven times. Esfoea strummed the pages of her *Pippi*, up and down. Why would a knockout sweetheart like Margarite be interested in Julia Inkster, she found herself musing. And since when was Julia gay? The same little bitch that had poached on Danny two summers ago? How did this make sense? Along West Harrie rumbled a flatbed truck with that dusty RV on the back of it. This guy Dog's side door flapped loose as the truck turned up the sloped drive into the county lot. The driver jumped out, hit levers, started things hissing. The truck bed began to tilt.

"If we can keep him safe in there, he's going to be ok," Margarite said with a tip of her head toward the hospital.

"Really?"

"Very likely, if he can avoid infection. He's sedated for the time being. They're going to see how the salt crystals behave beneath his skin. He should recover pretty fast after that."

"Good."

"Yes. Good. And lucky."

"Who me?" Esofea said. "Lucky?"

"Yes, you. He was running away from you, not a threat. Anybody else would have let him go, but you pulled the trigger. And you're lucky that I'm the one to ask you about it. Now I need you to go back inside the bookmobile and remember everything that went on between you two."

Esofea swallowed a giddy burp. That was a funny way to put it: *what went on between you two.*

Like Margarite could see into her mind and watch Esofea and Dog having their little Smithback-Tervo relationship workshop, compacted into twenty minutes at gunpoint within the bookmobile, and marvel at how it had ended with Esofea in this strange and exiting new place.

But of course her deputy friend could not see into her mind.

People just thought other people could see what they were thinking.

But they couldn't.

Esofea's mouth was dry. She should drink more water. And never smoke, of course.

"He told me everything," she said.

Deputy Margarite DuCharme reached into her shirt pocket for a pen.

"Really?"

"Yes," Esofea said. "Starting with when he met Danny Tervo."

6

Brent Takahashi was knee deep in the reed river, taking a water sample, when he saw the silver tanker glide into the parking lot and scatter a group of ladies coming in for the Ikebana Club breakfast.

Essence of Soy. This idiot is so lost, Takahashi thought.

The tanker turned in from Santa Rosa Boulevard and plowed through the boughs of Big Red, the western red cedar that anchored the east side of the entry into the gardens. Then the tanker's mirror clipped the hedge of rhodies, causing brittle leaves to clatter like playing cards onto the driveway.

Takahashi's heart went heavy at the sight of it. He couldn't water everything. That was the new reality. He wanted to shout at yesterday's board meeting, amidst the budget dithering: Idiots! Have you ever seen *Sophie's Choice*? Where the mother has to choose which of her children will live and which the Nazis will take? That's what I'm doing out there every day without enough water! Choosing between life and death!

He was keeping the reed river alive, for example, but any green on those rhodies was a photosynthetic mirage, a backlog of chlorophyll in a plant that had an underappreciated degree of succulence.

Of course everybody's precious water lilies had to survive, and the scum-sucking koi were sacrosanct, which meant keeping the entire six ponds in full circulation, while the alpine prairie flowers, which looked fine today, were getting shorted on the moisture they required to bloom next month.

Takahashi watched the tanker in disbelief.

Also, dryness in the understory around the tea house was killing the Rock Cap moss that Takahashi had nurtured against incredible botanical odds. Green moss in Phoenix, caressing the visual of a Japanese chashitsu. No one seemed to get how surreal that was. Even with the retreads and slackers they gave him for staff, Takahashi made it all look effortless—that was his problem.

The gardener was primed to holler at someone, so he came up out of the reed river in his hip boots, tossing his water sample—the water was little better than piss, there was your analysis—and he came right through that rhodie hedge himself, scattering leaves and yelling, "Hey! Hey, asshole!" at the tail end of the tanker. Goddamn milk tanker! Michigan plates! What the hell?

The Ikebana Club breakfast ladies had to scatter a second time as Takahashi clomped through with his nasty language and his uncouth scowl. No *wa* today, ladies. No escape into your fantasy of being delicate Edo princesses arranging sublimated vaginas into negative space. This is your scrub-bucket garden troll, coming through in the heat of the greatest drought in a hundred years.

Enjoy your ice water, he wanted to roar at the cringing trust-fund biddies. Savor your precious muskmelon. Flush your every fart.

He was blowing up. Finally.

But he saved himself for the idiot truck driver. This turned out to be a mellow-looking long-haired dude about Takahashi's age, obviously a stoner, easing down from the cab in cargo shorts and flip-flops, fishing a pack of American Spirit from his open shirt and broadcasting a monster dumbshit grin. For a moment, Takahashi wondered if he were going apply for a job, say he was sent over from the Huber Center.

"'Sup, bro?"

Takahashi was not in good control of what he said. It was garbled and off kilter, profane and unhinged, oaths and curses rattling to the asphalt between them like desiccated foliage cast off from the root of his sanity.

But it felt good. And whatever he said, the truck driver didn't seem to take it personally.

This Dead Head lit his smoke in the middle of Takahashi's barrage. He nodded slowly, in sympathy. He said, "Yeah, I figured you'd be about at wit's end, dealing with this water shortage."

He extended the cigarette pack.

"You want one of these?"

Danny Tervo walked the garden with this guy. Pretty much the same scene as Tucson, he observed. Things looked ok to the innocent eye—like Bob Marley looked just fine until the day you heard the news about his lungs. The deal here, with these exotic gardens in the southwest, was they were miniature counterfeit ecosystems worth millions of dollars, delicate sisters of the golf course, which obviously was the holy emblem of what would soon become known—to Tervo's thinking—as the "water class." The *noblesse de l'eau*, as he was calling them in his mind.

Shit was coming down. People couldn't see it. Wasn't rain, either.

A Japanese garden like this, for example, was no mere ornament. It was a yin in the wholeness of privilege. It was the feminine, the Apollonian, the restful summer palace of the pillaging extractionist yang-wise brain wave. Any of that. Think about it. Water was the new oil, Tervo concluded.

Brent Takahashi didn't disagree. He seemed a lot like Armando, the hands-on guy at the garden in Tucson. These dudes spent their days taking care of plants. They got pretty wise. They saw the way things worked. They looked a little like village idiots with their muddy knees and squeaking wheelbarrows, but they had the insights of prophets, and they would just about die for their botanical children. Only type more committed, Tervo imagined, would be dope growers.

"So that's not a milk truck," Takahashi said. "Soy or otherwise."

"Nope."

"I get it," he said. "You have what I need. Now what?"

They strolled along the reed river to the chashitsu, Danny Tervo beginning with geology and the essential differences between the southwest and the Midwest. He covered the thin soils and shallow aquifers of the desert biome. He noted the eco-drain of misplaced agriculture and disastrously mislocated population centers. He mourned the "tragedy of the commons" represented first by the Colorado River and in turn by numerous other western water "resources." All of this had been perfectly obvious for minimum a century, Tervo said, but suddenly it was on the mind of Pop-Tart Joe, now that there was a monster drought to pound a little truth through all the government and corporate smokescreening.

Takahashi was down with all that. Tervo paused to look across the sculpted river at a yawning kid dragging a bamboo broom over a stone path, stirring up the prematurely fallen leaves of an ornamental maple. The kid's Phoenix Suns jersey, orange as a poppy, was the most vivid color in the scene. Tervo noted the tattoos and the sullen, listless sweeping. "Our board is into socially conscious hiring," Takahashi told him. "That piece of work is less than a week out of the Arizona Boys Ranch at Oracle. Starts work with me at six AM. If you want to call that work."

Tervo met the kid's sulking stare. "Cool."

Takahashi telegraphed an invigorated sweeping motion. The kid sat down on a rock in the shade.

Tervo whistled softly to himself.

"Number thirteen. Is that a Steve Nash jersey?"

"Yeah."

Tervo whistled again. Nash was a player. He gave the kid a little nod and proceeded on to the Canadian Shield and then to the wonder of Great Lakes hydrology. Long story short, he told the gardener, as they arrived at the chashitsu, there was enough clean, limestone-filtered agua in Lake Superior alone to cover the entire United States seven feet deep—and that was without recharge. There was no water shortage, Tervo said. There was simply a water distribution problem, not currently addressed by the market.

Takahashi dug it. He took his hip boots off. Tervo released his flip-flops. As they stepped up from the genkan of the tea house, Tervo made a nifty move: he turned, bent, and reversed their footwear so it pointed neatly out, a subtle Japanese courtesy he had picked up somewhere and squirreled away in the Tervo brain for a moment like this.

Takahashi cleared the DO NOT ENTER signage and they sat cross legged on the tatami. Takahashi slid open the paper-paned shoji door before them, revealing the garden. Tervo observed that the kid in the Nash jersey had relocated. He had crossed the reed river into a wilting stand of Egyptian lilies nearer to the tea house. Tervo could see his acne from this distance, his close-set eyes and busted nose, his greasy brown hair pinched by an orange headband. The kid was maybe five-seven, a hundred and thirty pounds. But he was squinting back with some big attitude now—larval, ready to hatch—squinting right at Tervo.

"Billy Rowntree," Takahashi said, noting Tervo's continued interest. "His first day on the job, he figured out how to smoke weed behind the waterfall. But I had to turn that whole re-circ system off. Now we're finding burnt matches in the rhodies."

Tervo nodded. "Been there, man."

"Huh? My rhodies?"

"In juvie. And *out*, man. Out is the rush. Out is like, What did I miss? Where did everybody go? It's like you gotta suddenly *be* somebody, figure out how to be a player again."

"Oh, he's a player all right," Takahashi said. "He's selling skank to my whole damn staff. Now everybody's playing."

Tervo watched Rowntree a few moments longer. Rowntree watched him back. Tervo pantomimed a free throw, Nash-style, caused the kid to look away.

"Anyway, what I offer is primo stuff," he continued. "Verified by state-of-the-art hydrologic analysis. Super-low TDS, virtually toxin-free. Some of the very finest mizu in the world."

Takahashi was a Copenhagenite. He went into the pocket of his coveralls for a tin. He tucked a dank pinch beneath his lip. "Watch this," he said, looking across the garden before he shot a thin brown stream into the ashes of the fire pit, which primly swallowed the evidence. Tervo smiled. Choice.

"You get a five-thousand gallon tanker down here about once a month, it would be like a regular blood infusion." Tervo got a lotus going: cross-legged, erect, thumbs and forefingers encircled over his knees. His scrotum felt entirely normal again from the surgery. He exhaled from his diaphragm. "Keep all this lovely shit alive."

Takahashi spit again. "It's illegal?"

"Don't know."

"What kind of crime would it be?"

Tervo laughed. He didn't know that either. That was the truth. Nobody knew. This was the future, man. This was the kind of landscape you traveled into when you got out ahead of the curve. Trucking water was interstate, federal—that was as far as he could guess.

Takahashi said, "I'm not a criminal. I don't want to deal with criminals."

"Totally understood, my brother."

"How can I be sure you don't rip me off, stop at a pond somewhere in Oklahoma and stick a hose in the tank?"

Tervo laughed again. "I came in the driveway earlier," he said, "you were using that new Hach spectrophotometer, am I right? That's how you be sure. Verification, my brother. Like a fingerprint. You test my stuff on the spot. It doesn't meet your specs, I turn the truck around."

"It's gonna be you?"

"Nice," Tervo said. "Nice question."

He did a bit of Drishti gazing. Billy Rowntree could connect him. That is what he saw.

"Actually, due to some new circumstances up in the U.P., it looks like I'll be expanding over the next few months. Not sure I could guarantee the driver would be me. Could be a totally cool homeboy of mine."

Tervo watched as Takahashi gave that a long bit of thought. If this were anything like the situation in Tucson, the gardener was past deciding and into wondering where the money would come from. So now Takahashi would want to know …

"How much you asking?"

"The thing is," Tervo said, "even if I expand to two, three trucks, I'll still only be able to service a handful of clients. Round trip with no down-time takes about three days. Work in a little sleep and it's five. Gotta give the trucks time off for maintenance. I'm thinking since currently I just have the one truck, I'm looking at a three-client limit. I got one on board already, with sales calls ahead at Albuquerque, Amarillo, Wichita Falls, and Tulsa. I'll have my schedule filled by the time I get home. If you can't commit now, then in a couple months maybe I can afford to put another tanker on line and work you in."

"Shit." Takahashi worried his lip and spat. "A couple months?"

"This is a highly capitalized business," Tervo told him. "The minimum down on a tanker is twenty grand, man."

"So how much you asking?" Takahashi insisted.

"How much can you afford?"

Now Takahashi was looking out at his garden. His vegetation was on the very brink, like everything in the southwest that hadn't already perished. Tervo had driven past golf courses in small communities, city links, that were brown and brick hard, completely dead. Lakes had shrunken and scummed over. Swimming pools sat empty and filmed with dust. Whoever grew the weed Billy Roundtree was selling had to be in panic mode, ready to throw money at water. Tervo mimed another free throw across the garden.

"Keep this in mind, my friend. You don't have to ask anybody or tell anybody. You don't have to fight with some mall worm who wants to wash his car. No conflicts. No politics. No paper trail. You just get water."

Takahashi was nodding, ruminating. He kept that up for a long time. Meanwhile Tervo did some chakra breathing. He watched a dozen or so ladies exit the café and totter blinking onto the garden paths, fitting on big sunglasses and holding one another by the arm.

A group of them seemed pleased by the overheated koi that straggled up to suck at food pellets hanging in the algae, tossed there by a little boy with his mother.

Tervo exhaled slowly and completely. He inhaled the same way. Then he exhaled again. After a few more, Takahashi was doing it too.

"Your infinity is inside you, man, it really is."

"Yeah," said Takahashi.

Tervo watched Billy Rowntree drop his rake in the Egyptian lilies and skulk away toward a high hedge of rhododendrons. Tervo put two fingers in his mouth and whistled one short, high note. The kid kept going.

Tervo smiled at Takahashi. "Tell you what," he said. "How about I make you an introductory offer?"

7

Dog awoke at the exact moment of catheter insertion with a sense of something gone horribly wrong. It was an abstract, druggy feeling, presenting with severe nausea and primal fear, but no specifics.

He lay on his left side. Someone steadied him from behind. A very large nurse held his skewered penis in her blue-gloved hand. She swabbed brown goo around the glans. She tossed stained cotton in a trash can.

Then she trailed the catheter tube off the side of the bed. A small foam block appeared over Dog's shoulder. They rolled him on top of this, his right hip bone on it. They inserted another block under his left hip. "Just enough space for Mr. Wee-Wee," the big nurse said as she fit Dog's face into a padded window at the head of the bed.

He stared beneath, watching his urine drip into a bag. A door closed. Church bells rang. Then it was quiet. Dog began to holler at the floor tiles until they brought him a doctor, who sang to him in flawless Bombay English.

"You were injured dorsally by a twenty-gauge shotgun filled with sharp chloride crystals at a distance of approximately ten meters," the doctor told him. "This is why you are here."

"I don't feel much. What am I on?"

"You have been administered Percocet intravenously at ten milligrams per two hours time."

Dog's mouth was dry. A pair of brown shoes appeared beneath his urine bag.

"I counted eleven bells."

"The current time is 11:26 AM."

"What day?"

"Your injury occurred yesterday. This is Thursday."

So he still had time, Dog thought. It took him another few moments to figure out what he had time for.

Mary Jane. Eamon's birthday. The grave.

Call her. Let her know what happened. Dog thought: Christ, M.J.—and off wandered his mind.

She was picky when he met her. Rich, spoiled, Catholic, icy and hard to get. Fastidious and repressed. She was air-brushed pretty in the mode of a Land's End catalog model whom you could not imagine out of her high-cut panties, no way. This was the force field of conceit and inhibition that Dog had risen to, like the macho fool he was, and battled through and exhausted himself against until he had little left for marriage and none left when motherhood unleashed M.J.'s fury and Dog was the only target over ten pounds in the house. M.J. hadn't ever *not* been angry, Dog discovered in retrospect. She needed a fight.

"Grab the bag, doc. I'm gonna sit up."

He felt a small, cool hand on the back of his neck. It was enough to pin his face through the hole. He seemed to have no strength.

"Your buttocks have been injured somewhat as well, sir. We will see, but it is quite likely you will have to remain face down for at least two weeks following debridement without closure." The hand lingered. "In addition, the multiplicity of sites for potential damage to underlying structure mandates diagnostic arteriography."

"Uh-huh. Yeah. I need to make a phone call."

"I am sorry, sir."

"I need to make a phone call."

Dog strained against the hand on his neck. He saw the brown shoes move around the front of the bed. Dimly, Dog understood: the IV stand. After the brown shoes disappeared, Dog wrapped one hand around the aluminum post and the other around his catheter. But he could not remember why he had done this. He felt too pleasant to think about it. He counted the church bells ring twelve and he was fishing.

He was on a river in Spain. He had never been to Spain, but he was in Spain. He was fluent in the language, telling Mary Jane why mortar shells exploded along the river bank. She rode his back, nails like claws in the flesh of his chest. Dead fish floated in the river. Many dead fish, large as torsos. But Dog was spot-fishing. He told Mary Jane, "As soon as I hook one, the rest will spook, and we'll never see him again." He never hooked the one he wanted. She cursed him as he sank underwater, down with the big Montana sturgeon, touching their rough plates as they finned behind boulders. These were ancient creatures. These were present with the dinosaurs. Apatosaurus. Stegosaurus. Triceratops. Fossils in the limestone—see? Ancient sea bed. No one listening any more. Dog in troll-mode, alone in rough weather, off the map. Huge Dog stepping like Paul Bunyan in a tiny spring creek, all rock and cress and glass-clear water holding big, migrating browns in such chromatic fall splendor they were hard to look at, Dog snicking a chewed black wooly bugger along the edge of a cress bed in the wind and rain and hooking a savage, kipe-jawed, twenty-inch brown painted by Gustav Klimt that thrashed, thrashed, spilling sperm through Dog's net. He couldn't stop it. *Thrashing.*

He came awake. The silver IV pole lay on the tiles beneath the bed, aligned with a trickle of clear fluid. Dog's back formed a sheet of dawning pain. The catheter squirted, bent double in his fist. For a moment he observed his thought-stream: cloudy but fishable, like a river after a rainstorm. The room contained a phone.

"This is me again. Put on M.J."

Dog recalled his name was Ray. Ray laughed. "She ain't feeling too good right now."

"If she can talk, put her on."

A door closed, cutting unclear sounds in half. Ray was chewing something. "She can't talk."

"Why is that?"

"Because I said so."

Standing, Dog felt hung from the skin of his back, like a Sioux brave in the Sun Dance, his feet not quite touching the floor.

"Look," he said. "I'm going to be late. But I'm coming. You can count on that. You tell M.J.—" Dog went into a woozy spin, staggered into a cabinet full of swabs and needles and latex gloves "—and then you pack your shit up and get out of my house."

"I ain't going nowhere, ya focking needlenose." The guy spoke pure Boston twelve-pack. Dog saw Narragansett in cans, gold chain, and diamond ear stud, Bruins Starter jacket with a .45 in the pocket. Good chance M.J. had rediscovered cocaine.

Dog heard her voice: "I want to talk to him. Give me the phone."

"You don't need this jerkoff. Get over it."

"Give me the phone, Ray. Please?"

"He said to tell you he ain't coming."

"He can tell me himself."

He heard a smack. A cry. Another smack and a silence. Dog hung onto the counter, his forehead braced against the cartridge of hand sanitizer. He felt far away, but not in any normal sense. He felt like he could fly there. Like if he could leave this room it right now would happen.

"Don't call again," Ray threatened.

"Oh, I won't," Dog promised.

He hung up the phone. For a moment his certainty dissolved and reformed as the mental image of Curious George in a palm tree. Then he was speaking with his tax guy, Harvey Digman.

"Harvey, I think I'm going to need bail money."

The old man sighed. Dog heard rattling, then aerosol. Then more rattling.

"I got shot."

"Jennifer," said Harvey away from the phone, "regretfully, love, we'll have to finish this later." The rattling stopped. He was back. "This lovely young woman has agreed to spray her erotic graffiti art on my wall." He coughed. "Shot by whom?"

It came to Dog: "Pippi Longstocking."

"That's quite an accomplishment, my friend. Even for you."

"And I think I'm a murder suspect. I'm going to need a hundred grand or so."

Another sigh. "Where are you? What's going on?"

Dog paused to answer this question as precisely as possible. This was a simple hospital room on the ground floor. He was in an open-ass gown and white socks. An IV needle was taped to his left forearm. The link lay leaking on the floor in a curl of Velcro straps. He was rigid with stinging pain across the back. The pain grew stronger every moment.

Dog let go of the phone and tried the windows. His back split open as he reached. His organs hung out in the air. No. That didn't happen. He was ok.

The windows were pin-locked. Dog backed up with eyes watering. Shit. He looked at the IV link, dribbling onto the floor. It was so far down. He did not believe he could bend over.

He found a blood pressure cuff. He dangled it. He got Velcro to touch Velcro. He raised the IV link, dropped it, raised it again. He got the drug back in him. He felt the surge. Ok. *Go, Dog, go.*

The whole IV stand had to come with Dog as he hobbled to the door and opened it. A sheriff's deputy looked up from his magazine and reached for something on his belt.

Dog closed the door. He soared above the room. Through blurry vision he looked for something he could swing and hit the deputy with. He settled on a bed rail. But the rail would not detach. Not for Dog, who suddenly had no strength, no logic. Not even memory.

He only had desire. And wings. He flew at the deputy head first, missed, and was put back to bed.

"Harvey?" he said.

8

All of these being actions that pointed a large flashing arrow at guilty, reflected Deputy Margarite DuCharme after Tim Shrigley, the part-timer, reported Oglivie's feeble attempt at escape.

When, with nothing more potent than your ass hanging out of a hospital gown, you attack an armed man as big and ugly as Tim Shrigley, you have obviously done something you can't afford to pay for. Most likely that something was exactly what it appeared to be, except a little worse. At least this was true about ninety-eight percent of the time, in Margarite's experience.

CrimeNet had come up with a little more on Theodore "Dog" Oglivie. Brushes with the law in Wisconsin, Montana, New Mexico, Washington, and Colorado. The kind of minor stuff that drunks and drifters got into—vagrancy, disorderly, driving without a license, fishing without a license, urinating in a public place, a gas station drive-off—but none in the last year, as if he had cleaned up his act— plus an ancient, unviolated restraining order filed with police in West Newton, Massachusetts. He had behaved himself on that one.

So feel good about it, Margarite told herself. She had in custody some kind of transient fishing hobo nicknamed Dog who had twice already attempted escape. She had a librarian for a star witness, and in Danny Tervo she had an up-and-coming career criminal as a conspirator and/or accomplice. Plus the crown jewel: Heimo Kock was dead. She really didn't doubt it. He would have turned up by now if he weren't. How much better could it get?

Which meant she could just relax, put the kiddie puzzle together for Fritz Shunk, close out the arson case, get it all wrapped up in time for an October yacht cruise with Julia over to Duluth, where they would go to the casino, check out the Tweed Museum of Art, do burgers and microbrews at Sir Benedicts overlooking that awesome harbor and then make love in a hotel room, somehow Margarite's favorite place of all. That would get things going back in the direction they were headed during the dating phase, before Margarite landed the Luce County job and moved north so they could be together.

With these thoughts, driving north past Oswald's Bear Ranch under one of those late summer Superior skies, Margarite took a big gulp of Pepto. Then another.

She met Greg Bright from the Michigan DNR at the entrance to the Reed and Green Campground on the main stem of the Two Hearted River. The ranger led her in about a quarter mile along a soft sand road. On the river side, illegal campsites had been carved out of the brush and pines above the river. Each site was posted with a statement of the DNR rule prohibiting exactly such activity. Graffiti scrawled in charcoal over the postings screamed out DIE, GOVERNMENT TROLLS! and U.P. SECEDE! The resistance was alive and well, obviously.

Reed and Green was tiny, six or eight campsites on a tight loop around pit toilets, a trash depot, and the iron ranger—hollow, lidded, and locked—inside which campers dropped their registrations and payments. Margarite parked behind the DNR pickup. She suspected what was coming. Greg Bright didn't know her yet, didn't live in the county, wasn't in on the scandal. So, predictably, he would work from the rubric of an obviously well-formed female sheriff's deputy, pretty in the face, friendly to him, and not wearing a wedding ring.

Sure enough, the ranger became a stammerer in the face of this impossible planetary alignment. Margarite was going to have to finish his sentences.

"When was the last time you opened this thing?"

"Every two weeks on, let's see, uh, Fu-fu- ..."

"On Friday."

"And Saturday. It ... it takes two days. This one I get Fu-fu- ..."

"Friday. Got it. Ok. Do you keep records?"

"N-name, address, license plate. Phone and email if they ... they ... if they, uh ..."

"If they provide it. Good. And those are kept where?"

He was sorting through his keys like he had never seen them before. "Uh," he said. He gave the iron ranger's cap a hopeful tug, though anybody could see the whole cast-iron setup would still be there, lock and all, after the apocalypse.

"Marquette? Or the regional down in Newberry?"

He got out "Newberry" and wiped his palms on his jeans. "Ok," he said.

"People always pay?"

"You gotta be kidding," Bright said, getting his breath back finally. Then with a big, wild smile, he held up the proper key for her to see.

He reached down the iron tube. He brought up a small handful of tiny manila envelopes with carbons affixed. He sorted them and showed her six with Ned Oglivie written in, the expired Massachusetts plate number, no address, phone, or email.

He stuck the others, the non-Oglivies, in his shirt pocket. "Something funny here," he said, and Margarite could see what he meant. Oglivie's envelopes were slightly puffy, as if he had paid his twelve dollars in ones every time. Greg Bright tore one open and said, "Oh, Christ. Now I've seen it all."

"What?"

"P-p-put your ..."

Margarite put her hand out. He upended the envelope, shook it, and out fell six dry flies. All six were big and bushy, with red in the body, brown and white in the wings.

Margarite laughed. "Royal Coachmen. So, two bucks apiece? Are they worth it?"

Greg Bright picked a bushy fly from her palm. He inspected it. "Heck if I know. I use worms."

Margarite looked at the dates on the envelopes. Oglivie's unorthodox payments began the previous Wednesday and went in perfect sequence right up to the day before Esofea had caught him dumping Heimo Kock in the Two Hearted River. So where was Oglivie the final night? Margarite was betting on Tervo's place, in Deer Park. She opened the trunk of her cruiser and brought back an evidence bag. She felt jittery, her legs weak. Not much get-up-and-go in Pepto-Bismol.

"Those are classic, old-school flies," she said. "They're attractors. Brook trout love them. But I'm going to need all the envelopes. Everybody. Thanks."

Greg Bright stared, his lips parted, his face flushed. Nice guy, she was thinking. So learn from the Lodge mistake. Folks up here just didn't see it coming. Clue him in as soon as possible.

"S-s-so," he said, "you like to go fishing?"

"I do."

"You got someone to go with?"

"I'm teaching my sweetheart."

"Lucky guy."

"Gal."

"Oh."

See? It came out of nowhere.

"Her name is Julia."

Margarite was almost too exhausted, but she made herself smile at Greg Bright, show empathy for his distress. She was getting better at this. She gave him a little chuck on the arm. "But thanks."

Dolf Cook's summer place was close by. Greg Bright retreated and Margarite walked over there.

The gay mosquitoes found her. This was a joke she and Julia had developed during steadier times. In a little-known footnote to the

Book of Genesis, God had made it ten percent across the board, right down to tomboy porcupines and butch-dyke butterflies. This was the moment when God's work went from "very good" to "excellent."

Everything's fun when you're in love, Margarite mused. When she was coming up from Milwaukee once a month, their dates were wonderful. Julia was often a little sick, but they did fun things together. They tried out different bed-and-breakfast places. They played snowmobile poker. They went moose watching in the Seney Swamp. They kayaked at Pictured Rocks. They snuggled, made love, laughed together, looked at real estate, and dreamed about the future. And God had stricken neither of them dead, obviously—though, speaking of the Royal Coachman, one of those dates had involved a thrilling close shave as they were fly fishing on the catch-and-release water on the lower Escanaba River.

Margarite thought of the incident now, one of those near-death experiences that that gave you the priceless gift of awareness. She had been using the Royal Coachman because it was big and bright, and she was hopeful that Julia, who was learning, could follow the fly on the water.

To her surprise, Margarite had raised a good-sized brown from one of the cracks in the river's limestone bottom. Julia was wading over to take the rod and fight the trout, for the experience.

They were catching a trout together. Nothing more, nothing less—but a thrill for Margarite. The sky had not been particularly threatening. Or maybe Margarite hadn't noticed the storm building over the western tree line. In any case, as Julia fought the trout, a lighting bolt had snapped above them like the business end of a hundred-mile whip. Crack! Boom! Technicolor! Ozone! For an instant their surroundings were luridly colorful, like a retouched photograph.

Then they were holding each other against a sheet of hot rain. They staggered, deaf and shaking in the current, feeling each other for a pulse. Somehow Julia still held the rod, but that big trout was struck dead at the end of the leader—and here is where the event became a story they could cherish.

"Ma'am," Deputy Margarite DuCharme had drawled eventually, "this section of the river is a no-kill zone. I'm going to have to take you into custody."

"Oh, no," swooned Julia. "Not again ..."

Heimo Kock's older sibling, his only sibling, was a mess—though Margarite could see that Dolf Cook hadn't exactly been a Swiss-watch kind of guy beforehand. He answered his summer cottage door in mis-buttoned satin pajamas with a burn hole in the shirt tail, plus a sizable damp spot around the fly and down one leg. Kock's brother had located only one slipper in which to present himself, and his first words from behind the door—"who the hell's it?"—sounded chunky and wet in his mouth.

"Mr. Cook, I'm Deputy Margarite DuCharme from the Luce County—"

Jowly and red-eyed, Cook garbled right over her: "Ah, Christ, you're a woman. The hell they send a woman for, so I can embarrass myself?"

Of all the potential corrections to be made by a self-conscious gentleman, Cook threw off his solo slipper with a furtive little kick. It landed somewhere near a kindling box in the foyer.

"Forgive my language and come in please, young lady."

Cook turned and slung an arm with a highball glass at the end of it. The gesture upset his balance and launched a gout of liquid toward a cluttered table. Margarite smelled scotch. She checked her wristwatch: a little after one PM.

"Thank you. As you know, we have a report that your brother's body was seen in the river. I'm so sorry—"

"Bit of a hash," he interrupted. "At Yale they called me Pig Pen."

"I'm not so neat myself," Margarite admitted.

She smiled. He glinted back and struck: "But you didn't go to Yale, though, did you, missy. Probably University of Western Southern North Dakota, or like that. Huh?"

He was shambling away from her with a limp. Near the crown of his head, a freshly broken scab stained a spot of oily dull gray hair.

Margarite found it grimly interesting that this was kin of Heimo Kock. The man presumed dead had been stylish and hearty. Kock always looked like a NASCAR driver, except with fishing logos. And, in Margarite's limited experience, Heimo Kock, unlike his brother, would gladly insult a person directly to her face.

"No, sir. I went to the University of Wisconsin at Stevens Point."

"So sad for you," he said. He made it to his bar area and did a Y-turn. "But here you are. You married?"

Margarite retried the smile. "Who's asking?"

"I had four wives," Dolf Cook answered, pointing a belligerent finger at her. "None of them regrets a goddamn moment."

"I'm sure."

"I got a little chickie, plays with me every summer while I'm up here." He was drifting on his feet, tracking Margarite with the finger. "I don't pay her." This was a denial, indignant. "I give her gifts. Because I love her. Whaddya think of that?"

"I think that's great."

"I own restaurants in fifteen states. You don't believe me, do you?"

"Of course I believe you."

"You married?"

"Nope."

"Bring it on, chickie-babe," Cook said, and then he turned, finding himself misaligned with the bar, reaching his glass toward the dusty snout of a musk ox.

Good god. Margarite had had an inkling of this. She knew Bruce the Moose had handled a call or two regarding Dolf Cook from the tavern at the White Pines Hotel in Newberry. And a few weeks back, the sheriff had driven up to deal with complaints about an old man harassing campers at the Reed and Green. But relax, Margarite told herself, observe. On this bright day the man's living room was dark with game trophies and weapons, a shrine to the male *à la* Teddy Roosevelt—or no, up here it was Hemingway who set the standard. Margarite meant to check out a book or two, try to understand the whole Hemingway thing.

"I'll have straight tonic water, if you're pouring that for me."

She watched Cook turn his back ineffectively and splash scotch into the glass, as though he could slip her alcohol without her noticing. She wondered: what kind of woman goes for that? He handed her the drink.

"Shall we sit down?" she suggested, already taking a seat at Cook's cluttered dining table. A half dozen dry flies in a saucer caught her eye. Here again were Royal Coachmen, tied in the same way as the flies in Oglivie's payment envelopes.

Cook began pawing documents into a heap. Innocently, Magarite caught the corner of a glossy photo and drew it toward her, just beyond his reach. The photo showed Cook anxiously gripping a large brook trout, his rod across his chest, the trout extended toward the camera to make it look bigger.

"Wow. Nice fish."

His hand said gimme-gimme. "Goddamn right it's a nice fish."

"That's a big brookie."

"It's a coaster."

"A what? I fish, but I'm still learning the ropes up here."

That pale hand went gimme-gimme, Cook lurching around the table. "A coaster is a brook trout that eats in Superior, like a salmon. They're rare. Very few fishermen are good enough to find one, let alone catch one. Come on. I need that."

She took another look and let him have the photo.

"You caught that?"

"The hell's it look like? That's me, isn't it?"

"Where?"

"Near the coast. Christ. It's a coaster."

"Who took the picture?"

"My brother."

Then he dropped his woozy head to his chest and began to spasm—or no, he was crying, or trying to cry. Was this odd, when they hadn't confirmed that his brother was dead? Or, like her, did he just feel sure of it?

She was so sorry, Margarite began again. She was sorry his brother was missing and the subject of all these rumors about a body in the river, so sorry to come around asking questions at a time like this. But they had a person of interest in custody, and she was collecting information on that person's whereabouts and activities.

"Naturally since your place is right beside the campground, I'm just wondering if you ever noticed an old RV in Site One, just by the canoe launch."

"Piece of crap? Massachusetts? Yeah, I saw it."

"Do you remember about when you first saw it? Who you would associate with it? And about when you noticed it was gone?"

"I'm not some old woman peeking through the curtains," Cook huffed, offended. He slurped at his scotch. "He was here and then he was gone."

"He was right here in your house?"

He looked startled.

"The hell. I would never let a bum like that into my house."

"Can you describe the person you're talking about?"

"I never met him."

"But you saw a him. Because otherwise it might be a them. Or a her. And a guy, not a bum. What did he look like?"

Kock's brother glowered at her from a tear-stained face, his lips working on what she figured would be some foul and juicy indignation—and she somewhat deserved it. In Milwaukee, Margarite had always felt guilty, wading into collateral damage.

"Mr. Cook, I'm truly sorry to trouble you like this. Just give me a race, an age and a size range, the kind of thing he was wearing. It's really basic. Connecting the dots. I need to establish if the man we have in custody could be the same man you saw here."

He tossed back his drink. "What're ya, stupid?"

"Trying not to be," she said.

"Caucasian, for Christ's sake. You ever see a colored around here? Pretty good-sized sonofabitch with long hair, in a straw hat and old clothes. Patches on his waders. Smoked cigars. That's all I can tell you."

As Cook lurched back toward his bar, she picked one of the Royal Coachmen from the saucer and inspected it. He was lying to her. Oglivie had tied this fly.

She said, "Gotta love a Royal Coachman. My dad's favorite."

Cook swung around from his liquor bottles just like Margarite, as a kid, saw cattle swing their heads around in irritation when yanked by the tail. They staggered a little, thrown off balance by their own surprise.

"I've got nothing to do with those people." He pointed that finger at her again. "You hear me, girly? Nothing. Crazy assholes. I never even heard of them."

Which people, she could have asked him next. And how do you know they're crazy assholes if you've never even heard of them? And do you realize, old man, you've got shit on your tail?

But her radio was making static on her shoulder, conveying every third or fourth word from Sheriff Lodge, so instead she said, "Thank you, Mr. Cook. That's probably all I'm going to need. You take care of yourself."

"The hell's it look like?" he demanded, following her to the door. "Fifteen restaurants," he reiterated, yelling it at her back, "in fifteen states."

Outside, as she cut across the Reed and Green campground, the signal cleared and Deputy Margarite DuCharme heard Sheriff Lodge grunt, "I don't know where you're at, uh …" He was avoiding her name. "…but they're bringing up a body."

Two divers borrowed from the Alger County Sheriff's Department relaxed on a root-heave, sand and rusty spruce needles stuck all over their wet suits. One smoked a cigarette. The other was telling a joke but stopped as Margarite walked by.

Heimo Kock's body lay inside a half-zipped body bag. The ambulance guys got quiet too. Lodge did not make eye contact. He said, "Strangled."

One thing Margarite knew from growing up around trout streams: clean and cold, they were nature's morgue, preserving small dead wonders for her to find. Kock's corpse was intact and firm, unbloated. His guide-wear was hardly soiled, still clearly plugging Bass Pro Shops, Scientific Angler, Mercury Boats, Evinrude Motors. It was above the shoulders that defined the death.

Margarite changed her angle. Kock's face was swollen nearly to shapelessness. His skin was a pale shade of black. His eyeballs had popped hugely forward, as if from a fright mask, each one encrusted with tiny snails. Ten or more twists of fly line had accomplished this condition, each round sinking deeply into the flesh of Kock's neck and cinching off his airway. Someone strong had done this. Margarite herself had recovered Oglivie's reel out of brush by the road, where the RV had been blocked by Esofea. That reel had no line on it. So there you go. Ninety-eight percent of the time, a man who ran was guilty.

Hell, she revised, ninety-eight percent of all men were guilty, of something. Any good-looking woman, gay or straight, knew that. These divers for example. Eyes digging into her like a piece of exotic meat. And Lodge, disowning her.

"Hey, gentlemen," she called out. "You hear the one about the fly fisherman, the worm dunker, and the tackle rep?"

This was her Milwaukee PD persona. She squatted beside the body. It gave off no smell, except faintly like mineral and wet polyester. Right here the phrase "sleeping with the fishes" came to mind— the idea of a Yooper mafia, rumors that seemed far-fetched until she began to explore the dealings of Heimo Kock. Now it fit with what Esofea had just told her about Danny Tervo wanting to start up an outfitter and Kock trying to scare him off. So it might have gone like this: Tervo hires Oglivie to do Kock for a thousand bucks. Oglivie, needing Kock in a remote place, hires him as a guide for about three hundred. Kock, believing he is with a customer, turns his back, takes a six-weight floating double-taper fly line to the neck. Oglivie retrieves his three hundred from the dead man and is on his way. Neat. Until Esofea sees smoke in a strange place and stops the bookmobile.

"See, the fly fisherman, the worm dunker, and the tackle rep are having a drink together in a bar. Suddenly the fly fisherman puts down his fly ..."

Margarite fingered the trailing end of the fatal line. The monofilament leader was still on it, brownly opaque and wind-knotted all to hell. Not only those knots but the line itself reminded her of something off her dad's reel. One old Royal Coachman on a wind-knotted leader, a twenty-year-old fly line on a creaky bamboo rod, a fresh pint of J&B for himself and a Mello Yello for Margarite, all aiming at a nap in the grass. This line trailing from Kock's neck, pale orange and cracked, might have suited her father, but it would have been tossed into the trash by any normal fly fishermen. She figured thirty feet of it encircled Kock's neck. Where was the rest?

"…and then the worm dunker jerks out his worm …"

She straightened up, feeling both heartburn and dizziness. This stomach problem of hers: up here, unlike Milwaukee, you couldn't just duck into a deli or a 7-Eleven and take the edge off when you needed to eat. You had to plan ahead. Take stuff with you. Or suffer and then eat too much, too fast, too late. She had been in Newberry not an hour ago, and once again she had left town without food. Just Pepto.

"Ok," she told Lodge, who seemed to be waiting for more than the punch line. "We'll see if the ME tells us anything else. I'm heading over to Gwinn to talk to Rudvig, then up to Grand Marais to interview Kock's wife. I'll take her to ID the body if we're ready. And then I think you and I should have a beer tonight, talk over my status and future in the department."

She could almost hear the sheriff's mind go *huh?* The divers were all ears.

She said, "So when the fly fisherman puts his fly down and the worm dunker jerks out his worm, the tackle rep says "Oh, shit!" and starts running. You know why? It says on the back of his jacket Master Bait and Tackle."

Walking away, she heard the divers get the awful joke and laugh. That's how you did it. You got out ahead of the whole male hetero-sexual bonding thing. You raunched it up. Showed you were just another one of the guys.

And all that. Over and over. Up here too, apparently. God, she was tired. And now Rudvig.

Margarite drove west along the big lake, then dropped south into the sandy-soiled forestland of the Hiawatha National Forest.

She headed west again, alone on the roads, thinking of bears. Rudvig, the would-be Luce County Attorney, got the nickname "Donuts" because he baited black bears with five-gallon buckets of day-old bakery from Munising and Marquette coffee shops. Julia had explained it to Margarite one night while they were drinking beer on the deck. Rudvig had bait dumps all over Luce and Schoolcraft counties. He used game cameras to watch the bears binge on sugar, Julia said. Clients picked which dump to hunt from by viewing video highlights. Rudvig had six radio-collared Rhodesian ridgebacks trained to track on command, and Julia had explained that in terms of "hunting" and "guiding," Kock's top bear man had only to take those dogs to the chosen doughnut pile, let them pick up a scent, and turn them loose. In a half hour or so the bear would tire and tree itself above the ridgebacks, who would bay and froth and hurl themselves at the tree trunk until Rudvig and the shooter, following by radio at their leisure, would arrive ... and that's where Margarite had stopped Julia. She got how it worked. It made her sick.

In between times, Rudvig drank at the Full Throttle in Gwinn, and that's where the deputy found him, wedged at the rail between his buddy Ron Lindgren and another man Margarite didn't recognize. She spoke mostly to the greasy back of Rudvig's camo-pattern Superior Outfitters cap. He didn't know his boss's schedule yesterday. Hadn't seen him lately. Didn't know where he was now. Rudvig hunkered and sneered, glancing at her once or twice in the smoke-hazed bar mirror. Why? Was there a problem?

"I'm sure you've heard," Margarite said.

A headache had formed to counterweight the burning in her stomach. Her voice felt strange coming out. "But in case you haven't, we just pulled his body from the Two-Hearted near the Reed and Green campground."

Rudvig grunted. He looked unsurprised.

"Can I have you step outside a minute and talk to me?"

"Would but I'm kinda busy right now," he told her.

Lindgren snickered, clinked shot glasses with Rudvig. He could be Rudvig's admiring little brother, the way it looked. Both men were bearded. Both were dirty as little boys. Both dressed like loggers with caps tugged low over furtive, smart-ass blue eyes. Wallets on chains. Skoal bumps. Lindgren added the spooky touch of a zirconium ear stud. Donuts Rudvig, a few years older and a few inches shorter, was missing two-and-a-half fingers on his left hand, the one tossing back the shot. To Margarite, these didn't seem like the kind of guys who would want to take over a complex outfitting operation. That was desk work, PR work, people work, all kinds of work. It would make more sense—if she forgot about Tervo for the moment—that they took out Kock because they didn't want to go down for the Pine Stump Junction fire.

"You don't look busy."

"I'm in a meeting. Strategic planning."

Lindgren bumped his shoulder into Donuts. Margarite met Rudvig's eyes in the mirror.

"And I'm investigating the suspicious death of your employer. The office tells me you're the man in charge now. You want to step outside, please?"

"Do I want to? No, I don't want to."

"Step outside," Margarite said.

"Say please," he answered.

"Better watch out, Rudvig." This was the other man knocking elbows at the bar, pink-faced, big-shouldered, draining a shot. "She'll go all bull dyke on you."

"Can you train a dog to hunt that?" Lindgren wondered. "Bull dyke?"

Margarite hesitated, tried to calm herself. This was no time to confuse things with a bad reaction.

"Tell you what," she said. "You come to the sheriff's office, tomorrow morning at ten. I'll get the paperwork started on a subpoena in case you're unable to make it."

She looked at the three of them, their heads atop liquor-bottle necks in the mirror. She told herself to stop right there—but here came Milwaukee again: "By the way, you boys sit any closer, you'll get your dicks tangled."

She walked out. She passed a jacked-up black pickup in the parking lot—nearly jumped out of her duty boots as a big snout lunged out of a steel cage in the truck bed. Teeth bared, the dog snapped as she backed away. Inside the cage, pandemonium broke out, yelps and jaws emerging from every opening.

From a safe distance, her mind settling, Margarite identified them: Rhodesian ridgebacks.

By evening, nipping Pepto all the way, Margarite had swung past Danny Tervo's place in Deer Park—Danny not home—and then dropped in to visit Kock's wife over in Grand Marais. Here was another U.P. element that was hard to get used to: a fifty-mile round trip just to talk to someone "in the neighborhood."

She tried to unpack that visit afterward as she drove the last leg home. She had expressed condolences and made silent observations—and she had driven away startled and troubled and needing to replay the interview in her mind.

The dead man's wife was the rare woman who looked ten years older than her husband. June Kock had appeared ready for a walker, some bingo, and a nice buffet, while her husband was still out slaying game, messing with girls a quarter of his age, intimidating and possibly even killing people. The pairing gave off a Barbara and George H. W. Bush vibe, Margarite decided. The husband out selling arms to the Contras and invading Kuwait while his wife worried about illiterate children.

The house was on pricey real estate, on the bluff over Grand Marais, looking out on Lake Superior. But it was bland and middle-class as a structure, a well-kept standard ranch that disappointed the expectations of all the KEEP OUT and NO TRESPASSING signs Margarite had passed along the asphalt driveway up the bluff. Rumor had it Kock spent his money on boats and parties, and parties aboard boats. Rumor also had it June Kock didn't drink and would not set foot on a boat. Therein worked the raw mechanics of relational discord. Margarite wondered: how was the Kock couple in their first year? Like she and Julia? Could they see it coming?

"I'm so sorry to bother you with questions at a time like this."

June Kock had inspected Margarite, up and down, like almost every woman did. She said, "So you're Bruce's girl?"

"Not exactly." Margarite had tried to smile, be warm. "But I am the new full-time deputy, yes."

"And you were sniffing around him."

Margarite hesitated. Him? Then she got it, avoiding the name. "I was investigating your husband, Mrs. Kock. He had some unusual business practices."

Kock's wife had scoffed—or agreed. Her tone had not been clear. She limped away on unbalanced hips, and Margarite, guessing, had followed her into a dim living room, lit by the light of a television. June Kock had been watching Dr. Oz discuss "The Power of Infidelity." She tipped back onto her sofa and changed the channel. *Jeopardy.* Changed it again. *Oprah.* She turned the sound down and sat back.

"Go ahead then."

Margarite had gotten a partly familiar read, that was for sure. In Milwaukee, in the city, women with dead men often seemed bitter more than anything: *I told him so, he didn't listen, and now look.* Then, with an opportunity to shine a light, to facilitate justice, they usually stonewalled. No, June Kock's husband hadn't shown any unusual behavior lately. No, he had no business problems that she knew of. No, there had been no conflicts at home. No, she had no knowledge of a relation between her husband and someone named Theodore Oglivie. No, she had never heard of Danny Tervo. Just like those central Milwaukee women.

But those same women, Margarite found, would stick a knife into the heart of their man's killer if he walked through the door—because they knew exactly who he was.

"Mrs. Kock," she said, attempting to trigger that response, "your husband was strangled with a length of fly fishing line."

"Oh, sure," the old woman had muttered toward the TV. "Didn't I know it."

"What do you mean?"

No response. Margarite waited. Sometimes simple silence was all it took. But not today. "Mind if I go outside and look around?" she asked eventually.

"You do that," June Kock told her.

There wasn't much to see. Kock's wife was a decent gardener, with a taste for petunias, geraniums, and ceramic baby animals. A head-high cedar fence surrounded the property, but Margarite guessed that might be to keep deer out more than anything. You could drop this house down in Brookfield, Wauwatosa, one of the Milwaukee suburbs, and no one would notice. Then she found Kock's white Yukon in the garage. That surprised her. It scotched the highway robbery idea. It raised the possibility that Oglivie had picked his cargo up here.

With that in mind, Margarite had come back inside the house—warily—and found June Kock still on the sofa but with a reading lamp turned on and aimed into a large shadow box on her lap.

She waited. Kock's wife looked up. "You asked what do I mean. Well, you can't see it from over there, missy."

Taking a seat beside her on the sofa, Margarite had looked into the shadow box—the kind of thing that often displayed stamps, or butterflies, or medals from a war—and to her surprise she had seen dry flies.

Not any dry flies.

Royal Coachmen.

She counted two dozen of them, in various styles. There were traditionals and Wulffs. There were parachutes, wets, at least one trude, several steelhead streamers, other styles she couldn't name, but almost always with the golden pheasant fibers making a long and showy tail, the two bumps of peacock herl bracketing a red floss abdomen—the design signatures of the Royal Coachman.

"So it was one of them," June Kock said. "I knew it."

"I'm sorry?"

"Each one of them is a member. Half of them wanted him out."

"A member of what?"

Now, heading home, taking the big swing south around Muskelonge Lake, Margarite found herself disbelieving what June Kock had told her. No—not disbelieving exactly. Finding it fantastic. Feeling like she had when she first heard about "getting Hoovered in" or "sexed in," or about the "lights out" method for selecting initiation murder victims—gangland stuff that had seemed made up by television producers until she got involved and enlightened. Joining, belonging, being left out—few things, it seemed, drove human beings to higher heights and deeper depths.

According to June Kock, each fly in that shadow box represented a member of a secret fly fishing brotherhood called The Royal Coachmen. Her murdered husband had at some point become "keeper of the box." Only he could allow new members or expel old ones. There were blanks in the box where flies had been removed. It was one of them that he kicked out, she said. Or it was one he wouldn't let in.

The identities of the members, she told Margarite, were unknown to her. She knew only that a Royal Coachman was another man like *him*. Period. Using *him* again instead of a name. She had stopped there.

Margarite had taken the box in her hands and looked at each fly carefully. The Royal Coachmen that her suspect Oglivie had dropped into the Reed and Green iron ranger and given to Dolf Cook—that fly was not beneath the glass. She had handed the box back to June Kock.

"Is that your husband's Yukon in the pole barn?"

It was, the widow said.

"Did he park it there?"

Who else would park it there, she said.

"When?"

He came and went as he pleased, she said.

"Is there any way you can think of that I can find out who these people are?"

Sure, June Kock said. Wait by the door. The one who did it will come for the box.

Margarite told her that sometime tomorrow, at her convenience, they would need her at the morgue in Munising, to officially identify the body.

"Here's my number," Margarite had said, trying to hand her a card. But Kock's wife had sunk back onto the sofa with the shadow box on her lap, her eyes closed, her mouth set—she was done.

Lost in these thoughts, Margarite found herself home finally.

But Julia wasn't. Her truck was gone. Four Bud bottles stood neatly aligned in the sink. That tidiness was Julia's tiny apology for drinking them.

The deputy made a simple round of inspection, the bathroom, the hamper, the Camel carton, the shoe closet, hating herself but discovering that Julia had showered, changed her panties, put on her cowboy boots, and left with a fresh pack of cigarettes.

Margarite started water for pasta, thinking her stomach might take something bland. While the water boiled, she made phone calls to the four other campers who had dropped envelopes into the iron ranger during the time Oglivie was at Reed and Green. Two were bogus numbers. One was a honeymooning couple from Rheinlander who had kayaked from High Bridge. The lovebirds had arrived after midnight and remembered little else but fumbling through clouds of mosquitoes to set up their tent and then building a fire to dry their clothing out. The husband was still unhappy about the estimated time-on-water that the outfitter had given him. The trip had taken twice that long, he said. He wanted Margarite's estimate of the mileage between High Bridge and Reed and Green.

Julia had just come in. She was gargling in the bathroom. Margarite put her hand over the phone. "Sweetie?" she called. "What's the river mileage from High Bridge to Reed and Green?"

"Three times what it looks like. It takes even longer after a storm if there's a lot of crap in the water."

Julia yelled her answer moving from the bathroom into the laundry room. She had stocked trips for Kock while she was in high school and gotten herself fired. Her story was that Kock had cornered her in an equipment shed, over a pile of life jackets. She had kicked him in the caviar.

"About three times map miles," Margarite told the husband. "Was it Superior Outfitters?"

"Those jerks," the guy said. "I shove off, it turns out my paddle is bent. My wife, her seat doesn't adjust. She goes the whole way with nothing to brace her feet. They said five hours, it took us ten. My God, how do these people stay in business?"

You don't want to know, Margarite said to herself, hearing the lid on the washing machine thump down. But maybe if he came back next year, she told the husband, there might be some different outfitters in the business.

"Did you see anyone else at the campsite that night?"

Checking her notebook, Margarite realized this was the night when Oglivie had not paid with Royal Coachmen. So was he not there?

"Oh, yeah. We just get settled down, this drunk old man comes up to our campfire and talks us right into the tent. We get in there, zip it up, say goodnight, he keeps talking. Helluva good time."

"Did you see an RV at any point?"

"We would have hijacked it," he said, "and got the hell out of there."

"What are you washing?" Margarite asked Julia as she quick-stepped into the living room wearing the robe they left in the mud room for instant laundry occasions. The deputy watched her little free bird skitter past. Julia's skin was flushed rosy pink against the white robe. Her tiny calves knotted hard, feet squeaking as she turned.

"My clothes, obviously."

"Any room for mine?"

"Go ahead."

"Four beers is a lot. You ok?"

Julia went a few more steps before she said, "And how do you know I drank them all myself?" and continued into the bathroom.

A moment later the shower started. Shit. Julia didn't act out like this when they were dating once a month. She was mellow and cuddly. She wanted Margarite around her all the time. She wanted back rubs that went all the way.

Margarite forced herself to call the fourth number from the campground registrations, the one that came with no more address than "Gwinn." Another phony number.

Her mind was a muddle as she went to the deck, where she could look out on the Tahquamenon River. The slow, ale-colored water caught the orange hue of another perfect sunset. A trout rose.

Into her mind on the general theme of discouragement drifted the threats Kock had directed her way for investigating the Pine Stump Junction motel fire.

What did it mean that she had hidden those threats from Julia? That she loved Julia? That she needed to protect Julia? That she didn't trust Julia? That she was over-functioning, once more, in a relationship with a drinker who would end up resenting her?

Margarite had blamed the first broken window on a pigeon. She had tossed the heavy stone back into the river. This was June, pre-Labor Day. As far as anyone knew, she was just renting a room to Julia, who before had been staying with assorted friends, as Margarite understood it, or with her parents at Boney Falls.

Early one weekend morning not long after that, patrolling for sticks before using the mower, Margarite had found dead suckers rotting on the lower lawn. The suckers had been gut-slit with a knife, their organs pulled out before they were tossed ashore. That evening, waiting for Julia to come home, Margarite had answered the phone to "Back off, sucker." "You'll have to do better than that," she snapped back, and right away wished that she hadn't. There had been a looming silence from Kock's people since the outing at the brat fest, as if something better was in fact in the works. Some "strategic planning," maybe.

She leaned on the deck rail and put her chin in her hands. The trout rose, and rose again. So alone, she thought, and these stupid threats, and she felt her eyes tear up.

You're just tired, she told herself. Hungry. And that water boiled a long time ago.

Over an early dinner of garlic pasta and steamed kale from the garden, the clothes drier clanking distantly, Margarite led with the bad news first.

"I have to go back in first thing after supper, look over evidence again, meet with Fritz Shunk and Bruce the Moose. We have to decide how we're going to charge the trout bum."

Julia looked cute with her wet, mouse-brown hair, one of Margarite's big white shirts on as a dress over black panties and nothing else, her bare feet curled and scratching each other's mosquito bites under the table. Never mind the fifth beer, Margarite told herself. Never mind the distant scowl.

"But I'll be back as soon as possible. And the good news is—" Why do I lie? she asked herself "—this should be an easy case. There's the usual higgledy-piggledy at the beginning, but it'll sort out fast. It's just a question of connecting the dots for Shunk and getting the trout bum to tell us who put him up to it. No reason he won't talk, soon as he understands he's looking at life in prison."

"So how do you know he did it?"

"He did *something.*"

"How do you know?"

"I really shouldn't talk about it."

"Then why are you bringing it up?"

"Because you—" Margarite stopped. She took a bite of pasta but didn't notice swallowing it. Her eyes were open, but she could not have named a single thing in front of her, not even Julia's little black-and-bondo Toyota pickup with brand new tires below the deck in the driveway—except suddenly she was saying, "You got new tires? When did that happen?"

"I didn't use your credit card, if that's what you're asking."

"I'm not. I'm just surprised. They look nice."

"Tires look nice?"

"Big and shiny. That's nice in my book." Margarite wanted to ask where the money came from. She blurted instead, "Do you know Danny Tervo?"

Julia put her beer down on the handle of her fork and nearly tipped the bottle. "The hell's that got to do with anything?"

"Just tell me. You think he would kill somebody? Or be involved in it?"

"Why?"

"Just something Esofea mentioned."

"Oh. Esofea, huh?"

Julia's eyes flashed their mean glow suddenly. "I wouldn't believe a thing that girl says about Danny. I went with Danny Tervo once when they were broken up. He was sweet to me." Petite, fierce Julia lighting a Camel now. "Reminded me I sometimes have a taste for it."

It spilled out of Margarite. "Why are you hurting me?"

"Why are *you* hurting *me?*"

"I'm sorry," Margarite said. "I didn't think I was."

Her eyes followed Julia's blast of smoke toward the river. That trout still rose, chasing around a wide slick of water for some emerging insect that came along about every twenty seconds. Margarite—suddenly, powerfully—felt the urge to fish. To chuck it all and be a trout bum. Fish wherever, whenever. Swill Pepto and sleep alone in a camper, move on down the road.

"You ever see Danny these days?"

Another blast of smoke. "Never."

The drier buzzed. Margarite said, "New tires do look nice."

Julia said, "But you see Esofea every day. Am I right?"

"I guess. We both work for the county."

"Nothing you can do about it, huh?"

"Should I? I like her. Did you know she's trying to revive Pippi Longstocking as a hero for girls? Dresses the part, drives that book-mobile around pretty much the whole eastern U.P. and reads the stories? That is so healthy for little girls."

Julia chewed her lip. She shook her beer bottle, heard the swish inside and drained it before she tapped in cigarette ash. A bat swooped right in front of them.

"Healthy little girls, huh? So what?"

After two or three deep breaths, Margarite thought of something to say. A way, just for now, to bridge this gulf she was failing to understand.

"So Pippi reminds me of you. She's this little red-haired pip-squeak so strong she can pick up a horse, and *nobody* tells her what to do. She is completely independent, the way you are. She lives all alone in this big old house ..."

Margarite took Julia's non-smoking hand. As she pulled her lover closer, she felt—still felt, thank God—a rush of desire.

"... but her beautiful friend Annika visits every day—" now she was twisting the story, leaving out Annika's brother Tommy "—and they have all these wonderful, silly, naughty adventures that Pippi dreams up ..."

Stiffly, Julia came closer. Margarite kept pulling. "And she is so brave you can't believe it—like you are. She doesn't care what anybody thinks."

Her lover on her lap now, one hundred and three pounds of lean and stridently horny Yooper girl, fresh from the shower, Margarite began to nuzzle.

"It's a kid's book," she murmured, "so they don't tell the whole story. But Pippi is outrageously generous, just like you are, letting me share life, your mind, your body ..."

Margarite stroked Julia's back. She shut her eyes and plunged through an awful flash of feeling that she had been in this moment before: Georgia, Karin, Deb ... each love somehow arriving at a sick place within itself and falling to pieces ... Margarite doing something to these women, hurting them somehow, obviously ... proud Karin getting bombed and screaming in a bar that Margarite was so beautiful she could have anyone in the world, woman or man, *"So what the hell do you want from me?"*

She stroked Julia's shoulders and neck. She went down the tail of the shirt and up the cool skin of Julia's back. She could claim full credit for their current troubles—there was a strategy. Say this tension was all her fault, now that she thought about it. Mention Kock's threats against her, against them, say Kock had her worried and distracted and she had been working too hard to nail him, ignoring Julia. Now he was dead. Happy days were here again. Sorry, sorry, sorry. They could take a yacht cruise to Duluth and—

Julia broke into her thoughts. "You didn't know that, did you?"

"I'm sorry. I didn't know what?"

"That Kock was threatening you."

Margarite's hand stopped. Her eyes opened. Her pulse sped up.

"He called here," Julia said, "and then he stopped by here. You weren't home. He tried to mess with me, gave me some bullshit about how if you really want to know how somebody dies in a fire, he can arrange for you to find out …"

Julia's voice trembled and trailed off. She sniffled hard.

"I didn't tell you. I'm sorry. I didn't want you to worry. I wanted to take care of it. I told that shithead he had to go through me, he wanted to try some bullshit like that."

Julia reached away for a new cigarette and shakily lit it. After a puff she held the cigarette between them, waiting, waiting, until Margarite reached out.

9

After talking to her friend the deputy, Esofea had waited almost all afternoon for Lakeside Auto Glass out of Munising to fix the bookmobile's windshield. Knowing that the county board would stall a simple disbursement for weeks, she had gone into What Would Pippi Do mode and paid from her own pocket, four hundred dollars of Blind Sucker trust money to a pair of nice old gentleman who puttered and dithered and took two hours to do the job. She nearly had to call the Deer Park Day Care and cancel Thursday "Hop on Pop."

In the meantime, one block away at home, she used a coat hanger to make her pigtails perfectly horizontal. She put on a white blouse and a short plaid skirt, one brown knee sock and one that was black, and her black army boots with the scuffed-out toes. She freckled herself with brown washable marker.

Done with that, she returned to the county building and used the internet to look up Theodore Oglivie, forty-two, last-known address in West Newton, Mass. Scarcely trying, she found his name in a *Boston Globe* obituary, the father in the "survived by" roster for the death of Eamon Theodore Oglivie, four years old. She found a divorce record, from a Mary Jane Broyhill Oglivie, thirty-five, who also appeared as M.J. Broyhill in several court records for the kinds of things a person might do in extreme pain. And losing a child would certainly suffice. Even with her smallish piece of the experience, Esofea knew enough to fathom that.

She went outside to check on the window repair. Her Pippi skirt was very short, and Esofea had legs. She never needed Danny Tervo for male attention, that was for sure. One of the old men winked as he slid his van door closed.

"You be careful, sweetheart."

Which she never was. Never. Always zigzagging up and out, amplifying her life.

For example: next she bought a sandwich and a drink and dropped in on part-time Deputy Tim Shrigley at the hospital, sitting outside Dog's room reading *Car and Driver*, looking for an edge over Newberry Motors. Timmy fixed used cars and resold them off his front yard, handling turkey hunts for Heimo Kock as available. In high school, he had wanted Esofea so badly that after one lucky kiss he had self-tattooed her name over his deltoid, but working upside down he had gotten the "s" backwards. "Because you'll come *back* to me some day," he had claimed, after the fact.

"You just gotta sit here doing nothing all day?" she asked him now.

"Holy wah, Sofi. Guess it's Halloween already, eh?"

She could smell the hose-monkey grime on him ten feet away.

"I brought you Pickleman's."

"Oh, yah. Then I guess it's my birthday, eh?"

"No. But Danny Tervo sure is an asshole."

"Oh, youbetcha, girl. You just get reborn or something?"

The smells of corned ham and American cheese swooned the part-time deputy. Esofea gave him a Cherry Coke, too. "Don't mind me," she said, handing Timmy the screw cap. "I had a little swallow."

That excited him. She could tell by the way his eyes slid to the side and back. She had touched his hand in the transfer, too, working that old history up to the surface: *You'll come back to me some day.*

She read "Pippi Finds a Spink" on the day care story rug, making two kids wet their pants laughing and a third one get to jumping and flapping his arms so much he had to take some medicine.

Afterwards, the girls mobbed her, tiny hands touching everywhere. The boys made elaborate plans for Mr. Nilsson, Pippi's monkey, and her horse named Little Old Man. They went outside and filed through the bookmobile, confused at first by its vintage impression. They were each allowed to take out one book until next week.

"Now, excuse me," Esofea announced, shooing them out, "but I have to leave right away! I have to go and take care of my prankle!"

"What's your prankle?" the children cried as she pulled the lever and closed the door. She waved, tooted the horn as she pulled away. What was her prankle exactly?

She drove by Danny's. Nobody home. The tanker gone. The fucker gone. No call. No explanation. No change from status quo. No make-up from the break-up this time.

Ok.

She used her cell phone to call the Superior Adventures outpost in Munising, which of course was closed due to the tragic loss of so-on and etcetera. It was odd, Heimo Kock being dead. Esofea hadn't hated him as much as, for example, her Granny Tiina, or Danny Tervo, or Fritz Shunk, or a hundred other people had. Kock had been very attentive and almost kind to her, a fact she had always found a little creepy and confusing. She had avoided him at every opportunity.

She left a voice mail: "I hope youse guys all realize Danny Tervo paid that apple knocker to off Heimo cuz Danny got pushed outta da guide business, ya know?"

That would spread like a black fly hatch.

From there her course was a straight shot west across State 407 to the Blind Sucker Resort to check on Mummo Tiina. Yesterday was too quick, didn't count. Probably Mummo needed groceries.

Highway 407 hugged the Lake Superior shoreline. It tunneled through a canopy of pines, with the white beach, the blue lake, and the puffy-clouded sky flickering like shiny postcards at the right-side edge of her vision. Now and then the view opened up. A big sailboat floated out there today, right where Esofea would put one if she were painting a picture. There were so many nice things she and Danny could be doing, the fucker.

Esofea opened the bookmobile's flap door to catch lake air. Turning off the highway onto Blind Sucker Lane, she could hear Mummo Tiina's shotgun booming.

Not the punt gun, thank God. Just her 12-gauge trap gun. So today was skeet-carp, Mummo Tiina's new passion. She was too old to beat the bush for grouse anymore. She was making the carp jump down in the flooding, blowing them out of the air.

This sport took place from the end of the pier by the old boat-house, so Esofea couldn't see it yet. The Blind Sucker Resort was set back on a sandy ridge with a deck and a gravel path that ran down to the flooding where a boardwalk stilted back and forth along an uncertain shoreline, the boathouse at its far western end. Today, the near end of the walk was thronged with Canada geese, brazenly shit-ting their little tootsie rolls everywhere. Esfoea gunned the bus at the hundred or so geese spilling out to clog the lane. They lifted into low flight, peeled away at savvy angles, skimmed down upon the turbid flooding.

She dreaded these weekly check-ins. She felt a little sadder and a little angrier each time—a little less in control. Things fall apart. Yeats wrote that. The center cannot hold. A fine and perky resort that once hosted Hemingway and Eisenhower could become a sink-ing scramble of dilapidating cabins, tended by two lazy swill-hounds and a hulking, menstruating twelve-year-old. The flooding, once a sand-bottomed paradise where lake and river water swirled together into a limpid amber, perfect for swimming, could clog and smell and, thanks to Uncle Rush, end up invaded by the monstrous, bal-listic Asian carp. Tiina Maria Smithback, once the stunner of the northwoods, could become the massive and demented old Mummo Tiina, who was just this moment in boxer's pose with her trap gun at the end of the pier screeching, "Pull!"

Thirty yards out in an aluminum Starcraft, poor Caroline, clad in a yellow raincoat, dipped the revving five-horse engine into the water and ducked. Within seconds, a great silver body exploded through the surface and went airborne, wriggling either in ecstasy or madness until Mummo Tiina blasted it into a thousand bloody pieces. Automatically she swiveled and shredded a second one too.

Caroline tilted the prop clear of the water and raised her head. Mummo Tiina had reloaded. "Pull!" the old woman screeched again. Appearing terrified and despondent, Esofea's cousin recharged the flooding with prop vibrations and sank below the gunwale. This time Mummo Tiina fired into a spurting profusion of airborne carp, like a fountain erupting. Caroline had nowhere to go as chum rained down upon her.

Actually Yeats wrote *centre*, Esofea remembered. She didn't care for Yeats, to tell the truth, actually, a whole lot more than she cared for Hemingway.

She went through Mummo Tiina's kitchen in the red cabin and made a grocery list. On the way back to the lodge, she trespassed into the green cabin and found what she expected: Uncle Rush and Aunt Daryline, hungover, propped up in bed, smoking and staring at the television.

"Sorry," she said. "I was looking for Caroline's parents."

"We got bad backs again today," Rush told her.

"Real bad," said Daryline. "Anyway it's after Labor Day, and we haven't had nobody since mid-August."

"We're closed," Rush said.

"Uh-huh."

"You goin' store now, FiFi?" Rush wanted to know.

"Nope."

"When den?"

"Never."

She closed the door. Mummo Tiina was now in the dusty great room of the lodge, conversing with the game trophies and the historical rods and guns. Caroline had showered. "Anything you need, sweetheart? Or you want to come with me?"

The girl shrugged. For eleven years she was a pixie who had looked at Esofea with flushed cheeks and adoring eyes. But lately she was heavy, growing, bursting, moody. Esofea had begun to avoid her and feel guilty for it. At the moment, Caroline was stepping on dead wasps beneath the window.

"I can't do it today," Esofea said, "but how about next week we go through all the clothes you have. We get rid of what doesn't fit anymore. Then we go to Target and restock. What do you say?"

Another shrug. More reason to feel guilty. A teenage girl, a shopping offer, and a shrug? Something wasn't right.

"You *are* coming with me to Grand Marais today," she told her cousin, patching it over with an action.

"Herman has a place in Grand Marais." Mummo Tiina piped up with this announcement, as if speaking to the head of a bull moose her father Elmer "Bud" Smithback had shot in the 1940s. "But Herman likes a ham-and-cheese sandwich, and I don't have one."

No one knew who Herman was. Herman was new.

Sighing, Esofea moved behind her grandmother and squeezed her heavy shoulders. The old woman's hair smelled like shotgun. Esofea reached for her rough and wrinkled hand, lifted it and kissed the back of it. "That's from Herman, Mummo. He sent it along."

Mummo Tiina pried off her ankle boots. "Turn on the TV," she told someone.

With Caroline Smithback sullenly on board, Esofea drove the Luce County Bookmobile to Grand Marais and left it in the empty public lot across from Superior Shores Market. Along the way she and Caroline never got beyond "I don't know" and "If you say so" and "Whatever."

Knowing this terrain, Esofea grew impatient and took a shortcut. "Is someone bothering you? Touching you maybe, or talking to you in a certain way?"

"I don't know."

"Well, who would I ask, then? Who would know the answer?"

"No one."

"Nothing's wrong?"

"I *said*."

Ok. Well, she tried. Esofea took a moment to shake off a heavy feeling and appreciate September in the harbor. The public boat slips had been relieved of gaudy cabin cruisers and fair-weather yachts. Those folks had trailered up and hauled back to Dearborn, St. Paul, and Chicago. A few of them would have hired sail-aways—like she and Danny had done since they were out of high school, a couple of adventurous lake rats navigating a rich man's precious vessel through the Soo and down to Bay City or Cleveland or Milwaukee for the price of plane tickets back to Marquette—or, in spring, the other way around. Only last April they had conceived on a run north from Port Huron. Drinking, smoking, star-gazing, screwing, arguing— *conceiving*. Shit.

Esofea turned away from the lake.

"What are you reading these days?"

"Nothing."

"Well you are in luck, my love. Come with me."

Esofea steered the girl into the treasure chest of books behind the seats, feeling the heat and bulk of her body. Aunt Daryline, this girl's mother, was the progenitor of the round and active hind-end that Caroline was trying to manage with every step. Uncle Rush was a long-legged, raven-haired, wide-shouldered man who was impressively handsome as long as he kept his mouth shut, completely. Caroline was all this in potential but burgeoning through her lineage into caricature, like an over-blown balloon, as if the food she ate was spiked with hormones, which it no doubt was. She looked more mature at twelve than Esofea had at sixteen. Essentially alone at the Blind Sucker with the phenomenon of her own body, with her dawning awareness of parental abandonment, the girl seemed numb with a fear that Esofea sensed but couldn't resolve. Caroline jumped as Esofea touched her shoulder.

"*Pippi Longstocking*," Esofea said, putting the book in her hand.

"You told me that before. Like a hundred times."

"Well now it's a hundred and one. Is that enough already?"

"I guess so."

"Be careful," Esofea warned her. "It's very silly. It might make you laugh. And Pippi is very naughty, as well as very strong. She does whatever she wants, no matter what people think, and *nobody* messes with Pippi."

The girl chewed her lip. She had a habit of picking at her shirt, pulling it away from her swelling body. She did that twice.

"If they try to mess with her ... what does she do?"

"Ha!" said Esofea. "You're trying to cheat. You wanna sit here and read it, while I get groceries for Mummo?"

A wondrous dream, a fantasy incarnate—Esofea found herself reciting Vargas Llosa as she drifted the aisles of the market—*fiction completes us, mutilated beings burdened with the awful dichotomy of having only one life and the ability to desire a thousand.*

Me in a nutshell, she thought.

Peanuts in aisle seven. Cheese in the dairy case. Mummo Tiina loved buttermilk and Triscuits. The old woman ate three oranges and drank one beer every day. Hot Pockets might be good: less could go wrong in the microwave. Caroline would probably like a bag of chips and a soda. A Blue Sky, though, with cane sugar. But where next? What next? Why?

That old feeling inhaled Esofea suddenly, that intermittent twister in her brain that sucked her up and away from the crumbling *centre* of the Blind Sucker, out of her unexamined past, into the spin of a future where nothing was clear, or right, or wrong—it just *was,* because, and she reacted with *whatever,* in the hope of knowing why. And yet, crazy as she was to fly away, some heavy thing kept her stuck right here in Luce County.

She drove these thoughts away with a glance at the headlines of the *Marquette Miner,* stacked by the door: *Northwoods Legend Dead, Drifter Held.*

Ok then. She picked up a variety box of granola bars, a liter of water, a bottle of extra-strength Tylenol, and an extra large t-shirt with the secessionist motto "Yoopers for the State of Superior." The hats were up front by the softener salt. She chose a brown-billed foam ball cap that said "I'd Rather Be U.P. North." Of course you could not buy pants in a grocery store, not even in upper Michigan, and for footgear, a pair of size thirteen flip-flops was the best she could do. She bought a road map and one that showed the snowmobile trails. She picked up a two-liter Cherry Coke from the impulse cooler. After she dropped off groceries and Caroline at the Blind Sucker—the girl suddenly clinging, begging to play *Chutes and Ladders*—Esofea winged that sloshing howitzer back to the Helen Joy Newberry Hospital and presented it, with a whirl of skirt, to Timmy Shrigley, thinking that inside that room behind Timmy lay this curiosity Dog, stalled in his journey to the pain-black *centre* of his universe. Was that how you did it? You spiraled in and down, not out and up?

Part-time deputy Shrigley, having waited fifteen years for Esofea to validate the backwards "s" of his tattoo, accepted the Coke and wasted no time becoming full of himself. "I gotta tell you up front, Sofi, I am a married man. This can't go no place."

Esofea performed a heavy sigh. "Yeah. I understand. How is Annette?"

She didn't listen to his fishing expedition of an answer. Six or so wife-related complaints later and with the words "what're ya gonna do?" he put his auto magazine down and released the Coke from captivity. Its aroma bloomed out and clashed with antiseptic and floor wax. While he took a big chug from the bottle neck, Esofea snuck a look up and down the hallway, checking angles and distances. They were in the northeast corner, ground floor. The emergency exit was about thirty steps left, away from the nurses' station. It could be done.

"You gotta stay here all night, Timmy?"

"They lock down at midnight. I'll be back at six-thirty AM, get in a shift in before I gotta haul damn Annette up to her ma's in

Gwinn. So I guess around ten Sheriff Lodge or Deputy Muff Dive is going to cover."

God help Annette, Esofea thought again while Timmy yukked. And may Deputy Muff Dive someday have the honor of serving your papers.

Esofea had brought along from her celery mansion the big chintz carpet bag that went with her Pippi look. Inside that, she carried the old canvas shoulder bag she used in high school, still scrawled with ballpoint and still smelling a bit like Canadian sticky nugs and Danny's Kenzo fragrance. Inside that she had stashed the granola bars and the water and the Tylenol, the shirt, cap, and maps, all that—plus one of the two-way tracking pagers from the bookmobile.

"I feel so bad that I shot him," Esofea said.

"Ice Melt ain't so bad," grubby Tim waxed philosophically, expanding on his make-believe reconquest of the cutest girl at Newberry High. "Trouble is, it's embedded under his skin and took some shirt in there with it. Some wadding too. But he won't die. Unless he gets infected, which he's in the hospital, so … ya know."

Esofea slid down the wall and sat on the floor. "Are you religious, Timmy?"

"Only when I need to be."

"What would you do if you killed someone?"

He put the soda down and folded his arms. "On duty or off?"

"Either."

"Innocent or guilty?"

"A life is a life in my book, and everybody's both."

"Both what?"

"Everybody's both innocent and guilty." She ran with it. "The only thing that's wrong is putting yourself above the flow of things, thinking you know what's right, and judging people, and believing that it's your job to fix things. There's no need for that. The karmic debt is always paid."

"Uh-huh." Timmy gripped the jug of Coke and told an obvious lie: "I know what you mean."

She volleyed a Tervo at him: "When ego is lost, limit is lost."

"Ok." He slid a glance up Esofea's long-stockinged legs. "Sure."

"And truth is limitless. Truth doesn't need anybody's help."

Timmy mashed his tobacco-stained lips in a seriousness of consideration normally reserved for scouting turkey blind positions or choosing musky bait—situations where he planned to score. Solemnly he told her, "No shit."

"If I killed someone," Esofea went on, "I would kill myself to fix it."

"Oh, come on now. You don't mean that."

"Sure I do. You know, pay the karmic debt up front, go on to the next life with a clean slate. I hope I'm a giraffe, Timmy, or a Madagascan pigmy, wouldn't that be fun?"

The part-time deputy took an urgent slug from the jug and made himself cough. Esofea held back a smile. Here he was, a self-respecting northern white man, caught mind-humping a Madagascan pigmy. Timmy recovered to say, "You can stop being so damn psycho any time now."

She sighed. She replayed the picture of Dog crawling away along the ditch as Sheriff Lodge pulled up. After a silent minute she said, "Timmy, that poor man just laid there until they carried him into the ambulance. So to my mind he's dead."

"Now, that's not—"

"So now I need to die myself. That's the way I read it."

"What the—" Tim sputtered. Esofea explicated the varmint vibe: Would he get to nail her first, though? Before she died and turned pigmy? "What the hell are you reading anyway?" he said.

"Oh, I don't know." She wrung her hands. She could make her distress as real as need be. Everything hurt so much anyway.

She stood and shouldered her carpet bag, like she was leaving. She looked at part-time deputy Shrigley and quoted the great philosifucker Danny Tervo: "We write our own book of life, Timmy. *We* are the truth."

Now Tim stood up, his face abruptly flushed. "The guy is just passed out, Sofi." He was reaching at her. He was begging her to believe.

Esofea shrugged away. "I never saw him move. So, well, I guess I'll see you on the flip side. Hope you're going to be a Madagascan pigmy too. They walk around naked, you know. They don't care."

The part-time deputy looked both ways down the short corridor. He jerked the door open.

"He's alive, Sofi. Damn it. Go see for yourself."

10

Luce County Sheriff Bruce "The Moose" Lodge built his and Charlotte's dream house up on Widgeon Creek, isolated and perfectly quiet, with bird feeders and mineral licks for the deer, with flower and vegetable gardens, and then sixteen months later Charlotte had her stroke and died. You know. That whole sob story.

He didn't care to go into it. What can you do? What can you say?

The sheriff did take longer getting through his day. That was one thing. He didn't hurry home. He kind of stretched things out. He knew every bridge in the county that had fishable water under it. There were eighty-six.

From the crime scene up on 410 he had followed the ambulance with Heimo Kock's body back to where the highway became paved and then turned to four lanes and swept between the Indiantown bluffs into Munising, toward the morgue and the medical examiner. He came back on 28 eastbound, flipping his big spoon three times into Prairie Creek and three times into the Creighton and Driggs rivers. Trout jumped all over but paid no attention to the Daredevil. It was brushy as hell after mid-summer, too, and his angles were bad.

He had a late lunch in Seney and might have felt a strike on his first cast into the Fox River before a call came about teenagers drinking at the Natalie campground on the Dollarville Flooding. Sheriff Lodge drove down there, poured some alcohol out on the ground, and caught an axe-handle pike in the flooding, casting from the boat launch.

In an hour he was back at his desk. The sheriff's big hands smelled like pike and schnapps as he put the word out to look for Kock's vehicle. It was a white GMC Yukon. Might have a food pantry delivery in the back. Canned goods and macaroni, that kind of thing.

That's when it hit him that Heimo Kock, a fellow he'd known all his life and dealt with for thirty years as sheriff, a fellow he both loved and despised, was dead.

What can you do? What can you say? Everybody had some good in them, and everybody had some bad in them, and everybody died.

Bruce Lodge did need to dab his eyes a little, actually. Blow his nose.

Couldn't argue with Fritz Shunk, though. Kock was without a question the biggest horse's ass Lodge had ever known. The man had to dominate every fish and mammal within about a two-hundred-mile radius. He had to have relations with every woman who would let him and with a few who wouldn't and with far too many who weren't even women yet. He had kept cranking up his machine to get Bruce the Moose re-elected, term after term, the sheriff neither asking nor giving permission for the help, no discussion between them on the topic, ever. Winters, when outfitting was slow, Kock loaded up that Yukon at Dobber's in Escanaba and drove Cornish pasties all over the whole U.P. to folks shut in by the weather, dropped off fruitcakes at all the resorts and motels and sports shops, bought rounds in all the taverns. In summer he collected for food pantries, passed out free hats, tuned his political engine. Kept himself on people's minds. Gave the sheriff the cover of saying he was a good man. Hell. Who wasn't, in some way?

In the afternoon, the school bus to Curtis broke down near the north shore of Manistique Lake. On his way out, the sheriff stopped at the bridge over the East Branch of the Manistique River. One cast. Two casts. Bad angle again. He went up and across the road to get a better look from the upstream side. His third cast overshot and hung up in alder branches across the river. It came out, but with a big green leaf attached, wobbling back across the current like something even a musky wouldn't look at. Strike three. Suck a duck.

He delivered half a dozen kids to their houses and the driver home to Engadine. It was after five o'clock by then. At Furlong Creek, first cast, his spoon hit the concrete bridge abutment and returned with its treble hook broken off. Climbing back to the road, the sheriff stumbled in the jagged chunks of concrete fill. His big body toppled hard.

He lay there. Nothing serious, just pain that went away, and a broken rod, but he lay there longer than he needed to, exploring the dimensions of a quiet disappointment that dwelled in the cold shade beneath the bridge. He watched swallows swoop under to their mud nests, trailing little wakes of sunshine, and eventually he thought about You-Know-Who.

The lady-lover.

The impostor.

The lesbian.

The one who should have told him.

Margarite.

Maybe a half hour passed. Eventually he noticed that of all those names, it was the last one, Margarite, that returned to his mind and then his tongue, made him feel like standing up, going home, getting on with it.

Margarite. She had a name again.

Hell, though, he still felt angry.

She was sitting on his porch when he arrived home at dusk. They crossed words as he limped up his little bark path.

"Funny seeing you here."

"You broke your rod."

"Really?" He scowled at her. "I didn't notice."

"I brought beer."

"You're on emergency tonight."

"Right. But you're not."

Here came Goldie, Charlotte's ancient kitty, trotting across the lawn. Her half-cup of Friskies was sometimes the only reason Lodge came home at all. Though where else he might go was unclear to him. He turned on the porch light.

"You're in my chair."

"I'm not contagious. But ok, I'll move."

"That's Charlotte's chair."

"You can make me stand, Sheriff, but you can't make me leave. We're going to talk."

Lodge went inside and got a bowl of cat food. He set it on the deck and collapsed down heavily in his chair. His knee hurt, his elbow. His rod was busted. He was hungry without a clue what he had in the house to eat. So he just said it.

"You should have told me."

"Why?"

"So I could have hired someone else."

There. That was one angry piece of how he felt. Making a fool of him. A dunce. Bruce the Moose. He had enough of that.

"Ok," she responded at last, slowly. "By that you mean to say there was someone better?"

He looked at his deputy. Such a goldarned beautiful young lady, first class in every way. Polite too: holding out an open bottle of beer from some pissant teriyaki brewery that thought too highly of itself.

"You mean you had a better candidate than me, but you passed that one over and hired me for my looks? And it turns out you did that for nothing? Because I do it with girls? Tell me, Sheriff. Was I supposed to do it with you?"

Lodge gripped the arms of his lawn chair.

"You should have told me, that's all."

"Why?"

"Because it's the right thing to do. Be honest."

"Really. Then you should have told me Heimo Kock ran this county, got you elected to pick off downstaters for speeding tickets and stay out of his way. Be honest."

Lodge clenched his jaw. Goddamn Heimo Kock had pushed him around since grade school. His wife had always said that. "Sit down."

"Charlotte won't mind?"

Lodge sighed. "Charlotte is dead."

His head drooped to his chest. He had never said that before. Almost seven years now, and those three words—Charlotte is dead—had never left his mouth. Now, as Margarite sat, he felt a presence in Charlotte's chair beside him, and he knew what he had done. Another truth just flowed from his mouth, on a plan of its own.

"You reminded me of her. That's all. When she was young."

He covered himself with a swallow of the beer. Crap with bubbles, teriyaki dark and weird, just like he imagined. The bottle trembled in his big fist.

"She was so pretty," he said. "That's all. So graceful."

He raised his head to look across the creek. There it was, the sunset, lighting the treetops on fire. This is what he tried to miss. He tried to come home after it was over.

"She was fun to be around. Smart kid. Decent." His voice shook. "She always said what she was thinking."

Lodge took a deep breath. He looked away from the western sky. Another swallow of that beer took the edge off, for sure. Powerful alcohol. Almost made you forget you were surrounded by teeny brook trout and teriyaki everything, by lesbians and civil rights lawyers and beer the color of tobacco spit. Heimo Kock was finally dead. Next up: Bruce the Moose. Was that it? Join Charlotte in heaven? He was supposed to believe he would see her again, but he had found out that he did not. He ought just as well to lie down beneath a bridge, become mud, turn into swallow nests.

A mosquito lit on the sheriff's finger. He blew it off. It flew over his deputy's way. Now they were looking at each other. "She wouldn't have told a dirty joke like you told to the divers. She wasn't like that."

"Of course not. She didn't have to be like that."

"She wouldn't."

"No, she didn't *have* to be. You don't get it, do you?"

"I most surely do not."

She sat forward. "I get hassled a lot. Men think I'm straight. When they find out I'm not, they're cheated, they feel they have a license to attack. Sound familiar?"

Lodge stared at her face: she stared clear-eyed right back at him. He never felt like attacking. More just jilted and hurt, now that he thought about it.

"A dirty joke like that?" she said. "That's how I let men know I'm not afraid of them. And you want to know one reason I wear my vest all the time? I don't need the extra attention my body attracts. I tell the dirty jokes first, before they get told on me."

Lodge rubbed his face. Goldie finished her food and jumped up on the porch rail. She tight-roped to the middle and then sat down. Here was something the sheriff felt he could say: "Well, I just thought you were real pretty and real smart and a very nice person who wouldn't normally say things like that."

"Well, thank you."

Lodge tried the beer again. So bitter it climbed up in his sinus. He looked at the bottle. It had won a blue ribbon somewhere. Lord help him.

After a moment his deputy said, "Listen. The problem is that when you find out who I'm in love with, you want to take all those things away from me. You want to say I'm somehow counterfeit. I'm not who I claim to be."

"I just thought you should have told me."

She sighed and Lodge felt bad. He couldn't help it. He just thought she should have told him. It wouldn't go away.

"You didn't inform me, did you, Bruce, who you were sleeping with?"

"I'll tell you now. Goldie."

"But you had plans for me?"

Lodge groaned and stood up, waving at mosquitoes. He turned

off the porch light. He didn't know what he had plans for. Even
though she reminded him of Charlotte, his feelings weren't ever like
that, and it made him angry and confused that she thought so. He
wished he hadn't admitted anything. He dumped the rest of that
yuppie swill down his throat. It had a kick. He sat back down and
looked at the sky, a little dizzy.

The sun was gone, leaving a dome of deep, glowing indigo that
felt closer than any other sky ever did. It made your eyes give in.
It made your heart open up. Charlotte said this late summer deep
indigo was the color she wanted to paint the bedroom in the new
house behind him. She never managed to get it right, though. So
they had to come outside all the time, make love right here. But only
a year and a half of that, two summers, and then …

Margarite hit two mosquitoes, slap, slap, and then she stood up.
Sheriff Lodge tried to make out her face in the dark.

"Are you asking me to resign?"

"No."

"Good. Because I'd sue the roads right off Luce County."

"That's what Shunk says."

"Listen to Shunk," she said. She stepped off the porch and
crossed the grass toward her cruiser. She turned. "And don't forget
we're meeting him tonight."

He was relieved that she couldn't see him in the dark: Sheriff
Lodge had started to smile a little. He felt proud of her.

He drove with his window down so the night chill could contest
with that ridiculous bottle of beer. It had an aftertaste he could not
identify as something that belonged in his mouth.

By the time he sat down in his desk in the Luce County building, another bad taste had entered his mouth. Julia Inkster. A little
shitbird like that, what was Margarite thinking?

The deputy entered his office carrying an evidence drawer, Shunk
behind her, and behind the county attorney some hotshot who
Lodge understood was the new tri-county medical examiner. Shunk
cradled soda cans in his left arm, balanced a carry-out container on

his briefcase, keeping it all together no problem despite that alarming hitch in his gitalong.

Cokes and deep-fried mushrooms from The Log Jam. That should kill the beer taste. Lodge studied Margarite, tried to see how the taste for shitbird showed itself in her.

He couldn't see it, really. He took a Coke, tapped a thick, yellowed fingernail against the top, working his memory. Julia Inkster had stocked trips for Heimo Kock at one point. As far as Lodge knew, she still partied with Paul "Donuts" Rudvig, Kock's main bear guide, and with a few other of those nasty—

"Ok, folks." Shunk interrupted the sheriff's thoughts, setting the treats down on Lodge's desk and pulling up a chair. "We're twenty-four hours in. The law says we have to charge this guy or we can't hang on to him. This is Doctor … sorry."

"Boyd."

"Sorry. Dr. Boyd has come down from Munising, so let's hear what he has to say."

Maybe I'm just an old pump handle anymore, Lodge thought as he tried to focus. This Dr. Boyd was gay too maybe? He dressed like he was off a page from one of Charlotte's catalogs that kept coming in the mail, seven years later—like a downstater on a sailboat vacation, wrinkle-free trousers, topsiders with perfect leather laces, open coral-colored shirt with sleeves three-quarter rolled—or maybe the shirt was "puce," the sheriff studying these matters on the shitter—an exquisitely trim fellow with a nifty dark beard and smooth, expressive fingers, a cool impatience in his manner until he got a look at Margarite. Then he showed off big, hungry teeth. So not gay? Was that it?

The top of Bruce Lodge's head grew hot as the doctor explained directly to his deputy and no one else how Kock had died from ligature, yes, but not from tracheal closure, which required at least thirty-three pounds of pressure. Kock had no neck injuries. There had been no significant pressure. His hyoid bone was intact.

Hyoid bone. Now there was a new one on Sheriff Lodge. Thirty-some years in the business without hearing about the hyoid bone.

He tried to wink up Margarite. Teriyaki sauce all over this fellow. But she didn't look at him.

"It's a small, horseshoe-shaped bone in the neck, Sheriff, that helps support the tongue."

"Sure. Thanks."

"It is normally broken in a tracheal strangulation. We would also see damage to the cartilage of the larynx."

"Ok then."

"Only ten pounds for ten seconds." The doctor returned his attention to Margarite. "That's all it takes to compress the carotid arteries and cause unconsciousness. Sustain that state for four to five minutes, and the brain dies."

Margarite nodded. "He didn't struggle."

"Correct." Dr. Boyd flashed his teeth for her. "The bumps and abrasions happened after death. The skin on the back of his head is a paste. His buttocks and calves show post-mortis bruising."

Suddenly the doctor seemed fascinated with himself, leaning back and crossing his perfect pants at the knee, fondling his beard. Good golly, Lodge erupted silently. Enough already. He stood, his entire head feeling hot as Dr. Boyd said, "He had soil and pine needles in his underpants that didn't come from the river. My guess it he was dragged around quite a bit. I saved the soil in case you'd like it analyzed."

Lodge put out his enormous hand. Dr. Boyd looked like he would rather not, and the sheriff confirmed that worry for him, made it absolutely real as rain with a bone-crushing handshake.

"We'll let you know, Dr. Boyd, if we need any more of you."

The sheriff started the computer Margarite had been teaching him to use. Shunk became talkative.

"Dragged around, to me—I mean, dragged around for a significant period before Oglivie dumps him in the river—to me, that doesn't fit a simple robbery."

"Plus his vehicle is in his garage," Margarite said. "Up in Grand Marais."

Lodge looked up, surprised.

"Well, shit," Shunk said.

"And his sunglasses were in his jacket pocket," she said. "He wasn't driving. He was inside somewhere."

Lodge let them go around with it while he tried to remember how to get into the circuit court records. Onto the internet, and then ... He glanced up to see Margarite lift a chain-of-custody envelope from the evidence drawer. "My guess is we haven't even found the light switch on this one yet. That might be because it's down in Chicago."

"Chicago?" Shunk laughed explosively, staccato and loud, like a startled kingfisher. "I thought I was done with Chicago. I practiced there in the eighties. Got the heck out and went to Detroit. Like that was better."

There. Lodge's big fingers had found their way. *Inkster, Julia.*

"Here's the situation," Margarite said. "Esofea says that Danny Tervo's mixed up in this. He wanted to guide fly fishing on his own. Kock was threatening him. That's one piece. Then June Kock tells me this afternoon that she believes it's about some secret society of fly fishermen, which I take to be rich guys from Detroit, Chicago, places like that, and Kock was the head of this. The Royal Coachmen. I don't see Tervo involved in that. But still, that's piece number two."

While the computer system went on its shitbird hunt, Lodge looked up at his deputy. Margarite's lady friend was from Boney Falls, last he heard, lived on-and-off between man friends with her folks in the dam keeper's house there. Margarite had bought the old Gavinski place on the Tahquamenon. When had Julia moved in with her? No—that wasn't his question. What he didn't get was why.

"On top of that," Margarite was saying, "Dolf Cook lied to me and said he had never met Oglivie when clearly he had. Cook says he owns restaurants in fifteen states. I'm guessing Illinois is one of them. He has a home address in north Chicago. That's three. Now here's piece number four: before I left home tonight I got a call that places Oglivie in suburban Chicago around the time of the murder."

She flattened the chain-of-custody envelope so Shunk could see inside. When the sheriff looked back, Inkster's record had come up. Now where were his reading glasses?

"A gas receipt from the Schaumburg Road Ranger. Exactly the amount deducted from the thousand. Management down there had to track down the clerk and the security guy working that shift. They both saw Oglivie, no question. So he went down to Chicago and back, and then we had a corpse. We have no clue yet where Kock was that night. I can't find Danny Tervo, either. I need to go back and ask Dolf Cook where *he* was two nights ago, and I have to be prepared for him to lie again. Now … ready for piece five?"

Out came a larger chain-of-custody bag with the pale-orange fly line from around Kock's neck. She played the leader out through her fingers, handing Lodge the narrow end because his hand was out, searching under papers and files for his glasses.

"See? Wind knots."

Wind knots?

"Sure," Lodge said, not sure what he was touching. They were rock-hard bumps in thick monofilament. They were simple, too. A twist or three. Not the loose and messy Chinese arithmetic that came off his spinning reel about once a week.

"What the hell's a wind knot?" Shunk said.

"You make one by mistake."

Margarite put her right arm in the air.

"By bad casting. There's supposed to be an open loop up here."

Her arm went back and forth in an elegant motion. "You get sloppy, your loop collapses and your fly goes through it, making a knot. You blame it on the wind. Sometimes it is the wind."

Her arm came down. Lodge found his glasses behind the take-out container. Margarite passed the line to Shunk, who shrugged. "So?"

So … *Inkster, Julia. DOB July 3, 1983. Sex: F. Records: 13.*

"So Oglivie's a trout bum," Margarite said. "He's been fishing almost every day for five years. He wouldn't cast this badly. I counted seventeen wind knots on this leader. Maybe if the guy was fishing drunk, blindfolded, in a hurricane, in the dark ..."

"Maybe he was."

Lodge glanced up to see Shunk scowl and work his mustache back and forth.

"Small chance," Margarite said.

Record 1: December 14, 1997. Class Code Description: Possession. Status: Closed.

So ... age fourteen. Over in Schoolcraft County. When kids got started that early, Lodge reflected, they were going to be on the radar a long time.

"Maybe the guy was broke and couldn't buy a new line," Shunk said. "Maybe that line was five years old."

Now Margarite lifted another out evidence bag with spools of line and what looked like a measuring tape for sewing inside.

"I don't think so. He *was* broke, and the line itself looks ancient, but he had leader-building stuff in his cupboard. He made his own, for pennies apiece. One wind knot and he would have built a new leader. It takes five minutes, and I don't think he was watching TV at night."

Record 2: June 3, 1999. Class Code Description: Possession with Intent to Deliver. Status: Closed.

Record 3: Sept. 10, 2003. Class Code Description: Aggravated Battery. Status: Closed.

Record 4: Sept. 16, 2008. Class Code Description: Attempted Arson. Status: Dropped.

The county attorney said to Margarite, "You don't think Oglivie killed Kock."

"No. I don't. I think someone else did."

Shunk tossed his folder on Lodge's desk. "Well he must have done something he didn't want to pay for, or he wouldn't have been rolling a body into the river."

"Right," Lodge's deputy said. "With a thousand bucks minus a tank of gas in his glove box. Just upstream from Cook's place. After leaving the campground and driving to Chicago and back the night before. With Danny Tervo nowhere to be found. With Kock's vehicle in his garage. With a piece of ancient line around Kock's neck. Only he wasn't really strangled. Not with any force."

Shunk scowled. "Shit. I'm in the dark here."

"Exactly," Margarite said. "And no light switch."

Sheriff Lodge felt her looking at him now—as in, what did he think? He had gone into the Wisconsin circuit court system, where she was from, and typed *Margarite DuCharme*.

His big ears felt hot. He made some kind of twisted grimace as he hit *search*.

"Hey," she said to him. "You're the one in charge here. You gonna be ok?"

Margarite was yawning almost painfully, her brain dying to shut down as she pulled up outside the old Frens Mansion on East John Street few minutes later.

She sat in the cruiser, staring at Esofea's place and thinking involuntarily about celery. Who cared, but she had heard somewhere that "celery money" built the fifteen-room folk Victorian, and she was still getting her head around that bit of U.P. history. Iron ore, old growth timber … and celery—before a blight wiped out Otto Frens in the '30s. She yawned again. Get out of the cruiser, she told herself. Then two decades later, Esofea's great-grandfather Elmer Smithback, the guide, had bought the Frens Mansion on the cheap so his family wouldn't have to winter at the Blind Sucker Resort. That made sense. Esofea owned it now, her piece of Elmer Smithback's estate. But the next fact was some serious mental celery for Margarite to gnaw on: Esofea had lived there, solo, since her *sophomore year in high school.*

"Really? What?" Margarite remembered asking her, thinking she must have heard wrong.

"I just moved down here one day and nobody said anything," she explained.

"Not your Mummo Tiina? She was senile already?"

"No. She was ok then. I think." Esofea had shrugged. They were in the break room of the Luce County office building, bonding over the theft of two spoonfuls of the sheriff's powdered Sanka. There was a high window in the room, showing a windy sky. "I guess she just wanted me to go."

"But only so far, huh?"

"I can't really leave," Esofea said. "I don't know why."

It seemed obvious. This was after Julia's public humping of Margarite at the Labor Day Brat Fest. They were talking about lovers. "Maybe it's Danny?"

She shook her head. "He had this idea to move to Alaska once. I wouldn't go. But anyway, here," she said, and she handed Margarite a small wad of tissue paper. Inside was a geode, the size of a walnut, sliced in half to show yellow crystals around a dark, vacant center. "Put that where the sunlight can find it. It will help bring your soul back."

"Thank you."

"You know what I mean? When somebody takes a choice away from you, a very personal choice, don't you feel like a part of you has been lost?"

"Exactly," Margarite said. "I feel amputated somewhere."

"But you are so much bigger and stronger than this moment," Esofea told her. "That's the thing. You are spiritually huge. We all are."

"Thank you."

"I believe that."

They sipped Sanka for a moment, and then Margarite pushed her cup aside, noticing the thin and bitter taste. That was the moment when she realized Bruce Lodge hadn't spoken to her since the brat fest, hadn't even looked at her. Then Esofea had compounded this feeling by saying, "Well, I *was* wondering how a woman as attractive as you could still be single."

Margarite had felt prickly and deflated for a moment. She got that line all the time. "You mean, there must be something wrong about a woman without a man?"

"No," Esofea explained easily. "A woman without love."

"Oh."

"But now I see you have Julia. So it's ok."

"Right."

Then after a sigh and a long silence, Esofea said, "Don't you want to have a baby?"

"I don't know."

This was true. Margarite had no idea. All thoughts in that direction became tangled in memories of herself cooking for her dad, washing his clothes, getting him to work on time. She couldn't fathom what a child was, exactly, or a parent. "I haven't decided," she told Esofea. "But what about you?"

"I want to have a baby *back*," Esofea said, and then she had told Margarite a sniffly, elliptical tale involving a sailboat, a moonlit night, a happy accident followed by a negotiation, an abortion ...

At this point in the story the sheriff had walked in. Bruce the Moose had come to a clumsy stop inside the doorway. He blinked at the two women holding hands across the break table, then turned and took his coffee cup elsewhere.

"So now he wonders if you're gay too."

"I'm not."

"Oh, I know," Margarite assured Esofea. "Not even."

She left the cruiser finally. The celery mansion's run-around porch groaned under the deputy's step. The small gray cat called Mr. Nilsson rode Esofea's shoulder as she answered the door.

"Hi," the deputy said. "Any sign of Danny yet?"

Mr. Nilsson vaulted off and skittered away. Margarite watched the cat dart down a dim hallway into a lighted kitchen with enameled sink and pine sideboards, a cast iron stove, old gingham curtains limp above a firebox.

"Nope," said Esofea. "The boy is laying low. Or laying Lois. Who knows?"

"Lois?"

"I made her up. She's easy. Her tits think Danny's a great philosopher."

Margarite's brain felt slow. She discretely sniffed for weed. "No idea where he might be? His tanker is gone."

"Hauling Wesson Oil, I guess. That's what he does when his cash is low and he can't con me—which he can't right now, due to certain reproductive atrocities."

"You sound unhappy with him."

"You sound, hmm, investigative. Wanna come in?"

"I can't, really. I'm allergic to incense."

"Oh, shit," Esofea said. "I didn't inhale. Really."

Margarite smiled, shifted questions around in her head, groping for the right one. God, she was so tired. That guilty old stump Lodge had taken over her emergency shift for the night, told her to go home and get some rest. He would sleep in his office. The hospital was locked up for the night, but it wouldn't hurt to stay close. That was his reasoning. Margarite would bring in Dolf Cook for formal questioning in the morning. What she asked now, though, was this: "You ever fly fish?"

"Me? Never."

"Ever fish at all, any style?"

"I'm a vegetarian. On moral grounds. I don't bother animals."

"That takes a lot of guts up here."

Esofea raised a lovely thin arm and made a muscle. "Guts and granola." Her smile was impish. "And coffee. And cigarettes. And chocolate. Plus naps. You look beat, girl."

"I'll be ok. The sheriff's taking my emergency shift. Really, no fishing, not even with Danny Tervo?"

"I'm sorry. Danny who?"

"Tell me you're not so angry with him that you made a few things up."

"Of course not. But you'd be angry with him too."

"I would?"

"You oughta be."

"I should?"

"Oh, never mind," Esofea said, stepping out on the porch to retrieve a half-pack of American Spirit cigarettes from a window sill. She lit one. "So, things are good with Julia?"

"Perfect."

She snorted smoke. "Now who's making shit up?"

"Nobody in my world."

"Now *that* sounded angry."

Esofea reached out with arms open. Margarite froze for a moment, her eyes falling closed as she felt the hug, long and solid, leaving her in a swirl of cigarette smoke.

Later, heading home, she stopped at the Holiday station and picked up more Pepto. *Lovers*, she thought, taking a heavy slug of pink about a mile down the highway—but before she could complete the thought she realized her headlights were off and she was driving sixty in the dark.

1 1

The silver *Essence of Soy* tanker barreled across the panhandle of Oklahoma, casting its afternoon shadow onto a vast, flat dryness that pleased Danny Tervo very much.

He thought about the Santa Fe Trail, all those folks moving great and perilous distances to be where the resources were. This made sense. This was the only choice up until outfits like the Atchison, Topeka, and Santa Fe Railroad introduced the idea that folks ought to stay put and let other folks bring the resources to them. Such socio-economic transformations were the work of visionaries, of course, and the making of barons—and such was the arc of yours truly.

But Billy Rowntree had been making Tervo's prepaid ring every fifty miles or so, disturbing his meditations on fame, wealth, and the admiring, hot-green eyes of Esofea.

Tervo didn't answer. He wanted no part of Billy Rowntree.

He had to unfuck that shit, fast.

Pardon my language.

Talking to Esofea. Doing ninety, alert to his new GPS detector with "points of interest" programmed into the Trinity database. The thing worked. He had slowed down three times: twice for radar cops in New Mexico, once for a Wal-Mart automatic door opener outside Amarillo. He hit a button, put that Wal-Mart door in the database for "ignore."

At the Kansas border, drilling rigs infested the horizon to the south. Half of them were dormant, pumped out. Naturally, Tervo had done his case study project with oil. But the parameters held for any finite commodity. A period of unconsciousness, low prices, and profligate waste: dripping faucets, water parks, irrigated crops a thousand miles from their natural habitats—shit, it was Rowntree calling again. He had given his prepaid number out, thinking he might do business with this Sinbad dude, who was dead.

I kid you not, girl. The dude's name was Sinbad.

Talking to Esofea now. Because come to think of it, she may have been pissed at him before he left. About the issue of reproductive freedom—as in his.

Right.

His offense: vasectomy performed without consent and authorization of girlfriend. That's what she had been all Miss Overdue Book about.

It had not been much of an argument, actually. Esofea had quoted recklessly from *Charlotte's Web*, calling him "some pig." Tervo had trumped that with Gloria Steinem: "Yeah, and 'I don't breed well in captivity.'" Then she had burst into shrieks and tears, right there in the Luce County Library, struck him on the side of the head with the toner cartridge she was holding, threw the inky thing at Tervo as he backed up.

But if she was pissed at him, all he had to do was tell her a story. Show her the strength and quality of his character. And he had a story. *Damn, girl. Listen to this.*

Tervo pressed the side of his prepaid and silenced the ringer. He got home he would throw the phone in the lake. Meantime, though, he was leaving it on in case Belcher called back with a weather report from the home front, where Heimo Kock had been strangled—and Esofea had told the EMS guys what?

The thought of Belcher out there attending to Esofea mellowed Tervo's jitters and added a little levity to his thinking. To watch Belcher try to figure out whether, on a given day, he was supposed to be agreeing that Esofea was an insane bitch or tracking down the bookmobile in some lost corner of Luce County and giving her flowers from Danny, who was real, real sorry—that was amusing. Ugly big guy cloaked in Realtree and Scent-Lok, polarized wrap-arounds and a grubby Remington hat, bearing a dozen yellow roses and a voice in perfect pitch for the act of apology, because Belch was born sorry, about pretty much everything that ever happened to anyone, anywhere. And he loved Esofea, guilty-puppy-style.

Quite hilarious, when Tervo thought about it, given that this same guy killed bear like nobody's business. Gun, arrow, trap—die, bear, die.

Pizza and Kool-Aid.

That was Belcher's secret bear bait. Day-old pizza with dry Kool-Aid laced across the top. Belch was always ahead of the curve, once you set him down in the forest. He out-beared everybody, even Donuts Rudvig. That's where he and Belch hooked up, Tervo thought. They were visionaries, out there alone in the next paradigm.

Southwest of Topeka, over the great Oglala Aquifer, a sky the color of cantaloupe filled Tervo's two tall side mirrors. He thought of being inside Esofea's head when she was wearing earrings this color: inside her mind, working brake and gas and gear shift, getting her all revved up. Then he thought of himself barreling in between two flaps of luminous, pink-orange girl skin.

The story was awesome. He had predicted ninety percent of what was going to happen. And the ten percent surprise, what could he do? She should just chill, climb up on his lap, and you know … *Baby, just listen to my story.*

Around eight that morning, returning across the parking lot of the Saseyama Botanical Garden with a personal check from Brent Takahashi folded behind his cigarettes, Danny Tervo hadn't been one bit surprised to find Billy Rowntree waiting at the tanker, sitting on the step-up, yawning like it hurt.

"Right on," he said to the kid. "The man behind the waterfall."

Billy Rowntree had come to his feet brow first, scowling at Tervo's chest. But the kid said nothing, just scowled and breathed heavily, and Tervo would tell Esofea that at first the sick little shit had let go of each word as if it would cost him an hour of standing in the hot desert sun holding a cinder block over his head. Arizona Boys Ranch. Look it up.

"What can I do for you, Billy? You holding? You shopping? What's up?"

Tervo had read the clouds in the kid's expression as cognitive resistance, presenting as rage, suppressed with some really good skank. Billy Rowntree was stoned, very stoned, but unable to get rasta with it. *And that response, Sofi, I'm telling you, it's rough. It's lonely. It pisses you off. It's a killer. Listen ... I said:*

"What's up, little brother?"

Billy Rowntree, looking all inflamed in his orange Steve Nash jersey and orange headband, said, "Sir."

"Nah, man. Just Danny."

"Sir, I have a question, sir."

It didn't fit, that kind of language. It came from a warped place, Tervo would explain. It came from a place where damaged kids learned that authority was arbitrary and would torture and starve them and demand blow jobs in broom closets.

"Well, maybe I have an answer," Tervo had replied, expecting it would be something like *sure, I'll take a half ounce.*

His brow low, his eyes on Tervo's chest, Billy Rowntree said: "Sir, are you selling water, sir?"

Startled, Tervo laughed. "You're kidding me."

"No, sir."

"Wow. Yes, I'm selling water."

"How much, sir?"

"Right on, man." Tervo had clapped the kid on his skinny tattooed shoulder. "Wow. Stevie Nash, making a play."

After that, seriously, Esofea would have found it cute how Billy Rowntree had directed the tanker through the city with the surly confusion of someone who had never driven a car before and thought that every one who did always knew where they were going. Did she remember the two of them, back in high school, jacking cars during the football games and discovering they had no idea how to get anywhere?

"Sir, sorry. Left."

"Okay, Billy."

"Not here. Fuck. Sorry, sir. Back there. "

"Let me turn this baby around. And Billy, no more 'sir.' Okay? I don't like getting lumped in with those people. Just talk to me like a friend."

Whereupon, Tervo would tell Esofea, over the next thirty minutes or so, he had gone from *sir* to *bitch*. Turns out the kid had only two modes, he would tell her. One mode was for camp "counselors," the *sirs* who actually killed kids and wrote reports up to make it look otherwise. The other mode—she would dig Tervo's analysis here—was inside Billy's head, his fantasy talk-back mode to all the teenage black criminals from L.A. County who outnumbered him a hundred to one, who stole his spoon and urinated on his pillow and squirted ketchup on his Steve Nash jersey.

Tervo had looked across the tanker's bench seat and seen the long, brown stain on the kid's orange jersey, under the lettering on the front. The blacks. The kid focused on them. The ones who called *him* bitch. Letting it out now, using the word on Tervo. *See, girl? How understanding I am?*

What Tervo did eventually was turn the tanker around and return to the garden. There, they chilled for twenty minutes waiting for the Number 72 bus, then followed that roaring, spewing beast through the shimmering Phoenix heat. Tervo would share with Esofea the facts ascertained during that time:

- Billy Rowntree's ankle bracelet allowed him to travel via that 72 bus from his stepdad's in north Phoenix to the botanical garden.

- He always fell asleep, so he didn't know the way.
- He was at the Boys Ranch due to an accident caused by a lie told by his mother.
- Sinbad was Billy Rowntree's *second* black stepdad. The first was Rowntree, who fucked with the kid, day and night.
- Sinbad and his mother weren't together because his mother went to Miami. She was supposed to come back to Arizona and pick Rowntree up when he got out, but she was having trouble with her transportation.
- Steve Nash had won two MVP's and been in the All-Star Game seven times.
- His mother sent him the jersey and headband, finally, after he had already done what he did to get in trouble.
- That ketchup stain had cost some black bitch a cracked skull and a busted vertebrae, and Rowntree had spent six months in isolation for throwing a chair.
- No, that Takahashi bitch was wrong. Sinbad was not a dealer. He was a grower. That's why the water.

Tervo, celebrating silently, had burped the tanker through a maze of closed streets and empty parking lots until they reached a chuck-holed gravel expanse littered with car parts and stripped-out machinery.

Eyes in the back of my head, baby, as always.

"Stop."

Rowntree pointed to a long, flat pole barn. The sign leaning against it said the place was BROWNSVILLE LIFT PARTS. A sun-bleached basketball lay among the PET bottles and glass shards, beneath a bent hoop screwed to the barn. Rowntree had gone inside and shortly returned to the tanker. Ramon, the Mexican, had told him Sinbad wasn't in yet.

So they hooped a little, waiting, the sun not yet too high or too hot. The kid played dirty. He carried the ball and took extra steps on every move. He elbowed Tervo and hacked his arms and hoisted goofy-looking long shots from waist-level. On the rare occasion when he made one, he circled his index fingers and thumbs and taunted Tervo with "threes."

Danny Tervo, all Upper Peninsula as a senior, was the prototypical hippie skywalker, the loose and shaggy white kid with enough hang time to light a match against the backboard and a bowl on the way down. He took it easy on little Billy Rowntree—*only one time, baby, did I turn it on and snuff the kid, blow past him and jam it. And he said, "Foul."*

"Bullshit."

"Foul, bitch motherfucker."

Billy Rowntree wasn't kidding, and things had turned unpleasant at this point. Tervo should have walked. He didn't need trouble. He had two orders already. He should have driven away. *But you know me, baby, always giving people a chance. Always being fair.*

"Okay, cool, man. I fouled you."

Rowntree had picked up the ball. He had smacked it between his palms. He had gone into a larval hunch, then straightened out and made a run at the hoop. No way, Tervo thought.

On his last step, Billy Rowntree strode wide and hard. He went up, and up, twisting and jackknifing his body—straining, climbing the air—and as he peaked he cocked the ball over his head—tongue out like Jordan—and slammed it well short against the bottom of the rim.

"Fuck!" he raged as he landed. He kicked the basketball.

"No, man. That was awesome. You almost had it."

"Fuck!"

"No, man. You were up there. Half inch. You were *so* close."

Rowntree trembled. His zits turned white inside the livid crimson of his brow and cheeks. *Then I made a big mistake, baby.* Tervo had looked down at the kid's ankle bracelet.

"All you need is that half inch. Seriously, my brother, nobody ever showed you how to take one of those bad boys off?"

Tervo pushed the tanker north around Des Moines, picking up Interstate 80, aiming his headlights into a moth-speckled dusky gloom toward Iowa City. He had crossed the entire Oglala Aquifer now. He had left behind the largest underground freshwater resource in North America, which was *dropping* by five percent a year. That was warp speed, unless you were an insect or a goldfish and planned to be dead soon anyway.

That was little Billy Rowntree's fate, Tervo found himself thinking, ignoring the phone again.

Dead soon.

Free of his bracelet.

A moth against a windshield, thinking it could knock a truck off the road.

But the kid would take a few people down with him. Like Sinbad, who had arrived in a gold Escalade and, clearly belligerent, had parked right under the hoop. Tervo and Rowntree had followed the man's waddle into his warehouse "office."

Things got out of hand in there.

Sinbad had dropped breathless into a wheeled leather desk chair, dug his heels in, and come after Rowntree first.

Baby, Tervo would say, *I'm sorry, but to understand you need to hear the hurtful terminology involved: little bitch, little Nash bitch, hippie white-trash motherfucker—that was me—little white-hope-trash Nash bitch liability like you, little bitch motherfucker—*

"Hold on," Tervo had interrupted. "Yo."

Sinbad was startled. He spun the chair.

"Say what?"

"I said hold on," Tervo repeated. He had put a hand up sharply. Just an open hand, but Danny Tervo could give a look like Charlie Manson on some real different tofu. "I don't care for your wording," he told Rowntree's stepdad.

This fat Sinbad dude just gaped at him, wallowing a sea of stupefaction while Tervo opened a door behind Rowntree and looked into the grow room. An older Mexican looked back, a dripping hose in his hand. Behind the Mexican was about five grand in equipment, Tervo figured, and about twenty grand in weed. Small time. Walk now, he told himself, closing the door.

But you know me, baby. Peacemaker. Do-gooder. Citizen.

He shut the door. Sinbad meantime had pointed a piece at him, some kind of trendy foreign-made assault weapon, to which Tervo said, "The only tool you need is kindness, my brother."

Then he made his sales pitch. This young man beside him, who was concerned for various welfares, but especially for the welfare of Sinbad himself, had brought Tervo here with the gift of unlimited, off-the-grid, premium grade water, at a reasonable price.

Fat Sinbad, of course, had defiantly motherfucked this and that and waved the nasty weapon, but Tervo had persisted.

The grow house was using city water, was it not? Large, illegal quantities, was it not?

It was only a matter of time, Tervo had pointed out, before City of Phoenix officials began tracking down restriction violators and making visits. At that point the various welfares went in the following directions: the Mexican gentlemen to a holding facility and then back to Mexico, Billy Rowntree straight back to confinement on parole violations, and Sinbad the Sailor on a twenty-year voyage into the seas of mandatory sentencing, Arizona-style.

"Not to mention the crop loss," Tervo concluded. "Very sad, given that I saw what looked like Burmese Kush." Here he had been lying. The stuff had looked pale and undernourished. "Real tragedy all around."

"I can't afford to pay for no water," Sinbad had snarled.

"You can't afford not to, my brother."

"I ain't got it. Man in Chicago owes me."

"Here's my number." Tervo handed the man a picture postcard of Lake Superior, shot from the Luce County shoreline, the beach near Deer Park. "That's your water," he said. "My number's on the back. When your man in Chicago comes through with your money, you call me."

Tervo had moved toward the outside door. "You gentlemen have a nice day."

Iowa, the endless corn-tundra, forced a leftover half-joint upon him. How to put it, the little problem that came next? How to narrate his response? But wait: Esofea had said something? Enough to worry Belcher? And this was linked, apparently, to the fabulous gift of Heimo Kock's murder?

For a guy who could normally put pieces together in a hurry, Tervo was stumped. But maybe there was an angle here.

He powered up his laptop and set it on the dash. Around midnight, coming through Dubuque, he scored some solid unprotected wireless.

He pulled over and Googled Heimo Kock. Both the *Marquette Miner* and the *Detroit Times* had online pieces. *The Green Bay Gazette*, too. Typical carbon copy stories—anybody's guess as to which fifty percent of the "facts" were accurate. Every story had the same quote from Luce County's new dyke deputy, who said she was "unable to comment further at this time."

Typical media junk. But the "fact" that interested Tervo was this one: the suspect was apprehended in a citizen's arrest by a county employee, who shot the suspect in what authorities are saying was self-defense. The suspect was alive, but word on his condition was unavailable.

County employee?

Esofea?

Shot the suspect?

Could that be it?

Shit.

Well, no. Perfect. If she had her own little problem.

So, what the hell, he'd pick up a bottle of Pino Grigio at the all-nighter in Manistique, drop in on the girl before breakfast if he hustled. She'd be excited to see him. She always did get worked up for Danny Tervo, one way or another.

Tervo's problem being that he had stopped at the warehouse door when Billy Rowntree spat out, "Bitch."

He should have kept moving. But Tervo had looked at Rowntree. Rowntree had glared at Sinbad.

"You got that money up your ass right now," the kid said.

"Motherfucker—" began Sinbad.

"Fat-ass bitch," interrupted Rowntree.

Tervo put his hand up again. "Gentlemen—"

Rowntree kept his mouth going, clearing a backlog of thoughts: "You keep talking about this dude Quality in Chicago owes you money so you can't do this, can't do that, you can't send my momma money for transportation, you can't get water to save your own fat ass. What about Ramon? What about me? Dude in Chicago owes you money, get the money, fat-ass bitch. Quit making excuses."

Billy Rowntree gasped for air at the end of this. But Tervo had noticed that the kid's mouth, off on its own, had curled into a grin.

He was letting something go, baby. He was unhooking the wagon.

Tervo would report to Esofea his feeling that next, when Sinbad set that automatic weapon down on his desk, the man had made the fatal mistake of deciding to mess up Billy Rowntree later, as soon as Tervo walked out the door. That was the scene on Tervo's inner eye—that was the reason, he would tell her, that he had continued to linger in the office.

I was concerned about Billy Rowntree. At that point I was proud of the kid. He was cracking the cocoon, baby. The little grub was growing wings.

Then Sinbad said, "Your momma ain't coming, boy. It ain't about transportation. You telling me she can't find some nigger to fuck for bus money? You stuck in *my* house, Billy Nash."

Suddenly it was too late, baby.

Rowntree sprang past Tervo with that crude basketball quickness. With one forearm he struck Sinbad on the shoulder and sent the chair into a spin. With the other hand he grabbed the weapon. Exactly one second later, as Sinbad spun around, Rowntree scattered bullets into the fat man's belly and chest.

Tervo would have a hard time describing himself from this point on. He had no memory of what he said or did. He was a spectator in the scene, a sputtering camera.

He remembered the Mexican rushing out of the grow house, seeing Sinbad gripping himself, seeing Rowntree turn toward him with the weapon, fleeing back in among the dope plants.

He remembered Sinbad falling face-first off the chair, landing with a splat on the concrete floor, both shoes flopping off.

Now Tervo did remember one thing from himself. He had said, "Not cool. Not cool, Billy. Not cool at all."

He remembered Billy Rowntree pulling a fat wallet from the dying man's pocket, Billy Rowntree turning to Tervo with a handful of bills, saying how much?

"Not cool, Billy."

"Fuck cool, bitch. How much for the water?"

And Tervo said ... Tervo should have said ... Tervo would say, when he told the story to Esofea, *How much? I'll tell you how much, Billy. Five dollars a gallon, at the 7-Eleven. Because I don't do business with killers.*

But he had taken the money, hadn't he?

Yes.

Shit.

He hadn't meant to. *See, I don't operate outside what I'm about, baby.* But there it was, two grand cash, between Rhode Island and Tennessee in his atlas.

So now what?

12

Later, inside of a memory, Dog recognized the voice.

The librarian, the one who shot him, had been talking to the big deputy with the smell, the one who in some distant time zone had caught Dog's wrists and steered him back to the bed. After that he had returned to a sleep the librarian had infiltrated, first her voice outside, the one he now recognized, and then the blurry hindsight of her black clodhoppers and sloppy stockings appearing through his face-hole beneath the bed.

Snap-snap!

She had snapped her fingers right beneath his face.

Her hand opened. Written in pen on her palm was I CAN GET YOU OUT. She held it. Then she closed her fist and pointed with her thumb out at the head of the bed.

The clodhoppers and stockings reappeared there, against the cream-colored melamine cabinets that now held Dog's woozy gaze. A flowered shoulder bag hit the floor. Just beneath the line of his eyebrows Dog had caught a glimpse of the rest of her as she popped in and out of a squat. In that motion she shoved a second bag, worn-out canvas, into one of the cabinets and closed the cabinet door without a sound.

Then her fingers again: Snap-snap!

Her other palm appeared: AM, 6 BELLS, GO LEFT ON VIBRATE. Then she was calling out toward the hallway. "You're right. He is alive. Oh, Timmy. You saved me."

Her breath arrived hot against his ear. "In the morning—can you hear me?"

Dog said, "Nnn." She withdrew. He felt her lift the back of his gown.

"Oh, shit," she said aloud. "But listen, I've heard it's not that bad. Just don't get infected. Ok?"

Then her palm appeared again beneath his face: AM, 6 BELLS, GO LEFT ON VIBRATE.

Dog was dosed enough to arch his face up out of its hole and see the pleats of her skirt as she darted from the room.

Dog turned his face the other way. The window was luminously pink. So this was dusk again. This was the hour to quit fishing, mix a vodka-Tang, put his brain in the pickle jar for the night. He might sit up another hour or two, empty-headed, smoking Swisher Sweets. He might watch the bats and the stars. He might sleep in his lawn chair until frost pinched his nose—then jerk awake, wondering: Couldn't I have heard something? Splashing? A struggle? Didn't I? How long have I been out here?

Now, Dog took a series of small actions, testing himself. All he needed was Dolf Cook's fly reel—needed to find it in the kindling box where he had dropped it, possess it before Cook did, match it with the line around Kock's neck, and he was on his way.

Esofea had fed Mr. Nilsson. She had cleaned her inky palms and scrubbed her freckles off with Palmolive. She had poured a jelly glass full of red wine, drank it down at the kitchen counter, then poured another and took it upstairs.

In her bedroom she smoked a leftover half-joint. She removed her contact lenses. Then she stripped off Pippi and slipped into the bath, thinking about a man who had lost a little boy and still knew *McElligot's Pool* by heart—who would no doubt stand at the edge of that pool for eternity.

Shit. Was that how it was? Then where would she stand?

Esofea sank below the surface of the bath, blowing bubbles. Underwater, she straightened her hair into a long slick strand and thought of a kelp, its hold-fast cemented to the stone of her head. As the bathwater sloshed lazily to and fro over her submerged body, the coppery hair between her legs unmatted like a sea flower and swayed in the waves. Anemone was *wind* in Greek. Seahorses held on against the sea wind with their tails. The males got knocked up and had the babies. That was it for nature. Just that one tiny turn-about, down in the weeds at the bottom of the ocean, and that was it. God, how she wished all the chemicals had turned Danny Tervo into a seahorse.

"Were you worried?" she said in a splash and a gasp of breath to Mr. Nilsson, who, from atop the toilet tank, only blinked.

"The fucker did this to a stranger, used him, planted a body and left him to deal with it. Right in character, don't you think? Disrespect for human life? That's why that karma thing, one life for another, I believe it—as I know you do, too, Mr. Nilsson. Agree with me. Unless you think you can swim, you little shit."

She sank back to the ocean bottom. Did it matter, now that her bag was in the hospital cabinet? And where was Danny, by the way? Mysteriously gone? Was not that a supporting fact?

A half hour later, when the water was tepid, Esofea climbed out and dried off and lubed her skin and put on her nightgown and her glasses and confronted the stack of books on the night table. All at once, in her style, she was reading *Guns, Germs, and Steel*, Hemingway's *Death in the Afternoon* (nights when she believed she could understand Danny through "the metaphor of bullfighting"), and Dr. Seuss's *There's a Wocket in My Pocket*—actually not so much reading that last one but absorbing it into her memory for future professional use.

She felt too sleepy tonight, though. Didn't even remember to take her glasses off. Just turned the light out and had the bright idea to hook her tail on a weed to stop the spinning and murmured, "Goodnight, lady seahorse," and swayed, and swayed in place, until some small pre-dawn hour when a semi honked and he pounded on the door, hollering, "Hey, Sofi. Open up, baby. I got a bottle of wine!"

13

Tervo knew women. Women made you wait when they were pissed at you but didn't know why and had no better way to express themselves.

"I know you're up there, Sofi." Crooning at her window on the second floor. "Hey, lovely girl, I got Grigio."

He did this loud enough, Esofea would worry about the neighbors, come down to hiss and scowl, say shut up and get inside.

Not yet though. Maybe she was zonked. Good times, then. As in likewise.

Tervo had pulled his tanker into the big empty corner at Engadine and hot-boxed a bud of that new Tucson skank, making his own buzz official, putting stupid Rowntree to the side of his thoughts and letting his mastermind out for a run. Point: canibinoidal thought conferencing; point: global climate change; point: as for the droughts of the future, b-b-b-baby you ain't seen n-n-n-n-nothing yet; point: water was the new oil. Question: Who was the new Exxon? Who was the new Al Capone? Who was the new Ray Kroc? Fact: in Barcelona, in 2008, tankers convoyed water from distant rivers to save the city. Desalination? Really? Could anyone afford that besides the Saudis?

No, ma'am. All he had to do was get upstairs with that wine and put his hand in the right place and say, baby, come on now, I know you see it: my purpose, all I got time for, I'm the father of an *idea*.

He called up there, "Baby, must I yodel?"

Apparently he must. Finnish folkways being another of his areas, Danny Tervo cut loose in the Laplander style, speaking reindeer about the size of his horn.

That did it. Baby opened the front door. Her glasses on. Naked.

See? The girl was crazy about him.

Esofea Maria Smithback, in love with him since fifth grade, since she had breast bumps and he had cigarettes and they slouched up and down Main Street Newberry after school like a couple of midgets with their arms around each other. She never had done a single one of those nasty things she promised when she was mad at him. Never even dated someone else.

Girl took off ahead of him toward the bedroom. He slapped her fine bare tush about halfway up the staircase.

"Looking good, baby."

Pursuit. Yeah. He tried to get a grip, reach through and grab that bony redhead pubis like a handle. She sped up, shanked his hand between her thighs, almost broke his thumb off.

"Damn, baby. You gonna say hello or anything?"

"Hello, Danny."

"Guten abend, my love."

"You've been busy?"

"Been out of town, you know, hauling shit around the country. It's what I do."

"Hexane to the Wesson plant?"

This water thing would be a surprise, Tervo had decided, after he had his Rowntree problem worked out. She would dig his ingenuity.

"Isohexane, baby. It's healthier."

They were in the bedroom. The reason she was slow to the door: she had been busy torching up some romantic candles. Light flickered on her pale skin. Her glasses held points of flame.

"You really care, don't you, Danny? About your fellow man?"

Lord God on a stick, there were handcuffs on the bed. That game dated back before the accidental fertilization and the drop-off in action. "You know how I feel, baby. Uplift everybody, and you uplift yourself."

She jumped—talk about uplift—and wrapped her legs around his waist. Tervo fell back on the bed. She crawled over him like a monkey, her little breasts dangling cutely. Tervo nipped at one as it passed above his face.

Then—"Damn, baby! Ouch!"—she was sitting on his collarbones. Her pubes prickled his chin. His windpipe flattened as she leaned and reached for his left wrist, pulled it to the headboard of the bed. He felt a cuff come around, cool and hard. He heard a click. Ok. Playing rough. He could dig that. He volunteered his other wrist before she crushed tracheal cartilage.

"Been a long time, baby. I take this to mean that you finally dig my purpose. You understand how I was born for—you know, how my destiny is not the minivan—how, you know, I'm into some very big ideas, some very big money. Grounded by my principles, right? So listen, I got a story—"

She muffled him. She put Madam Ovary right square down on his face. This position, Tervo found, was not the same as when it was your own idea, not the same at all. In his fog of distress, he revoked the offer of his right wrist. But she lunged and caught it. As she closed the second cuff, Tervo felt his jaw wrench, her entire 112 pounds bearing down.

Now Esofea looked right down the middle of her pale and freckled self and into Tervo's blue Finlander eyes. She looked enormous. Even her breasts looked huge. Her taste and smell filled his senses. Which was way different, the prize, when it wasn't—

"We've had this conversation before, Danny. Nothing ever changes with you."

He pulled in air through one nostril and tried to correct the record: he was change. That's what she was missing. He was change itself. It was a question of her keeping up with him. But the words backed up in his throat until he was yelling formless sounds straight into her cool, sour—she slid off suddenly—"cunt!"

She said, "Pretty much sums me up. Do you like my candles?"

Tervo rolled his head to one side. She had a row of votives along her dresser edge. A large black one, thick as a tanker flange, burned on the nightstand. That was the one that danced in her glasses.

"Incense too," she said.

"Yeah," Tervo said. "Cool. I dig it, baby."

She slid down his body until she sat on his ankles. What that did, basically—Tervo also somewhat of a kinesiologist—was incapacitate his hip flexors, muscles that could not lever well from a flat position. Esofea's one twelve now stopped his legs completely. Turned out next she had laid a bathrobe sash across the bottom of the bed. She whipped this around his shin bones and tied a knot. Then she slid off and produced a bungee cord. She hooked one end to the mattress frame—as far as he could tell—and then like a trucker strapping down a tarp she stretched up and over at the ankles and hooked the other end to the frame on the other side. Now he couldn't move much at all.

Tervo laughed without certainty. "You got me."

"Well, I'm working on it."

"Do me good, baby."

"Yup," she said.

"I'll just lay here and take it."

"I guess you will."

Tervo's spine felt uncomfortably bent as he humped his hips at her. "Bring it," he said, but she came back at him with scissors, working up the right leg of his jeans—"Hey, those are my comfort pair, for driving!"—cutting from ankle to waist.

"Everything ok between you and me, babe?"

"Ok as ever."

"That's really good to hear." She yanked the jeans out from underneath him, leaving a little denim burn on the backs of this thighs. "Really excellent to hear. Fine music, baby. Hey, I wanna tell you a story—"

But the scissors bit into his boxers. They were brand new, an organic hemp-silk blend with natural dyes that Tervo had scored at a co-op in Tucson, killing time while his first hydroponic client got comfortable with the price point of his product. Awesome moment: the sun beating down, the greatest drought in a lifetime turning everything to a crisp, Tervo with one big deal already in the works. He thought of telling Sofi this instead, impressing her. This guy, this wealthy Arab businessman, Ali Ali Fahm from Syria, sixty years old, builds his twenty-five-year-old blond wife a garden with figs and kumquats and birds of paradise, clipped white swans in one pond, giant Asian lotus in another, and now, losing it all for lack of water, is presented with the offer of a six-month "resource membership"—the way Tervo decided to set it up, like an exclusive club, a privilege only the few could access. Tervo had cruised the co-op for only about thirty minutes, had just picked out these very boxers, before Ali Ali Fahm came back on the track phone, joined the club with a two-grand cash deposit. But now Rowntree—

Esofea had shredded and stripped away his boxers and she was telling him, "Things have pretty much been excellent, I'd say, since after I let you talk me into having the abortion and I didn't feeling like screwing you for a while but I had to anyway to keep this bad boy out of the Petri dish, meanwhile realizing that deep down I must have wanted the baby, because I had stopped taking my pills, and also realizing that even though I don't know where I'm going in life, you and I are born to take totally different paths but I've been following yours. I just wasn't appreciating how excellent that was."

"Huh?"

"Crazy me."

"I got no idea, babe, where this is coming from. You doing ok? You on some shit without me?"

Esofea just looked at him. She was still naked. But it didn't seem like she was. Also, de-tumescence was now in progress.

"Darling, aren't you gonna cut my shirt off too?"

"Why?" she said, and kept staring until Tervo got the idea they were into a different area of human sexuality here. Like a breast

cancer exam or a pap smear—or when the doctor squeezed a tes-
ticle like a kiwi fruit. He tested the bungee cord. He had the all the
strength and mobility of a tarp, for sure.

"Hey—we talked about the abortion. We talked and talked. Life
should not be an accident. You agreed, babe, it wasn't the time."

"That's right. Rather than be alone with it. Then, while I was
thinking about what I wanted, you went and had your surgery. Only
this time we didn't talk at all. You just did it, and told me later."

He had her now, Tervo thought. You fight feminism with feminism, a trick he learned at UNM before he decided that college
moved too slowly.

"Hey—" he gave her a big grin "—my body, myself."

But Esofea, no reaction, moved away from the bed. His comeback slumped onto the floor and lay there, flat and dirty. At her
dresser, she put on her panties—left foot, right foot—and looked at
him over her shoulder. She said, "Feels weird to say that, doesn't it,
when someone else is in control?"

She put her nightgown on. She tied her hair back. She set her
glasses on the dresser and began rubbing cream on her face.

"Baby, what's wrong?"

She came back by the bed and looked down at him, crossing her
arms.

"What are you up to, Danny?"

"Help me out, Sofi. What are you talking about?"

"Don't bullshit me, Danny Tervo. I'm done with that. We're into
a new chapter here. You're not trucking hexane to Oklahoma anymore. Or you never were. Tell me what you're doing."

"I'm not doing anything."

"You can lie better than that."

"Ok, look. Don't worry. I'm not doing anything wrong. How's
that?"

"Bullshit."

"I'm telling you the truth, Sofi."

"Are you serious?" The glasses went back on. "You never tell the
truth."

"Au contraire," argued Tervo, and immediately he regretted the smart-ass linguistics. She had him tied down, for Christ's sake, his clothes off, his giblets sitting out there on a platter.

But he really had to dispute the "never tell the truth" remark: "The truth *beneath* the truth, Sofi, that's the one I tell."

Goddamn librarian now, tight hair and glasses, tight dry lips, looking at him like he'd wiped a booger in a book. Then she startled him.

"Sure. That's about where I figured we would end up. So, speaking of the truth beneath the truth, I told Deputy DuCharme you paid that guy to kill Heimo Kock."

Tervo's head came off the bed, his eyes bugging with surprise as she went on.

"Which is so much the truth beneath the truth that the deputy didn't even blink."

"You little witch. I wasn't even involved."

"Which is exactly what you would say if you *were* involved."

What the hell? Tervo tried to rise up and shake her, slap her, whatever it took—something inside him still not getting the situation, not believing it.

"Jesus, Sofi—you told the cops I paid for a hit?"

"That seemed like a real good guess."

"I didn't."

She shrugged. "Oh, well. I *said* you did. I told her that the guy told *me* that."

Christ. She was stupid. She would get felony obstructing. Wasn't she smarter than that? Now he couldn't tell his Rowntree story, either. So fuck it. Throw the phone away. Keep the money. Never see the sick punk again.

"He won't back you up, Sofi, because it's not true. And he's in custody. They'll talk to him again before you do. You're screwed, girl. I can prove where I was."

"Where?"

"I mean if I have to." But shit, then ... his alibi would expose Mr. Ali Ali Fahm, Takahashi, and lead eventually to the scene at

Brownsville Auto Parts grow house. And it would give up the empire. "What do you want, Sofi?"

She didn't answer. She studied his naked lower half, shaking her head slowly side to side and looking sad. She reached out with a toe and gave his giblets a jiggle.

"Isn't it a weird feeling, Danny, when those private parts that want to be touched so badly, that really define what we're here on earth for, that we share with the people we love the most—isn't it the weirdest feeling when they just hang out there, like raw meat, in the middle of nowhere, with no purpose other than to amuse another person? Doesn't that just suck to the core?"

"You're sick, Sofi."

"How about if you reverse it, Danny Tervo."

"Huh?"

"Your snip job. Which stands for all this bullshit with me. Fix it. Yes or no. Decide you can be good to me or I will put your darling ass in prison. Because if you didn't kill Heimo Kock, you'll have to say what else you were doing. And I'm sure it's not legal."

Ok. Shit. Follow her here. "So you tell the truth and I reverse it?"

"First you reverse it, Danny. Then I'll tell the truth. Unless I change my mind and think of a better deal for myself. Isn't that the way you'd play it?"

Ok, Tervo thought. He had it now. So it was about reversing history, getting a replay on life. This shit was easy. Girl just needed a little philosophy lesson.

He opened his mouth wide to take a deep, compassionate breath. He closed his eyes to concentrate on his access point to truth and wisdom. "Sofi … girl … what you don't understand … I mean—ok—let me put it this way: in the words of the great Lao Tsu—"

She stuffed a lighted votive candle into his mouth.

All the way back to his molars.

"Shut up, Danny."

And turned away to search the pockets of his shredded pants.

Tervo thrashed against the cuffs and the bungee. Wax scalded his chin and chest. He screamed in the dark back of his throat. "Oh, sorry," she said, and blew the flame out.

He watched her. She found his prepaid in his pants pocket. She took it. She took his keys. She grabbed her alarm clock and a thick book from the nightstand. A pager too, one from the county office. He heard her heels strike wood in the stairway, going down.

"Nighty-night," she called.

14

Deputy Margarite DuCharme often fly fished in her dreams. This meant that she dreamed of love. That's exactly how it felt, anyway. Her dreams ran like stage plays where the parameters of love were revealed inside the depths and corners of fishing stories—the unknowable complexity and helpless attraction, the going out and the coming back, the blank faces of rivers and their explosions into idiotic joy, the heartbreak, the yearning, the fleeting moments of *grasp*—and, in Margarite's really juicy dreams, the tackle.

Oh, the tackle …

The part you carried with you. The part you touched. The part you could touch when you weren't fishing. The part you dressed and sharpened. The attraction, the connection—the barb, the hook.

The Tahquamenon River, a long cast beyond her window screen, now moved through Margarite's dreams. That lovely beer-brown water flowed around her as she eased over the muck-and-sand bottom, tipsy Julia behind with chipped-lavender fingernails through Margarite's wader belt, complaining all the way—why didn't they just go back to the porch for another drink?—stumbling and slipping, about to lurch completely out of balance and dunk them both.

Margarite spoke to a half-dozen lovers every time she spoke to Julia: "Come on, girl. Hang on to me. We're going to make it."

Why did they always ask *make it where?*

Or when? Or how? Or why?

None of those questions mattered when Margarite stepped into a river. As a girl, when Reggie DuCharme was still around, she had heard him say *here we are* over and over. Her dad said *here we are* when he parked in the weeds beyond some bridge and they put their waders on. He said *here we are* when he handed Margarite a rod, and again when he handed her a fly. He said it when she caught fish and also when she stripped in clots of water weed. He said *here we are* when rain burst over them, *here we are* when they sat to undo tangles and wind knots, *here we are* when he chugged his flask and stretched back for a nap. It was Margarite's experience that she and her dad were always where they wanted to be, doing what they wanted to do. That was her singular sensation when fishing—and when loving, too—*here we are.* Satisfaction was simple. It was everywhere. Or she wanted it to be.

Every woman she fell in love with, Margarite had tried to take fishing. Down at Madison, at the Barrymore Theater during intermission of the Tori Amos concert, this cute little tipsy shitkicker Julia Inkster had told her, "Do I fish? Are you kidding? I'm from the U.P., woman. I was born fishing."

"Come on, sweetheart. You said you could do this. Can you get one foot here?"

"It's cold."

"We'll get warm later."

About once a week through the summer, after dinner, drinks, and wheedling, Margarite could get Julia into a pair of waders and across the yard, into the smooth Tahquamenon just as a high northern sunset flushed through the jack pines and reflected in the big curve below the house. Every night trout rose down there. Julia could catch one on a fly—maybe, hopefully—if they could only make that one small journey together.

This dream skipped and Julia was casting. She was using the rod like a badminton racket, swatting and swatting harder. Of course that wasn't working. Then her style shifted to something that might have worked for throwing cats. Her line snagged the water behind her. She ripped it out, flung it yowling in an arc overhead and smacked it to the surface in the short foreground. Her leader and fly fluttered down around her shoulders. Margarite picked it free with calming talk. *Ten o'clock and two o'clock. Pretend you're in a phone booth. Lock the wrist. Load the rod.* There were at least a dozen wind knots on that leader, some of them doubles and triples, so dream-big they filled Margarite's palms and thwarted her fingers. She let go. It was too dark to go on. Anyway, the line was cut, about thirty feet missing— and the rest was a cracked, pale pumpkin color, like the line around Heimo Kock's neck. "No!" gasped Margarite, and she jerked upright in bed, her heartbeat a hot sting in the tip of her left ear.

Cracked with age, faded orange—that dream line was Julia's real line. That line was on the cheap old Cortland reel Julia had discovered at her parent's house at Boney Falls and insisted on using.

Margarite eased away from her lover in the bed. The left side of her face was hot. Her left arm was asleep. Holding herself against the early morning chill, she stepped outside in her nightgown. It was foggy in the river bottom. When she hit the yard light, the same old coon wobbled away from the garbage cans, and Margarite's temper flared out of nowhere. She chucked a stick of firewood at the creature. She missed it not by much. The firewood cartwheeled across the driveway, whanged off the wheel well of Julia's truck.

New tires? Four of them? For a girl who scrounged through pockets and ashtrays for beer money?

Don't go looking, Margarite told herself. That was a personal rule. You investigate criminals, never friends.

But she was moving into the fog toward the little black Toyota, pushed by a wave of morbid disbelief. She could not be this unlucky in love. She could not possibly deserve another failure. It had been settling in with her. Esofea nearly blurted it just hours ago. The greatest surprise to locals seemed to be not that Margarite was queer, but who she was queer with. Like Julia had another life, obvious to every-one but her.

There would be a credit card receipt on the floor of the pickup, and it would be Margarite's card, if Julia's habits held. Or did these tires come from the same unspecified source as the Oakley sunglasses that showed up two weeks ago, or the bottle of Hennessey and the leather jacket Julia brought home back in July? She had clerked at Pickleman's since last November, abruptly quitting in June for no apparent reason. *Don't go looking.* Margarite had held to that guide-line—until now.

She found nothing related to tires amidst the junk on the pas-senger seat and on the floor beneath. Margarite popped the glove box. An empty Bud longneck rolled out. There behind it, startling Margarite, was Julia's loose-screwed old Cortland fly reel.

As Margarite removed the reel, the knob snagged inside the glove box and the spool spun freely. Through her mind ran Julia's words as they discussed Kock's threats: *I told him he had to go through me, he wanted to try some bullshit like that.*

That old fly line—with its wind-knotted leader—it was gone completely.

Sheriff Bruce Lodge, taking the emergency shift, had been blink-ing dry-eyed at his computer screen when sleep at last forged its way through his fog of irritation and felled him backwards in his desk chair at 4:02 AM precisely. His great soft dewlap stretched out. His jaw hung open, flecked by a few scraps of deep-fried mushroom. His dingleberry red nose plumed snores at the ceiling.

His deputy, Margarite DuCharme, was completely clean. She had left no legal footprints along her path toward lap-dancing in public with a delinquent little shitbird drug-eater like Julia Inkster.

His Margarite was a good girl. In the dream he was having, Sheriff Lodge was shaking her by the shoulders. He was pleading with her. Then he was in his cruiser, on the highway somewhere, screaming up behind Inkster's little black pickup and pulling the shitbird over. He was stepping out into the swampy dreamscape of a high-risk vehicle-approach when a shout and a gunshot rocked him awake.

He spun his desk chair slowly until he faced the window. There was a fire in the middle of West Harrie Street. Lodge ran a big mitt over his face. He stretched his eyes open. He pinched his nose, back-handed the last dream-words from his lips. Flames leapt six feet high, right in the middle of the street.

Lodge bowled the chair back. His shoes were off, lost deep beneath the desk. One of his guilty secrets with his wife gone: peeling his shoes off while they were still tied, leaving them anywhere and going around in his socks, even out to piss on the dewy lawn after dark.

He staggered groggily across the damp grass of the county building's lawn toward the fire. It leapt higher, reflecting in the glass box of the hospital emergency entrance. The cold wetness against the bottoms of his feet woke Lodge fully. He looked down. Suck a duck. No shoes.

A few more befuddled steps and the sheriff found himself stranded in the middle of West Harrie Street.

Probably that was a firecracker, not a gun. Because there was a fire, not a body, in the street. But what was he planning to do, in sock feet, his hands empty, with a fire?

The Pine Stump Junction fire flashed through the sheriff's mind—the astounding heat of it when he stepped from his cruiser, the hungry violence, the awful feeling that he might have let this happen but was helpless to stop it now, his despair as Farooq Kalim's wife hurled herself against his belly, shrieking and clawing while the motel roof caved in.

Then in the dark behind Lodge, from the direction of Saint Gregory's, an engine revved, revved higher, and then a vehicle surged from the church lot on a neutral-drop and a howl of rubber.

By the time the sheriff turned, a square-nosed pickup with its lights off accelerated straight at him, sucking up the pavement beneath its squealing tires.

Lodge stumbled back. He raised his palms. The vehicle's head-lights blazed on, blinding him. He was going to get hit. Killed. Like

Kalim. He got it now, that instant, in his gut: Heimo Kock had been a killer. Now he lived on through his people.

But then the inevitable seemed to fly to pieces—brakes screeching and tires smoking, the pickup spinning, Lodge falling away untouched on his own power, scraping his elbows and braining himself on the street as the truck slid around, slinging something from the bed that clanged and bounced into the grass of the hospital lawn.

Lodge crawled to the curb and sat. Tires squealed again. The truck backed up enough that Kock's filthy shitbird Donuts Rudvig could leer out the passenger window and hiss back at the driver, "Dumbass. That ain't her."

"This is her night, man. Thursday night."

"It's Bruce the Moose. He ain't a problem." Rudvig raised his voice. "Right, Bruce? And you're gonna make good and sure that fuck in the hospital pays for what he done. Am I right? So we don't have to?"

Lodge crawled to a sign pole and raised himself to standing as the truck peeled away. It was a blowtorch that had bounded over him. He found it in the dark wet grass.

It was true. He wasn't a problem. Never had been. Yet.

Thirty minutes later, Sheriff Lodge parked at the road to McPhee's Landing, angled across Margarite's driveway, blocking it. He brought his service shotgun up from the trunk. He loaded it. He watched the road, incoming, his cruiser shrouded first in darkness and then in fog as the sun began to emerge above the vast stillness of the Hiawatha National Forest.

Gradually, colors emerged. Blue sky, white vapor, black river—and in his mirror something pink out there beyond the house, moving.

Her.

Lodge started the engine and rolled up the driveway to where his deputy stood shivering in a pale pink nightgown dotted with dark red hearts. He ran his window down.

"Morning."

"Hi."

"You ok?"

"Sure. Yeah."

"You going fishing?"

She looked at the reel in her hand. It was a fly reel, Lodge noted. Pretty useless article, as far as he was concerned.

"No. Sleepwalking, I guess."

"Everything ok at the house?"

"Uh-huh."

"Nobody bothering you?"

His deputy didn't answer that, except to turn away toward the shitbird's little black Tacoma. The passenger door was open. She put the reel in the glove box and then took care of the door.

Lodge levered stiffly out of his cruiser. Pain arced from his right hip across his pelvis. He had lost skin from his left palm. His elbow on that side was so swollen his shirt was tight. His head ached, and his heart felt about to burst, but his thinking seemed clear.

"Somebody's bothering you," he said. "Tell me. We can take care of it."

"I'm ok."

"Listen," he began. "You said I'd been letting Heimo run things around here."

"Never mind," she said, her voice flat and quiet. She was shivering, looking toward the Taquahmenon. "He's dead."

"No. There's truth to it. I guess I was just too happy, all those years. I didn't want to spoil things. I liked driving around the county, chatting with people, being helpful. Those days there were some decent trout beneath the bridges. I liked to bring a good one home to Charlotte."

"Don't worry about it."

"I was lazy."

He looked at her feet. They were bare and wet, flecked with cut grass and sand from the driveway.

"Heimo did pretty much whatever he wanted. I can't deny that. He got me elected, then had his way, and I loved my wife and built my house and … but he never … he pushed people around a little, sure, but … I never thought he'd hurt anybody …"

She exhaled, looking exasperated, and turned away. A little trout jumped all the way out of the river. Suddenly, after all these years, going all the way back, God almighty, sixty years to the "Bruce the Moose" playground taunts, Lodge was ready to knock Heimo Kock's teeth down his throat. He'd been clenching his fists, hadn't he, since Charlotte was gone? Now it was too late.

"Listen." He started over. "You and Shunk might be right about Pine Stump. I can see a good chance that Heimo had someone light that fire, and I just missed it."

That turned her. She pulled hair from her face and looked at him with puffy eyes.

"Rudvig is probably dangerous," he admitted. "He might do a thing like that, especially for money, in the winter, when money's hard to come by up here. And if he thought you were getting ready to arrest Heimo, Rudvig might have killed Heimo so Heimo wouldn't give him up." He paused to get his phrasing right. "I guess you might be a target too. They've been bothering you. I'm pretty sure."

Again, she turned away toward the river. The fog lingered heaviest over the smooth, black current. She and shitbird had a bench beyond the tall grass over there. A fire pit. A lantern stand. A coffee can in the grass for shitbird's butts.

"No. We're fine."

When Lodge cleared his throat his entire neck hurt, reminding him that this pain he felt was supposed to be his deputy's. It was her turn to take emergency calls. They knew that, and they meant to run her over.

"If Rudvig and them ever threaten you, we can arrest them."

She didn't answer. That same little trout did a flip, missed the bug it was after. Lodge rolled his neck around. He felt the back of his head—a ripe scab there. She was looking.

"You're hurt. What happened last night?"

"Not a thing. Quiet. Fell asleep in my chair."

"Tell me."

"Oh, that. Some punks lit a fire in the street. I fell down chasing them. You?"

"Couldn't sleep."

"She come home late, wake you up?"

Margarite just shrugged. Lodge said, "Love can be the damndest thing. Charlotte was married and divorced before we settled down. Twice."

The sheriff felt himself chuckle softly. He hadn't looked back at this stuff in a long time.

"She liked to drink, get into a lot of drama. We didn't have drugs in those days or she would have been into those too. But she settled down. So you know, maybe ..."

"I said we're fine."

Margarite turned, zombie-walked into tall wet grass toward the bench. "It seems like you don't know who you're with," Lodge blurted, following.

"Don't worry about it."

"Julia Inkster hasn't gone two years since junior high school without getting arrested. Did you know that?"

"Of course."

"She isn't all ... you know, like you are ... all for women, either."

Her nightgown was wet to the waist when she turned on him, her face abruptly ruined and ferocious: "What do you want?"

Lodge blinked at her. Blinked again, opened his mouth, tasted salt and by God he was falling all apart suddenly. He was shaking, his thoughts and vision blurring, his big hands open and extended, groping into this space between them.

"I ..."

"What?"

"You just reminded me of her. That's all. You filled my heart up when I saw you. I felt happy. But ... I'm sorry ... I want you to forgive me."

He wavered there, blind and lost until she caught his hands and held them.

"Stupid old man," he choked out.

"No."

"I'm sorry."

"No. I understand. It's ok."

"It's not. I'm sorry."

Cautiously, deliberately, she moved against him. The side of her face pressed his chest. Her hair caught in the stubble on his chin and smelled like lilacs. Her hands skimmed like feathers across his back and then suddenly she gripped him, squeezed him, her pulse hammering at his belly.

"It's nice to feel cared for."

"Forgive me, Margarite. Please."

She rested against him, breathing deeply. She said nothing for a long time. Only the humming of mosquitoes, the cawing of crows, reached Lodge's ears. At last she pushed away to arm's length. She shivered hard. That ruined look was still there, but she was trying to smile.

"Think you could take me fishing someday?"

"Me? Take you?"

"Right."

"I'm a one-trick wonder. Spoons, which you don't like. And I don't catch much."

"I don't care."

"I don't know how to wave a fly rod. What is it? Wind knots?"

"I don't care. Could you?"

"I guess I could. Sure."

"Isn't it Coho season? The run?"

"Almost. They're bunching up outside the rivers."

"You know a place?"

"I can look around a little."

"And we bring a picnic? A few beers? Some teriyaki snacks? Take a nap in the grass?"

Lodge's heart beat too fast. And suck a duck—his hands were trembling.

"Sure."

Her teeth chattered. Her chin was blue. She squeezed his hands and said, "And I talk. I tell you what I should have told you before

… I mean … and … what I should have told my dad, I wish, before he …"

That was it. She turned away, sat down on the wet bench.

"Sure," Lodge managed. "You got a deal." He walked back to his cruiser. He tossed his radio on the seat and opened the trunk. He forgot the radio when he brought his duty jacket over. On the way he looked up at the house she shared with Julia Inkster. Its green roof glowed wet in the sun. The windows below were black, night still inside them.

He put the jacket on Margarite's shoulders. He stood over her, watching the house, the road, the river.

"Sit down," she said at last. "Tell me about the Coho run."

"I gotta go back and get that first," the sheriff said, because wouldn't you know it, you leave your radio behind, it starts to squawk and complain, like one of the ravens across the river.

15

Agnes Cunard knew it would happen someday. The Newberry State Correctional Facility would send some sick or injured psychopathic criminal down the road one mile to the public hospital that backed up against her yard. That criminal would escape out the rear exit and trespass into her garden. For a hideous moment he would freeze there in his white socks upon her dirt, peeping around just like this one did, his ugly hind-end buck naked, just like this one's was. Though she had imagined the bare ass would be colored.

Gang bangers, they called these criminals on the television. In her day, gang bang meant something regular men could get away with on the likes of Agnes Cunard, landing them in trouble only if they did it to the daughter of a mine owner, say, or the wife of the foreman at the Newberry celery farm. The likes of Agnes Cunard had better watch out for gang bangers—exactly what she had done for ninety-two years, a full third of those without her beloved Sten. It would be a colored coming after her, Sten had told her. But she should hold her fire, Sten said, until the criminal hit the top step of the porch.

This fellow went into the pole beans first, staggering and knocking things over. He had shaggy hair and a beard. Maybe this was a hippie, Agnes Cunard thought, though it had been quite some time since she had seen one. A hippie was the next thing to a colored, in any case.

The pistol was heavy. This was one reason Sten taught her not to set up too early. She might get tired holding it. It was Sten's revolver from the war, a Smith and Wesson .38 that fired 200-gram bullets. Dearest Sten made her remember the bullet type, for after he was gone. He had left her ten of them in a dominoes tin.

Here is what the hippie did: he went into a canvas bag he was carrying, dropped a few things out on the dirt, then stripped off his hospital gown and crouched there, bare naked now except for socks, looking her direction. Slowly, from a squat, he peeled off the socks.

Agnes Cunard sat motionless in a webbed chair against the house in the far back corner of the porch. Above and beside her, sweaters and jackets and coveralls, mostly Sten's, hung on hooks. If she didn't move she might look like one of these, she hoped, like an old gray sweater. To fire the pistol, though, she would need to lean her arms forward onto the television tray where she had laid out her solitaire game. So while the hippie tied his hospital gown around his waist and put on a t-shirt, hat, and a pair of thongs, Agnes Cunard got set up, because otherwise, if she waited until he got close, he was going to see her move.

Now here he came—thongs popping—out of the pole beans and onto the grass. He stumbled around the bird bath and walked right through her purple asters as they were starting to open for the day. As per Sten, she was using the porch screen door as a target, going to shoot right through the center of the top panel the instant the door moved inward.

But the hippie fell down somewhere. She lost sight of him below the half wall of the porch. She wrestled opened the pistol's cylinder. What folks did these days, she recalled suddenly, was call a number on the telephone, 911, for help. Sten never thought much of this idea, didn't trust it, but that was what they told you to do. Lately when Agnes Cunard went to the senior center they gabbled on about it, these young people waving tiny telephones that had no cords and lived in their pockets.

Or was this a while ago? Quite likely, she began to think, they had changed the number by now. But changed it to what? And, oh yes, load the bullets first. Her stiff fingers cracked the dominoes tin and made one fit. And suddenly there he was, his hairy face at the screen right beside her, so close she could smell hospital and see crazy in his eyes.

"Hippie," scolded Agnes Cunard, closing the cylinder.

He punched his hand directly through the screen—then he had Sten's pistol. The other hand came through, toward her throat, and she ducked. He yanked Sten's coveralls off the hook behind—Agnes Cunard felt the straps across her shoulders—and next he tore out more screen to grab a pair of fur-tipped boots that Agnes Cunard could not recall seeing before. When she raised up and the dizziness went away, the hippie was gone. Only his socks, his hospital gown, and his thongs remained in the yard.

Arrayed across the dew-soaked side grass of the house next door were snowmobiles, ATVs, mini-bikes, and hobby tractors—but Dog didn't have the time. He jacked a kid's one-speed bike from the driveway. Standing on the pedals, he wobbled up to speed and cornered into West Truman.

In coveralls, mukluks, and a ball cap that said "I'd Rather be U.P. North," Dog herky-jerked that little blue bike toward the west end of town, the long-barreled pistol flopping heavily in his bib pocket. Several people saw him. No one seemed alarmed. This was the U.P. after all, Dog thought vaguely.

Two blocks, three blocks, a crumbling, trash-strewn dead end, and Newberry was behind him, Lake Superior State Forest ahead.

Dog did not slow or look back. He transferred the pistol into the horn mount over the handlebars, where it wedged and stayed still. He crouched like a jockey, spun those deflated mini tires down a wide trail into jack pine forest before the bike fizzed to a stop in heavy sand.

Dog pitched to his knees on the trail, dizzy for air. Ahead of him sprawled the pistol and the bag provided by his local librarian. The bag was still fat with items.

Dog shook a map out, spread it on the sand. Luce County ORV and snowmobile trails. Yellow highlight pen traced a route north maybe twenty miles to a place called Blind Sucker Flooding. Ink pen circled spots where the trails crossed roads.

Dog's finger followed the yellow path to a junction south of Dawson Creek. There he broke away on his own, east toward Dolf Cook's place, plotting snowmobile trails across what looked like wetland. He had no way to resolve the question of whether only winter's frozen ground made those trails passable. Swamps and bogs sucked at his mind, but the map was silent. Should he go back, he wondered, and carjack? Should he go back and surrender?

The canvas bag began to vibrate. He pulled it to him. In a small outside pocket he found a pager. He pushed buttons haphazardly. The pager buzzed out.

More items in the bag. His dirty palm caught Tylenol capsules, like tiny red-and-white bobbers. He washed down six with the bottle of water. He fit the pistol into the bag. Once you ran, you were guilty. Dog comprehended that. *So go, Dog, go.*

He pushed the bike for solid ground. When the trail forked a mile or so later, he found the sun. He checked his map and peddled north, his distance measured by an assiduous deer fly that bit his neck at twenty-yard intervals. When he killed that finally, another rotated in. And another. In a short while more, it was yellow jackets that ascertained the meaty scent of his wounds and circled him like reef sharks. In a slow spot, where the bike bogged down, a nimbus of mosquitoes caught him and charged their toll in blood, left him slapping and scratching and wobbling one-handed over the asphalt dome of the first paved road with the dignity and control of a fugitive circus bear. On the other side, the shoulder was too steep. He had to lift his feet and let the pedals spin, jittering at high speed down into the shelter of the opposing forest. At the bottom, the little bike stuck its front tire into mud, flipping Dog onto his back.

His back. Two hundred wounds spraying mace-hot pain to his brain until he rolled over and made it only slightly better.

As Dog lay there the pager went off again. Pain masked the complexities of the situation, revealing a simple thought: the librarian. She was tracking the pager. That was it. The pager was sending back its coordinates. She was looking for him.

He pulled the bike out of the mud. The rim of the front wheel had buckled. He traced the seep that made the mud, away from the road through high brush to a small bog, pretty with yellowing bracken ferns and darting dragonflies.

He flung the bike toward open water. It floated like some strange Schwinn swan in the soft grip of lilies, then slowly began to sink. Watching the bike inch under, Dog thought he too could sink down in that cold black muck. Do that now. Sink. This was too much pain.

But the image of the old Pflueger reel at Cook's place returned him to task.

No. Not now. *Go dog, go.*

A short distance up the trail, a big tamarack had died and tipped over. Dog got behind the root ball and waited. The pager buzzed. It buzzed again.

The Luce County Bookmobile rumbled along the adjacent paved road maybe ten minutes later, stirring Dog from a swamp of mental numbness. The librarian parked at the trail crossing. She left the old bus running, came down the steep shoulder, jumped over the mud, then changed her mind. She went back up and shut off the engine. Then she blew the horn twice and came down onto the snowmobile trail again. She looked up the trail, over toward the bog, then picked up her pace, trotting as she passed the root ball.

She stopped when she saw Dog there. She looked full of ideas. Her mouth started up, but Dog raised the pistol and said, "No."

"Wow. You got a gun?"

"Turn around."

"What? Do you realize what I just—this is the second time I saved your—"

"Walk," he rasped, turning her. Then he shoved her in the back.

On the way to the road he threw up twice, water and Tylenol—keeping the pistol on her. Inside the bookmobile he got her in the seat behind the wheel. He was nearly blacking out. She was streaking words past his ears.

He backed up a few steps. He got around the checkout counter and leaned on it. The sound of her voice overwhelmed him. He cocked the hammer by way of interruption. That made things quiet.

"Go on," he said. "Drive. Dolf Cook's place."

16

Deputy Margarite DuCharme said to Donuts Rudvig, when Rudvig surprised her by appearing at the county building exactly as requested, at ten that morning, "I should have called you, Paul. I'm sorry. We're too busy right now, so we'll have to talk later. Thanks for coming though."

But she got the sense right away that Rudvig hadn't come to be questioned. He was with Ron Lindgren again. The two of them looked like they had been in a swamp all night, taking charm lessons from a rabid possum. Margarite peered past them out the lobby doors. That jacked-up black pickup of Rudvig's was parked wrong-way on West Harrie in front of the county building. The deputy observed dog snouts in the cage. Across the street had to be Lindgren's rig: four animals in that one, coon dogs it looked like, tethered and frantic. She brought her eyes back to the short view again: both of Kock's bear guides were mouth-breathing, their bloodshot eyes darting around the sheriff's office.

So this much was clear to Margarite: news of Oglivie's escape was out among Kock's crowd.

No surprise, really. She and Lodge and part-time deputy Tim Shrigley were just back from a Keystone Kops ninety minutes of gunning both Luce County cruisers plus the sand-and-salt truck in random patterns through and around greater Newberry. The suspect, the witness, whatever Oglivie was at this point—he was gone. Bruce the Moose, seeming on the verge of a stroke, had retreated to his office with the door closed. Margàrite felt like she had barbed wire in her esophagus. She had been interviewing Shrigley, who was adamant that no one had penetrated his guard before the hospital was locked down. Not one single person. A simple no, of course, would have been more convincing.

Margarite met Rudvig's possum leer. She was comprehending Esofea's varmint thing. She said, "If you're here to help look for him, the answer is no."

"Look for who?"

"This is a law enforcement job. You guys stay out of it."

Lindgren wanted to play too: "Stay out of what?"

"You gentlemen interfere, you're obstructing justice. We are busy, but we'll make time."

Rudvig pulled a paper cone from the water cooler and spat brown goo into it. He stuck the mess through the trash can flap. "Ok. The guy slipped away from you. Everybody knows it. Now you got who? You got Bruce the Moose, you got Half-a-Sandwich in there—" he jerked a black thumb toward Tim Shrigley in the break room "—and you, hell, you gotta keep your finger in the dyke, am I right?"

Gotta love the deep north, Margarite thought, forcing a breath. Everything so fresh for people. Lindgren stared bluntly below her utility belt.

Rudvig continued: "What're you idiots going to do, drive around some more, hope the guy is out there in his hospital gown, hitchhiking? We can nail his ass inside the hour, soon as we get the sighting from you people."

"Go home," Margarite said. But *sighting? You people?* Oglivie had not been seen. No one had called in. The sheriff's department had no clue where he was. "We've got the state prison K-9 team getting ready now," she said. "Go home and stay out of the woods."

Here the sheriff's door opened. Bruce the Moose looked ok, but in a vacant, inappropriately contented kind of way. Maybe he had his stroke already and this was the ominous outcome: the howdy-do smile, the acetylene torch in his hand.

"No, no, no. Paul's right," he said, waving a big freckled paw. "I was just coming out to tell you, deputy. We're understaffed. I asked Paul to come in and give us a hand."

"You—"

"He's the best," Lodge said. "Right, Paul? Those ridgebacks of yours could track a fart in a windstorm. Hey! Ronny Lindgren, how you doing?" The sheriff extended his hand for another shake. "Long time, no see, pal. How's things over in Baraga? Pretty bearable? Get it? Bearable?"

Margarite, stunned, said, "Sheriff, you can't—"

Lodge interrupted her. "Now, now. I'm in charge."

And she thought: You are? Since when?

"Here's your lighter," Lodge said, and he handed the torch to Rudvig. Rudvig took it warily. Margarite's jaws clamping together, fighting back a surge of acid. A torch like that—the fire investigator's guess—was used in the Pine Stump Junction fire. What the hell was going on? Lodge had evidence? And now he was giving it back?

"Why, thank you," Rudvig said. "Hang on a sec." With the dirty pinky of his three-fingered right hand, he scooped out his dip and flicked it through the flap of the trash can, leaving half of it to hang there. Next, smirking at Margarite, he fished a wrinkled box of Phillies out of his saggy shirt pocket. He stuck a cigar in his mouth. Lodge said jovially, now handing over the torch, "Be careful with that thing. Might be set a little high."

Margarite blurted, "Sheriff? You've got to stop this right here."

All three men looked. She crossed her arms over her vest. It was Lodge she looked back at.

"You can't send a civilian posse out there. It's illegal. It's dangerous. Especially not these nutjobs."

"Fuck you, lady," said Lindgren, the kind of man who waited until he had enough cover. "By the way, just for my information, what's it take to get a pretty one like you to do it regular?"

Margarite glanced at Lodge. The sheriff's placid look had abruptly vanished. He was leaning onto his toes, his jowls reddening, his hands flexing. Let it go, she told him with her eyes. Don't defend me. "Just give us the sighting," Rudvig said.

Lodge blinked, looking disoriented for a moment. Then he walked Rudvig over to the county map on the wall inside the door. He raised his chin. He squinted at the map, his big pink index finger coasting over it like Braille. Then he stopped.

"Right here," he said.

Margarite moved close enough to see. The sheriff's finger trembled under Camp Seven Lake, near the old Chevrolet Hunting Club.

"Motorist saw him cross the highway there, westbound."

Margarite thought: who says *motorist*?

"Here's a radio you fellahs can use."

Lodge took one off his belt. Lindgren grabbed it.

Margarite felt desperate, confused, deceived. "Sheriff—can we talk?" She came right up to the map as the others pulled away. Oglivie was there? That far? How? "Could you just slow down and talk to me?"

"Certainly," Bruce the Moose said, but when she looked again he was holding the door, and Rudvig and Lindgren were through it already. Rudvig sparked the torch and lit his cigar from the concrete apron just outside. Lindgren hooked the radio over his belt.

She watched them all the way to the trucks. They bumped shoulders once, again, high-fived each other. They would have a bullet in Oglivie's back by noon.

Margarite turned to the sheriff. "Yes?"

"Well, you know," Lodge said with a shrug, "they were going to hunt for him anyway, whether we liked it or not. They might as well hunt in the wrong place."

Rudvig's truck roared obscenely. His dogs yelped. Lindgren and crew added to the din.

"With a dead radio," the sheriff added.

Margarite backed up and sat down hard on the edge of the reception desk. She felt a blast of sweaty heat rise from under her vest. Now Lodge was kind of grinning at her, giving her that old jam-on-the-face look.

"That was good," she told him. "That was real good. Maybe you ought to stay up all night and bump your head more often. Wow."

She expected a comeback, or an explanation, or the next strategic step, or even a wet tongue to the face. Something relevant to the moment at least, to the triumph of Sheriff Bruce Lodge dialing in on some real sheriff-style action.

Instead he said, "Meant to tell you. I called up to the Rainbow Lodge. The Cohos have been trickling up river since last evening, so the run is about to get going. And it looks like a good one." He smiled at her. "Just to let you know."

He was heading back into his office.

"Sheriff? Bruce? You ok?"

She phoned Danny Tervo's home again. No answer. She checked with the library. Esofea had logged in a bookmobile run to the Ojibway charter school at Brimley. The deputy pushed her speed dial number for Julia but hung up before it rang.

Don't go looking.

She crossed the street, took statements at the Helen Joy Newberry Hospital and got circuitous dithering about security procedures and shift changes and work loads and so on. The escape had occurred at six sharp. Staff was minimal. The sheriff's guard wasn't in yet. No one had seen which way Oglivie went. She left the hospital in frustration. It was nearly ten o'clock.

But along Oglivie's escape route in back of the hospital, Margarite found an old woman she hadn't met before, a Mrs. Agnes Cunard, ninety-two years old and hopping mad. Oglivie had tricked her, popped right up, busted her window screen, and taken her late husband's favorite pair of coveralls. And, oh, yes, a pistol. That she had loaded, yes, to the best of her recollection.

"Did you see which way, Missus Cunard?"

"Why, yes, I did," the old woman said, and she pointed directly at the hospital, which had to be wrong.

Shit. Double shit. And a pistol.

Cussing for all she was worth, Margarite cut through back yards to the county building. Someone had helped Oglivie escape. That was all she could think of. Someone who knew the hospital. The timing. Someone with a motive to get tied up in Kock's death. Oglivie had no friends around here, she was pretty sure of that. Her darkest guess was someone had turned him loose, knowing that a hunt would break out.

It could be Tervo, sure. She hadn't found him yet. But Kock had a hundred other enemies. And it was Julia's fly line that was missing. As deeply as Margarite would like to bury that fact, she couldn't. *Don't go looking*—she had to let that go now. This was new ground. Julia knew the hospital. She knew Tim Shrigley. She hated Kock. She played with Tervo. Did she know, then, where Oglivie was?

Rename that woman, the deputy thought grimly. Code name *Pepto.*

She hit speed dial again and let it go.

"What?" snapped Julia after the first ring.

Margarite was startled. Her throat felt rough and sour. "Where are you?"

"Margarite, where are *you*? You just took off, no shower, no note, nothing."

"I'm sorry. But by now you know why, right? Where are you, sweetheart?"

"The White Pines. Subbing for Angie."

"Oh." Margarite looked at her watch. It had somehow become a few minutes before noon. The bar had been open nearly an hour.

"Is there a problem? That I have something to do with?"

"Well ..."

"Well what?"

"Well, I guess I'm coming over."

"It's a free country."

She took the cruiser but parked on Main a block away to get some breathing time. It was still clumsy for her, working in a town so small. She still drove places and on arrival realized she could have walked. But then what if something happened and she needed to move fast? Except that nothing ever happened. Except that something was happening now. Like that, back and forth in her mind.

The White Pines Hotel bar, once an elegant saloon, was in Margarite's experience a dark and smoky warren for serious daytime drunks. "Subbing for Angie" meant Angie Miner was too hungover to function today and Julia, who took her place as needed over the last few years, would be in that same condition tomorrow. Margarite and Julia had clashed over this, but anyway the deputy tried to be positive coming in.

"What's going on? Ladies only today?"

One of the women at the horseshoe bar slurred, "Soon as they saw it on the news, they all left to go hunt some escaped convict. Driving drunk maybe they can hit him. 'Cept for one slacker in the can."

Daryline Smithback, Esofea's aunt, turned on her stool. "Yeah, Rush's in the can. He's been on the potty all day. Liquid in, liquid out, that's what they say. A bunch of them others went out to form a perim … a perim … a perimeter."

A hacking laugh erupted from down the bar, beneath the television. Ice rattled in a glass. Margarite blinked. Her eyes stung. Julia came down the bar and stopped across from her. "Drink?"

Margarite felt her stomach foam. "Pepsi," she said. "And can we talk over here?"

Julia dug out some ice, hosed Pepsi into a beer glass. Down low behind the bar, she poured something for herself into a coffee mug, and they took a table beside a burgundy curtain stiff with dust. The Main Street sidewalk was an arm's length beyond the window. Margarite could see her cruiser through a wedge of sunlight.

"I didn't know you were in town."

"Was I supposed to tell you?"

"That's not what I meant. I'm just surprised, that's all." Her first sip of the Pepsi tasted soapy. "I don't know," Margarite said. "I don't know whether I'm ... No, I do know. I'm just asking this you because I love you and I'm weak and I'm worried."

She stopped. That was neither a lie nor the truth. She had power here, legal power, supposedly, but she couldn't feel it. She had urgency, but she was moving backwards.

Margarite tried to gather herself. Julia had been drinking already. She looked good in the first phase of a drunk. Her eyes narrowed and her skin flushed and she got this expression that was a mysteriously attractive combination of come-hither and get-lost. She looked exactly the way she had—tipsy, it was evident now—when Margarite met her in Madison at the concert two years ago. Julia had been leaning against the wall in the lobby of the Barrymore, a plastic cup of beer in her hand, an unsmoked cigarette behind her ear, scoping the crowd for five or ten minutes before Margarite moved in to say hello and was she with anyone. She wasn't. She had come down from the U.P. solo, Julia had said, just to be someplace else.

"Well ..." This was so dumb. So awful. "I just was surprised that you got new tires for your truck. I mean I've known you two years. I've been living with you coming up on half that. You've needed new tires that whole time but you didn't care."

"You came here because you're surprised I bought new tires for my truck?"

"Yes."

Julia shrugged. "Ok. Was there anything else?"

"Was there a certain reason you didn't buy them earlier but you did now? Anything I should know about?"

"Nope."

"You washed your truck too. Why?"

"I gave Jim Grove a ride home from softball. His Doberman yakked in the box. I got going with the hose, didn't feel like stopping. Goddamn, Margarite, are you interrogating me? What do you think I did?"

"Hit something on the road," Margarite lied, snatching a plausible excuse out of nowhere. "That's all. I just worry about you driving when you go out partying."

"Hey, I like to party."

"Yeah. Well, I'm on the other side of the party. I have a job to do."

Julia took a long gulp from her mug that left her lips red. When her chin came down it stopped a fraction of an inch above normal. "You're checking up on me," she said. "Which you promised never to do."

It was a reflex to lift the Pepsi and drink. Margarite's stomach returned the bubbles hard against the back of her mouth. Her eyes watered. *Maybe I wouldn't have to check up you if you still had your old tires and the line wasn't gone from your reel.*

"Sweetheart," she managed to say, "I'm sure you have good reasons for all of this, but I think you're lying to me."

Julia laughed loudly and falsely.

"Share the joke," droned a woman from the bar. "We're plowed. We'll laugh at anything."

"Barkeep!" roared Esofea's Uncle Rush. He had emerged from the toilet. "I need a freshener-upper!"

"Can't you people just chill out?" Julia snapped over her shoulder. Then her voice came down to a rough whisper. She looked Margarite hotly in the eye. "You're safe now. Relax. Heimo Kock is dead."

"What happened to the line on your fly reel?"

Julia lit a cigarette. She leaned back and spoke normally. "I should have known better than try to fool a frickin' detective. Ok. I went out fishing."

"Fishing ... by yourself?"

"By myself."

"That's a first."

"First time for everything."

Margarite turned her Pepsi glass. "I can't imagine that. I have to drag you out. You don't try very hard to like it. What made you go fishing by yourself?"

"Impress you."

Margarite didn't know which objection to start with—or should she be happy? Julia exhaled smoke toward the stiff curtain. She pulled it open a little, squinted across Main Street. "I wanted to practice and get good at it. So you're not so frustrated." She looked back at Margarite. "I love you, woman."

"Where did you go?"

"Did you hear me? I said love you."

"Thank you. Where—"

"Thank you? Shit. Ok. The Two Hearted. Main branch. Frickin trees behind me everywhere."

"I'm gone all day," Margarite said. "You could have practiced in front of the house."

Julia nodded like all this had been foretold. Her buzzed eyes narrowed to red-rimmed slits as she looked toward the bar.

"Now you're trying to tell me exactly how I should do all the stupid little things I do to show you I'm crazy about you. I don't believe this. You wanna know something? When you used to drive up here once a month? Wasn't I sweet?"

"You were very sweet. Yes."

"Like a kitten?"

"Tiger, maybe, and you were a good listener. But—"

"See, I used to party my ass off for a couple days before you came, so I wouldn't want to drink and smoke too much while you were here. I would just let you take me places, and hold me and talk to me, put me to bed early and get it on with me. You didn't know that, right? I did that for you. For us. So we could get along."

Margarite might have thrown up if she hadn't been so startled. Instead, her breath stuck and the acid crept up like a slow, hot knife into the center of her chest. Her eyes flooded and she put one hand to the base of her throat.

You are a sheriff's deputy right now, she said to herself. You are a sheriff's deputy investigating a murder. Cry later. Get yourself back on point.

"Why the Two Hearted?" she persisted as soon as she could speak evenly. "I told you, it's too hard to fish. That's why we never go there."

"See what I mean? Twenty questions suddenly."

"What happened to your line?"

"Shit, girl," Julia said. "You went through my truck."

"I did. Your whole fly line is gone."

Julia lurched in her chair, standing halfway up. "Yeah—well that ain't all that's gone—" She snatched at her cigarette. Margarite caught her hand above the ashtray.

"Where is Oglivie?"

"Who?"

"Sit down. Tell me why you went all the way up to the Two Hearted to practice fishing, and tell me what happened to your line."

But Julia wouldn't budge. Into this small tussle arrived the full tension of their time together, both of them trembling.

"Just be straight with me one time," Margarite said. "See how it works out."

"I don't talk to cops," Julia snarled back.

"Right now you'd better," Margarite said. "So that if you did what I think you did, I can figure out how to help you."

They held like this, staring each other down so long the drunks took note. "Uh-oh," sang Aunt Daryline Smithback. "Uh-oh, SpaghettiOs."

"Busted," cackled Uncle Rush, turning from a glance out the window.

"Busted at what?" Margarite said it quietly, gripping Julia's hand. "Tell me what they're talking about."

"They're just making noise."

"Hey," blared a third drunk in their direction, "she's a good girl. She don't hurt nobody. She's just a free spirit, that's all."

"Tell me, Julia."

Now inebriated singing carried from the sidewalk beyond the open front door. Here came Dolf Cook, tottering, blinded by the sudden darkness, extracting from his wallet some quantity of paper money.

Cook held the backs of stools and bantered with the ladies as he began his way around the bar—"Make way for royalty. Care to kiss my thing, love? Now where's my little chickie-babe? She's got something for me—" and then he saw the deputy.

Heimo Kock's brother wavered a moment, focusing, as Julia wrenched her hand free from Margarite and spun to face him, her whole body tensed. That move straightened Dolf Cook. He proceeded in a drunk's cautious steps toward a small paper sack on the bar. He snatched the sack, shoved it in his pants pocket. He laid the money on the bar, patted it three or four times. Then he managed a U-turn and puttered back the way he came, butchering some moldy tune through the door and down the sidewalk.

Julia turned back to retrieve her mug. Margarite spoke almost silently, aiming the words. "What the hell was that?"

"What the hell was what?"

She bustled away from Margarite, around the bar. She put out her cigarette and poured Rush his freshener-upper at the far end.

Margarite set her Pepsi at the rail. She could hear Dolf Cook starting his car. Julia came back scowling. She put her elbows on the bar. She raised her eyebrows, like *what the hell else do you want?*

"I need to know where your line is. Now."

Julia put her chin in her palms, closed her eyes, opened them to a squint: "Sweetheart, you don't believe me, my line is in the dumpster at the Reed and Green campground, I fucked it up so bad."

17

"Pull over," Billy Rowntree told Ramon. "We got time. 7-Eleven."

Ramon still looked startled. Only yesterday, Rowntree was wearing an electronic arrest bracelet, taking the 72 bus across the city to the botanical garden, coming home and sleeping next to Ramon on the peat moss bags at the rear of the grow house. Now he was in the back seat of Sinbad's gold Escalade, in a brand new home warm-up, orange with purple piping, purple Nash number 13 in a white outline, leaning up into Ramon's rear view mirror and telling the Mexican, "I said pull over, bitch. You didn't hear me?"

Then he sat back, realizing the 7-Eleven was across on the opposite side of this wide street with lots of traffic and an island in the middle. Ramon was working on it. Cool. Ramon knew how to go places.

Inside 7-Eleven Rowntree said to the clerk, "Gimme a Slurpee, man, red and large, and we in a hurry."

"So very sorry, sir. Under Level 5 restrictions, we may not serve ice drinks."

"Then why you keep the machine on?"

"Sir, if we should drop to Level 4, then we are ready to serve—"

"For that matter, why you open at six AM when you a 7-Eleven?"

The clerk scowled. Some kind of turban on his head. None of that at the ranch. Rowntree poked a sweet little Sig he found at Sinbad's house out the pouch of his warm-up jacket.

"Bitch," Rowntree said, "I asked you gimme a Slurpee. And pull a blue one for my driver, yo."

He walked out with his hands full, *NASH* across the back, basketball exploding like an angry sun. Fuck Level 5 restrictions. He had water coming.

"Here you go, my brother," he told trembling old Ramon. "American Airlines. I believe that's Terminal Three."

Then Billy Rowntree slouched across the leather back seat of the Escalade with a straw in his mouth, replaying the speed and beauty of his moves. Telling Ramon, yo, old man, go put Sinbad in a hole in the desert. A *big* hole. Pick up some gorditas on the way back. And then take me to Sinbad's place. That's where I live now.

Ramon eased the Escalade off Interstate 17 onto the airport exit. Rowntree blew soft bubbles in his Slurpee, gazed out at the hot blue sky. He was baked real good, to last all day. He wondered at all the cell phone calls flying through the sky. Riding the lasers. He had called his mother, but she hadn't answered—probably, Ramon told him, because it was Sinbad's phone. He had left a message: *Let me know you still need money to get here, cuz I got it. Call me back.*

Now he called her number again. He was getting better at finding the keys. A recorded voice told him what number he had reached, which was hers. Cool. At the message tone, he said, "Call me back. I'm going on business to Chicago. So, um, call me back."

He forgot something and repeated the process: "On the airplane. Dude there named Quality owes me money. But don't worry, I got some already. So call me back."

When Billy Rowntree stepped into the heat in front of Terminal Three, he left his Suns warm-up folded neatly atop the seat for Ramon to take back to Sinbad's house. He left his game jersey and his orange headband on—keep his luck running, keep Nash in the game. The Sig went back with Ramon too. "And keep that city water off, man. We got some on the way." Ramon nodding, his brown eyes wide open. "And take good care of shit, man. I'm gonna call you every hour, make sure you do it right."

Rowntree closed the car door. The linen suit he bought at K&G Fashion Super Store was a cool gray, pant cuffs sweeping the airport floor because they told him to come back tomorrow and they would have the length fixed. Fuck tomorrow. Tomorrow he was in Chicago, up in Quality's shit. Underneath he had the Nash jersey. Over that, his shirt, grapefruit pink, for Florida, piled up a little at the wrists. Ramon had knotted the tie for him, silver with fine pink dots. The Brutini shoes, with two-tone blue panels, clicked nice on the tiles, slipped when Billy Rowntree changed directions.

What he thought about, strolling toward his boarding gate, was his deal for five thousand gallons of black-market water. Four bucks a gallon. Two grand deposit to this hippie from up wherever. Ramon said where do we keep the water? Rowntree said figure it out. Maybe put it into pipes or something.

He got back from Chicago tomorrow night, Rowntree was thinking, that truck better be filled up and on its way.

Put some pressure on, Rowntree decided as he reached the gate. Call him.

He had a phone, man.

He stepped out of line and dialed. He did it with his thumb this time, leaning on a wall, sending out the lasers.

Just beyond the road to Sleeper Lake, still a good ten miles from the turn to Dolf Cook's cottage, Danny Tervo's cell phone rang. Esofea grabbed it off the flat dash. She waved it at Dog. "Come on. I need a man's voice. Say hello."

But he wouldn't. He kept his arms braced on the checkout counter and the barrel of that big revolver wavering like compass needle in the direction of her head. He might not have heard her. His eyes were beyond bloodshot. His sweat had soaked the shirt she gave him.

Maybe he couldn't hear her. Oh, well.

"Tervo Enterprises, this is Sofi," she answered, one-handing the clumsy old bus around a mild curve with a pulp hauler roaring past the other way.

"Bitch," said the voice on the other end, "where's my water at?"

Esofea said, "I'm sorry, and your name is?"

"My name is Where's My Water At, Bitch."

"Which water is that?" Esofea inquired—and the dude was gone.

Esofea glanced over her shoulder. "See? Six-oh-two area code. Where's my water. Danny's got fishing clients calling already."

She wasn't totally sure, though. That didn't sound like a fisherman. She goosed the Luce County Bookmobile down the dip into High Bridge. She could tip Dog over, she thought, maybe at the Perch Lake corner. She could bury him with an avalanche of Michener from the Fiction section and take his weapon away. He looked that weak.

She started talking again, working it through. "Heimo Kock was in Danny's way. He always was, anything Danny tried to do, guiding, stealing snowmobiles, bringing weed from Ontario across the lake, whatever, Kock would bust his balls. It went way back to when we were in high school, but I'm not sure why they hated each other. Danny wanted him dead, but of course he wouldn't do it himself. Now look—" she held up Danny's business phone "—he's got fishermen calling. He's in the guide business, like he always wanted."

"Nobody paid me to kill Heimo Kock."

"Ok, dispose of, like you said."

"Nobody did that either."

"Hey, I'm not convicting you here. I'm saying maybe you met a guy named Belcher? Grimy, short, with a beard? He protects Danny, so maybe he never mentioned him. He just showed up and wondered if you'd like some cash to take a body somewhere far away? You said yes, but then you went down the road a little ways and—"

Dog fired the pistol. Esofea hit the brakes. The bookmobile skidded. Its tires shrieked. She shrieked too but then felt nothing. She turned her head warily and saw smoke curling from the cover of the

Webster's Unabridged, the twenty-five pounder.

"Turn right," he told her.

"Here?"

"And shut up."

That did it. Esofea took the right onto 414 East with a jerk of the wheel that sent all forty million words of Michener down on the varmint's head. She stomped the brake pedal all the way to the floor this time. Her fishtail onto the shoulder dumped on Harry Potter and Philip Pullman, burying him in a pile of wizards.

The bus was hardly stopped when she sprang over the checkout counter into the heap of books. He moved erratically beneath the sliding spines and covers. Accustomed to bed-wrestling with Danny, Esofea was startled by Dog's strength. She tried to pin the wrist with the pistol. But when she grabbed him, her arm moved with his arm, light as a cuff on his sleeve. But then he twisted his back to her, and she grabbed a fistful of perforated skin. He stopped fighting. He looked at her, his sweat-streaked face turning pale and tight with pain.

"Actually, Dog, Bingo, Balto—" Esofea caught her breath "—nobody tells me to shut up."

"Let go."

"Get that thing out of my face."

"I had nothing to do with the death of Heimo Kock."

"Ok."

"Ok?"

"Ok. You're not going to shoot me, so get that thing out of my face."

"Let go."

"I did."

He lowered the pistol. She took the weapon from his hand and snapped open the cylinder. Empty. He saw it too—one bullet, used on Webster—closed his eyes and swallowed.

Esofea said, "Did you find the Tylenol?"

He began to shake. He closed his eyes and tipped his head back. She pulled her canvas shoulder bag across the floor. "I grew up around shotguns," she told him. "I thought I waited until you were good and far away." She opened the bottle of water and touched it to his unresponsive hand. "My grandparents built a resort on the Blind Sucker Flooding. Can you hear me? There were so many ducks and geese around the cabins—you've seen Hitchcock's *The Birds*?"

No answer.

"Picture geese instead," she said. "Ridiculous."

He sputtered water when she put it to his lips.

"You want to hear something wild?" She shook him by the arm. "Balto, listen. Don't tell anyone this, but my great grandpa basically lived in the nineteenth century and had a big old punt gun. You know what that is? It's a shotgun the size of a fire hose. You could take down the Detroit Lions with one pull. Those geese were ruining the business. My GG had to shoot a couple thousand before the collective birdbrain got the message."

This time he admitted a sip. She popped the lid off the Tylenol.

"After that it was my job to wing a couple honkers with sidewalk salt every now and then when they got too brave—with a regular twelve-gauge, of course. I packed the shells myself."

She withdrew the bottle as water began to run down his chest.

"In fact, I dropped you with that very shotgun, a 1955 Savage, with a shell I packed when I was about fifteen. Kept in the bus here for varmint control. Legal with salt in it."

She paused to shake out three Tylenol.

"Look. Ok. We need to get out of the ditch and go somewhere. I can help you. You can help me. Bingo? Buddy? You're not just any dog anymore. You're my dog. Ok? You listen to me. So what should I call you?"

His head lolled.

"Ok. Buckles. I'm Esofea Smithback. You can hate me all you want, Buckles, but you'd be dead now if I hadn't shot you. Now why Dolf Cook's place? What's there?"

Dog gathered himself slowly until he could explain it. She listened, quiet for an unusual stretch of time. He started with his visit to Dolf Cook's cottage, the night he burned his fishing gear.

Cook hadn't been there when Dog arrived. Dog figured he must have strangled his brother at the cottage sometime while Dog was out fishing, then stashed the body near the garbage box or the outhouse. Then he invited Dog over, to "give him something," which had turned out to be the reel that contained the line that strangled Kock. While Dog waited in his cottage, Cook had circled back to the campground and wrestled his dead brother inside the Cruise Master. From there it was driving, discovery, more driving, until Dog was back in Luce County, rolling Kock's body down the sand bank into the Two Hearted, meaning to put the ball back in Cook's court where it belonged. That was end of his story. He needed Dolf Cook's reel to show where the murder weapon had come from.

When she started talking again, Dog begged inside his head for Esofea Smithback to make sense.

Which she did, to a degree.

She believed his story about wanting to make it home in time for Eamon and M.J. But she also believed, she said, that it was not Dolf Cook but her boyfriend, Danny Tervo, who was behind Kock's murder and that Dog, knowingly or not, was part of it. Fair enough, Dog allowed, as long as she delivered him to Cook's for a chance to prove otherwise.

She turned the bookmobile around without getting stuck. She headed back out to 410 East and through the Perch Lake intersection onto 410 West.

Dog rode standing with his elbows on the checkout desk. A pale blue sky filled the windshield, agitated by a front off Superior. Treetops trembled. The bus felt a small gust broadside.

"You feeling ok now?"

"I'll make it."

"You move quite a bit slower than a goose," she told him, "so actually you were closer than I thought."

"I was only twenty feet away."

He focused on her. No pigtails or paint-on freckles today. But the copper hair was really hers. "Well, I had to knock you down," she explained. "Otherwise what was the point?"

She had convinced him, too, that he should approach Dolf Cook's indirectly, with stealth, from the Two Hearted River. They had kayaks at her family's resort. She would dump the bookmobile, use a pickup to drop him with a kayak, retrieve him later, downstream. In between that she expressed ominous plans involving the release of this guy Danny Tervo from some form of captivity, followed by the diversion of bear hounds—something about donuts— she was sure they had gotten her message at the outfitters by now and those donuts and hounds would be looking for Tervo's trail. Not Dog's. Because the donut guy believed her. She hoped.

Dog tuned out, backsliding into pain. The sky had faded to a dull gray by the time they turned off 410 West and bounced a half-mile on gravel to a shabby old lodge and bungalows that a weather-beaten sign said was *Blin ucker ort, Cabins, Boats, ips, Est. 1937.*

"Just stay inside here, out of sight," she said as she parked behind a row of tiny cabins. Each cabin was a different faded color, trading sun for shade and sun again under a turbulent sky. Dog moved back from the windows.

"I might be a little while," she said on her way out the door, but then she returned within minutes bearing two large blue capsules that Dog swallowed without asking.

"Now I *really* might be a while," Esofea said. "I've got a bit of a mess to sort out, as you can see."

Dog inched forward enough to look out the windshield. A large old woman in a nightgown paced the grass in front of one of the cabins, holding an armload of cordwood and shouting in a foreign language.

"That's my grandmother, Tiina. She's taking the woodpile apart. Something on the TV about an escaped murder suspect. You get my drift? And she does not use rock salt. So find something to read. And oh, practice sounding like this."

She made a low and dopey voice like she had already taken a few pills herself: "Live to share, brother. Your infinity is inside you."

Dog could not locate a response.

She patted him on the arm. "You can do it. You're on Percocet now. Actually, work on this." Out came the same stoner voice: "'What water you talking about? Dude, we gotta communicate better.'" She caught his chin, made him look at her. "Remember that phone call from the six-oh-two area code? When I come back, we're going to return the call from Danny's phone, and you're going to say to the guy, 'What water you talking about? Dude, we gotta communicate better.' Ok? Be ready."

Dumbfounded, Dog watched her out the door.

Billy Rowntree, aboard an airplane for the first time, flying the red-eye from Phoenix to Chicago beside this retired truck driver, turned on Sinbad's phone and used the chance to figure out some math. They taught that, at Oracle—how to use a calculator. Rowntree said, twenty thousand to make a run from the Midwest to Arizona, how would a trucker make out on a paycheck like that, figuring mileage and keep-up? This trucker driver just chuckled and winked and rattled his plastic cup of Bloody Mary and said, "When do I start?"

About a half hour later, Rowntree's eyes closed, the trucker tapped his arm.

"You gotta figure in the cost of the cargo, though. What you're hauling ain't free."

"Bitch," said Rowntree, "can't you see I'm trying to sleep?"

But he was thinking, actually. The hippie's water *was* free. After road costs, Tervo's operation was pure profit. Then he noticed something on the phone: a tiny picture of an envelope. A message. His mom had called him back.

But when Rowntree arrived at O'Hare another two hours later and checked Sinbad's prepaid, the phone said it was Tervo who left the message: "What water you talking about? Dude, we gotta communicate better."

Rowntree shouted, "Motherfucking bitch!" and nearly threw the phone. A rent-a-cop followed him, keeping a distance. Outside,

Rowntree snapped at the Sinbad Junior who picked him up in a Hummer at Arrivals: "Let's go. I got business. Where's Quality at?"

The Hummer was yellow. This fat black banger just stood beside it in his baggy pants and crooked Sox cap, looking at Rowntree with no expression.

"We're going where Quality is at," he said.

"That don't tell me where he's at."

"When we get there, then you'll know where he's at."

"Yo," Rowntree said. "Yo, Buddha."

As he said it Rowntree remembered Buddha was this fat black giant on the ranch at Oracle, Rowntree's first couple years. Calm as hell. Got out at eighteen, like Rowntree. Next day he busted somebody's neck, Rowntree heard. That's how calm he was.

"Yo, what?"

Rowntree backed off. "Just drive, man. All right?"

"I'm driving."

He did, for an hour or so more until there were Chinese signs everywhere, old Chinese people in the street, Chinese laundries, Chinese food on every corner. Outside a kung fu gym this Buddha stopped the Hummer, everything quiet for a moment until he said, "Ok, man. Listen. I'm going to tell you something. Quality don't got your money. He didn't agree to see you because he was going to give you something."

Rowntree stared out the window. He felt the sweat roll beneath his new suit. He had wanted to carry Sinbad's Sig, but Ramon told him on the plane you couldn't. He wondered could he take Buddha barehanded, peel off whatever his weapon was. Fat bitch might bust his neck.

"Don't fuck with me," Rowntree said.

"I'm not fucking with you, man. He says he never got any stuff from Phoenix. He's gonna, you know ... when you walk in there, man, Quality's gonna, like ... cancel the contract."

"When I walk in where? This kung fu place?"

"Naw. We ain't at Quality's yet. I'm just telling you something, man."

Rowntree looked out the window. The kung fu gym was murky behind dusty glass with peeling gold letters and curled-up Chinese posters taped everywhere. Down the sidewalk this old man carried an umbrella like he expected rain. Rowntree looked up at a cloudy sky. He hadn't seen rain in five months. The ranch, they rationed the showers. Rowntree got shit.

"So why we stopped here?"

Buddha hesitated. Rowntree stared into the low gray clouds through the windshield. Cancel the contract. Anybody could do that. Tervo too. Or Rowntree.

"Because you just got off a plane, man, so I know you're not carrying nothing right now. And they sell shit in there, which you need."

Rowntree looked at Buddha.

"Man, he's gonna cancel the contract," Buddha said. "You know? I'm *telling* you something here."

"Yeah?" Rowntree said. "Why you telling me?"

"You don't believe me?'

"Why should I?"

"You came all this way to die?" Buddha said. "You ready?"

"I said why."

"He thinks I stole the Phoenix shit, man," Buddha said, his voice rising. "But I never stole it. Lately, he thinks everybody stole some shit from him. That's just where the dude is at. That's why he sent me to pick you up. Which one of us he's gonna take out first, that's the only question."

The rest was fast and simple. They pulled up at Quality's crib three blocks away. The door opened on darkness and smoke and lazy music, Mr. Quality a smooth, pot-bellied, Dr. J-style bitch with one hand behind his back, all cordial in the doorway until he was dead from a bullet through the forehead.

Back at the Hummer, his jacket pocket heavy with the pistol on one side, Rowntree leaned through the window. "What's your name, brother?"

"Mike."

"Mike?"

"Yeah. My name's Mike."

"Buddha Mike."

"Just Mike."

Rowntree got in. His ears rang from the pistol shot. His heart flew around in his chest. He found Tervo's postcard in the pocket of his suit coat. "Yo, Buddha Mike, I'm gonna be needing me some more of this ride here. Now Michigan, where's that at?"

18

The Newberry Correctional K-9 unit took off from the back-yard of Mrs. Agnes Cunard on West Truman Street. Sheriff Lodge watched from the window of his cruiser. Three German Shepherds lunged ahead of three young officers in fatigues and jackboots who reminded him of guys like Tommy Woods and Mitchell Svjosej, half-backs he used to pull-block for in high school. Did they wear helmets then? He couldn't remember. That was funny. Couldn't remember if he wore a helmet. Get it? He and Margarite shared a chuckle inside his dizzy head.

The dogs crossed the yard of Mrs. Agnes Cunard into the neigh-bor's driveway. The guards followed at a slow trot, yipping encourage-ments. Then the dogs stopped. They circled. They picked something up and surged again. Off charged the prison K-9 team out West Truman Street onto the Tahquamenon-Pike Lake snowmobile trail, the way Oglivie really went, apparently. The Luce County sheriff watched them out of sight.

Oglivie had shucked his hospital gown beside Agnes Cunard's screen porch. Lodge had ripped the gown, given half to the prison team, and kept a piece. Now he levered out of his cruiser and limped on that sore hip around to his trunk and opened it. He lifted out his spinning rod and hooked the gown shred to the treble of a new

Daredevil spoon. He brought all that back to the front seat with him, got it situated, got on the radio with Tim Shrigley.

"Timmy?"

"Yessir."

"Where you at?"

Like he hoped. Rudvig was milling around in frustration west of Camp Seven Lake on the land where Chevrolet big wigs used to hunt back in the '50s. By the sheriff's instructions, Tim Shrigley supported them on the county's ORV.

"We have another sighting. You tell Donuts for me that he was just seen crossing the highway a little northeast of where you're at, exactly at that dirt road into Sleeper Lake."

When Lodge arrived by cruiser at that point, he opened his window to a wall of fresh wind that meant a storm was coming. Gusts from the north punched back the baying and hollering of Rudvig's Rhodesian ridgebacks, but Lodge could hear them coming. They were close.

He cast the shred of the trout bum's gown out the window with a little backhand flip. Not far enough into the ditch. He reeled in. He reversed the cruiser a few feet. He flipped again. Farther. Better.

He opened the bail on the reel and pulled forward. Maybe thirty feet or so behind the cruiser would be right. He hit the reel handle, tripped the bail, set the rod butt down between his leg and the door. He would drive on the wrong side of the road.

"Timmy?" he said into his radio as he pulled away.

"Yessir?"

Been a long time since he trolled, Lodge thought, looking back in his mirror. That was lake trout, with Charlotte and another couple. The pale blue shred dragged and fluttered along the shoulder of 407. Trolling for shitbird now. Rudvig and the rest of Heimo's people. They would not touch Margarite. He would stop all that.

"That's all I need, Deputy. You go help the prison team now."

Your infinity is inside you?

High on Percocet, staring out the window of the Luce County

Bookmobile with a book in his hand, Dog began to feel the spiritual gravity, if not the purpose, of Esofea's maxim.

Your infinity is inside you. Yeah.

A person's outer, actual life was such a narrow slice of what could really happen.

A person's limits lay far beyond where they were presumed to be.

Compared to the errors we feared, the errors we could actually make were completely more splendid.

These are not actual errors ...

Stamp that on the forehead of any man enjoining middle age, Dog decided.

Before long, vast thoughts such as these had replaced the pain in his back.

But—oh, yeah. The book. The guide book. *U.P. Trails and Treasures*—he had been looking up Heimo Kock.

"Outfitters" listed *Superior Adventures*. On that page was a photo of the man, barrel-chested and silver-bearded, jibbed out in technical fibers, big amber sunglasses—his arm cozily around, the caption said, actress and fly fisher Jane Seymour, star of *Dr. Quinn, Medicine Woman.*

"I'll take your word for it," Dog murmured. A gust of wind broke around the bookmobile's prow-shaped window glass. Thunder rumbled. Dog could not feel his feet.

Superior Adventures was the Upper Peninsula's "oldest and largest outfitter of ..." What followed seemed like every conceivable outdoor activity: hunting, bear hunting, fishing, fly fishing, lake trout fishing, musky fishing, walleye fishing, cruises, snowmobiling, rafting, canoeing, snowshoeing, cross country skiing, tubing, spelunking, backpacking, horseback riding, off-road vehicles, orienteering, rock hounding, even bird watching. Kock had outlets in Eagle River, L'Anse, Munising, and the Soo. He was pissing on every tree in the forest.

Dog's eyes chased the swimming words. The man's bio, headed "Guide to the Stars and Heroes of our Time," informed him that Heimo Henrich Kock was born in 1914 in Marquette. He had a degree in mining. He had hunted and fished around the world, claiming numerous fish and game records. He began guiding at age eighteen. In his fifty-five years of "service" he had "introduced to the U.P. such stars and heroes as Jane Seymour, Jimmy Carter, Merlin Olsen, Ted Williams, Bobby Knight, Dick Cheney, Joan Salvato (Wulff)—and even Ernest Hemingway!"

That last claim lifted Dog's buzzing head from the page. Kock guided Hemingway? That could be. But no—it said that Kock had "introduced" Hemingway to the U.P. Not possible. At the museum in Seney, Dog had learned that Hemingway first traveled to the Upper Peninsula in 1919, as a young man, with some buddies. Writing much later in Paris, he had based "Big Two-Hearted River" on that trip. Kock would have been five years old during Hemingway's first visit. So what did that mean, *introduced*?

He was too near the window, Dog realized. A heavy young girl stared at him from under the eave of the Blind Sucker lodge. Above her, the big lake seemed to be sneezing. Fine spray swirled over the lodge and cabins and hit the bookmobile in soft gusts. In the way of pebbles dipped in a stream, the cabins had brightened. The most distant one glistened like a new robin's egg. The next one was a wet, faded yellow, like a glass of lemonade. Then came a rain-warmed green, and after that a cabin the color of an old red barn in a fresh oil painting. The cabin nearest to the lodge had taken on decades of soot from the lodge chimney, achieving the sheen of a wet black bear that Dog had startled a week ago on a dark corner of the Fox River. That was the river Hemingway and his friends had fished, with fly rods and live grasshoppers, taking trout so big they could swallow the ones Dog had been catching.

He was getting loopy on this stuff. But the girl. Her eyes remained on Dog. She stepped inside the lodge's main screen door as Esofea emerged from the red cabin and hustled past around the downhill side of the lodge. A moment later, just a shape now, the girl held still as Esofea returned dragging a red plastic kayak, which she dumped over the tailgate of a drab green pickup that advertised *Blind Sucker Shuttle* across its rusted tailgate.

In through the door of the green cabin Esofea went, then out again she came, carrying a mixing bowl with a plate over the top. She pinched her face against a lake sneeze. Dog dimly registered a thumping at the bookmobile door. Oh, yeah, open it.

"I think this is edible." She handed him the bowl and a fork. "I nuked it good. Now, more practice."

Dog dug into macaroni-and-cheese with cut-up hot dogs. He tasted nothing, but his appetite was surprising. "Practice what?"

"I looked up the six-oh-two area code in the phone book. This guy called Danny's cell phone from Phoenix. We're going to leave him another message. Or maybe he'll answer this time. We need him to tell us what water he's talking about."

Dog said through a mouthful, "What water?"

"Heimo Kock owned certain rivers in his mind. He scared people off them. Maybe Danny ran into him there. Maybe that's where you got the body."

"Besides guiding—" Dog was burning his mouth, not feeling it much "—what does your boyfriend do?"

"He jerks me around."

"I mean for a living."

"He borrows money from me. Then he jerks me around."

Dog hung his mouth wide, letting in some air. "And his infinity is inside him?"

"That's pretty much the situation, yeah."

"He does drugs?"

"Religiously."

"You find out what he's up to, that he killed Kock or whatever, that he set me up, what do you do with it?"

"Concessions."

"Concessions—?"

"Long story," she told him, "involving private parts. Or else I let him loose and tell Donuts Rudvig that Danny can run those hounds instead of you. Oh, by the way. The TV says there are two dog teams out after you, both of them looking in the wrong place."

Dog beheld her in a kind of fuzzy wonderment. She opened the boyfriend's phone.

"What?" she said. "You're confused?"

She pressed a key. She put the ringing phone in Dog's hand. "Phoenix answers, or you get the service again, you say, 'Let's work it out, my brother. We had a misunderstanding. What water did I promise you?' Then when Danny lies to me, I'll know exactly how to play him."

"Play him. Sure. But for me, how—"

Motherfucker, what the fuck?

Dog stared at the phone's tiny speaker. Esofea rushed her lips to his ear: "Let's work it out, my brother."

"Let's work it out, my brother—"

Motherfucker, fuck you, I ain't your motherfucking brother. The voice came to Dog like from a bee on its hind legs, shouting. *Where's my water at?*

Esofea hissed in Dog's ear again. Dog repeated it: "We had a misunderstanding. What water?"

Motherfucking motherfucker!

That made Dog laugh. Esofea gestured wildly at him to stop.

You got my deposit, bitch!

"Yeah?" Dog said as Esofea grabbed at the phone. "Well, I'm keeping it." He held the phone away. "What do you say to that?"

For moment the speaker played miniature road noises, wee honking, petite obscenities. At last the bee voice came back: *What I say is we almost in Green Bay, bitch, and that ain't far from where you at.*

Then Phoenix snapped it off.

Now Dog let Esofea snatch the phone.

She appeared to think things over for a minute. "Green Bay?" she said. Then she pecked a kiss onto his forehead. She took the bowl, fed him the final forkful of macaroni.

"Good boy, Cujo," she said. "Perfect."

Now she had to hurry. Into Mummo Tiina's red cabin went Esofea and back out with the first-aid box. She noticed Caroline under the eave of the lodge.

"Sweetie, your mom and dad still have bad backs, right? Go see if they're ok."

The girl gave a pouty shake of her head.

"What's that mean?"

"They're not home."

"Where'd they go?"

She shrugged. "Where do you think?"

"Ok, then. I'm glad they're better. But Mummo Tiina seems a little upset today. Maybe read her a story."

Just that sullen, accusing, hormonal stare. Esofea fought a heavy, pulling feeling.

"What then?"

And the girl said, "Who ate my macaroni?"

Shit. With her cousin now lurking suspiciously outside, Esofea lay Dog on his belly on the bookmobile floor. She stripped the coveralls to the tops of his thighs. She uncapped a bottle of hydrogen peroxide.

"Our story," she said, answering his question, "is that after his Pulitzer and his Nobel, Hemingway took an assignment from *Esquire* to come back to the U.P. and revisit the Big Two Hearted River stories that everybody loves. He hired Heimo Kock to take him fly fishing. That was the hot thing then, fly fishing, and Heimo was the hot young guide. But I have no idea what to do here without hurting you."

"Just dump it on."

"You can't scream, then. My cousin Caroline is suspicious. She says anything, my Mummo Tiina will come out with a shotgun, except it will not, I repeat, be salt."

"Just dump it on."

Esofea held the bottle over his back. She said, "I'm so sorry," and poured. He gasped and his fists clenched and his naked ass went tight as a walnut. The dozens of inflamed wounds fizzed like tiny volcanoes. Esofea heard his forehead grind against on the floor. "More of Uncle Rush's stupid pills for you," she said. Then she heard a door.

She rose. Caroline had gotten into the resort truck, was fiddling with the lights and wipers, pretending to drive.

"So Heimo Kock … took Hemingway fly fishing?"

"Yes. And he couldn't catch anything. When he tried to blame that on his guide, Kock told the whole world that Hemingway couldn't cast a fly rod."

"Again," Dog said.

She repeated the procedure. This time his hand shot out and grabbed her ankle. He pinched his butt and whimpered and said, "Perfect, thank you. And then?"

"The *Esquire* article Hemingway was supposed to write never happened. But Kock did an interview with *Playboy* where he said that Hemingway was strictly a bait guy, and the best he could do with a fly rod was down-and-across with a wet fly. My great grandpa kept the issue. Kock called Hemingway 'the wind knot champion of the world'—or something. I don't know what that means exactly, but I'm sure you do."

He let go of her ankle. "That's why I want to get to Dolf Cook's place. Dab it off."

"Ok."

"A wind knot is made by bad casting like Cook's. The line that strangled his brother—it had wind knots in the leader. Cook tried to plant the reel with the rest of the line on me. I wouldn't take it, but I know where it is."

Cotton balls from the first-aid kid clung wrongly to his wounds. She unwrapped gauze, cut a strip and folded it into pad. Better. She dabbed him dry, worrying again that Danny really wasn't involved. Would that be a problem?

"Where we come into the story is when Hemingway returned the next summer and hired my great-grandfather to teach him proper fly casting. This was before Kock muscled everyone else out of the guiding business. Hemingway was going to disprove what Kock said to *Playboy*. We still have the rod and reel he used, hanging with the rest of the junk in the lodge."

She helped Dog roll to his side and sit up.

"You're all clean."

His voice was small and hoarse. "Thanks." He looked at her dizzily. "And?"

"But it didn't work out. Hemingway acted crazy. He said Kock was with the FBI. Kock was working for Castro. Then he messed around with Mummo Tiina—that's what I think—she was just sixteen, a big, pretty girl. My great-grandpa Smithback threw him out after a week, and he shot himself shortly after."

"In Ketchum, Idaho. On July 2, 1961."

"Oh, god," she said. "You too?"

"Me too what?"

"Admire that crap."

"What crap?"

"Come on." She pulled him to his knees. "This was my great-grandpa's shirt."

She helped him into a dark brown flannel. She stood him up, lowered the coveralls, helped him step out. He was naked beneath. And how.

"And GG's boxers," she said, holding his waist, guiding him into a pair of fifty-year-old underpants.

"Belt or suspenders? Which do you think? Belt? Good boy. So here's what we do. The bookmobile stays here. I already put a kayak in the back of that pickup out there. I'll drop you off upstream of Dolf Cook's. You come up on his place from the river. He won't expect that. There's a steep bank there. You'll just have to climb it. Meanwhile I continue to Newberry in the truck and do my business with Mr. Tervo. Then I come back here, pick up the bookmobile, drive it to the campground at the Mouth of the Two Hearted. That's where you are, because you've gotten back into the kayak and continued downriver to the lake. Ditch the kayak at the end of the spit. I'll pull through the boat launch parking lot, you'll get on board—"

A honk startled both of them. "That's just Miss Caroline," Esofea said, "making things difficult."

Dog looked at her.

"Admire what crap?" he asked again.

19

By the time Conrad Belcher approached Danny Tervo's house, Danny's tanker had been parked in its turn-out on the lake side of H58 for nearly seven hours.

This observation permitted Belcher, returning from a deer scout in Schoolcraft County, to draw near at a perfect moment that balanced the possibility he would wake Danny and piss him off against the possibility that Danny was already awake and already pissed off that Belcher had waited.

This was the "rabbit hour"—when the risks of acting and not acting equalized and became *now.*

So Belcher moved in, intending to ask Danny if he was supposed to run the hose across the beach tonight, fill the tanker for a delivery to those poor bastards down in drought-country.

Or did Danny want him to drive to Grand Marais for pizza and beer?

Or should he just give Danny some space to work on Esofea with a bottle of wine and a bag of weed?

At the roadside, he called Danny's house, gazing across the highway at where the phone rang.

But no Danny. Strange.

Belcher's inner rabbit hesitated now—there was a balance here too, where his empathy for the hunted leveled perfectly with his instinct to kill, the equilibrium forming a surreal and intoxicating oneness.

Belcher returned to his truck. He strapped a .45 Magnum side-arm under his left pit. From the compound bows and mineral licks and other junk in the truck box he sorted out a hickory-handled musky gaff. He slipped the handle up the sleeve of his Realtree jacket, cupped the hook in his palm.

He held still against a ninebark shrub as a couple of minivans convoyed west toward Munising. At his back, an autumn storm had begun to squat and piss on the lake. Electricals snapped a mile or two out. It would rain in thirty minutes. Maybe thirty-one. No one saw him cross the road.

Belcher felt annoyed, as always, approaching Danny's house. Here was another balance: friendship. It used to be a nice old sum-mer house, one of the best. Then Danny's mom got the place in a divorce and didn't take care of it. Then she got remarried and moved, and Danny—alone as a senior in high school—took over the house. It looked terrible now, the way Danny kept it up, meaning he didn't. The shrubs rose to the gutters, blocking the windows. The stone path was shagged with salt grass. Invasives claimed the gardens, Japanese knotweed and garlic mustard up to Belcher's waist as he stepped through, phragmites clogging what used to be a minnow pond, kudzu going up the trunks of the old growth pines in back of the driveway. And that was just the vegetable neglect. Windows were broken, screens hung loose, the septic line was ruptured. Bricks from the chimney had popped out and landed on the roof so long ago that pine and maple seedlings grew around them. All this called attention to Danny—which you did not want if you were into the stuff Danny was into—which was inconsiderate—think about it—to the people who cared about Danny and basically believed in him and supported him in certain risks—people such as, for example, his best old friend, Conrad Belcher.

But try to explain this to Danny.

When you called attention, you got attention, eventually. That was a law of nature. When you made trouble, trouble made you back.

Belcher kicked through newspapers in plastic sleeves and knocked.

No sound. No movement.

Once more he called the house. No.

He circled outside, muting his footfalls on fallen leaves—yellow beech, red maple. Heineken bottles on the deck table, labels faded. Black panties in a stunning red viburnum.

Goddamned Danny. Sofi wouldn't do that.

The back door was ajar. With the gaff raised in one hand and the .45 cocked in the other, Belcher went in. He stalked through the place, room by room—thinking, The tanker is here, and that means Danny. But no …

So why does the enlightened man not stand on his feet and explain himself?

Earlier, by about five that morning, using a meditation on this kōan from Shogen, Tervo had worked his legs free of the bungee cord. This was just after he heard Esofea pull away in his tanker.

Because when the feet of enlightenment move, the great ocean overflows.

And people drown in that shit, Tervo thought. It's too deep for them.

In any case, he could then twist to one side and loose a screaming piss off the side of the bed, fire-hosing some jewelry off the top of Esofea's bureau. Awesome.

After that he took a little nap, thinking Esofea would be back any minute, the truck in a ditch, all sorry, all done riding the estrogen rocket, or whatever. And she had come back, just before sunrise. Tervo recognized the sound of his own Kawasaki Ninja 650. He should have never taught her to ride *that* rocket, obviously. He recognized the sound of the heavy carriage doors on the mansion's garage. Then she had left again, he didn't know how or where to, and when the St. Gregory's bells woke him at ten, Esofea wasn't back yet.

Tervo registered this unpleasant surprise in his molars, grinding inside a dry mouth. Maybe he really had a problem.

So break it down. He still had about twelve hours to get the tanker filled and back on the road to Phoenix. If he got Belcher going now, the truck could be rolling by midnight. The ornamental gardener, Takahashi, could not afford to be patient. Avoiding that psychopathic insect Billy Rowntree—he hadn't figured that one out yet.

But maybe, speaking of insects, he could try an inchworm. Like that. Yeah. He used his hips and ass to work the mattress off the box spring beneath. Finally the mattress slid to the floor. These activities took until noon and exhausted him. But now, in a deeper pocket of space atop the box spring, he had enough play to roll back like a pill bug and see what he was dealing with.

So this was his strategy: he pushed hands and cuffs as high up the brass spindles as they would go. Then he put his feet to his wrists and pushed them higher, until he could get into *sarvangasana*, the Ashtanga yoga shoulder stand. From here, spreading his feet down the arc of the top pipe, he created enough knee bend to kick toward the ceiling. He hammered the piping upward in its sleeves. It popped out and fell on top of him.

Tervo rolled off the bed. He was a free man, aside from the fact that he was cuffed to his batshit girlfriend's antique brass sex-handle.

But he could swing the thing sideways and hammer his way down the staircase to the ground floor. He cracked plaster. He smashed light fixtures on both landings. He fractured the bottom banister, booted the newel knob into the next hallway.

Then Tervo took measures. First, he rehydrated. He drank water at the kitchen sink, lifting the whole headboard with the cup. He knew where Esofea kept her weed, and he burned some of that, the antique pipes moving like the complex armature of some fantastic bong. As Tervo, now stoned, entered the front parlor, the kitty Mr. Nilsson startled, ran across the rug and turned to look again.

Which gave him a thought.

An awkward, hilarious, impossible, perfectly vengeful thought. Sensing something, Esofea's kitty cat fled to the next room. But—headboard and all—he would catch it.

Caroline rolled down the pickup's window. "Oh, *finally,*" she said. "You were like in there forever."

"Caroline, honey, can you get out of the truck?"

"Who's in there?"

"No one."

"Is Danny in there?"

"Why would Danny be in there?"

"Because he's your boyfriend and you guys do it."

"Danny has a house. I have a house. If we were going to do it, sweetheart, we would do it in a house. In a bed. That's how people do it when they love each other. Come on out now and go inside. I need the truck."

Squinting as the drizzle sailed sideways, Esofea opened the pickup door. Caroline didn't get out. The girl wiggled the shifter, jerked the steering wheel left and right. Then she said, "I wouldn't do it unless somebody made me."

"Good girl. Come on out."

"They went to the White Pines," Caroline said. "Again."

"Who did?"

"Mom and Dad."

"That's nice. So they're feeling better. Now, please—out."

"Then who's in there?"

"Nobody."

"It's that guy, right?"

"What guy?"

"You shot him and then he escaped from the hospital? Mummo's watching on TV. He has a gun and everything? So, are you guys doing it now?"

Esofea took her by the arm—this suddenly heavy, stupid girl—gripped the baby fat below her armpit and tugged. For a few ugly moments, Esofea's cousin resisted, clawed the steering wheel, tried to hook a foot through it, called Esofea a stupid twat and a *houkka*, until at last Esofea extracted her and steered her inside the great room of the lodge, where the girl tore away and stood hulking and trembling amidst the rods and guns and game trophies.

"Keep your mouth shut, Caroline, and stay right here."

"I don't like it in here."

"It's fine in here."

"It's ... it sucks in here. It's boring."

Esofea slung open the drawer where the games were kept. She pawed through playing cards, dominoes, Laugh-a-Day books of riddles and jokes, Don't Spill the Beans, Operation, Chutes and Ladders, a bb pinball game—heaped this stuff out wholesale onto the sawed-pine lodge table. "Keep busy," she ordered the girl. She left behind the empty pint bottle of Bailey's Cream. Uncle Rush probably. But no time to wonder.

"I want to go with Mummo."

"Mummo's sleeping."

"She is not."

Esofea pushed her toward the deer-hide sofa. But the girl fought again—as if the sofa would burn her—then twisted loose and fled into Great Grandpa Smithback's old rocker.

"Leave Mummo alone. Don't upset her. Play some games."

"That junk?" Her voice cracked and she sniffled. "No way."

Caroline adjusted the bloom of her rear end and from a pocket there produced a pink electronic game of the type Esofea sometimes competed with at library story time.

"Who got you that?"

"Who's in the bookmobile?"

Esofea backed up inside her mind. The girl wasn't sassing her, she realized. She was negotiating. She had something. Some knowledge, some information, some trouble. It just wasn't free. "How about we tell each other tomorrow?" Esofea asked her more gently. But a heaviness flooded her heart. Tomorrow. Tomorrow she would play the games, ask the questions, do what she should do for a girl growing up in a way she, of all people, ought to understand.

"I'm sorry, Caroline. And I mean it. We'll talk."

Caroline kept her head down over the game, her thumbs a blur. "What*ever*."

Dog let Esofea help him aboard the pickup. She drove hard, lake wind whipping from behind. The kayak hammered in the box, sending vibrations to the cab. Loose firewood slung around back there too, and what sounded like a maul, pounding back and forth between the wheel wells. Dog's wounds got wired again. His pain rewound.

"Any more of those pills on hand?"

He asked this twice. He needed to brace against the dash.

"Somebody's messing with her," she said through gritted teeth. "My little cousin."

"Messing with her?"

"Do I have to explain?"

Dog lost the thread of this. "Any more of those pills?"

"And I think I know who. After I let Mr. Tervo out for the dogs to play with," she said, "you can find me at the White Pines Hotel."

That didn't seem like the plan that Dog remembered. Ten rough and worried miles went by, his eyes closed and his teeth locked. He thought about the cold water of the Two Hearted River. Lie down in it. No—the big lake, Superior. Now that was cold water. If he got that far—if that was still the plan—he would stretch out in lake water, go numb.

"Get down."

Dog opened his eyes.

"Down!" She caught a fistful of hair, yanked him apart from a blur of sound and image: dogs yelping at the roadside, men in camouflage, someone hollering.

"Shit," she muttered grimly. "You should have disappeared right where I picked you up. Somehow those psychos got way up here."

Five miles on, she threw the kayak onto the road at the Reed and Green Bridge. "Don't drag it. You'll leave a mark in the sand. Carry it overhead and put it down in the water so they don't know you have it." She gave him the boyfriend's phone. "Use that if you need it. I made myself speed dial number one."

"Number one?"

"You find that funny?"

Then she left him, the kayak paddle going with her on the way to Newberry, slamming around with the firewood and the maul.

Dog lingered on the bridge beside the kayak, shivering on a wave of pain. Should he hit number one and call her? Or should he find a good branch, pole the kayak downriver? Call her, he decided, studying the phone keys—and then the damn thing rang.

And rang again louder. And louder. Until Dog pressed something and it stopped.

"You took the paddle—"

Bitch, I get to Iron Mountain, which way I go next?

"Take a left and go to hell," Dog said. The screen said he had another call. Trying to get it, he pushed OFF. He said, "You took the paddle."

Silence. Blank screen.

So OFF was off. He pushed ON, but that didn't bring the call back. He lingered, hoping Esofea would reappear on a fishtail of sand and throw the paddle out.

But no. He carried the kayak to the Two Hearted. He set the boat in a little slip of backwater, its nose on a mat of gnat-infested flotsam. He was sorting through deadfall along the riverbank, looking for a pole, when the phone rang again.

"The paddle. You took it with you."

The what?

"Who is this?"

This is Takahashi. From Phoenix? I gave you two grand, remember? You said seventy-two hours. The koi are floating on their sides. The rhodies are dropping petals all over the parking lot. Can you make it sooner?

Conrad Belcher located his pal Danny Tervo inside the kitchen of the Frens mansion a little after noon. His first thought: turn around and leave.

Because Danny was stoned and handcuffed to a brass headboard and in the midst of doing a very bad thing.

"Let the cat go, Danny. Let him out of there."

"I caught him while I was attached to this thing, Belch. Do I have talent, or what? Can you believe it? Now watch."

Handcuffs clattered on brass spindles as Belcher's buddy pumped the plunger on an extra large salad spinner. Danny's arms and hands were scratched and bleeding. Mr. Nilsson, mashed inside, became a yowling whirl of gray fur.

"That's messed up, Danny."

"He fell into the bathtub, Belch. He got all wet."

Just coming in there, after searching several bars for Danny, Belcher had felt extremely tense. He hated bars. Give him a pint of Schnapps and a tree stand. In those bars, there was hardly anyone to ask about Danny, and Belcher had learned that the suspect in Kock's death was loose in the woods with half the gun nuts in the county out after him. Bear dogs and ORVs. Talk of spotter planes. Boats heading out from Grand Marais and Deer Park to "patrol the coastline." It hadn't felt right—the guy escaping from the hospital, vanishing. He had help. Only way it was possible. And this shit here looked connected. Which meant Esofea was in trouble.

"Come on, Danny. Knock it off."

"Give me your phone, Belch. I'm gonna take a picture."

"Danny, I found that cat, begging for graham crackers in the Pratt Lake Campground. I gave him to Sofi."

"Give me your phone."

"Hell no."

"Then take a picture for me and send it to Sofi." Danny pumped the plunger again. This time Mr. Nilsson whirled in silent terror. "Text message: sorry baby, your pussy got wet."

"Where is she, Danny?"

"Cut me out of this thing, Belch."

"Where is she?"

"I can't hear you, buddy."

"Where is she, Danny? She's in trouble, right?"

"Cut me out, Belch."

Belcher turned his back. He stormed outside, stood on the porch with tears in his eyes. He spat out his Skoal. Like Esofea always said: *fucker.*

Then he went to his truck and got the cutters.

20

Careful not to spook Dolf Cook, Deputy Margarite DuCharme left the White Pines Hotel by the rear door, drove the opposite way around the block, then fell in and followed Cook at a distance.

The dead man's brother drove erratically. She should have pulled him over, gotten him off the road. She didn't.

She stayed a quarter mile behind the dust-caked silver Jeep Cherokee—Illinois plates, taillight out—watching a dangerous drunk speed and slow, catch the shoulder, drift over the center line, perform the entire gamut of DUI maneuvers—because she had to find out about Julia.

Which meant, really, that she had to find out about herself.

Which meant she didn't know.

There. Now it was on the table. She didn't understand her own self. The why. The who. The where it was that she always went wrong in her life.

Cook took the first big turn north of Newberry from the left-hand lane, but Deputy DuCharme allowed him to drive on. Several lucky miles later, going eighty on a straight, he swerved around Donuts Rudvig and his bear hounds as they surged along the shoulder. What were they doing all the way up here? And on the roadside? She heard Rudvig curse a particular female sexual part as she flew past, nearly clipping a Rhodesian ridgeback. First she had lost Julia, Margarite decided. Then Oglivie. Now she had lost her mind. Next would be her badge.

Everything hurt suddenly, but all she had was Pepto. Then Cook made it worse. He deepened her morass of doubt, following 424 to 421 past Deadman's Lake to 422 and onward past Peanut Lake into the Tahquamenon chain, into the middle of nowhere.

She went too far, too fast, with the wrong one. She always did.

Margarite fell way back and followed, racking up a brutal list of should-haves. She should have grilled Julia harder about all the men she liked to mention, especially Tervo. She should have grilled Julia harder about Julia. She should have stayed with the Milwaukee job and made Julia come to her, not the other way around. Long before that, at the Tori Amos concert, she should have asked herself why is this perfectly hot grrl just leaning there on the wall, alone with her beer, nobody coming close to her?

Nobody but me.

Why?

At State 77, Dolf Cook turned north toward Grand Marais, and suddenly Margarite guessed where he was going. She picked up her radio.

"Sheriff? Just checking in. I'm in Grand Marais, headed for Kock's house."

She heard nothing back for five or six miles, driving into a misty squall of lake wind, the beginning of a storm. She was right, though: Cook had just crossed Wilson Street and turned right past the West Bay Diner, headed for his brother's house.

"Sheriff? Bruce? You copy?"

She turned behind Dolf Cook up the hill on Morris. He maneuvered a drunken left onto Burton Street, clipping the snow stake but otherwise making the corner. His brother's house was up the long private drive from there.

Margarite pulled over to watch, her brain a messy swirl of duty and doubt. Did June Kock know who killed her husband? *Wait by the door*, she had said. *The one who did it will come for the box.*

"Sheriff? Damn it, where the hell are you?"

Her windshield was misted over. Two hundred yards up the bluff, Cook had disappeared through the gate to his brother's house.

"I'm going in on Kock's house. You copy?"

Margarite pulled ahead and took the hill on foot. She charged up the steep incline, through dune grass and shrubby red pines. Sure enough, when she looked over the cedar fence, Cook was leaving his vehicle, heading up the front walk—dithering along, unaware that June Kock had appeared in the picture window, standing against the drapes to watch his approach—not with a knife, though. The widow dropped shells into a shotgun.

Neither of them saw Margarite clear the fence. She landed in soft landscape bark. Wind noise covered her dodge through shrubbery and her sprint over grass.

June Kock opened the door.

Dolf Cook skidded tipsily to a halt.

June Kock raised the shotgun.

Cook said, "It's only me, dear," and he was doffing an invisible cap as Margarite took a last long stride and laid herself out in the air. She heard June Kock pump the shotgun. The deputy slammed into Cook at midsection, a full-out tackle, heard his breath squeak out as she landed hard on top of him. The shotgun tore a hole in the air above, spraying lead against the fence across the yard.

Beneath her, Cook made a bawl of angry sound and began to thrash. Margarite twisted his head and shoved his face into the grass until he went fetal. She looked up. "No. Mrs. Kock. Wait."

June Kock, in her lumpy stretch pants and slippers, pumped the weapon a second time: "Clear outta the way, missy."

"No. Please. Wait."

Margarite struggled up into the line of the shotgun. She squared her vest to the barrel. Her chest heaved.

"Mrs. Kock, please."

The woman's brother-in-law unreeled from his fetal position and corkscrewed a swing at the deputy. Margarite caught him by the forearm. With her free hand she pushed the gun barrel down. She tried to recover her breath.

"He's ... he's ... we're going to take care of it."

"Take care of what?" Cook thrashed feebly. "I didn't kill him! Get your hands off me!"

She bent Cook's arm until he yelped. She wanted to snap it.

"The sheriff's department is taking care of it, I promise," she panted at June Kock. "Now put that thing away. Unload it, put it away, and don't answer your door. Lock your gate. Please let us take care of it."

"I didn't touch him! He's my brother, for chrissake!"

She spun Cook. She shoved a hand down his baggy pants pocket. She withdrew the paper sack from the White Pines and tore it open.

Julia's empty reel.

"Come on." She pushed Cook ahead. "You're riding with me. We're going to do this at your place."

Dolf Cook blubbered all the way from Grand Marias to Deer Park, then said he was going to piss his pants. Deputy Margarite DuCharme stopped at Deer Park Lodge and let him go inside the general store.

He didn't kill his brother. He swore to God. His brother hated him—he had told Margarite this much so far—because he changed his name from Kock to Cook. Because he went to a fancy college. Because he owned restaurants in fifteen states. His brother hated him because he was acquainted with better and richer celebrities. The restaurants, you know. His brother hated him because he had had so many good-looking wives, whereas his brother's wife, June the Goon—and here he had managed to stop himself, possibly realizing that "June the Goon" had nearly killed him.

But then Cook got going again.

His brother wouldn't let him into the Royal Coachmen Society.

His brother wouldn't even admit there was a Royal Coachmen Society. That was a dirty lie. Dolf Cook knew there was. He knew they met once a year on Isle Royale, flew in during the coaster run with high-class working girls and casks of twelve-year-old scotch. But he didn't kill his brother. He swore it. His brother was his brother, for chrissake. Then he said he had to piss.

Margarite kept her mouth shut. She watched Cook wobble inside the Deer Park Lodge general store. She left the cruiser running, went around behind the store, and waited in the drizzle by the LP tank. She caught Cook by the back of his neck as he tried to sneak out the delivery door, slapping at a wet circle on the crotch of his trousers.

"Be gentle," he slurred at her. "For chrissake, officer, be a lady."

"I'm a dyke, you idiot." She hurled him onto the back seat. "So is Julia Inkster."

"You mean—"

"No. I'm sure she can just barely tolerate you and your restaurants in fifteen states." Margarite twisted from the front seat to glare at the fool. "Your clue is when the sex costs you truck tires."

He lay there the last five miles, silent except for gasping sounds. This last hour, since the deputy left the White Pines in pursuit of Cook, Julia had been pounding Margarite's cell phone with messages. She let them go. But she couldn't stop herself: "I know it's hard, Mr. Cook. But look on the bright side. At least you're a dishonest drunk."

She turned off before the Reed and Green bridge—she glimpsed someone in a flannel shirt down there at the river, launching a kayak—and took the campground road. The same short drive that she took two days ago to meet the DNR guy, Greg Bright, now seemed to take a thousand heartbeats and a hundred acid swallows. *God damn you, Julia. God damn you.* But there weren't words for it.

Cook shambled to his door. He took a key from his pocket. He inserted it. Apparently the door had been unlocked—he had now locked it. While he sorted out the whole conundrum, Margarite looked over toward the campground dumpster, just visible through the trees. But she had to stay here, make sure Cook had no wiggle room.

"Don't touch anything."

"It's my house; I'll touch what I want."

Margarite reached for her cuffs.

"All right, all right. Lord God, why do people despise me?"

She stepped inside. Was it two days ago she had first come here? It was a harmless mess then. Today the place groped and leered. Its breath stank. Goddamned Julia.

"Stop. Sit there. Put your hands on the table top and keep them there."

Margarite left the front door open. Wind whipped jackets in the foyer, sleeves slapping a kindling box below them. She drew back a curtain and let in the approaching storm's skidding light. By this she reviewed the photograph of Cook holding the large brook trout—and now she saw the pale, cracked, pumpkin-colored fly line draped over Cook's arm at the margin of the picture. Was this the line that killed Heimo Kock? Or was this Julia's line? Or …

"You said your brother took this photograph."

"Well, I—"

"Then you wrapped that line around his neck?"

"Huh? No. No, I—" He lurched in the chair. "May I stand?"

She let him. She stepped aside as he puttered nervously behind her, reaching into a cabinet cluttered with fishing gear. He returned to the table. "Oh, yes," he said. "Now I recall. My reel … that reel … I gave that reel to the fellow with the RV. I'm sure you've found it in his things by now."

Margarite stared him back to a sitting position. "No. We didn't find it. I don't believe he had much of anything to do with this. Who took this picture?"

Cook jerked his head toward the window, where a gust wobbled grimy window panes in their mullions. "He did. The trout bum."

"Who caught the fish?"

"He did."

"You gave him a thousand bucks cash?"

"Yes."

"Why? And why did you lie to me?"

Cook stood again. Drifting unsteadily toward his bar, he asked, "May I?"

He poured himself a scotch.

"In answer to my own question, why do people despise me," he announced, tossing down the drink, "I cheat. I always have. It began, you might say, when I changed my name from Kock to Cook—though of course I was still one hundred percent Kock, spell it any way you like. But it was a manner of misrepresenting the truth, et cetera, et cetera. It all follows from there. I couldn't catch a fish like that in the picture to save my life. I can't even figure out how to cast a goddamned fly rod."

Margarite released her mind a little further into the room, easing up to the fact that Julia had moved around in here, with a drink and a smoke, her buzzed eyes and her party voice. Julia had breathed this air, touched these things, touched this man. For a leather jacket and sunglasses, free booze, and truck tires. And then *touched me.* Margarite wheeled around at a sound: coat sleeves, slapping in the foyer.

"Porn," Cook said.

"I'm sorry?"

"That's called porn. Fish porn." He slopped his drink toward the brook trout photograph. "In the trade, pictures like that, that make a fisherman drool—pornography."

"And fish porn is part of your application to the club?" There was the dish of the flies tied by Oglivie, still on the table. "The Royal Coachmen?"

"You have to get something published." Cook tottered over from the bar. He poked through the mess on the table and tossed a newsprint magazine toward her, a pretty picture of a spring creek on the front. *Midwest Fly Fishing.* "Has to mention Hemingway, the Royal Coachman, and use the word 'ass.' The keeper of the box has to see it. He has to contact you. Tough shit if he doesn't. You can try again. Look at page three."

"This is just a letter to the editor," Margarite said. "That counts?"

He was silent as she read. Adolf Cook of Chicago (winters) and

Luce County, Michigan (summers), was correcting a previous letter to the editor (Ed Smith, Joliet) containing the false information
that Ernest Hemingway was indifferent to fly fishing. *In point of fact,*
Cook wrote, *the famous author, disgraced in print by a young UP guide
named Heimo Kock (my brother), had visited three weeks in 1956 at
the Blind Sucker Resort, where with a guide named Elmer Smithback
he worked his illustrious ass off to learn the craft of fly casting and repair
the damage to his ego and reputation. However, Mr. Hemingway—who
favored a Royal Coachman, wet—left abruptly upon discovery of his
affair with an underage local beauty. Mr. Ed Smith, though well inten-
tioned, and undoubtedly a gentleman, should get his facts straight.*

"Apparently my brother felt a letter to the editor did *not* count,"
Cook said, "and I heard nothing."

"I'll bet you were Ed Smith, too."

Cook merely shrugged. His hands trembled. Thunder boomed
from the direction of the big lake.

"How did you know your brother was keeper of the box?"

"I couldn't get in, that's how. I had my first piece in the *Marquette
Miner*, Outdoor Page, fall of 1997. I had another in 2000. Nothing.
Nada. Rejection like that, it had to be him."

"Somehow you knew the application requirements."

"Rumor," Cook said with a shrug. "That stuff's been out there
thirty years."

"You finally got something else in print."

"Goddamn right. And nothing again. Nada."

Margarite set the sack with Julia's reel on the table. "Tell me the
requirements again," she said. "Fish porn and what else?"

"Porn, pelt, and press," muttered Cook. "Porn and pelt to a P.O.
box in Detroit. Along with a perfect fly for the box."

"Pelt?"

"Pelt."

"As in beaver?"

"Correct."

"Meaning woman?"

"The very thing, yes." His head hung, eyes on his piss-spattered slippers. "That's just the sort of thing we men do, you know, among one another, powerful men like my brother and the rest of us."

Margarite's breathing felt cut-off, shallow. This horrid drunken pal of Julia's had assumed almost a British accent. Apparently it helped him express depravity. Along with the rattling windows, and the empty jackets dancing in the foyer.

"You know at Yale, we Bonesmen gave George H. W. Bush the name Magog for a reason. He had a third leg, that rotter, and he knew how to use it."

Cook began pushing papers aside, gearing up for more. Margarite snarled, "Stop."

He did, limply.

"You disgust me."

"I know."

"You were never in Skull and Bones. Not a chance. You read about it, that's all."

"I was not. No. Yes, I'm something of a reader."

"You went to Yale?"

"U of Illinois."

"Do you know who killed your brother?"

"I do not."

Margarite abstained from believing that, or disbelieving it. Her mind was leaping forward. The Hemingway thing. It was time she got it.

"Hemingway's underage beauty. Tiina Smithback?"

Cook looked surprised. "That's what my brother claimed. He was hot for Tiina but she didn't like him. He was jealous. He blamed it on Hemingway, though I don't think anyone really believed him by that point, with their feud and all that."

Margarite measured one raw breath—in, out—and pointed at the mess of paper on the table.

"Your pelt is in here too?"

"Yes, I believe it is."

"This woman is a regular visitor?"

"A bit of one over the years, yes. Various activities."

"Julia Inkster?"

He shrugged, stared at his slippers. Margarite felt tears building behind her eyelids. Shit. She opened the sack, rolled out Julia's reel.

"What's this for?"

"Verification," he muttered. "Because I'm not in the picture with her. Could be anybody's pelt. Figured that might hang me up. Paid her for the reel. You saw that. Paid her for every goddamn thing."

Then he reached into the slew of documents again.

"No. Move your hands back."

Margarite would do this herself. She lifted one piece of paper after another and another—until at the top of one sheet she saw a woman's sunburned bare arms lashed with pale orange fly line to a tree trunk. That line came off a fly reel, gripped in one of the woman's fists. The reel, the fist: Julia's.

Margarite pulled the sheet from the pile by millimeters. Beneath a pair of dirty, reddened elbows appeared the top of Julia's head. Strands of her frizzy hair had snagged in the tree bark, the way they had sometimes snagged in Margarite's eager fingers.

Suddenly the wind released the windows. Outside the trees stopped thrashing. The jackets sleeves fell still. Margarite looked no further.

Dog winced and cussed, stabbing along the river bottom with a dead branch. Five years and not a single phone call. Now he couldn't keep up with them.

Some guy named Belcher, expecting he was Danny. Now another call.

As the ringing of Tervo's phone intensified, Dog levered to the bank. He looked for gravel where the kayak wouldn't leave a nose mark. He caught the tip of a spruce bough and pulled himself aground. He had passed the campground. Now he saw it. That was Dolf Cook's place, ahead on the left, up an eroded bank about a hundred feet high.

"Hello?"

"The fucker's gone!"

Esofea shrieked this—and Dog stowed his first thought, which was *good*. Also his second thought, a complaint involving his lack of a kayak paddle.

"And ... he hurt my cat ... and Caroline is mad at me so she told my Mummo Tiina that I left the Blind Sucker in the pickup with a strange man who wasn't Danny so I called and said you were Danny, for sure, but Caroline got a stool and looked in the bookmobile window and said she saw Danny really in there with his friend Belcher but Mummo Tiina believes me about Danny, that he's with me—she hasn't seen Danny in I don't know how long—so Caroline thinks she's been called a liar and she's sulking while my mummo's getting out the punt gun and I think she's about to blast the—"

"Punt gun?"

"I told you. It's a—never mind."

"You're at the Blind Sucker now?"

"I'm driving there. Get your business done. I'm going to swing through the campground and pick you up. You can't come back with me, but I know an empty cabin on Muscalonge Lake, so you'll jump off—"

Her voice cut out. Dog waited: only wind and river noise and the high-pitched static of his pain.

"Hello? Listen, I can't—"

"—later, then I'll—"

"A different guy called—"

"—Mummo Tiina blows Danny and Belcher into a million—"

"Hello?"

But she was gone. A gardener down in Phoenix, he meant to tell her, was expecting Tervo to deliver a tanker of water from Lake Superior. This guy had paid four bucks a gallon. Twice the price of crude oil, the guy had pointed out, furious because he thought Dog—thought Tervo—was stonewalling. Now the gardener wanted out, wanted no part of whatever Tervo was into, wanted his check back—and Dog, who had nothing to say to the guy, had finally figured out how to hang up.

Brilliant. Insane. Visionary. Criminal. No wonder Esofea loved Danny Tervo, Dog thought. And hated him.

He returned the phone to his pocket. He beached the kayak. He clawed his way up the sloughing sand bank toward Dolf Cook's cottage. By the top his wounds had cracked their peroxide husks and dissolved and bled and stung themselves up to a new level of hurt. Dog hid within a sumac thicket, did not move again until he had measured the additional burden. He disconnected his legs, his brain, his hands, checked their function, then carried his pain away like a sack of red-hot nails slung over his shoulder. The pain was on him, not in him. He could stand it a while.

The cottage was quiet. Cook's vehicle was not there. At the corner of the house Dog found a rusted axe, wedged deep in the grain of a cedar stump. He worked that loose and took it to Cook's door, which stood open.

Cook sat at his dining table, but he did not see Dog step in. The little automatic pistol Dog had given away two nights ago was there on the table, heel down, Cook trying to jam in the wrong end of the magazine. Dog silently pushed jackets aside. He reached down into the kindling box: the Pflueger reel was exactly where he had dropped it.

He kept his eyes on Cook. The old man's scalp bled thinly behind one ear. The cheek on that side was inflamed, and the eye watered. His clothing was grass stained, as if he had fallen. His hands trembled too much to discover that the magazine didn't fit because it was backwards. Dog rapped the axe against the door jamb.

"Nobody home."

"Guess who."

"Go away."

"I will in a minute. I've got the reel you tried to plant on me. Look. Now give me the print of you with that brook trout you paid me to catch. I'm going to undo your set up before I get killed for it."

Cook raised his head.

"You can take any goddamn thing you want. Help yourself."

"I'll take my pistol back too."

"The hell you will."

With a hard metallic click, the magazine inserted on its own. Cook looked up. He looked back down at the pistol. Just as he realized he could shoot it, Dog stepped in, went low in a dive and then exploded up. His head and shoulders connected. His thighs drove hard. He flipped the table over on top of Cook. He charged across the tipping underside with the axe butt ready.

But nothing moved. Cook had disappeared completely, just a soft and whimpering fulcrum beneath Dog's weight. He stepped off.

He looked at the reel in his hand. The old Pflueger held a cracked orange line—yes—but that line was un-cut, whole, fastened with a leader, wind knots and all.

He was wrong.

Cook hadn't killed his brother. Not with this anyway. Maybe the reel was a true gift. Maybe the old liar beneath the table had been reaching out for friendship.

This knowledge came over Dog like a deeper silence than the room could hold, and in poured sounds: Cook's windows rattled. Treetops whipped and swished. The garbage lid clanged at the campground. Thunder rumbled from the lake. Dog eased to the side of the window and looked out. A sheriff's deputy circled the trash box.

"Who killed your brother?"

The table slid a centimeter, rose and fell minutely. Cook was muttering.

"Come on, old man. I'm taking the fall for it. Who?"

At Dog's feet was the photo he had wanted: Cook the cheater, with his trout-for-hire. A secret fly fishing society was made up of just such men, Dog imagined. Maybe the secret was how appalling they were. It didn't matter now.

Dog nudged an upside-down table leg. He eased around a corner of the pale wood slab, watching out for Cook. If the pistol showed— with a wrist, an arm—he would chop down with the axe.

"They're on me with bear hounds. A posse. And there's a cop outside. I deserve a lot of things, but not that. How did your brother end up in my vehicle?"

The next photograph Dog retrieved from the floor was the image of a young woman lashed to a scrawny tree trunk, naked except for hip boots. She gave the camera a disturbing smile: insincerely lewd, subliminally enraged. Above her head, her wrists were lashed to the tree with a pale-pumpkin-colored fly line. That line trailed from a reel in her right hand. Not the Pflueger. A different old reel.

So maybe that line killed Kock.

"Who is this young woman?"

Silence.

"Okay, I'll keep looking."

Dog's eyes found bookshelves. The sadsack drunk was a reader, it seemed. Melville. Thackery. Jack London. And there was Hemingway's *In Our Time*, the collection with the Big Two Hearted River stories. Dog touched the book, had begun to pull it from the shelf, when he was swamped by a sudden wave of his own despair, of his exhaustion with himself, his pain and his failure to relieve it. Sadsack drunk? Who? Running for his life. Why? Those Nick Adams stories had sent him out here—to this negation of personal progress. To shameful absurdity, meaningless danger, exhaustion and pain.

The sensation was complete for a long moment, debilitating. Then Cook groaned beneath the table, bringing Dog back.

Why did he go on? How?

On the floor beneath the window he saw a business card. Bewildered with himself, Dog sidestepped toward it, holding the axe two-handed like a club. Exposed to the window in this position, he moved slowly. He let go of the axe with one hand to pick up the card. After he read it, he nudged the table again.

"Hey. Cook. Can you hear me? Can I ask you something? So which fifteen states do you own restaurants in?"

Cook moaned. The table shifted slightly and went still. Dog knocked on it with the butt of the axe. "Hello? Listen, you can come clean with me. I don't think I care anymore. But I found your business card, and it says here you sell napkins, coasters, and plastic dinnerware."

Beneath the table the pistol went off.

Dog jumped back, the axe raised.

The pistol spun out from beneath the table and Dog snatched it. Cook's blood wandered out across the floor.

A second time the garbage lid crashed down. Dog bent and crawled to the window. The sheriff's deputy had heard the shot. Her hair whipping across her face, she jogged toward Cook's. She glanced away, upriver, and now Dog heard hounds baying. Somehow, they had come all this way already. They were on him. And the deputy—had she seen him?—wouldn't she have to assume that he had just killed Cook?

Shouldn't he run?

Why?

He was running. He dropped the pistol, kicked it back beneath the table. He re-entered the wind head down. He stumbled through toppled firewood, cornered the house, kicked over a ruined old canoe. He ripped a wooden paddle from a tissue of spider silk.

A half dozen reckless strides carried him to the high sand bank over the river. He punched number one on Tervo's phone—again—until he got Esofea, heard her voice, and then he launched—getting off one word in midair before he hit the sand bank and tumbled and lost the phone into the Two Hearted.

"Don't—"

21

Sheriff Bruce Lodge had been trolling Oglivie's hospital gown across the Reed and Green Bridge, drawing Donuts Rudvig and the Heimo Kock era ever closer to the end, when dispatch asked him to stand by for a phone call.

This was a little over an hour ago. Lodge had pulled over, thinking, Phone call? Oh. Right. His onboard computer. The thing could teriyaki up a phone call, like a real phone except you touched a spot on the screen and then held nothing in your hand.

"This is Luce County Sheriff Bruce Lodge."

About the last person he would have expected was a captain from the Arizona State Police. He felt weird making listening sounds at a computer screen. *Ok. Sure. That so? Uh-huh.* A gardener from Phoenix had told law enforcement down there that Danny Tervo was selling water brought down in a tanker from Lake Superior.

Lodge said, "Wait a minute. What?"

Tervo had taken two grand from this gardener, who now had second thoughts, based on a hunch about who Tervo's other clients might be. And just a short time ago, someone answering Tervo's phone had denied knowing anything about it. The gardener wanted to file a fraud charge.

Lodge had checked his mirror. The gown was still back there. It was brown now and stuck with burrs. Lodge wondered if it retained enough scent to pull the dogs along. "Not sure I see the crime," he said. "Unless the guy never gets his water."

"We're not sure either," the police captain said. "Just wanted to put you in the loop. We're going to investigate."

"Good idea."

"Any clue up there if he can do that?"

"Do what?"

"Move water like that?"

Lodge checked his mirror again and told himself to relax. Rudvig was coming. Only problem was if it rained too soon.

"Not sure."

"One way or another, you folks are going to make a fortune off us poor suckers, that's a bet. We're in a world of hurt down here, Sheriff. Folks are stealing water, right and left. "

"I'll look into it," Lodge promised. Once he figured out how to "hang up," teriyaki style, he touched numbers on the screen and had dispatch hook him up with the Michigan DNR. He got a nice young fellow named Greg Bright. "Do me a favor?" the sheriff asked.

Now Lodge at last had reached the bridge he favored for Coho. This was 412 over the Little Two Hearted, just west of Culhane Lake. He parked the cruiser. He cupped his hands around his eyes and peered over the rail. Bingo. There went a fat silver hen, gliding upstream.

The sheriff reeled up Oglivie's gown and unhooked it. He tied the gown around the bridge rail. He changed his mind. He untied the gown, made a little sack out of it—filled that with sand and stones and tossed it into the river. It all stopped here, one way or the other. First the dogs, milling for the lost scent. Then Kock's boy Donuts Rudvig tramping down underneath this bridge, maybe with others, their eyes adjusting too late. Lodge would pick out Rudvig. Donuts could make one final threat if he wanted to. Raise his weapon if he thought that was a good idea. See where it got him.

Lodge made a quick trip home to Widgeon Creek. He changed

out of his uniform—this was civilian work—and swapped the cruiser for his old blue Ford pickup with the tackle rep stickers all over the black topper. *Mepps. Rapala. Firm Worm. Rooster Tail. Mister Twister.* There was a lot of Bruce Lodge represented in those stickers, he observed, a lot of show and not much do.

Well, then.

He returned the Luce County Sheriff's shotgun to the cruiser's trunk and loaded his own beloved twelve-gauge. He pulled Goldie's sack of Friskies out of the cupboard, cut it wide open, left it on the kitchen floor. That would tide her over.

The sheriff was back at the Little Two Hearted inside of thirty minutes. Now he parked his pickup crossways, blocking the road. The posse's ORVs would have to stop here no matter what.

His Daredevil spoon was worn to a dull, pockmarked silver. It looked more real than it ever had. Lodge retied it with a clinch knot. Getting down off the bridge and next to the river—rod in one hand, shotgun in the other—this was not a graceful thing. The big man went to his rump twice and stayed there the third time, scooting down a steep scree of riprap until he confronted a thicket of tag alder butchered by a beaver into short, sharp spears. Now he had to get up, watch himself, kick and stumble his way through, provoking a cloud of mosquitoes that had escaped the first frost.

But there was Sheriff "Bruce the Moose" Lodge eventually. Beneath a bridge again, flushing swallows from their nests and breathing in that cool, earthy air. But this no longer seemed like a stolen moment. These seemed like the sensations of a new beginning. Charlotte was dead now. Heimo Kock was dead now. A certain amount of criminal dignity had gone with him, the sheriff guessed. And Luce County had itself one hell of a good new young deputy. It was high time for things to be different.

He set the shotgun down. The dogs would appear first. Then Donuts would come down. He would be armed and he would make his lethal threat, never expecting Lodge to shoot first. Anyone of the rest of those shitbirds could have a go, too. The sheriff—the ex-sheriff—the retired sheriff—he would shoot until they stopped him.

But in the meantime, he had maybe a couple hours. One cast, two casts, three casts, four, five, six—a dozen—Coho squirting past—in the meantime—teriyaki!—hot damn!—he had a fish on.

The roads in Luce County turned to dirt and Buddha Mike had to slow down. Billy Rowntree, crashing hard, took a nap, woke up, took a nap again, woke up and stared blearily out the window until a small animal hesitated at the dusty edge and then darted in front of the Hummer. Buddha Mike swerved but he hit it.

"Damn," said Rowntree, perking up, "pop goes the weasel."

"I didn't mean to."

Rowntree gestured at the dusty windshield. "What is this shit, Buddha Mike? You got lost."

Quiet, too damn calm, he drove a minute more, steering between wheel ruts and potholes. "Was I going someplace I didn't know about?"

The postcard had fallen to the floor. Rowntree put it back where Buddha Mike could see it: a huge blue lake.

"You supposed to find somebody, ask them where Tervo is at. Who you found so far?"

"Nobody here, man. What can I do?"

"Take some turns, fool. Get busy."

Buddha Mike turned down a side road leading to the edge of an ugly swamp where they had to turn around. The Hummer caught on a bump of sand and hung there spinning.

"Get behind the wheel," Buddha Mike said.

Rowntree put his hand in his jacket pocket, touched the pistol, watched him. Buddha Mike got out and looked, slapping mosquitoes off his round face. Rowntree twisted, following him as he climbed into the back seat. The back end of the Hummer sank down. "Pull forward," he said.

Rowntree looked around the dash. Pull forward? How?

"Get behind the wheel. Put your foot on the brake. That's the gas. The brake. Pull the shifter back. Yeah. Now hit the gas."

The Hummer jerked forward, spun a ways up the road, and stalled.

Buddha Mike got out, came to the driver's door. But Rowntree had already turned the key and heard the engine start. Easy. He laughed. Damn. He said, "Other side, bitch. Rowntree's driving now."

It was real easy. He could even drive one-handed. He fished out Sinbad's phone. "Hey," he said after the tone at his mother's number, "I had to drive up to Michigan. In a Hummer. Do some business. But call me back."

Buddha Mike was looking at him.

"What?"

"You're going eighty, man."

"So?"

"You see that? Coming? That's a truck."

Sure enough here came this motherfucker high with shaggy logs and blaring his horn. Rowntree froze. Then he found the Hummer's horn and pushed it hard. The next moment was all noise and hammering shadow, air sucked out of the Hummer, a sharp metallic snap, an instant of weightlessness. Then open road again, the Hummer's side mirror spinning behind them and the truck disappearing in a whirlwind of dirt.

Laughing, Rowntree looked over. "See, Nash gonna take the charge," he said. "Don't care how big you are."

It was like Buddha Mike had never stopped looking at him.

"What?"

"Steve Nash? Phoenix Suns? That who you mean?"

"Damn right. You got something to say about that?"

Buddha Mike shrugged. "I knew a dude like you once."

"Dude like what?"

"Never mind, man."

"Dude like what, I said."

Buddha Mike looked away, silent. Rowntree felt his brain get hot. His mother wouldn't answer him. He had called like, what, six times? It was like when he called her from Oracle. Two weeks later, maybe, she might call back. It was like the jersey, like everything, the whole reason he was in there in the first place. And then, a year later, she *really* orders it.

"Little white dude," Buddha Mike said finally. "Talked all ghetto cuz he was trying to sound tough. Like he was raised by wolves or some shit. Overcompensating on every front, man, seriously."

"Man, fuck you."

"Like the black man was gonna respect him someday."

"I got my respect, man." Rowntree shook his jacket pocket.

"Yeah," said Buddha Mike. "That kind of shit. And everybody just played with that dude. Nobody said to him, this just ain't working, brother. This just ain't your game."

Rowntree said nothing, couldn't, just put his hand down in the pocket and touched the pistol and drove on, his brain feeling like it itched and burned, just like that hot Arizona morning when he was thirteen and he walked out of his fat-mouthing stepfather Darrell Rowntree's apartment with a small heavy pistol and shot the UPS driver who had returned to the apartment parking lot to sort through the boxes in the back of his truck. Rowntree had been waiting three weeks. But just like the driver had told him, not one of those boxes contained the Steve Nash '01 All-Star jersey his mother told him she had ordered five weeks ago. Then she tells the police that actually she had just *meant* to order it five weeks ago but she had forgotten. Next January that jersey shows up at Oracle. Merry Christmas.

"Fuck you, man."

"Ok," said Buddha Mike.

Rowntree drove down dirt roads, turning randomly, going as fast as he could on straightaways, until they passed a lonely trailer with a roll-away adjustable hoop on the gravel driveway, a flat orange ball in high weeds. He figured out how to stop the Hummer. He lifted the pistol from his nice gray jacket, put it in Buddha Mike's face.

"Get on the court, Buddha Mike."

"I don't play ball."

Rowntree adjusted, made a target out of one black ear, the little diamond stud in it. Buddha Mike closed his eyes. He held very still, breathed slowly. "That's somebody's driveway, man. They looking out the window."

"Get on the court."

"I got no ankles, man. Leave me alone."

"Then, you gonna die now, Buddha Mike. I don't take the kind of shit you just said. Not any more."

"The truth ain't ever shit, man."

"Get out."

"I don't do sports, man. Please."

Rowntree left the Hummer and walked around, leaned in the window and focused on the same little diamond in Buddha Mike's other ear. "You doing sports now, bitch. Get out."

Buddha Mike put his palms together. It looked like he prayed. Then he walked slowly into the driveway and stood there. Someone watched from the trailer's window—a bony white man in stubble and a hat. Rowntree put the pistol on the hood of the Hummer. He unbuttoned the coat and hung it on the side mirror. He dropped the keys into his pants pocket. Then he picked up the ball.

The stubbled man had opened his door.

"What ya think yer doin', eh? That's my grandson's ball."

Rowntree pounded the ball between his palms. He snapped off some crossover dribbles. Buddha Mike followed the ball with his eyes but didn't move. "That's all you got?" said Rowntree and went around him. He elevated, rubbed the ball in over the rim, and tore the feeble thing off on the way down. He kicked the ball at the old man in the trailer doorway.

"See?" he said when they were back in the Hummer, Buddha Mike driving again so Rowntree could watch him. "You see that, bitch?"

"I saw it, man."

"Good."

Buddha Mike drove on at about thirty-five with his mouth shut. Rowntree watched the identical trees go by. Goddamn this Michigan. Bad as the desert. Nothing nowhere. They hadn't seen one building in an hour. Phoenix, you rolled in a yellow Hummer like this, you just pulled into an area and started asking where a man was at, you got the man. At least that's how it was when Rowntree went away. Nowadays maybe you got shot, lost the Hummer.

Rowntree checked the phone. No messages. He used the calculator. A tanker held about five thousand gallons. Trucker at Shell in Green Bay said that. Five thousand times four bucks a gallon was twenty thousand. Water was free. The shit was everywhere up here. Cost of diesel three bucks a gallon on the pump in Green Bay. Figure five miles per gallon on a tanker, the trucker said, from up here to Phoenix about two thousand miles. That's four hundred gallons of diesel one way. Twelve hundred bucks. Two thousand four hundred, round trip. Add costs up to three thousand, total expenses per round trip.

Twenty thousand coming in, three thousand going out.

They did money management at Oracle. That was a seventeen grand profit. Then he had it: enough money to *buy* a car, drive it from Miami. And it was water, man. What everybody needed.

See?

So find this Tervo bitch, right? Cancel *his* contract. Take the keys to his tanker.

A loud flash in the sky got Rowntree's attention back on the moment. A boom of thunder followed. Goddamn. Lightning and thunder. He had forgot. The Hummer rolled into an open area where the forest had burned. "Look at that, Buddha Mike. Stop."

Rowntree had been over a river before, but dry and empty. The Salt ran through Phoenix once but they built whore houses over it and then malls and highways until it all disappeared and now there were memorial markers. But look at this.

It was a small river, quick and shallow and loud, brown as bong water but somehow clear at the same time. Cool air rose off it. Rowntree kicked a stick over the bridge. Before he crossed to the other rail, that stick was twirling away around a bend, as if he threw it down there.

That's when Rowntree got a glimpse of the big postcard lake.

"God*damn.*"

It was *right there*. Hell, he could hear it. Waves crashing. Gulls crying. This little river, trickling down through burnt trees, opened to a mind-blowing horizon, water touching sky. So much water Rowntree followed its pale blue body around the curve of the earth.

"Mike," he hollered, scrambling onto the roof of the Hummer. "Mike, you seeing this?"

So much water it went around the curve of the earth *in three directions*, and at the same time, right here, water flowing under the bridge, steady, not giving out, and now another crack of lightning and ok, here we go, *water falling out of the sky!*

The first drops were cold. They soaked him in seconds, and Rowntree felt good. Droplets streaked down inside the open spaces of the suit, tickling Rowntree and making him smile. Fat drops smashed his head. Bitter juice ran out of his headband, but in a few seconds more it ran clear and sweet.

Rowntree turned to the sky, flinching, shutting his eyes. Water, water, water. He felt his underclothes turn wet. He smelled minerals as the dust jumped. He smelled green from everywhere. He raised his arms. He hooked the two-tone blue Brutinis under a bar of the luggage rack. He got his balance. He opened his jacket. He unbuttoned his shirt, letting out the jersey.

"Mike! Drive!"

The Hummer began to roll and Rowntree rode up there, his arms raised like Nash at that '01 All-Star Game, hearing it.

At the next bridge, this old blue pickup blocked the road and stopped them. Rowntree jumped down and walked to the window. Nobody in it.

He blew the horn. He looked over the rail. Old white man down there, fishing.

"Yo. Yo, Homer Simpson."

Stumbling a little, making a stiff-necked turn, the old man looked up at Rowntree and hollered, "They're running! The Coho!"

Rowntree scowled down at a big silver fish, dead in the rocks.

"You blocking me, Homer."

"Oh, gosh. Sorry about that."

He came up, big monster marshmallow man, huffing and sweating.

"You ... you fellas ... lost?"

"Yeah. Danny Tervo. Friend of mine. Where's he at?"

"Well, he's got a place ... over in ... Deer Park." Old man looked at the Hummer, the Illinois plates, Mike behind the wheel. "Hey ... what's going on? You guys ... fishermen?"

"You got a map?"

"Sure do."

Rowntree looked again inside that old blue truck. It was radioed. LED dash strobes down on the passenger floor, like on some of the trucks at Oracle. Old man opened a map stamped on the top *Courtesy of the Luce County Sheriff's Department*. He was off-duty law.

"Where I find the nearest cop up here?"

Old man laughed.

Rowntree looked in the truck again. No weapons in view. He reached under his wet jacket to get hold of his own.

"You can show me where is Tervo at?"

"You betcha. You're headed the wrong way. Deer Park is right here."

This old cop put his finger on the map.

"Appreciate it," Rowntree said, tossing the map back into the pickup so it wouldn't get any wetter.

He put the pistol to the old man's head, and for a long, beautiful moment it was like he was calm, floating, seeing everything, his options, his plans, his goal, all his messages, his mother in Sinbad's house—and then he walked Homer ten yards up the road so Buddha Mike could have a good study of a man's skull when a bullet went through it.

"Get out," he told Buddha Mike. "No, leave the keys. We changing vehicles," he said, and then he pulled the trigger.

22

"Don't," Dog told her, and Esofea stuffed the brake pedal once, twice, fishtailing the Blind Sucker pickup on the wet road and fumbling her cell phone to the truck floor right at the Whiskey Creek and Pine Stump Junction—but she was already committed to the back route to the Reed and Green Campground.

Don't?

She retrieved the phone but Dog was gone and didn't answer back. Esofea felt a hard stitch in that heavy region of her heart. Don't what?

With a lunatic like her, a Pippi disciple, a Tervo casualty, a woman cut from the cloth of Mummo Tiina, the possibilities for *don't* seemed endless.

There were so many things Esofea felt she should not do, many more she never should have done, and countless things yet to arise that she should not consider doing in the future. Yet somehow the idea of *not* doing something had never occurred to her. Dog's one word—*don't*—struck her as an epiphany of such appalling significance that she could not bear witness and remain whole, in charge of a speeding pickup.

Not *What Would Pippi Do?* This seemed easy, in a way. Or at least natural.

But … What Would Pippi *Don't?*

She had no idea.

How about *don't stop?*

She drove faster, that's what, the wrongness of it gnawing at her. She made that old pickup fly over chuckholes, smashing puddles, taking a washboard corner so fast the truck slid sideways and nearly rolled before she yanked it out and sped on.

So here it was. Forget grad school. Something was wrong with Pippi. Esofea could not deny that. Something bad made Pippi act out the way she did. Injured girl, being delightful. Cut to Esofea dressing up in costumes, driving a fifty-year-old bookmobile around a county where nobody cared, going home and screwing a criminal. Exactly which *don't* ran through all this?

She couldn't see it, and in blindness she flew across Wabash Creek to the Uhl's Camp corner, where she stamped the brakes in startled desperation, nearly colliding with the ambulance from Rainbow Lodge as it churned past.

In anxious silence now, Esofea followed the ambulance toward the Reed and Green Bridge. Then in a single booming instant the entire sky fell and the windshield blurred. The ambulance glowed wet-red around the turn into the campground and Esofea's heart sank.

Dog. They caught Dog. They hurt him.

Don't come for me. That was what he meant.

But here she was. Esofea pulled into the campground. The rain came straight down, deafening against the truck roof. Beyond the last campsite, Deputy Margarite, in an orange slicker, urgently flagged the ambulance into Dolf Cook's drive.

Seen through the downpour and the trees, the scene at Cook's was only indistinct dabs of color and movement. Stalled like this, unsure and near to tears, Esofea thought: but I am all *do.* Wasn't that true? Wasn't that how she had managed to let Caroline down? And now, had she gotten someone killed? Plugged him with rock salt so that a pack of Yooper varmint hose monkeys could chase him down and bag him with the real thing?

Because she craved Danny Tervo and never heard the thousand don'ts?

Don't go out with him. Don't kiss him. Don't let him touch you there. Don't fall in love. Don't put up with that. Don't trust him. Don't take him back. Don't go off the pill. Don't abort for him. Don't try to fix him. Don't try to outsmart him. Don't listen to him. Don't make him mad. Don't believe him. Just *don't.*

She, with her fabulous actions and distractions—where was the *don't* part of her? Where was the stop, look, and listen?

Esofea watched medics blur the gaps in Dolf Cook's windows. Families had stories. Pippi's mother had died when she was a baby, and Pippi "lay in a cradle and howled so that nobody could go near her"; Pippi's father was "blown overboard in a storm and disappeared." Esofea thought, So what is my story?

She saw a camera flash inside Dolf Cook's cottage. Now came a smear of action through the front door: a gurney, a yellow body bag, red ambulance doors swinging open, a swim of bodies in the hammering rain.

Esofea left the truck and began to run. She passed the bear box and the outhouse, her feet flailing in the slick mud ruts.

But then she stopped.

Don't?

She turned, scrambled on a crash of lightning back into the pickup. She was reversing, bucking and spinning through a desperate Y-turn, when Margarite pulled her Luce County cruiser in front and blocked the way out.

And like that they sat, rain plunging between them.

Greg Bright of the Michigan Department of Natural Resources fiddled with the water export problem an hour or two, tried a few things on the web and with a calculator, then grabbed a rain skin and went out to do his regular iron ranger collection route.

In his region, collections south of Highway 28 included Big Knob, Hog Island Point, Garnet Lake, Manistique Lake, Manistique River, and Germfask. The campground at the East Branch of the Fox River was a spur, out of his way. Nothing he could do but drive up and back. Returning to Newberry then and moving north, he faced the puzzle of Natalie, Sixteen Creek, Bass Lake, Three Lakes, Soldier Lake, Pratt Lake, Pretty Lake, Perch Lake, Pike Lake, Holland Lake, Bodi Lake, and Culhane Lake, mostly small and sparsely used campgrounds where the iron rangers might be empty. But he had to cover them anyway. In the far northwest of his region, Bright was responsible for Blind Sucker 1, Blind Sucker 2, and Lake Superior. Then along the Two Hearted River, he had to collect at High Bridge, Headquarters, Two Hearted River, Reed and Green Bridge, and Mouth of the Two Hearted River.

Of course there was logic to his approach, a sequencing that minimized his mileage and routed him first down to the Lake Michigan coast and up to Andy's Seney Bar by early dinner time. Then in the evening he would do the Blind Sucker circuit. He picked up Pratt Lake, Pretty Lake, and Holland Lake, then caught the sunset on Superior at Blind Sucker 2 before heading to the Dunes Saloon in Grand Marais for microbrew and then to a sofa at his buddy Paul's place up on Masse Hill Road.

In the morning, the plan required driving all the way to Bodi Lake, out by the eastern edge of Luce County, nearly to the Crisp Point Lighthouse. He rigged his rod and dug some worms at this point. From there he would work back along the Two Hearted watershed, fishing the Little Two Hearted by Culhane Lake, then the main stem of the Two Hearted, and then finally the West Branch of the Two Hearted above High Bridge.

This was the optimal way to go about it. You studied the maps the way Greg Bright did, you had that figured out.

But the call from Sheriff Lodge had really goosed his thought process. It sounded like a hoax at first. What the sheriff said had seemed garbled, actually, but Bright had followed up with the phone numbers Lodge had given him. The captain from the Arizona State

Police had been a prick about giving out information. The gardener from Phoenix, on the other hand, had been grimly patient with the details and fiercely insistent on the name: Danny Tervo.

Bright only knew *of* the guy. Danny Tervo was the name that Esfoea, the cute girl at the library, had dropped on Bright the time he suggested a drink at The Log Jam. The name was meant to shut him down. And what the hell, it had. He was easy.

Heading north out 123, disrupting his route today, the ranger glanced at his notes. Brent Takahashi. Saseyama Japanese Garden. He had scrawled *wrst drought in recrd hist* while Takahashi explained that his entire region of the country was dying of thirst. The golf courses and ball diamonds were long dead. No one had washed a car for a month. It was illegal to serve water in a restaurant, and bottled water was up to five dollars a gallon. Politicians were at each other's throats, as were whites, blacks, and Hispanics, the wealthy and the poor, the city and the country—everything was coming apart.

Fnd rsing Bright had scribbled, letting Takahashi continue to vent about the malfeasance of Danny Tervo. The gardener had hit up the Ladies Auxiliary to the Saseyama Japanese Garden for two thousand in cash donations to reimburse his personal check, promising them the koi would live and the rhodies would be holding blooms by the end of the week. Takahashi had a receipt. What he didn't have for much longer was a job.

Bright had to speed up his wipers. The numbers had been in his head for a good while now, puzzling him and then fascinating him. There was big money in this. Huge money. Like booze in prohibition.

But was it a crime actually? Bright had Googled the Great Lakes Water Compact, glanced through it: ratified by Congress and signed by the President, it was complex and vague, straining to satisfy its multi-state and bi-national signees. It was conceptual and feel-good broad policy, Bright thought, like the Kyoto accords, lacking in the specifics necessary to identify and prosecute crimes. It wasn't really law. Was it? If it was, who was the enforcer?

Not him, Bright had decided by Eightmile Corner.

He didn't have that kind of clarity, or authority.

And that was the thing. Lacking a clear legal basis, no small bureaucratic body was likely to take it on and get entangled. Not Luce County, that was for damn sure. Probably not the Michigan Department of Natural Resources either—and definitely not through the person of yours truly, Greg Bright, here and now.

So he would modify his iron ranger collection route to check out Takahashi's story. That was all. Talk to this Danny Tervo. See if it was really happening. See how it was done. Collect a little information. Put together some observations. Kick it ahead and see what gave. Then talk it over with Paul later at the Dune Saloon—whether or not he was right in thinking that this Tervo guy was an outlaw ahead of the curve, the bootlegger of the future.

Tervo's place was an easy find. It was one of the classic old beach cottages across H58 from the big lake. Wow, Bright told himself. What a place. He had lived in the U.P. all his life and always dreamed about a place like that. It was run down, sure, looked soggy under a heavy rain like this and probably needed about a thirty grand in upgrades—but wow.

Bright parked behind a massive silver tank truck, tucked into a turnout on the lake side of the highway. Wow to that too. Tervo was an independent trucker, Sheriff Lodge had told him. With a property like this.

The DNR ranger wrestled into his rain skin and stepped out. The tanker had its own rotary transport pump. How it worked, probably, is at night Tervo ran a hose right across the beach into the surf. It wasn't but a couple hundred feet. A pump like that probably did about four hundred gallons a minute. So within a half hour, including hook-up and take-down, the tanker was full. And big old Gitche Gumee, of course, felt nothing.

Wow, wow, wow.

Bright stepped around the tanker and looked at the cottage across the highway. A blue Chevy pickup with a topper sat in the driveway. Hard to say, though, if anyone was at home, or if it was safe to knock on the door. But he had cooked up an idea of what to say, so what the hell. He practiced it once across the road: "Mr.

Tervo, I'm Greg Bright from the Michigan Department of Natural Resources. We're concerned that a sudden beach erosion might tip that tanker and we'd have a spill. Can I get a manifest, let my bosses know what's inside it?"

Wow—when it rained on the big lake you felt overwhelmed with water. You could do with a mask and gills, Bright thought, getting blown herky-jerk into a rut in Tervo's driveway. The tailpipe of the blue pickup was still steaming. So the guy was at home. He was a fisherman—all the tackle decals stuck to the topper.

"Mr. Tervo, I'm Greg Bright from the Michigan Department of Natural Resources. We're concerned that a sudden beach erosion—"

This strange-looking kid wearing a slack gray suit and an orange headband raised a pistol into his face.

"Mr. Tervo, I'm—"

The barrel surged close.

"I ain't asked you nothing yet."

"Ok ... ok ..." Bright felt his legs fail. A mammoth black kid stepped out to look.

"Where's Tervo at?" said the kid in the suit.

"I don't know."

Now the barrel touched Bright under the chin. "Don't look at the Buddha. He ain't gonna help you. Look at me. Where's Tervo at, I said."

"I don't know. I don't know the guy ... except he goes with the girl at the ... at the library."

"And where's she at?"

"She works at the library."

"Not where she works. I said where's she *at?*"

"I ... I ..." Bright had no idea. But she was chatty sometimes, talked about all the stuff she had to do for her family, the old resort they tried to keep going.

"She ... she ... she might be at her grandmother's, the Blind Sucker Resort ... right down the road here."

"Where?"

Bright saw the black kid turn away with a frown and disappear inside. This other kid moved the pistol up to align with his head. Bright lifted his arm and pointed west—just like pulling the trigger himself.

Tervo, waiting with Belcher for Esofea in the bookmobile, was startled by what sounded like a cannon shot. He bent the page over and put the book down. Belcher was already at the window, looking out at the rain-drenched Blind Sucker Resort.

Jeheezeous Christ, to quote the great scholar Tom Waits. There lay Esofea's deranged grandmother Tiina on the concrete floor of the fish-cleaning shelter, underneath what looked like Paul Bunyan's shotgun.

The little plumper, what's-her-name—Caroline—sprawled about ten yards out in the wet grass, like she had been shot-put. Now Granny Tiina was back up already. That gun had to be twelve feet long. The stock was thick as cord wood. A guy could shove his fist down the barrel.

"Shit, Belch—"

"I know. Look."

Across the yard, what used to be a kiddie basketball hoop was now a decapitated plastic stump. Behind that, the tool shack where Tervo and Esfoea used to smoke and fiddle—the near side of that was shredded chipboard now, the shack's roof slumping over a swirl of atomized motor oil and ant poison.

Belcher stammered, "Th-that, Danny, that's a punt gun, man. That sucker can take out a hundred ducks at a time."

Rarely was Tervo speechless, and to the same small degree did Belcher get excited and talk. But off went Belch while Tervo, dumb-founded, watched the old woman order the girl to drag over a picnic table. "You can thank that sucker for the extinction of the passenger pigeon, Danny. They roosted so tight together, you just lined that thing up, blew off the whole treetop, you got maybe a thousand birds with one shot. That's how it happened. Took two or three guys to hold one. For waterfowl, you know how they would do it, they would attach it to a punt, a little rowboat, and row the punt out—"

Tervo put his hand up. He reshelved the Hemingway. He had been reading aloud, soothing Belcher with the poetry of extreme manhood, as expressed in *The Old Man and the Sea*. The old Cuban was on the second night of his struggle with the marlin, towed maybe fifty miles out to sea, eating raw dolphin off the blade of his knife and jabbering to himself.

"Thanks, Belch. That's fascinating. She's gonna aim that thing at us, you think?"

"I don't know why she would," Belcher said, but he sounded uncertain.

Tervo was watching Esofea's cousin drag a picnic table backwards over slick grass and under the shelter. When the table was in place, Granny Tiina hoisted that gun like she was a Scotsman in a pole toss. She balanced the butt between her feet and tipped the barrel down, barking at the girl to adjust the line of the table. Then damned if the mad old bitch didn't swab out that barrel with what looked like mitten wadded around a musky rod. Off the cleaning table she grabbed a brass-cased shell no less than a foot long. "Let's get out," Tervo said. "Shit, Belch, I wanna shoot that thing."

"Danny—"

Tervo unlatched the bookmobile's front door and swung it open—and Belcher grabbed him by the shirt the instant before ten feet of flame erupted from the gun barrel and a blast of shot ripped the door off.

Tervo's hand was hit.

"My hand's gone, Belch!"

Belch began to moan and shake.

No, no, no—the hand was there.

Tervo showed Belcher through the whirl of smoke and rain and debris. His hand was nicked and bleeding, but it was still there.

"Don't cry, Belch. I was kidding. It's still there."

"You bastard, Danny. You sick bastard."

Tervo raised up for a peek out the windshield. Granny Tiina had already reloaded. She was lining up his very head.

They were done like ducks, Tervo thought. Unless. Yeah. No, actually, they were fine. That down there, that blue pickup down there with the stickered black topper, easing along the drive by the flooding, that was the sheriff. On the ball for once.

Bruce the Moose, Tervo informed Belcher as he dropped, was on his way up to make a save.

23

It tore the skin of Dog's back to work the paddle. The sky broke and rain drove down, stinging every wound.

A long stroke to clear a deadfall pine made him think of ripping the skin off a bullhead ... with pliers ... with Eamon... out in Concord ... on Walden Pond ... a million miles away ... and when Dog cleared that deadfall hazard there was another, another, again, the river replicating its corners, its complications, until he was delirious and stroking blindly as the kayak surged downriver.

Now that his innocence project had failed, and he would miss Eamon's birthday, confirming his reputation with M.J., where was he going? What was his purpose?

A shoal of gravel caught the kayak's bow. The hull slung broadside to the current. Then nose and tail realigned backwards and he was riding fast into a deep corner packed with flotsam that glinted black in the rain.

Dog slashed with the paddle.

He back-thrust, throwing water.

He snatched at a wind-whipped cedar bough overhead, caught it, tried to yank the kayak three-sixty. His grip held him long enough to see the wreckage of stumps and limbs ahead, the torsos of full-grown trees, sharp branches jittering over dark cavities of swirl and foam, behind it all the vast black cauldron of a northwoods swamp.

Then the bough stripped through his fingers.

Dog plunged away helplessly, full speed and stern-first—twisting, seeing it all before it happened—slamming into clubs of deadfall that cracked against his head—raking over clawed and bladed branches that tore him open—the current shoving and dragging—jamming him deeper—pinning him against a root ball that lashed its rotting tendrils across his face.

For some time Dog remained numbly defeated in that place. The rain stung him everywhere now. Blood ran down his arms and down the paddle. He turned feebly and watched it curl, then catch the current and stream away into the swamp behind him.

Faintly through the mashing rain and water he heard the bear hounds baying—and Dog thought, I was wrong. This is where the fishing has brought me. This is the healing. If he sat here, stopped struggling, let the river hold him here, they would catch him soon. They would shoot him. He could let them. He could pay for a life he had not taken, to account for the one he had. One little backward push of the paddle and he could slide into that swamp, out of the flow, and await his perfect tragic end.

He could do that if he wanted.

On that thought, Dog's head jerked up.

He peered upriver into wet forest. He scanned the towering sand banks. Or instead was *this* the point of the story?

It was. It had to be.

Hemingway wrote about choice. Not fishing, not healing: choice. Choice was the stump at the edge of the Big Two Hearted River where Hemingway sat his boy Nick Adams down—injured, remorseful, at the edge of despair and full of the impulse to vanish. If he chose to.

Dog raised his head on a shiver of guilty thrill.

And the boy said no. He said no more tragedy.

Luce County Attorney Fritz Shunk put the bar phone down. He chewed at his mustache and limped out between empty tables to the window. Surging, swirling, pounding rain. The Luce-Schoolcraft shared dispatcher could not raise Sheriff Lodge. Deputy DuCharme had made an EMT call, but was not answering. The Newberry Correctional K-9 team had lost the scent north of town and called it off because of the rain.

"Pal, I'm telling ya. Guess the date on this—"

Shunk turned to watch as Rush Smithback slapped his driver's license on the bar. "Says I was born on January 2, 1958, that's what it says. And you know when the 'real Rush' was born?"

On the stool beside him, the lovely Daryline hung onto the bar with her armpits, smoking a cigarette and staring into the big mirror, where Wheel of Fortune clues ran backwards. "Gimme a K," she slurred.

Rush yakked at a young guy reading a map while he ate a burger two stools over. This kid had asked Shunk about fly fishing guides. They had chatted a bit over the bar. Earnest kid. Bit of a Hemingway pilgrim. But Heimo Kock was dead. So the field was open. Shunk told the kid, try Uncle Ducky's in Marquette.

"Daryline, tell my friend when Limbaugh was born."

Shunk's phone rang. He hustled down and grabbed it. Consolidated dispatch said a Schoolcraft County deputy had found Lodge's cruiser at his house on Widgeon Creek. No sign of the sheriff. As for Deputy DuCharme, Rainbow Lodge EMT had gone to a cottage up on the Two Hearted, near the Reed and Green Campground. An elderly gentleman had been fatally shot and his body transported to Munising. Deputy DuCharme was at the Reed and Green, apparently, but not answering. Shunk, getting worried, said thank you.

Daryline Smithback droned, "Limbaugh was born in '51. Cape Girardeau, Missouri. How'd he supposed ta copy the name of a seven-year-old a thousand miles away? Think about it. Such bullshit. Let's go home, Rushy. Or else we gotta call Caroline."

Her husband had squared up on the fly fisherman. He loomed until the kid looked up from his map.

"You telling me my momma got my name from a seven-year-old fat kid in Missouri? I mean, I love the man, but screw that. Rush is *my* name. I ain't copied nobody. Lady, call the daughter, damn it. I ain't going nowhere." Shunk watched Smithback find himself suddenly amused. "I came in town to drag *her* home, now *I'm* the one." He glanced at Shunk. "Lord, what a team. Frizty! Coupla beers!"

Shunk came down, twisting a rag in his fists. "Who's driving?"

Rush Smithback turned to his wife. "Bend over, hon, I'll drive ya home." He roared with laughter.

"Promises, promises." Daryline got off her stool. "God, it's coming down out there. Makes me gotta pee."

She couldn't straighten up, Shunk observed. She struggled like a sick little duck toward the restrooms.

"You're both driving? Is that it?"

"I believe that is the case," Rush Smithback said. "I also believe that I will have another brewski."

Smithback pushed his empty to the rail. Shunk shook the drips out, tossed it in the recycle barrel. He set up another MGD long neck but left the cap on. Smithback searched his pockets for money.

"Where'd you two stop before this?" Shunk asked.

"White Pines Hotel. See, I came down from the Blind Sucker to get Daryline but she wouldn't leave. So I hadda spend about three hours—"

"Yeah," Shunk said. "I heard that."

"Don't ya got an opener?"

"Of course I do."

Shunk had figured out what to do. Bad drunks on wet roads. No law enforcement available. There were murders you could prevent.

"Girls piss fast," Smithback commented as his wife returned. "You ever notice that, Fritzy?"

He eased off his stool like a ninety-year-old man. He helped Daryline onto hers. He winced and cussed himself back into position.

"We both got bad backs," he advised Shunk.

"I'm calling Caroline," Daryline said.

"You do that, lady. Tell her put in a couple Tombstones. Hey, Fritzy, I gotta bite the cap off this brewski or what?"

Shunk set up a second unopened bottle, this one in front of Daryline. She grabbed it like Shunk had seen people grab poles on a downtown Detroit bus. He was thinking: Louise could cover the bar. All this rain, they shouldn't be too busy. Up to the Blind Sucker and back shouldn't take him more than an hour.

"Those beers are on the house," he told the Smithbacks, "but only if you let me drive you home."

No more tragedy.

He stowed the paddle and levered his body out of the kayak. He stretched and splashed and crawled fast across a sinking mat of flotsam, pulling the boat after him. Slick branches gave the hand-hold he needed to worm up into the tangle. There he rested. Then he dropped the kayak into the mess of sticks and held onto its bow rope, dragging the plastic shell, jerking it after himself, tightroping a shivering log along the swamp edge until the tip was too small to hold him.

He tied off the rope and pulled the kayak toward him ... then up onto the log with him ... next out in front of him. Then he flung it toward the river. The current caught the kayak. The rope shot tight. The tip of the log disappeared from under Dog's feet and down he crashed into the snarl of water and wood.

But he was hollering. Cussing and hollering cusses and laughing. Hanging on and bleeding. Hauling himself back up. Stumbling and thrashing to a spot where he could jump clear of deadly timber. He splashed and rolled and snagged the kayak by its seat hole as he coursed past it.

Hell, just choose. Nobody else was in this. He was alone and the choice was his.

Enough pain, struggle, tragedy.

Enough.

Because it was enough.

He hauled in. He worked the paddle up between his legs. He untied the bow rope and— *Go, Dog, go.*

Stay in the river was how he figured to do it. Stay in the river and the next idea would come—and then a plan came in the dark shape of a Coho salmon slipping upstream over rippled sand.

Dog paused to watch the fish disappear. In its place arrived another. As he floated into the next deep corner, Dog adjusted his eyes. The river's sand depths were spotted with shifting black shapes. The Coho were running. From the lake. The big wide lake. That was it. The lake. He could go all the way. He could paddle out far from shore and travel freely back to the Blind Sucker.

Dog trimmed his stroke and focused. The Coho showed him lines. He saw the river in layers. The way snags split the current triggered directional decisions twenty strokes ahead. Cut left. Fade right. Dig forward. He was moving, keeping the kayak on a fast, high skim.

In a mile or so, the Coho massed more densely in the deep holes. Ahead, a fat hen left the depths and shot a gravel spit through shallow water. Dog watched. He could dart the kayak the same way, keep his speed. At the next quiet water he paused his stroke and listened. He could not hear hounds anymore. Only rain and wind.

Soon he heard surf over a high, pale dune. Against a river now sluggish with counter-current, Dog paddled harder. For a half mile, the river ran east, parallel, not reaching the lake. Dog was tempted: bail, ditch now, hike over the dune—but if the dogs came this far, that is how they would catch him. They would smell him on land again. They would know where he went.

Around a bend appeared a sodden orange tent. Then pop-up trailers, massive new RVs, and more tents and screened canopies. Campers huddled against the storm. A few hollered greetings at Dog. He kept his fugitive head down. This was the Mouth of the Two Hearted. Now he dug against a full lake wind. Ahead, beyond a timbered foot bridge, the river narrowed. The current surged across a bed of small round stones. A gush of speed and here, finally, was the lake itself, huge and wild and lovely.

But his trackers were out there already—a large skiff about a hundred yards off shore and maybe a quarter mile east, patrolling the beach.

Dog rolled out of the kayak into fast, waist-deep water. He went to his knees and let the kayak go. He couldn't watch it. The current shoved him forward, pushed his face under. He tried to brake with the paddle and had it ripped from his hands. Then the river roared over shallow gravel, spinning him into water so cold his lungs stopped.

When he recovered, Dog was waist-deep again. He crouched lower, forcing his shoulders under, fighting to hold steady and breathe in the clash of currents. He kept his eyes and nose above the surface and looked east, waiting, measuring, shivering—they were coming his way.

The kayak had to be visible from their distance. But it was empty. The red boat twirled out on the warmer river current until a swarm of milling Coho broke its drift and lake waves began to push it back toward shore. The search skiff was coming fast, seeing the kayak now, but they would have to guess. He could have bailed a mile upstream for all they knew. He could have drowned somewhere. They would have to guess—and he would have to gamble.

In slow motion, Dog breaststroked toward the scrum of Coho. Don't spook—come on, stay together. I'm not a threat. Don't spook.

A few fish bolted at Dog's approach. These startled others, who startled a few more. But it was spawning time. Instinct was strong and they were not a school, not coordinated. Dog slipped in among them. When he became still, they massed and slapped as if he hadn't joined them at all.

In this heavy chop of storm and fish, Dog hung hidden. The cold water stunned his thinking and stung his skin. Tails dragged and snapped across his face. Flanks and noses bumped and shoved. Underneath, his legs worked hard. He couldn't tread water forever. He wouldn't last ten minutes.

But here came the skiff. Dog heard it accelerating. He bobbed slowly, stealing mouthfuls of air, nervous salmon squirting across the top of his head.

The boat was straight out now, slowing. But they couldn't know which way he went—or whether he was somewhere upstream with the hounds after him. They couldn't know. Their eyes were off the water, searching inland. Their brains said man running. The last place they would expect him was right beneath them, among the Coho, in the mouth of the river.

He kept his face turned away. He bobbed deep and slow. Lecherous salmon brawled over him, swatting water down his throat. Then the skiff was accelerating along the west beach, three men in camo gear with scoped rifles and beer cans, no one looking back.

Dog waited. Waited. Then he sloshed onto the pebbled beach and stumped on numb legs in the direction the skiff had come from, away from the Blind Sucker. His gait was only functional, but his back pain had eased in the frigid water. He followed the beach until the mouth of the Two Hearted River was out of sight.

About there, a tea-colored creek flowed from a brushy bog. The bottom looked solid. Pines grew a short distance in, suggesting high ground nearby. The creek ran full with rain but clean.

Dog took it.

Inland he would find a way to move. He would steal something, he decided after a half hour slogging against current and brush— something such as the yellow Hummer parked beyond a bridge ahead.

He looked for the Hummer's fisherman. He whistled and called. He pushed through the deep water beneath the bridge. He passed a freshly dead Coho in the rocks. He waded on until brush closed the upstream passage.

Something was wrong. He could feel it.

No fisherman. Only Coho, spooking around his clumsy legs.

As he staggered back to the bridge, Dog's exhausted heart accelerated one last time. Could this be one of his hunters? He stopped. He eased his feet around on the stream bottom, eased his hips and shoulders around, brought his head around. Looked one way. The other. He took an audible inhale, expecting his bullet to the back.

But no. Only tiny thuds of rain.

He climbed over the dead Coho, through the riprap up to the bridge.

Keys hung from the Hummer's ignition, and on the driver's side, where Dog arrived in cautious strides, he found a long rut, puddled with rain and blood—

Sprawled across the puddle near the tailpipe was a large old man with the back of his head blown off.

24

Margarite watched Esofea grip the steering wheel, going nowhere.

"He didn't do it."

"Oglivie didn't?"

"Right."

Rain battered in a deafening rhythm against the roof of the Blind Sucker pickup. The truck's wipers slapped frantically. Esofea raised her voice. She was confessing. It looked so painful, like she was yanking loose a main thread in her own existence.

"As far as I know, he never even met Danny."

She put her head against the wheel. As if she smelled something there, someone's hands, she jerked back, looking repulsed and then losing herself to hard, choking tears. "Oh, God. I don't know why I—"

A jammed wing window on the passenger side dripped onto Margarite's knee until the gray fabric of her uniform turned black. She had been quiet long enough. Any more silence became her own deception.

"The one they took away in the bag? That wasn't Oglivie."

Esofea seemed to hear this with her whole body. She raised a flushed and tear-stained face.

"Not him? Not—?"

"That was Dolf Cook. He didn't do it either. But he shot himself."

"Why?" blurted Esofea, and she cried while Margarite numbly watched the drip strike her knee. Because the old man had wanted to be loved? By his brother? By Julia? By himself? Probably after a lifetime of trying to be appreciated by the wrong people, the poor fool had given up.

"Whenever somebody does that to themselves," Margarite admitted at last, "a part of me always knows why. I feel right where it comes from, inside myself. Don't you?"

She couldn't tell if Esofea meant to agree. This was a woman who could cry hard enough to hurt herself. Margarite had known a lot of women, too many, and the ones who cried like this were sometimes the strong ones. They were sometimes the ones who could *stop* crying—and move on.

"Later, I'll need to arrest you."

Esofea attempted to look at Margarite as she explained. "You told me Oglivie met Danny and Danny put him up to killing Kock. That wasn't true, and I think you knew it when you said it. In terms of sentencing, that could work out to anything from picking up highway trash to a year in prison. But I hadn't pursued your lie yet. I can tell a judge I never took you seriously so it didn't interfere with my investigation, and that will help. It will help too if you tell me where Oglivie is."

"I don't know."

"Tell me. He's in danger."

"I don't know."

Margarite stared down the campground road where the ambulance had disappeared with Cook's body. "This feels like the scene I read where the policemen chase Pippi around the house and up onto Pippi's roof and they get stuck up there until she helps them down. Esofea—don't play."

"I'm not playing."

Esofea moved in awkward bursts. She stopped her wipers and turned her headlights off. She rubbed her palms on her jeans.

"I was supposed to pick him up here. He thought Cook did it and he could get the evidence, a reel with some line cut off—and by the way, Danny didn't do it either. The fucker was out of town. God, how much I hate him."

Margarite sat, glumly lost in thought. Not Julia. Not Tervo. She and Esofea had both used the death of Heimo Kock to reach for some apocalyptic healing of wounded hearts. Now here they sat, returned to pain and ruins, darkness falling. They belonged in this place, hearts torn open, confidence drained away. This is where Margarite's thoughts went. This was how people like them were made. They couldn't help it.

She picked up Esofea's hand. She wrapped hers around it. She placed the pair of hands on the seat between them.

"You talk about your grandmother and your aunt and uncle. And your little cousin Caroline. Even your lost baby. Never your parents."

"I don't have parents."

"I didn't think so."

"I never have. I took care of myself. So there's nothing to talk about."

"Are you sure?" Margarite squeezed her hand. "Maybe you'll find something while you talk. Did you ever try that?"

Slowly, Esofea calmed herself. Margarite waited, watching rain explode against the windshield. Funny—Kock and Cook were dead, a killer was at large, Oglivie was lost out there—but all she cared about, right now, was hearing her friend.

"When my Granny Tiina was sixteen she got knocked up by a cabin guest."

Esofea sniffled, wiped her eyes with the back of her hand. Her voice sounded hoarse but determined.

"She never said who, except she always told people it was not Hemingway—which I always thought was her funny way of getting attention, you know, of having a brush with greatness, only not. Or else she was just lying and she had slept with him. Anyway, out of that came my mom, who did more or less the same thing, I guess …"

She glanced at Margarite, who nodded. "You know, got knocked up by a mystery man, probably a fisherman or hunter at the lodge—she never said who. Lack of sexual common sense is a trademark of the Smithback female, along with gunplay. Right? You know that, after dealing with me. So that's how I came about. Then when I was around two, my mother took off with a boyfriend to Detroit for a Fleetwood Mac concert and we never heard from her again. My mummo raised me. Sort of, as you can see."

"Fleetwood Mac. And *not* Hemingway. That's funny," Margarite said, and then—the story—all those variables out there—her path opened up. She saw a clear line from the famous author to Heimo Kock floating in the Two Hearted River.

"What do you know about Hemingway taking casting lessons at the Blind Sucker? Dolf Cook told me, so I can't count on it. Did he come here back in the fifties? And did Hemingway and Heimo Kock hate each other?"

Esofea's eyes darted over Margarite's face and down to their joined fingers. "Before my time," she said, and withdrew her hand. She began to rub her palms on her jeans again.

"Then," Margarite said, "I think I need to visit the resort and talk to your grandmother."

"Danny's there."

"You ride with me," Margarite said. "I can handle Danny."

Boom!—and the punt gun took out the bookmobile's window.

But Tervo held in his mind the image of Lodge's black-topped blue pickup creeping along the rutted gravel down by the flooding. This would all work out fine in a few minutes. Bruce the Moose would interrupt. He would buffer. He would corral the craziness of the Smithback girls.

Tervo sat back in the litter of glass and retrieved *The Old Man and the Sea*. He paged ahead. One thing that irked him about the story—irked and yet fascinated him—was the cheap-shot ending. Hemingway played it as if the old Cuban had never thought of sharks until that final moment. Like the old man knew the sea so well that he could lower a herring on a hand line and parse out a thousand-pound marlin, knew the sea so well he could see a hurricane coming five days ahead, so well he could stay alive by meat-fishing one-handed in the dark, in a near-coma, while being towed by the marlin, and know ahead of time which fish would end up on his hook and how it would taste—and yet after he catches the marlin, as he sails across the Gulf Stream, a bleeding carcass the size of a Ford Escort lashed to his gunnels, it never occurs to the brilliant old pedo that he will attract sharks. No. This obvious fatal complication does not present itself until Hemingway is ready, until the story is ready, and *then* the author places the long-overdue thought inside the señor's head, ending the tale right there.

It was a deliciously cheap out, Tervo thought, wholly artificial stuff, dressed up as brutal reality. It required a charmed and gullible reader—and it worked, obviously, to the tune of a Pulitzer and a Nobel Prize. All this told Tervo a lot about people, and about Hemingway, and it made him a fan.

"Belch," he said, sucking blood from the outside meat of his palm, "I'm sorry, man. I thought she hit me worse than that, I'm serious. I thought she blew my hand clean off. I wasn't effing with you."

Belcher was so upset he was ruminating for grains of Skoal around his mouth, ejecting them off the tip of his tongue with ferociously tiny outbursts of air.

"You're always fucking with me, Danny. Especially when you say you're not fucking with me. And now you're gonna get me killed."

"Ah, Belch," Tervo said, "dark words. Very dark. Turn the light on, my brother."

He beckoned Belcher toward the empty windshield. The rain had nearly stopped. Esofea's insane genetic source material was knocking another shell into her punt gun.

"Look down there."

"That's Sheriff Lodge's truck."

"Right. So everything's jake, is it not?"

"But that's not Lodge," Belcher said.

Tervo couldn't see anything more detailed than a truck, but Belcher's eyesight was legendary. He could probably read the decals on the topper.

"Who is it?"

"At the wheel it's a big black guy in a White Sox hat," Belcher said, "with a pistol to his head. Passenger seat, with the pistol, little greasy-haired guy in a gray suit ... and an orange headband."

Stunned, all Tervo could think for a good while was *how?*

How in the hell had she done this to him?

Buddha Mike's head stayed still. As far as Rowntree could tell, he was watching water falling on top of water on the lake beyond the truck's windows. "I ain't driving up there just to see you shoot more people," he said.

"At this point in time," Billy Rowntree said, "I ain't shot nobody, Mike, unless you tell somebody I did."

"Then how'd we get that Hummer?" Buddha Mike said. "And this pickup? I don't see no car lots. Man, a lot of shit just doesn't occur to you, does it?"

"By the time it occurs to me, I already done it," Rowntree said. "I'm ahead." He was feeling high, words just jumping into his mouth. "Man, I bought my momma a car already, while we been sitting here."

"Yeah, sure."

"Some kind of Oldsmobile or something. Red."

"Ok, man."

Rowntree looked across this lake where it curved and then narrowed toward some distant trees. He wiped fog off the window on his side. "You see that green shit out there on that water?"

"That's called lily pads."

"You some kind of plant scientist, Buddha Mike? Damn. Maybe I can use you back in Phoenix."

"Everybody knows lily pads. Except you. Seems like you don't know nothing."

Rowntree wiped off fog again.

"I could run across the top of that shit. Because I don't stop to think what's gonna happen. That's how I roll. That's how I *fly*, Mike."

Very slowly, Buddha Mike reached out and switched the wipers off. He turned his head so the pistol barrel was right at his chin. He looked at Rowntree through his fat-pinched eyes.

"That's how you fly?"

"That is how I fly."

"You the dumbest motherfucker I ever met in my life," Buddha Mike said. Very slowly, he shifted in the seat, squaring on Rowntree.

Rowntree moved the pistol up between Buddha Mike's eyes. "Here we go, Mike," he said. "Game on."

But on a knock on Buddha Mike's side interrupted this.

A woman's face, a cop in a gray uniform, telling him to roll it down.

"You gentlemen mind stepping out of the vehicle?"

From the bookmobile window, Tervo watched Esofea's lesbo deputy friend Margarite try to handle the situation without backup. That was Esofea, left behind in the cruiser.

Out the driver's side came the big black kid, moving real slow, raising big pale palms to show he had nothing going on, he just happened to be driving a pickup that belonged to the Luce County Sheriff. Don't know how that happened. Is there a problem, Officer?

Tervo tossed the Hemingway aside. Hell, yes, there was a problem. The dude still inside with a pistol was the problem. Billy Rowntree.

"Belch, we got issues."

Billy Rowntree came out the passenger side looking like somebody had pissed on a perfume commercial for midgets who dug orange headbands. He concealed that pistol behind his saggy pants as he came around the tail end of Lodge's pickup.

Esofea blew the horn of the cruiser too late.

Rowntree drew the pistol around and fired a shot that sounded like a cough in the wet air. Tervo waited for the deputy to drop—he had to know what he was dealing with, or without—and she did go down, very slowly. She bent forward to an unbalanced angle like she was bowing to a Japanese prime minister and then she sat back with a hard splat into a puddle on the road.

So she had a vest on. Sensible lesbian. It looked like she also knew to lie back and play dead until her faculties returned.

Now Tervo had to move before Esofea did. You could not expect good judgment from a girl who believed her father was King of the Cannibals, who fantasized about eating twenty-six pounds of candy and twirling robbers on her fingertips. Esofea might not have the sense to lock the doors and stay in the cruiser.

These thoughts propelled Danny out the shattered bookmobile door and beneath a blast from Granny Tiina's punt gun.

He felt a wicked stinging in a few places along his left side, but that was about it. And, glancing back, he saw good old Belch swarm right out behind him, heading straight down the line of that massive gun barrel toward the genetic base of Esofea's insanity. Cousin Caroline, drenched and screaming, hurled herself at Belcher and stuck like a tick, but Belch kept on trucking.

Tervo cut left, skidded, plunged inside the Blind Sucker Lodge and rushed through to the deck door, sliding it open and stepping out to a view of the scene below at the flooding. At the rail, he raised both arms into the rain.

"Billy!"

The gale-swept downslope between them defeated Tervo's effort. Rain, wind, water, everywhere you turned.

"Billy Rowntree!"

Now the kid in the sopping gray suit and the orange headband turned toward the resort buildings. It was him for sure.

"Billy!" Tervo bellowed. "Peace, my brother! Welcome!"

Conrad Belcher hadn't ever held a punt gun. In fact, he couldn't hold it. Not like a normal shotgun. The thing was ten feet long and at least fifty pounds. The butt was the thick shape of a skinned-out bear hock. The barrel could shoot tennis balls.

Belcher's hands trembled, and not because the nutty old Smithback lady had nearly decorated the trees with a thousand pieces of his dense and hairy body.

Belcher's own death had never occurred to him within the context of fear. Nor had Heimo Kock ever successfully frightened him. He guided for himself, his way. He had killed a thousand animals, each one efficiently and with its dignity intact. On dozens of occasions, he had stripped firearms from the hands of clients who were about to do otherwise, and he had driven these men back to their and bed-and-breakfasts and thrown their shit out on the pavement and kept the deposit. He would receive death as he had given it, Belcher believed—Kool-Aid and pizza would be fine—and he didn't worry.

No, his hands trembled because this was a punt gun, the stuff of hunting history and legend.

Only a few of these still existed in the world. Belcher had looked it up. Once at the Newberry Library, with Esofea's help to get started, he had gone out on eBay and Craigslist and failed to find a single intact punt gun for sale in the entire U.S.—only shells, or stocks, a few ram rods for the early black-powder models, never one whole and functional like this.

Now Belcher wondered, was there a punt at the resort somewhere too, a little wooden deadrise skiff with a barrel bracket on the bow, breech ropes, knee-marks from shooters skidding backwards when the big gun went off?

But ok—one thing at a time, the hunter's creed—Belcher took a breath and brought his thoughts back around. The heavy blond girl with the green Esofea eyes had stopped screaming, but now she started in again. The grandmother was tearing at Belcher's hands, trying to load in the eight-bore brass cartridge he had knocked from the breech.

Belch, we got issues, Danny had said. Then he had surprised the hell out of Belcher by doing something.

Now the girl and the grandmother began pointing together toward a man at the tree line of the resort grounds. Belcher wiped rain from his eyes and clarified the blur. Not a problem. The guy was shoeless and unarmed.

Still, Belcher studied patiently, as if the guy were an upwind whitetail. About six-two and wiry-thin, forty years plus a couple. Skin weathered the way fishermen's skin could get, a mask of white around the eyes from sunglasses. Soaking wet and dressed in clothes that didn't fit the time or the body. Behind him were segments of bright yellow—a vehicle parked back beyond the tree line. This had to be the fugitive, the guy who put an end to Heimo Kock.

Good deal.

Belcher pried the cartridge from the old woman's hands. He pushed the panicked girl behind him. He called across the wet yard, "We got issues, man. Come on. I need somebody under the barrel of this gun."

His mind stripped bare but for the image of the murdered old man, Dog had one concern.

"Where is Esofea?"

"She's in trouble. Get under this thing. Let's go."

The two other Smithback women—the grandmother, the cousin—gaped at Dog.

"I didn't kill anybody," he promised them.

"Yet," said the big man with the punt gun.

That's what it had to be—a punt gun—this colossal firearm that Dog held by a barrel bigger around than the exhaust pipe that whanged off the Cruise Master and down a cliff in southern Utah.

"Hey. You with me? You're bleeding through your shirt."

"Let's go."

Dog balanced the stock of the punt gun on his shoulder and followed the big man into a stand of hardwoods behind the tool sheds and the bookmobile. Concealed in this grove was the high ground of a prehistoric sand dune. Whoever this guy was, Dog thought, he knew where and how to walk. High and clear, soft and straight.

In stride, over his shoulder, he low-voiced a question for Dog: "These guys shot one officer right in front of us. So I wonder where the sheriff is at, since they're driving his truck. You got any idea?"

"That could be him over by Culhane Lake with his brains blown out."

"About what I figured."

They made ground south toward the flooding and the big lake. Soon Dog heard voices to his right, where the gravel drive climbed to the main cabin and office. Actually two voices. One of them—pretty sure—was the guy from Tervo's phone, the genius with the subject-verb-motherfucker grammatical habits. The other voice, on the move, moving parallel with the punt gun, called out, "Brother, put your weapon down. The only tool you need is kindness."

Tervo. The boyfriend.

"I'll put my motherfucking weapon down your motherfucking kindness, motherfucking bitch."

Wrong about the grammar, Dog thought as the long barrel jerked him off stride and down the far side of the dune. The big man mashed through heavy brush. Dog followed. Diagram a sentence like that, you had to take a shower afterward.

"Hey. Stay with me. You all right?"

"Not really."

"So here we go."

As they came up on an old wood-frame structure, Dog received a game-stalker's open-mouthed whisper. "Here's the boathouse. The punt's inside. I hope. Put it down."

With a sweep of the long gun, they folded over grass that grew on the muddy bank of the flooding. They set the weapon on that. On a blast of buck scent and body odor, the big man came right up in Dog's face.

"We go in together and carry the punt out and back over here. Only Danny might see us as far as I can tell. Esofea's still inside the deputy's car and the deputy is lying down in the road. She's hit but I think she's alive. The two guys we gotta watch out for are facing away." He hesitated. "Ready?"

They flattened against the front of the boathouse and slipped through the open door. In the dark and musty interior, Dog's escort stopped. "By the way, I'm Belcher."

The handshake was a bone-crusher. "Dog."

Belcher's wide pupils dialed in. "That's it. That's the punt gun's punt."

Dog took the bow as they lifted a flat wooden rowboat. Outside, rain spotted the weathered transom panel in Dog's grip and quickly turned it black, raising shadows of ancient duck blood.

"Belcher!"

Tervo hollered this suddenly, though they were well out of sight.

"Shit," Belcher muttered.

"Belch, come on down here!"

He was yelling up toward the cabins. Not toward the boathouse. Assorted hideous constructions from the criminal got swept up in a mighty lake gust that cleared the dune behind the flooding and flung rain into Dog's face.

"Listen." Belcher startled him. "I better get up there so I can answer Danny and come down. I don't, them guys are gonna head up where the old lady and the kid are. And that ain't the safest way I see this playing out."

He positioned the punt gun in the punt. He clamped the barrel in a wooden stockade anchored to the gunnels toward the front. "This thing'll float I guess." He roped the breech to an opposing pair of forged shackles at the midpoint, like he was anchoring a canon. "It's loaded," he mentioned before he turned and began to sprint uphill toward the cabins: sprinted like a bear, haunchy and low and fast, startling Dog in some deep place—and awakening him.

There were no oars.

The first observation of an alert mind.

There were small paddles fixed to crank handles, attached to the punt in the adipose position, toward the stern. Had to be that you hung your arms over the sides and cranked each handle, rotating the paddles.

There was no seat either.

Puzzling, Dog pushed the boat in. He waded beside it. When he stepped aboard he sat down anyway, seat or not. In this way— reaching emptily—he discovered that a punt gun pilot had to lie face down, to create the wingspan to reach the cranks. Now it all came together. Flat and quiet. Low and slow. Stealth.

Eager now, Dog navigated into the choppy gray water and turned against the lake wind. Broadside against the shoving air, the punt skidded toward shore.

That wouldn't do.

Dog backpaddled, sizing up the situation. There were two vehicles, a dark-blue Chevy pickup with a stickered-over black plastic topper, and a Luce County Sheriff's cruiser. The pickup appeared empty. Esofea's head showed inside the cruiser, front passenger seat. She was turned away from Dog, low as she could go and still see where the action was.

To see what she saw, Dog had to tack to stern and then forward with the wind for a net gain to the east. Now he had a thirty-foot window between the vehicles. The two young men with their backs to him—little one in a gray suit and orange headband, big one in a wet white cap—were the targets. The little one talked with jabs of a hand gun. Tervo, facing Dog, spoke back. Dog paused on him a moment. Esofea's man looked like Yooper Jesus, tall and loose, magnificently wet, spreading his arms and smiling.

Dog treaded, adjusting. A little more movement showed him Belcher, arriving out of breath with his hands up. Then the female deputy from Cook's place—she sat up in a puddle, her head slumped into her chest.

If he shot right now, Dog thought, he would hit them all.

Then Belcher made eye contact. Staring at Dog, he slowly tipped his head toward the east. *That way.*

Dog backed up farther. He let a new gust return him on a slightly flatter line. As Dog drifted closer, Tervo, Belcher, and the deputy disappeared behind the sheriff's cruiser. He couldn't hit them now if he tried. The cruiser would take any stray shot. Esofea twisted to see him, then lowered herself out of view.

Dog moved his face directly over the barrel. He fussed with his crank pedals, lining up. Suddenly from behind the cruiser Belcher hollered, "Shoot the damn thing!" and the guy in the gray suit twisted and Dog heaved on the trigger.

The blast singed his nostrils and snapped his head back and stunned his eardrums into a shrill flat silence. Recoil drove the punt twenty feet backwards into the wind. Dog could see no person left standing as he spun broadside and drifted out of control over the middle of the flooding, into a current.

It was baying hounds, the nagging sound drifting to him from the south above the cabins, that broke the seal on Dog's ears. As the spinning punt came around, he heard Belcher hollering at him and saw flashes of that saggy gray suit streaking between trees beyond the boathouse, away from the Blind Sucker.

25

"I'm Mike," the enormous black kid told Deputy Margarite DuCharme, "and I haven't done nothing but pick that psycho up at O'Hare Airport early this morning. He's killed three people and injured you since then. I'm surprised I'm still standing here, you wanna know the truth."

"How in God's name," Belcher ranted, "can you miss a person with a punt gun?"

"It's ok," Margarite told him. "It's good he missed."

Her inventory of body parts concluded, she had finally gotten to her feet to take back some authority. She had been shot somewhere—that was all she knew at first. Now she felt her lungs un-sticking and her breath leaking back in. She had taken it square in the chest, like a sledgehammer as hard as you could swing it. Knocked her down, knocked the wind out of her, knocked her heart out of rhythm—but that seemed to be it, aside from a wet ass and a numb left boob. She was fine. Her vest was a hero.

"He didn't even hit one of the vehicles!" Belcher was making himself hoarse. "He must have shot over the whole damn scene."

"Easy, Belch," Tervo said. "We didn't need a bloodbath."

Actually, Margarite wasn't ready to stand yet. She sat back down in her puddle.

"That's Rudvig, I'm sure," she wheezed, hearing dogs at the cabins. "I don't know why he's here, but we'll redirect him." She nodded toward Oglivie, churning paddles beyond the boathouse, the boat spinning out of control. "It's only about two feet deep out there. Somebody want to go help him get in?"

Esofea moved on it. Danny Tervo followed her. "Baby?"

She turned halfway, not quite looking at him.

"The power of love is infinite, baby. I saved you."

"Fuck you, Danny."

She walked on toward the whirling punt.

"*He* did."

Rudvig had left associates on the trail of Dog and split off to look for Tervo—something about a tipster's call to the Superior Outfitters home office, blaming Tervo for Kock's murder—but it was a simple matter of redirection, giving the man's ridgebacks a sniff of the seat in Lodge's pickup, a taste of some napkins Mike said the kid with the pistol and the headband had dried his face with, and then letting them run. Rudvig said he had a visual too and he expressed no doubts. His little fleet of ORVs barreled after the dogs.

With Mike's help, Belcher lifted Margarite onto the back seat of the cruiser. "A punt gun—are you shitting me?—a punt gun could take out a thousand passenger pigeons at a time! And he hit nothing! From less than a hundred feet away!"

Mike said, "Well, I sure am glad he missed, you know?" and Belcher finally shut up.

Fritz Shunk had arrived with Esofea's Uncle Rush and Aunt Daryline. He left them in his Subaru and drove Margarite's cruiser up and around the bookmobile to the door of the resort's lodge and office. A silent Danny Tervo manned the Subaru, delivered a matching set of drunks up the hill. Margarite, wincing with each breath, got more or less comfortable on a smelly couch in the lobby, beneath the musty snout of a bull moose. There was a difference between pain and injury, she had always assumed. You weren't really hurt if you could keep thinking and moving. Only injury stopped a person. But maybe she would rethink that. Later.

"You're the acting sheriff," Shunk told her. "Until we confirm what happened to Bruce."

"I figured as much."

"I ordered two ambulances."

"Good."

They shared a look at Oglivie. Their former fugitive sprawled face down on the floor across the lobby, Esofea stroking the back of his head. He was breathing. Just resting, Margarite hoped. Then, spacing out, gazing blankly beyond the reception desk, she saw what she should have looked for all along.

Above and behind the desk, mounted like a trophy, was a fiber-glass fly rod with push-button reel attached.

"Is that the one Hemingway used here?"

"Yes," said Esfoea.

"It's always been displayed right there?"

"Yes."

Margarite rose and hunched across the floor. She reached up through the incredible stiffness of her chest, took the rig down and laid it on the counter. She switched on a deer-antler desk lamp.

The ancient line came stubbornly off the reel: faintly orange, cracked with age—and sliced clean. She held it under the lamp. The cut was back toward the belly of the line, above the nail knot and the leader—and those parts, Margarite was certain now, were in a plastic bag in the evidence locker, back in Newberry. She found scissors in the drawer immediately below. This was the line that killed Heimo Kock.

"Esfoea? Can you get Caroline and your grandmother?"

Esofea stood over Oglivie. She took a long slow breath. Looking down at him with a trace of a smile, she carefully lifted a wet string of copper hair away from her face and hooked it behind her ear. She widened the smile at Margarite. Her face appeared flushed with relief.

"Sure."

"Your Uncle Rush and Aunt Daryline too."

"You betcha."

They made eye contact. Esofea looked giddy, a bit off-balance. Margarite didn't think, and it worked finally: "Ok den," she said.

"Here I go."

"You go and go," she said.

"You betcha."

As Esofea herded her ragtag little clan into the Blind Sucker lodge, she was surprised by an infusion of pride. After a promising historical start, represented by decades of impressive trophies, important memorabilia, and a celery mansion, there remained not a functional being among them—yet they had offed Heimo Kock, hadn't they? Wasn't that something a hundred smarter people had contemplated over the man's horrid seventy-two years?

Alzheimer's, alcohol, and adolescence—that's what it took to get the job done.

Go, Smithbacks.

But she kept all that to herself. It was story time, led by Deputy DuCharme, who told one ambulance to go on with Dog and asked the other to wait for her—maybe a half hour or so, until Tim Shrigley could get there.

Esofea's family pride turned out to be a flash in the pan, though, crowded out by worries as she listened. She withdrew to a dim post beside the reception desk, sat on the floor and chewed a lip, and experienced a fantastic and unsolicited Pippi prayer for Dog.

May he eat warm, enormous pancakes.

Mummo Tiina went in and out of reality, but Margarite was patient, as always. Mummo's replies muddled back to the middle of the previous century, when Great Grandpa Smithback was a legendary guide and Heimo Kock was a red-ass loudmouth—Esofea finally caring about the story—when the trout were big and plentiful, when fly fishing was in its popular craze and when Ernest Hemingway—freshly a winner of the Nobel Prize—had come north for some remedial casting lessons.

Into this patchwork history lesson, Dog somehow reappeared, glazed and trailing his ambulance attendants. He sat down in an armchair, changed his mind and lay face down again on the floor. Esofea said, "Everybody wait," knowing her mummo wouldn't, and she ran and searched in the green cabin and found him Pop-Tarts and a Coke.

Mummo Tiina had bedded the great Hemingway. Wow. That was the gist while she was gone. Esofea knew it anyway, somewhere inside. Tiina Smithback was sixteen and wild, and the legendary author-fisherman was at the Blind Sucker to learn from Bud Smithback, Mummo Tiina's father. Not a big surprise, supposedly. But wow.

Here the self-legendary Danny Tervo cleared his throat and scowled until he was recognized by the deputy.

"Hemingway hired Kock to guide him on the Two Hearted," he filled in sullenly. "In 1958. They got skunked and the national press made a big deal about it. Hemingway publicly blamed Kock. Kock wrote an article for *Playboy* awarding him the Pulitzer Prize for wind knots. They hated each other, and that made Kock famous. Hemingway shot himself a couple years later but Kock kept on hating him."

Margarite thanked Danny. He tried eye games with Esofea, who after another five minutes of story had become, conclusively, the granddaughter of his man crush. Esofea *Hemingway* Smithback. She stuck her tongue out. Fucker.

Mummo Tiina kept talking. Mummo's daughter with Hemingway—Esofea's mother, Ilma Smithback—was a happy child until Heimo Kock began to visit her, also at sixteen, when she was alone with Rush and watching the desk at the resort.

Esofea's heart clutched. Sixteen. The same age as Esofea when Mummo Tiina had let her move away to the mansion in Newberry. That had always hurt her, how Mummo Tiina seemed to want her gone from the resort.

The old woman paused here, as she had once already, to ask where Herman was. Nobody knew *who* Herman was. Maybe Rush's daddy, Esfoea thought. The stupid jughead was opening another beer now, doing what he did best while family women were molested.

"Did Herman get his meatloaf sandwich?" Mummo Tiina wanted to know.

"He did," said Margarite. "He loved it and said to thank you."

"He doesn't eat enough." That sounded normal for a grandmother. But then she said, "He can't do it but once a day without that meatloaf sandwich."

"Well, he got it," Margarite said.

"Good. Herman is very sweet. He waits for me."

There was a long and awkward silence—and into that, with no warning even to herself, Esofea again began to weep.

When her mom was sixteen?

And Esofea was born in '77?

"Shit!" she screeched through her sobs.

She came out of her chair and upended it.

"That sonofabitch always flirted with me, always had little gifts for me, while everybody else hated him, and I knew it meant something! I knew it! And that's why Mummo Tiina never left me alone at the lodge, and why she didn't mind that when I moved to Newberry, even though she knew Danny was over there all the time. Because she hoped Danny would protect me ... And I wonder why am I so messed up? Really? *Shit!*"

She collapsed to the floor. Maybe time passed. She had no sense of it. No sense of people waiting or people talking. Only her own horrid thoughts, all her life spent straining outward, spinning crazy words and acts around an unknown truth that pinned her straight through the chest. Esofea Hemingway *Kock* Smithback. Her mother *had* died, in a way, when she was a baby. Her father *was* King of the Cannibals. He had come to the door of the mansion on three separate nights and found Danny there each time. Danny had threatened to kill him if he came back a fourth. She remembered now.

Finally Esofea revealed her ruined face to the group. "Did he rape her?" Dog was beside her, his hand on her back.

"Did Heimo Kock rape my mother?"

"He did what he pleased," Mummo Tiina said. "But we didn't use that word in those days, dear."

"Did she love him?"

"Oh, no. She left because of him. By the way … Caroline?"

The girl slumped on the floor against the leg of her great-grand-mother's chair.

"What?"

"Did you eat up Herman's meatloaf?"

"No."

"Well, anyway," Mummo Tiina concluded, her tone revealing she was done with all this attention and talk, "I'm the one that killed him. Caroline was just trying to get him off her."

Esofea's heart began to hurl its awful heaviness against her chest. "Come here, baby," said Caroline's father, setting aside his beer can as the girl jumped up. She crossed the room with an unhinged fatty jiggle and sat hugely on her mother's lap.

So Aunt Daryline began. "She had been watching the desk a lot, you know, cuz me and Rush was so busy."

"End of the tourist season," Rush put in. "No time to wipe your ass. So much to do a man can't do anything, like read the newspaper or take care of his finances or nothing. Youse guys don't know the half of it. So yeah, like Caroline was here—well, because we was so busy that—well, even though we ain't had nobody since July, there's a lot of work goes into—"

Shunk took care of it. "Shut up, Rush."

Caroline's father wound down into non-words and was quiet.

"She was watching the desk, you know," continued Daryline, "the way Esofea always did before she went down to Newberry, and it seems Heimo Kock was coming in here and messing on her, believe it or not, an old man like that, and Caroline didn't realize she could say no."

"I *said* no." The girl's tone was fierce. "A hundred times."

Esofea began, "Are you telling me that neither one of you noticed—"

She stopped herself, unable to foresee anything less than an hour of unhinged screaming. She could kill these people. Daughter of Heimo Kock. Shit. She could kill herself. How had she missed all this? How had she let this girl down? Hanging around here while flying away in her mind, messing with Danny, being here but not.

She stared at Margarite, who stood gingerly, saying, "Ok. This needs to stop. This needs to be done properly. I have some basic private questions to ask. Then if the family needs to talk among themselves, they can do that. Then, with an attorney present if they want, we can get into formal questioning. "

"I said no a hundred times," Caroline repeated. "And I told you and Dad and you and Dad did nothing. You kept leaving me here. And half the time Mummo was asleep all the way over in the red cabin and—"

"Caroline—" Margarite tried to stop her.

But she was heedless, her story rushing into open air. She talked over Margarite's voice. "I saw him coming from the window that day and I knew he was going to do it, really do it, I couldn't stop him, so I just took some line off that—" she pointed at the Hemingway reel in Margarite's hand "—and cut it and rolled it up and I kept the piece of line rolled up in my hand and when he got on top of me I slipped it around his neck. I tightened it kind of slowly. I think he blacked out. I went to get Mummo Tiina, and she ... and she ..."

The girl glanced nervously at her great-grandmother. Mummo Tiina had her bony elbows up on the chair arms, her large arthritic fingers knit together. She was humming.

"Mom!" barked Rush. "Yo! Hello!"

"Huh? Yes, sweetheart?"

"You gotta do that now and then," Rush advised the group. "Mom, sometimes, you know—well, it's quite a bit of work taking care of—"

"Shut up, Rush," Shunk said.

Mummo Tiina said, "Me? Oh, I put my foot on his chest and wrapped that line around as many times as it would go and then I pulled and pulled, like starting a chainsaw." She went back to humming.

At Esofea's shoulder Dog cleared his throat. "I ended up with the body …"

He couldn't manage a full question, so Esofea added, "How?"

"Me and Rush come home to a situation," Daryline said. "As you may imagine. So we put that s.o.b. under a canvas in the pickup and convoyed his vehicle home, threw his keys under the seat. Then we took him down the West Fork of the Two Hearted to that big swamp across from Ohio Camp."

"Hell, you could lose a jumbo jet in that swamp," Rush said.

He stopped, glancing warily at Shunk. This time, the county attorney said, "Speak."

"But I guess it was this fellah's RV that was blocking the road and you know it's just a little sand road, no place to go around unless you want to get stuck, which of course is why he left his vehicle in the road in the first place."

Rush paused again. That her uncle expected to be shut up when he *should* go on told you everything. Esofea ground her teeth together. The moron could not distinguish meaningful from meaningless talk—and she had tried to grow up in that. In that, and in a silence that Caroline had finally broken.

Margarite said, "So you …"

"Yeah, so we, uh, I guess you could say we kind of panicked and did a bad thing."

"Well, the plates said Massachusetts," Daryline explained. "So, of course, in that case, you know, we …"

She stopped right there. Esofea never knew what she meant. Nor wanted to.

26

Each rock salt crystal embedded under Dog's skin would maintain a sufficient sterility within its own wound. This is what the doctor hoped. He wasn't sure. A great deal of sweat, sand, soil, blood, and other microbial carriers had gotten mixed into the deal. Debridement, at this late point, was not the automatic course of action.

Dog listened, belly-flopped on a bed at the Bell Memorial Hospital in Munising. His wounds had scabbed over beneath raised red bumps that by report were slightly hot to the touch and topped with crusts of drying pus. This meant some staph infection, though he was not feverish and was perhaps fighting it well. If Dog wished, the doctor could reprise the Newberry doctor's original debridement strategy—that is, open each of nearly a hundred abscesses with a scalpel, excavate any foreign matter, douse with antiseptic, allow to rescab—or the doctor could prescribe some ampicillin and painkiller and send him home.

Dog laughed weakly. Home?

Which option he chose, the doctor continued, would probably depend on his insurance.

Dog laughed a little more deeply. Everything hurt. His insurance? So which pharmacy did he normally use?

Dog made it back to the lobby on his own power. Esofea looked up from reading *In Our Time*. She was conducting a post-feminist reassessment of the author, she claimed, powered by the new light that events had cast upon the excellence of his gene pool.

Dog said, "I'm supposed to go home."

"Hmmm …"

"Can I come over?"

She fed him grapefruit seed extract, Echinacea, and Pickleman's pizza, with a tall vodka-Tang. She spread tea tree oil across his back and somewhat gratuitously into the firm curve at the top of his buttocks. They talked for an hour or so. Then she put him to bed in one of the downstairs bedrooms and read him to sleep with *McElligot's Pool*. He drifted off during the herd of whales and slept for two days. This was ample time for Esofea to help Danny Tervo adjust to a new set of ideas: Hemingway was ok, but he, Tervo, sucked possum ass.

"Intuition is my new best friend, Danny. And of course, there is no love without compassion. So I ask myself, intuitively, do I feel compassion for you?"

The deposed boyfriend sat at Esofea's kitchen table with his long brown legs stuck out so that she, the granddaughter of his hero Ernest Hemingway, had to walk around them as she crushed and steeped a pile of feathery yarrow stems, preparing to combat fever as needed.

"You want me to define compassion," Esofea continued. "Ok. *Com*, with, *passion*, to suffer. To suffer with another. So, do I suffer with you? Hell-no-are-you-kidding-me is my answer—I mean, if I listen to my best friend intuition. They're gonna confiscate your tanker, Danny. Property used in the commission of an interstate crime. An impressive one, I have to admit—but not admire. You'll probably do some time. And I do *not* feel your pain."

He wanted to argue this: trucking water—that part—was not for sure a crime.

Ignoring the topic, dripping yarrow juice across his legs on the way from the sink, Esofea said, "And by the way, you can keep your clipped nuts. I don't want them. Your testicles, yourself."

"Ok. That was bogus. I should have discussed it with you."

"Maybe not," she said. "If you had, I might be stuck with you for life."

She let this drag on because she wanted it all out and finished. She let Danny toke her up with some new Canadian junk and take her for drinks at The Log Jam so she could perform her liberation drama over again, as ripped as he could get her, thus eliminating that old Tervo favorite as a future strategy.

Fritz Shunk, one of Esofea's new heroes, was there behind the bar. "Hey, kids."

Danny, placing his silver Navaho money clip on the bar, said, "Legal opinion. Let's say there's a questionably ratified international agreement—"

"Nope," Shunk said. "I'm tending bar, Danny. After that I'm the county attorney, not the state attorney general or the FBI. You want a legal opinion, find somebody qualified and pay money for it. What're you kids having?"

"Same as you," Esfoea said and giggled. "None of Danny's shit."

She ordered a Bloody Mary. Tervo sucked silently on a Dos Equis with lime squeezed down its neck. He gave Esofea-plus-alcohol five minutes and then slung an arm around her shoulders. She bit his hand, hard as she could.

"Ow! Sofi! What the hell is wrong with you?"

"Less than before, that's for sure." She nipped the end off her pickle to clear the taste of his skin. "If you wanna beg me, Danny, let's get started. I repeat: you suck. You and I are history."

"Give me a break. We've been history about a hundred times before."

Esofea crunched her marinated celery. She loved the way her mind was working. "Actually, those were all times when I was just mad at you."

"Well—what are you now?"

"I'm Ernest Hemingway's granddaughter."

"And Heimo Kock's daughter."

"It skips a generation. Haven't you heard that?"

"You're a nut job, Sofi."

"No—*you're* a nut job."

"Fuck you, Sofi."

"Fuck ya back, bub."

He left his beer half-finished. Esofea took the rest of her celery to-go and walked back home to Dog.

Fritz Shunk had a quiet hour behind the bar, and then the Smithbacks, Rush and Daryline, came in with Caroline.

Shunk found himself gripping a damp towel as if he could break it. After a family catastrophe, this was the pair's concession to proper parenting: bring the child to the bar with them.

Shunk kept his mouth out of it as long as he could. He limped down to serve them. The girl's mom and dad seemed to feel quite grand in ordering the girl a burger and fries, setting her up where she could scowl at them in the bar mirror as they sucked down beers.

In a drawer at the other end of the bar, Shunk kept a sign that said THIS ESTABLISHMENT RESERVES THE RIGHT TO REFUSE SERVICE TO ANYONE. The sign had been taped to the mirror when he bought the bar. A guy like him, a civil liberties veteran, despised that kind of thing. A sign like that was a lawsuit waiting to happen, and rightly so. Nevertheless, Shunk retrieved the yellowed card, carried it down the bar with a marker and crossed out ESTABLISHMENT and SERVICE TO, replacing them with YOUNG WOMAN and ABUSE BY and handed it to Caroline, who just barely smiled under her bangs. Shunk smiled back and said, "High school next year?"

She nodded.

"Long bus trip down here from where you're at. About an hour each way?"

She shrugged.

"Some kids stay with a friend or a relative who lives a lot closer to the school, at least during the week."

Shunk had mentioned this idea to Louise, who said she would think about it. Or maybe Esofea, with all her extra space in the celery mansion, would be willing. Shunk was just floating the idea for now, guessing it would appeal to lazy parents.

"Sir? What are ... hey ... Sir, what are ..."

Rush Smithback leaned over the bar, trying to speak without slurring.

"Yes, Rush?"

"Sir, excuse me for interrupting your work, but you got any idea what the charges against us are gonna be?"

They didn't have a lawyer. Shunk knew that. They were going to get Kathy Medlar from the Marquette Public Defenders Office. Kathy would take proper care of them. Shunk and Kathy had already met on the phone and discussed his intentions as attorney for Luce County.

Nothing for Caroline, he told the Smithbacks. She had reasonably defended herself from an assault.

For the grandmother, Tiina Smithback, Shunk was going to file for voluntary manslaughter. Two to twenty years was the sentencing guideline, but there was age, dementia, and the arguable threat of continued assault on a minor in her care. She would get supervision, Shunk predicted. She would move to a nice facility in Marquette.

"Ya, ok, but then, you know, there was me and the missus. We didn't do nothing wrong, right, sir?"

"You two are accessories after the fact to a voluntary manslaughter. Which doesn't amount to much."

Rush looked at his wife. She raised her beer. He raised his. They hit each other's bottles too hard.

"But we'll see what else we can throw in," Shunk said, wiping up.

Dog awoke on a sunny September day that was chilly at the edges. Esofea's cat, Mr. Nilsson, had curled up in his armpit. He found a well-read newspaper under a pair of funky purple eyeglasses on the bedside table.

He rose to his elbows. Trying not to stretch the skin on his back, he pulled the newspaper onto the bed and worked it around to the front page, quickly updating himself on two topics. The lead national news was that drought in the southwest had rung up a tally of over fifty billion in economic losses. That was a shocker for a moment, and then on second thought it wasn't. The number was undoubtedly low. Irrigation sources had run dry. Tourism had dropped off. Investment was pulling out. Governors seeking cash for dams and desalination plants had begun to raid funds for social services, city infrastructure, and education. Migrant workers and illegal aliens, stranded with no work, festered in waterless tent cities. Fingers pointed. Legislatures gridlocked. Crime was up. So were taxes. That fifty billion, Dog estimated, was just the loose change on the floor.

The local news of relevance was that Dog's fantastic miss with the punt gun had triggered a manhunt that was still unresolved.

What?

Dog went back and read the item again. Acting Sheriff Margarite DuCharme identified William Rowntree, eighteen, of Phoenix, Arizona, as the triple murder suspect, still at large. The posse of Kock-loyalists that had chased Dog with terrifying efficiency all over Luce County had been unable to track down a city kid in slick-soled shoes who had no more than a ten-minute lead on eager bear dogs, and who couldn't have had the vaguest idea of where he was or where he might go.

> "He got away from us somehow," said local professional hunter Paul Rudvig, senior guide for Superior Adventures and leader of a volunteer search team that Friday ended its efforts in frustration. "We're stumped. We have no idea where he got to. But bear season opens this week and we have to get back to paying work."

The Michigan State Police Special Units K-9 Search Team was scheduled to retrace the suspect's assumed flight path beginning sometime Sunday. "It's like D.J. Cooper or something. All we can do is show them where we lost the trail," Rudvig said.

"Yeah, right," Dog commented to Mr. Nilsson, who switched his tail at the sound of sarcasm. "Vanished into thin air. Swallowed by a giant wolverine. Something like that."

"What?" said Esofea.

She breezed through the bedroom's doorway in a green robe. She had wet hair and two coffee cups on a tray.

"Hey, you're up."

"Hey, you brought two cups."

"Hey, I was going to going to tickle you until you woke up. I was getting bored."

She pulled what looked like a nineteenth century armchair close to the bed. She kicked her slippers off and put her feet right up on the peak of Dog's rear end.

"Make yourself at home," he said.

"I am at home. I don't know how a person can sleep like that on his stomach for so long."

"That wasn't sleep," Dog said. "That was a coma."

She shifted one ankle over the other, bouncing a little. "Me and my feet have been wanting to do this since yesterday. Dog is no good. I think I'll call you Otto. Short for ottoman. So, what is this about giant wolverines?"

"I read they couldn't catch the suspect. They can't find him. All that."

"You know what I think?" she said.

"Probably."

"I think what you and everybody else thinks."

"Those guys that were chasing me, they caught the guy and shot him—"

"—cut him into pieces with a dressing saw—"

"And dumped the pieces into five different swamps," Dog concluded, "each one at least twenty miles from where they'll send the State Police to look."

"That could be you, Otto," Esofea reminded him. "Instead you're here. I bagged you and made a footstool."

"I guess I appreciate it."

"I guess you should."

Mr. Nilsson decided to wake up. He arched his spine, extended one rear leg, then the other, then hopped onto Dog's back with claws open and began to knead.

"Mr. Nilsson! Bad monkey!"

Esofea kicked at him. He walked over Dog's head and jumped off the bed. Dog rolled onto his side and sat up. His face felt suddenly hot, his stomach twisted. Esofea studied him for a moment and said, "Let's have a look."

She kneed across the bed to get behind him. She lifted the shirt that he guessed had belonged to Danny Tervo. Esofea said, "Oh, boy. More tea tree oil for you."

She kept watch and made Moroccan lentil soup and wondered. Was she doing her Tervo thing all over again? Falling for the dodgy one? The project? Shouldn't she be up at the Blind Sucker, looking after Caroline and Mummo Tiina, jabbing sharp sticks in the direction of Uncle Rush and Aunt Daryline?

Don't.

That simple, common word had stuck with her. He had tried to save her with it. Not save her in an abstract or spiritual sense, he hadn't meant it like that. But it hit her in that way, like an oracle. It hit her like *Whatever you are doing, Esofea, don't.*

She sighed and stirred the soup as the afternoon turned cold. Had there ever been a single day in her life when she wasn't lost, passionately lost, and overcompensating with deeds and exploits and adventures? She felt enormously sad.

What Would Pippi Do?

Pippi would bake a cake so big it wouldn't fit out the door and so therefore a house party would be necessary and she would sing and dance and whip herself into a fit of preposterous activities involving a horse, a monkey, a policeman, a thug, and a Christmas tree in September.

Her Danny Tervo, Esofea guessed, had been all these things in one. Maybe her dog Otto was more of the same.

But she hated quitting. That was another thing.

And, to be honest: she was exactly the horny brat that Danny always said she was, and the very practice of loving a complete piece of work like Tervo—the difficulties, the regular bouts of hatred—had put some boundaries on how far she might go, had kept her somewhat wary and conservative and safe. God forbid, she mused, that Pippi Longstocking should hit puberty and get the itch. Bring on the horse, the monkey, the policeman, the thug—oh, boy—one just had to stop imagining.

Esofea sighed some more and stirred the soup until the lentils were soft. She took a bowl in to Dog. He woke up and she fed him some and he said he felt ok, and after she crawled over the bed and examined his back, she kissed his neck and said, "Hey, Otto."

"Hey what?"

"There's a wocket in your pocket."

And then, easily, calmly, they fell into making love, just as she knew-feared-hoped they would.

They whispered as if they knew some great secret.

They arranged careful positions.

They looked each other in the eye.

They lost track.

They chose a simple place to honor grief and let it rest.

Sometime long after it was fully dark and the room was quiet and cold, Dog came up to his hands and knees, between Esofea's legs and over her heaving freckled chest, his eyes glowing in the last flickers of a candle she had lit hours ago, and he told her:"Oh, the sea is so full of a number of fish, if a fellow is patient, he *might* get his wish …"

And she murmured, for some reason, "Seahorse ..."

The knock on the door a few minutes later was Margarite, in uniform, looking fatigued and in pain, her cruiser idling at the curb.

"Hey der," the deputy said.

"Hey der."

"How ya doin'?" the deputy said.

Esofea widened her eyes and whispered. "I'm doin' *it*. Ya know?"

Margarite smiled at that. "Ok, den." Wincing, she dropped the language lesson to deliver her message: "I'm the acting sheriff. You obstructed justice. I have to arrest you."

"I'll turn myself in tomorrow morning."

"Promise?"

"Oh, you betcha."

"Ok, den," Margarite said, smiling again. "Tanks."

27

The closed-casket funeral for Sheriff Bruce Andrew Lodge occurred on a morning that thick frost crusted the windows of the Luce Country motor pool, such as it was. Margarite's cruiser was still in the shade of the bookmobile at ten and she couldn't figure out where the scrapers were kept. She walked the six blocks to the Newberry United Methodist Church, knowing all the way that this was something she should never do as long as she was sheriff. Anything happens, she was thinking, she loses the ten minutes required to run back to her vehicle.

So this was it. This was her big dice-rolling walk through town. And tonight, the cruiser had to go inside the county garage.

Maybe she just ought to sleep in the office, she was thinking, until Julia cleared out of the house. Or maybe she ought to buy a used RV and go fishing. Or Milwaukee was always hiring. She just didn't know. It was hard to know how to heal.

Fritz Shunk was a little bewildered after the funeral to find the acting sheriff on foot and in tears. She didn't tell him how she had been reliving, the whole time, her father and his funeral. Double whammy. Shunk drove her in his Subaru to the burial, then back to the office.

"Are you ok?"

She said yes.

"Should I have some coffee and egg sandwiches sent over from the restaurant?"

Yes to that, too.

They ate from either side of what had been Lodge's desk. Margarite had clumsily filled two boxes with the sheriff's personal effects and then not known what to do with them. A son came from Atlanta, a daughter from Denver, both looking distant and rushed. Neither seemed good a fit for the stuffed northern pike and the U.P.-themed coffee mugs, and definitely not for the old cat, Goldie, nor the plastic tackle box strewn with swivels, battered Daredevils, and an empty spool of twenty-pound test. Margarite had felt oddly protective. Bruce Lodge, she realized, had been all alone when she showed up in Luce County. She had tilted his world, but he had tried to get his balance back. It was just too sad to think about.

For lack of anyone else, the new acting sheriff reported to the county attorney. She told Shunk that the hefty black kid, Michael Wilson, from Chicago, had a little bit of a record in the drug trade but nothing felonious or violent. All he knew: he made his pickup at O'Hare by holding up a sign that said Quality, the nickname of the first victim. Nobody next to Quality would make a peep. And that was all.

Margarite believed Michael Wilson. She believed Danny Tervo less when he told her he had recognized Billy Rowntree after meeting him briefly at a botanical garden in Phoenix. That was all, he said. He had no idea why Rowntree was in the U.P. If she caught him lying, Margarite warned Tervo, she and Shunk were going to make one hundred percent sure he got a chance to hone his tea-bag wisdom and general smart-assery in a State of Michigan prison.

"What I don't believe," she told Shunk, "is that Rudvig lost our guy out there in the swamps."

"I don't believe it either."

"I think he killed him."

"Me too."

They both chewed egg sandwich for a while, grappling silently with the large and obvious questions. What was in the best interest of justice here? What was worth the county investment? The egg sandwich settled into Margarite's stomach with only minor incident.

Shunk said, "Let's act like we know something and charge Rudvig with homicide. Start some fingers pointing. See what shakes out. We may get something on the Pine Stump case too."

"Ok. I guess."

Shunk gave her his bristly woodchuck smile, alert to energies. She looked away. "You know," he said, "I have to tell you, a lot of us were surprised about you, and not necessarily why you think. I think the big shock was that a person of your quality would come up here to be with Julia Inkster, knowing her as we do."

Great. Now Margarite wouldn't be able to eat any more. It was Pepto time.

"I'm sorry," Shunk said. "I feel bad for you."

"Don't."

"Too late. I felt bad for you the moment I knew. You were here about a month and I saw you two shopping at the food co-op up in Marquette. I go up there every Friday to play hoops with the kids at the university gym. Or Ultimate on the grass at Harbor Park. I scare the shit out of them. You and Julia were buying bulk grains and debating organic or not."

Margarite had to smile a little. "Dead giveaway. Yeah, I remember."

"You didn't try to hide it, though."

"I just don't advertise it. I guess I should been warned when Julia found the organic beer."

"Poor Bruce the Moose had it bad for you."

"I'm sorry. I reminded him of his wife. Which gender I sleep with wasn't a question in the interview."

"And better not be in the future, either," Shunk said.

They were silent a bit. Margarite couldn't see it yet, could not yet construct the scene, but she had begun to feel the exact moment when she should have told her father who she was, what was happening inside her—but then she didn't and then it was too late for anything but remorse—and a life, she realized, of trying to have him back. There was movement in the memory. They were going fishing in his truck. She knew she was sixteen. She knew she had felt anxiously happy. She knew now that her father had been sick from liver failure, but in the memory he was whistling with the radio—about to declare "here we are," and she hadn't wanted to interrupt him, hadn't wanted the moment to stop. Ever. Eleven days later he was gone.

Shunk said, "Julia cares for you. I'm sure. Who wouldn't? But for a person like her, the whole idea of love is pretty warped. When you're a kid and you get burned by love, it's pretty hard to handle the whole concept after that."

"You're telling me," Margarite agreed. She put a napkin over her egg sandwich, unable to look at it.

"I assume Julia shared the story with you about the time her father and one of her uncles spent some time in prison because they—"

"No. She didn't." Margarite forced a smile. "Let's leave it at that."

She drove down to The Log Jam later because, after all, talking to Shunk had felt good to her. He was tending bar. It wasn't busy. After Labor Day Louise went home and the Luce County attorney kept a waiter, a cook, and himself.

Margarite decided on the Cobb salad. She ate slowly, trying one morsel at a time, egg, ham, lettuce, carefully chewing and then dropping each softened bite into her empty, worn-out stomach.

"Back to Tervo," she said when Shunk had time to come down and lean on the bar. "He admits he took one tanker load of water out of Lake Superior and drove it down to Arizona, sold it to a guy in Tucson. Then he took a down payment of two grand from the gardener in Phoenix. But if that was all, what was Billy Rowntree doing in Luce County?"

Shunk grinned, raised his eyebrows. "Chasing Danny?"

"What else?"

"Why?"

"Not sure. But look at the numbers. Tervo told me he was projecting a profit of around fifteen grand per load as long as the drought lasted. You run only one truck once a week and the gig lasts a year, you're coming up on a million dollars. Maybe Rowntree was a partner, and Danny ripped him off."

The avocado felt best. Generous and silky in her stomach.

"Hmmm. That's some math," Shunk said. "Christ, though, what gets me is I can't figure out if Tervo is a genius or an idiot. I guess both—but water is water, so why not get it out of the Mississippi in St. Louis, or some other place that's much closer?"

Another chunk of avocado. Smooth touchdown. Margarite felt her whole bruised chest relax.

"Danny's plan was to call on high-end water users, ornamental gardeners with rare plants and million-dollar koi collections. I don't think he made the pitch to car washes. He sold the purity of Lake Superior. The water chemistry. The word 'superior' itself."

"And people bought it."

"Danny himself bought it." Margarite added what a helpful professor at UNM had told her. "And it's completely true, actually. His product was premium, as far as water goes. It's just one of those situations where premium just doesn't make much difference—except to a mind like Tervo's."

Shunk appeared quizzical. Margarite, having contemplated the phenomenon of Danny Tervo at some length, offered her private solution out loud: "The guys smokes organic cigarettes."

"Oh," Shunk said, and then he guffawed.

"So speaking of that," Margarite said, "and never mind that taking a few tankers of water from Lake Superior makes no difference whatsoever to the lake. Is it a crime?"

Shunk limped in his assertive and shocking way down to his home base at the other end of the bar. He limped back with a folder of pages from the internet.

"Any significant diversion inside or outside the watershed without the combined permission of—get this—the states of Minnesota, Wisconsin, Illinois, Indiana, Michigan, Ohio, Pennsylvania, and

New York, and the Canadian province of Ontario—that's illegal. Export is also not allowed. In the eighties, some Canadian actually loaded a super tanker and tried to take it through the Soo and out the St. Lawrence Seaway to Dubai."

Shunk looked at her, knowing she would have a hard time believing.

"No shit. This is true. He and Dubai had a contract. The guy got busted. Stopped, really. There were no applicable laws. The Great Lakes Water Compact came after that. But there are loopholes for beer, bottled water, possibly other containers, and agricultural products like apples or celery or Michigan blueberries, all of which move net amounts of water out of the basin, never to return. A lot of gray areas—that's the point—new legal territory, and a lot of wrangling."

He closed the folder. "You want my wisdom?"

"That's what I'm here for."

"Forget it. We're a small county with more muskrats than people. We as public servants plow snow and sit in dunk tanks at carnivals and serve child support warrants. It's not our fight."

That seemed right. When the avocados were gone from the Cobb salad, Margarite stopped eating. The situation seemed somewhat stable down there. Now she wanted Shunk to tell her one more thing.

"You think that's the big thing in life? Knowing what to fight?"

"Hey." Shunk gave her his bristly eager woodchuck look, drumming fingers on the bar. "That's what I'm doing up here. I got tired of fighting battles I couldn't win. I'm a guy who needs to win. Or stop fighting. That's just me. So I left Detroit."

And so Margarite made her mind up. She was leaving the U.P.

"You shouldn't go yet," Esofea advised Dog. "It's not the right time."

But by now she was loved up to the brim and heavily biased, if Dog might say so himself. He couldn't stop talking, storytelling, laughing. He couldn't stop touching her, couldn't leave any part of her alone. He couldn't—well, you know how dogs can get. He promised her he was coming right back, and he meant it.

"You still have some infection. The birthday you were worried about is long gone. Plus, your ex never believed you were coming anyway. And she didn't want you to. Another week is not going to matter."

Dog had reserved one fact as getaway material: "This guy Ray is abusing her."

"That's terrible. I'm sorry. But how is that your problem?"

Dog didn't know how to explain that it wasn't about a problem anymore. He was going home to substantiate his recent insight that going home was not the answer—that was no answer except the choice not to suffer. He was going back to tell Mary Jane this, to offer it, because he felt he had to out of kindness, welcome or not, and to tell her she would never erase her grief with suffering—and, yes, he would rope-a-dope Cocaine Ray if he had to. But pain proved nothing, and he would avoid it. Enough. And no matter what day he got there, it would be the anniversary of a day when Eamon was *alive*. And that's what he planned to focus on.

But he delayed leaving a couple more days. He got a little stronger. He fixed the damage in the Cruise Master. With Esofea still in the spirit of literary reassessment, they tracked down Conrad Belcher and invented a "Hemingway tour." Danny's old pal took them up the Fox River with tents and bedrolls, with whiskey, bread, cheese, canned kidney beans, and cigars in a rucksack. Dog ate painkillers as they hiked through ghost stands of giant white pine, imagining. They passed a lot of good water because the old-school guys like Hemingway fished downstream. They camped and cooked on a fire. They each told their Heimo Kock stories. Belcher set his tent up a bashful quarter mile away and no doubt heard them make love anyway. It was good.

In the morning, Dog and Belcher used fly rods with live hoppers, caught after the grass dried and kept in baking powder tins with holes in the top. They stalked and flipped and drifted hoppers into trout lies under a hot September sun. They caught a few little yearlings, not much to crow about, and carefully put them back under Esofea's stern supervision. The big trout were mostly gone.

They went to Seney afterward. In the museum they saw a picture of Hemingway in front of a tent with nine dead brook trout laid out on his jacket. The largest brookie was easily two feet long.

It had been like that, obviously, once upon a time.

Once more Dog left the Upper Peninsula too late at night to take the bridge into Michigan. He drove to Chicago. He got cloverleafed again in Schaumburg, pulled into a truck stop to get gasoline and check his bunk. He was alone. No dead bodies. He drank coffee and drove on into daylight.

By Cleveland he didn't feel so good. He felt hot. His fingers felt puffy around the wheel. Sweat dripped from his armpits and his eyes dried and itched. His body kept running out of fluid.

He checked a map. He dropped down into central Pennsylvania, figuring there were better places to stop if he needed to. Through the back of his mind flowed some still-unexplored trout water. But what he craved was the wet, the cold—the water, not the fishing. The water.

By late afternoon he needed to stop. He was shivering. He was seeing things. He was just nervous, he figured, that was all. A little freaked out to be really heading home. He needed to lie down under his sleeping bag. His heartbeat needed to level off. These visions of little Eamon riding his tricycle in circles on the driveway, crawling on a lap to read a book—these needed to stop their exact progress through time, allow him to focus on each one. He just needed to slow things down a bit. Cool off and rest, touch some water, get his legs back. Eat some warm, enormous pancakes like Esofea had cooked for him. That was all.

He found a little campground on a little stream. He parked and closed the curtains and crawled into his bunk. When he was level, blood galloped through his veins. His brain, infused with strange hot energies, performed spectacular trout bum burlesques. His mindspace tilted and cleaved and zoomed, an electronic atlas with a drunken pilot. He held things that held him. He said words that said him. He found things that found him. Familiar voices waited in circular silence, saying nothing.

At some point after the sun went down, every person Dog ever loved rose fully dressed out of a bathtub. Then he caught one. A nice one. He landed it. He embraced a fish so large that it pulled him through and embraced him back, his skin burning in the alien air, embraced him, his lungs burning to breathe, embraced him, his legs and arms jumping in the heat, held him and held him, and held him, until he said "Yes" and fell back where it was cold.

Alone in the office, Acting Luce County Sheriff Margarite DuCharme said aloud, "No way."

She was on Craigslist, browsing condo prices in far-away places. She had completed her resignation letter minutes before and saved it on a minimized screen, planning to read it over one more time before she printed. Stalling, just messing around, doubting she could live in a place without water, she was scrolling through the Craigslist entries under *Arizona, Miscellaneous.* There it was: an ad for "premium organic water" in thousand-gallon minimums, five bucks a gallon, weekly delivery to the Phoenix area. One number with a Phoenix area code said ask for "All-Star." The other, with an Upper Peninsula area code, said ask for "Fry Cakes."

Margarite copied the telephone numbers. She saved her resignation letter in a folder called *Now What?*

She called Esofea and rescheduled their daily Sanka moment. They had done it every day for three weeks straight now, Esofea rigorously refusing to worry about Dog, focusing on healing the pre-Dog portion of her life, Margarite sworn not to complain about Julia, who was such an easy and irrelevant target. Margarite enjoyed the affection between them, found it deflated the hurt of Julia and let her focus on her real pain, which acted out its secret existence from some dark and fatherless place inside her—an inner place that Esfoea, nodding, smiling, touching her hand, had called "your own Villa Villekulla."

"As in, symbolically, Pippi's mansion. Some crazy shit goes on in there. Not to get too grad school on you," Esofea apologized.

Which was an idea, Margarite thought. Grad school. Maybe.

Needing her Craigslist call to be untraceable, she checked around.

True Value couldn't help her. Nor Snyders Drug Store. She was *still* getting used to a town this small. She could not buy a TracFone anywhere in Luce County. She would have to wait for her day off duty, when calls were routed to Schoolcraft County, and go for a drive.

On a clear and chilly Sunday morning, the acting sheriff packed a lunch and cruised through sharp fall colors all the way to Wal-Mart in Marquette. Luce County, viewed at her leisure along the way, felt orderly, calm, familiar ... lucid, actually. Like she understood the way things worked. Like she could deal with whatever arose if she had to. And all the way she wondered excitedly which one of them she should call first: Billy "All-Star" Rowntree or Paul "Fry Cakes" Rudvig? Those two had cut a water deal in a buggy swamp somewhere. She knew it. She had them both nailed.

And after that?

Then, well, it was like the question she was already asking herself, only bigger. Life just got that way, apparently. Life got bigger and wider and more full of moments when you had to know yourself and pick your fights, when you had to relax and feel the trickles of yourself collecting into one whole, flowing, beautiful body, ninety-seven percent water.

So now what?